TWICE AS DEAD

TWICE AS DEAD

CITY OF SHADOWS
BOOK ONE

Harry Turtledove

ARC MANOR
ROCKVILLE, MARYLAND

SHAHID MAHMUD
PUBLISHER

www.caeziksf.com

Twice as Dead **copyright © 2025 by Harry Turtledove.** All rights reserved. This book may not be copied or reproduced, in whole or in part, by any means, electronic, mechanical, or otherwise without written permission except short excerpts in a review, critical analysis, or academic work.

This is a work of fiction.

Cover art by Dany V.

ISBN: 978-1-64710-123-7

First Edition. First Printing. March 2025.
1 2 3 4 5 6 7 8 9 10

An imprint of Arc Manor Inc.

www.CaezikSF.com

It had got dark outside without my noticing. Well, the venetian blinds were closed anyway. I didn't want whatever was out there looking in at me. I didn't want to do much looking out either.

The Santa Anas were blowing, hot and dry. They rattled the palm fronds on the overgrown feather duster stuck in a hole in the sidewalk outside my building. I hate that noise. It reminds me too much of skeletons.

I sat at my desk and tried to ignore it. The cat was asleep on the beat-up sofa next to the filing cabinet. The sofa is a faded lavender. Old Man Mose is red, and fuzzy. Except where he'd shed on it, they didn't go at all.

I shuffled the bills I hadn't paid. I looked at the bills I'd sent out to people who hadn't paid me. Even if a miracle happened and they all coughed up what they owed, I'd still be in the red. I haven't seen a hell of a lot of miracles lately. How about you?

"Shit," I said, which was just what I meant. I reached into the bottom left desk drawer and pulled out the fifth of Wild Turkey that lived there with the blackjack and the crucifix and the brass knucks. The then-current fifth, I should say. I took a knock and looked at the bills again. The bourbon didn't help. I took another knock. The bills still looked lousy. I felt better, though. The fifth was two knocks closer to moving out. Before it did, I'd have to buy a new tenant for the drawer.

But for the walking bones outside, the night was quiet. Then it wasn't. Shouts rose and fell back like waves on the beach at high tide. Two blocks up and one block over, the Coast League season was winding down at Wrigley Field. The Padres were in town to play the Angels. An awful lot of holiness going to waste in this sinners' town, you want to know what I think.

One more time. I still couldn't see how I was supposed to pay what I owed. If I didn't figure it out pretty damn quick, they'd throw me out of this office. They'd throw Old Man Mose out, too. Then I'd have to find honest work. I hadn't done that since I got out of the service. I wasn't what you'd call eager to start.

Somebody knocked on the door. Mose's greeny-yellow eyes went from shut to wide open and wide pupiled in nothing flat. He flowed under the sofa. He's a hero, Old Man Mose is.

"Who's there?" I said. It wasn't like anybody had an appointment for ten after nine or anything. Wouldn't be surprised if I was kind of wide pupiled myself.

"Someone who needs something from you." A woman's voice. She didn't say *Someone who wants something from you*, but that was what she meant. That's what they all mean.

"Come on in, then, and we'll talk about it," I told her. I could hope I wouldn't need the little persuaders in the drawer with the Wild Turkey. I could hope I wouldn't need the snub-nosed .38 under my left shoulder, either, or the bag of goofer dust in my inside jacket pocket. I could hope, yeah, but I couldn't be sure. Dames aren't trouble as often as men. When they are, though, they're worse trouble than guys ever dream of being.

Then I remembered, or thought I remembered, I'd locked the door. The corner of Forty-Third and San Pedro is a part of town where it's easy to get company you don't want. Any kind of company: white, black, brown, yellow, alive, dead, undead, none of the above. They're all in the neighborhood, and they're not all friendly. So I got up to let the lady—if she was a lady—in.

But I must've remembered, or thought I remembered, wrong. The door opened just fine without any help from me, thank you very much. And into the office walked a beautiful dame. I know, I know. That's how the stories always start, 'specially when the fella telling 'em's got a few under his belt.

She was, though, honest to Pete. Maybe the fourth most beautiful dame I've ever seen with my own two eyes. A blonde, which for me is usually a strike against, but not this time. Heart-shaped face. Big green eyes. Cute little nose. Kissable red lips. White, pointed teeth. Perfect skin, the kind velvet wishes it were.

I'm working my way down. Green linen blouse, tailored to flatter what she had up top. That was plenty without being too much. Black wool skirt that clung to her hips and stopped a little below the knee. It let me see her legs were as fine as the rest of her. Can't say anything nicer about 'em than that.

Oh. Silk stockings, not nylons. Don't know why I noticed, but I did. She looked twenty-eight, maybe thirty: all the way ripe, but with some of the bloom still.

No ring. I didn't miss that spot on the inspection tour. Only maybe half a second slower than I should have, I waved her to the chair on the other side of my desk and said, "Won't you sit down, Miss—?" I didn't go *What the hell are you doing* here? no matter how much I wanted to. I was proud of myself because I didn't, too. Oh, you bet I was.

"My name is Dora Urban, Mister Mitchell. Thank you so much." She had an accent, not a heavy one but she did. Something from the middle of Europe. The chair didn't creak when she parked herself in it. It mostly does, even with gals smaller than she was. But it didn't.

My swivel chair made up for it. One of these days, it'll fall apart and leave me on my ass on the floor. Hasn't yet, though. "Call me Jack," I said as I settled myself. "It's my name."

"Jack," she echoed. But she didn't go, *Then you can call me Dora*, the way I figured she would.

I took a pack of Old Golds out of the center desk drawer and showed 'em to her. "You mind?" I asked. She shook her head, so I lit up. She shook it again when I held out the pack. I shrugged and put it back. After I blew a stream of smoke up at the spinning ceiling fan, I tried again: "So what can I do for you tonight?" If she didn't want me calling her Dora, I wouldn't call her anything.

3

I didn't say *So what can I do to you tonight?* I was thinking it. A dame like that walks into your office, you have to be deader than I am or queerer than I am not to be thinking it. Did she know? Of course she knew. I wouldn't be the first with that in mind. I'd be at the end of a long, long line. Did she let on? Not even slightly. "You are a person who can find out about things that may not want to be discovered," she said.

The way she phrased stuff was as interesting as anything else about her, which is saying something. I sucked in more smoke and nodded. "I'm a detective, yeah," I said. "When people pay me, I am, anyway."

I wondered if she'd get up and walk out. When they're pretty like that, sometimes they think even the hope of some will wrap you round their little finger. A lot of the time, in fact. And sometimes they're right. Not with me, not that night. I was too broke and too blue.

If she *was* miffed, she didn't show it. "But of course," she said.

She opened her beaded handbag and pulled out a coin purse. She didn't rummage. Somehow, I got the feeling she never had to rummage. Whatever she needed would always be right there, at her fingertips.

Like me? The question didn't cross my mind—then.

Dora Urban took out a coin, leaned forward, and set it on the desk next to a coffee ring. It wasn't as big as a silver dollar. For a split second, I thought it was a half. Then I realized it wasn't silver at all. It was gold.

A twenty-dollar goldpiece. A double eagle. An ounce of gold. I hadn't seen one since I was a kid. They aren't legal tender. They haven't been for years. I couldn't take it to the saloon down the street and yell *Drinks are on me!* But still. An ounce. Of *gold*. Not legal tender. Not worthless, either, though. Oh, no.

She put another double eagle on top of the first one, and another, and another, till she had a stack twelve coins high. I goggled. You would, too, buddy. You ever see a pound of gold, all in one place? Neither had I. Twelve troy ounces. A troy pound. That's how you weigh gold.

"This will be enough for your services? And for your discretion?" she asked.

TWICE AS DEAD

"Hang on a second." I opened the drawer where I keep my smokes. This time, though, I wanted a paper clip. I unbent it so one end stuck out, then touched it to the coins. I made sure I got them all.

Nothing happened. They didn't turn to sand or fairy dust or lead slugs. They would have, too, if they were fakes. *Iron—Cold Iron—is master of them all.* That's what the poem says, and it knows what it's talking about.

"You are satisfied now?" Dora Urban sounded faintly amused that anyone could dare to doubt her.

"Just about." Now I touched the top double eagle with my fingers. I rang it on the desk. It sounded sweet. I bit it. The soft gold gave a little under my choppers. I did the same thing with a coin from the middle of the stack. Then I put them both back. I didn't want her to see how bad I needed them. "Okey-doke," I said. "I'm hired. What am I hired for? Talk to me."

Before she could, another swell of noise rolled in from the ballpark. Somebody'd done something over there. It seemed to distract her. It distracted me, too. I noticed Old Man Mose hadn't come out from under the sofa. He usually does when he decides I haven't let a cat killer into the office this time. Not that night, though.

As the cheering died down, Dora Urban steepled her fingers. Her hands were as perfect as the rest of her, as perfect as Bianca's. Her nails were long and painted red as blood. But then, every broad had nails as red as blood that summer. Cold iron may be master of them all, but fashion's the mistress.

"My ... half brother is missing," she said into the returned quiet. "If he is still with us, I want you to find him and do what you can for him. If he is not, find out what happened to him and who made it happen."

Who made it happen? That didn't sound so real good. I grabbed a pencil. "What's his name? How long has he been missing? When was the last time you saw him or talked to him or whatever it was?"

"He is called Rudolf Sebestyen." She spelled the last name so I wouldn't write it the usual way. "I saw him last this past Sunday night. He said he was going to Deacon's."

"Oh, he did, did he?" I didn't say *Christ, no wonder he's missing!*, but it sure as hell went through my mind. You get to Deacon's off of Central. If they decide to let you in, you do. If they don't, you've got other things to worry about. "Is he, um, the same color you are?"

5

"Rudolf? He has black hair. Otherwise, yes," she said.

That's the colored part of town. Where I'm at is right on the edge of it. Somebody as fair as Dora Urban would stand out on his way to Deacon's—or maybe not, considering it's off of Central. And not so much once he got there, if he got there. Deacon's is the kind of place that draws 'em from a long way off. Not everybody in our pure and decent city thinks that's a good thing. Of course, some of the ones who scream about it the loudest show up there themselves.

"Was he a regular there?" I asked, which was another way of trying to find out how much trouble I was likely to land in.

She shrugged. "It would not have been the first time he went. He did not go every night, or even every week."

"All right." I didn't think it was, but never mind. "Did he have any … particular friends there?" I was trying to stay as discreet as I could. The next questions didn't need discretion: "Did he have any enemies there you know of? Who *are* his enemies, there or anywhere else? What line of business is he in?"

"We do importing and exporting together," Dora Urban answered. "We know a lot of people in different parts of the city. We have had some permit trouble lately with the people in City Hall."

"Have you?" I wanted to reach for the Wild Turkey again. I lit another cigarette instead. Not as good, but better than nothing. They don't say *You can't fight City Hall* here. They say *You better not.* Because City Hall fights back. And it's bigger than you are. Odds are it's meaner, too.

Our fair city. Which would be funny, if only it were funny.

I let out a sigh of my own. "I'll do what I can for you. How do I get hold of you if I find anything or if I start running low on cash?"

She pulled a little spiral-wire notebook out of her handbag with the same deft touch she'd shown extracting the coin purse. A fountain pen followed, just as smoothly. She wrote, tore out a page, and put it on the desk facing me. *Dora Urban, MUtual 8273, evenings.* She had an elegant hand. Why was I not surprised? She crossed the seven like a European.

"What if I need to talk to you during the day?" I asked.

"I am not there in the daytime," she answered. "Someone may take a message for me, but there is no certainty."

She wasn't gonna tell me. I sighed again. "However you want. You're paying the freight."

"Yes," she said, as if I'd lost points for mentioning the obvious. She stood up. Her chair still didn't creak. So did I. Mine did. She turned away and walked out through the door she'd used to come in.

I don't mean she opened the door and walked through the doorway. I mean she walked through the door. It never opened, but one instant she was on this side of it, the next on the other. Hell, no wonder I thought her teeth were pointed!

Old Man Mose chose that moment to emerge from under the sofa and hop up onto it. He looked at me and shook his head. "You dope," he said. "You didn't even know what you were dealing with."

The hell of it was, he was right. All kinds of things all of a sudden made, well, more sense than they had. The way she talked. That she'd given me gold and not silver or even silver certificates. That she'd needed an invitation before she crossed my threshold. And that she wasn't there in the daytime. Oh, boy, she sure wasn't!

"How was I supposed to know she lives, exists, whatever the right word is, in Vampire Village?" I said. VV starts a few blocks south of the office. Yeah, I know, it's not the angelic part of Los Angeles. But I don't know what the angelic part of LA is, either. I haven't found it yet—I know that.

And I know I'd go out of business if I hung up my shingle in a nice part of town. Of course, I was too damn close to going out of business anyhow, so what does that prove?

As for Mose, the way he looked at me said I was stupid even for a human being. "If you didn't poison your nose and your tongue with those stinking cigarettes, you would have smelled what she was before she even came in."

"Do I bitch about your catnip?"

"You'd better not." He curled up in a doughnut with his tail over his mouth and his nose. Even if I did complain, he wouldn't listen. So I didn't.

The world looked better the next morning. A pound of gold will do that to you. I hadn't turned it into money I could spend, but I had it.

7

I knew I had it. I knew the kind of finagling I'd have to use and the people I needed to talk to.

So I splurged on breakfast. Two eggs over medium, a ham steak, hash browns, enough coffee to float a man-of-war. Came to forty cents. I left a quarter tip. The waitress looked at me funny. "You rob a bank, Jack?" she asked.

"Two of 'em," I said. She could do whatever she wanted with that.

But my good mood wore off when I went to the corner to wait for the Red Line car. The sun was shining through the smog. That meant I couldn't go to Deacon's. It kept vampire hours, pretty much. So I had to head downtown instead. Talk to the cops, talk to the clerks .... I would have had more fun at Deacon's, if I came out again afterwards. I couldn't very well have had less.

A dented old Black and White cab chugged by, belching smoke from the tailpipe. The colored driver looked a question my way and slowed down. I shook my head. He sped up again. He wouldn't have wanted to take me where I needed to go. Black and Whites cover the Negro part of town, and they're supposed to stay there. Yeah, and Sunshine cabs are supposed to stick to Hollywood. Somehow, it's not the same.

Ten minutes later, the Red Car clattered up. The motorman rang his bell. I climbed aboard and handed him a quarter. He thumbed the coin dispenser on his belt without even looking at it. "Out of zone?" he asked. When I nodded, a dime and a nickel went into the fare box. The other dime came back to me.

I sat down. The motorman clanged the bell again and got going. The trolley wasn't crowded. No surprise. He'd just come up through Vampire Village. VV hopped at night, but not much went on there during the daytime.

The seat was too hard and too straight up-and-down. They didn't want you getting comfy. They wanted you to get off quick. As I shifted, the coins in my pocket jingled. It made me wonder how vampires ever rode the Red Car. Silver isn't good for them.

No sooner wondered than answered. Up above the windows, with the advertising placards for hair restorers and crystal-ball readers and Jim Clinton men's clothes, was a sign from the Pacific Electric Railway telling people—and anyone else who happened to get on—they could buy a passbook: forty in-zone rides for three bucks. So vampires could use the trolley, all right. They could even do it at a discount.

North up San Pedro we went, stopping every half a block or every block or every other block, depending on who wanted to get on or get off where. It's a scuffling part of town. Shoe-repair places, hex joints, storefront churches, saloons, paper and magazine stands, little groceries, fried-chicken places and burger shops, secondhand stores that *were* secondhand stores, secondhand stores that fronted for the numbers runners, a Technocracy meeting house that couldn't have looked more out of place if it tried, and more crystal-ball readers.

Why do so many crystal-ball readers work out of places that look like somebody ought to tear them down? For the same reason some of 'em troll for suckers on the Red Car lines, I figure: they're lousy at what they try to do. If they were any good, they could see the future well enough to take care of themselves. I'm not talking about their clients.

Don't get me wrong. There are good crystal-ball readers, damn good ones. They don't advertise on the trolley, though, and they don't work out of filthy shacks with dried-out weeds for a front yard. They take care of themselves real nice. Or the fat cats in places like Detroit and Wall Street and Washington—oh, yes, and Moscow, too—do it for them.

Things only got scruffier as we came closer to downtown. What had been Little Tokio before the war, they were calling Bronzeville these days. Soon as the government cleared the Japs out, Negroes started moving in. Sometimes they did it legal, sometimes they just squatted. Nobody fussed much. There was a war on. Lotta jobs to do. You had to squeeze people in somewhere.

Old colored part of town, along Central and through there, they knew their place. It wasn't a great place, not even a good one, but it was a place where you could get along if you didn't make waves. Bronzeville .... When Bronzeville opened up, everybody who was new and everybody who was uppity jumped in.

In Bronzeville, the numbers runners and the boys who sold reefers don't bother to hide. They stand on the corner like respectable folks. In Bronzeville, they are. What makes you respectable faster than money in your pocket?

9

Girls paraded in dresses down to here and up to there. They left no doubt about their assets, so to speak. The guys who ran them paraded, too, in rolled-brim fedoras, sharp-cut suits, and spit-shined shoes. They say a good pimp doesn't need to keep an eye on his girls. This was Bronzeville. Good pimps didn't come here.

At least the trolley car was quiet. We didn't have anybody from the Pushers and Shovers Society riding with us. They're punks, is what they are. They see somebody who looks weak or meek, they push him around, they shake him down, they rough him up, they lift his billfold and they run like hell. Punks. Colored punks. Oh, there's white punks, too—you betcha—but not in the Pushers and Shovers.

When we got to Second and San Pedro, the trolley took a diagonal on Weller to go to First at Los Angeles Street. I rode it one more block west, then hopped off. The trolley would make a right and keep on heading north up Main past City Hall. The main police station was on First, three blocks west.

I hoofed it. The building looks like it'll fall over the first time the earth elementals get mad at us again, or maybe just if the Santa Anas blow harder than usual. It goes back before the turn of the century. Here, that makes it ancient. So they're gonna tear it down and build a new one. They've got the land. They've got the money. Pretty soon, the flatfoots'll have a fancy new place to drink coffee and beat on prisoners in.

Pretty soon, but not yet. They overflow the old station like a twelve-year-old in a nine-year-old's clothes. They've split off some of their operations (not the ones I wanted—I hoped) and moved 'em to City Hall. I don't know of any twelve-year-old who can do that when he gets too big for his britches.

The sergeant at the front desk was eating a jelly doughnut and smoking a cheroot that smelled like burning dragon turds. Made me sick to my stomach when I saw him. Do one, fine. Do the other, fine. Both at once? I started to understand how much Old Man Mose loved my cigarettes.

The sergeant looked as thrilled to see me as I was to watch him. "I thought they hauled the trash away today," he said. "Instead, it comes walking in."

A private eye who expects a cop to be his pal is in the wrong line of work. When they get under your skin, you can't show it. Might as well pour gasoline on a fire. I gave him my best you-dumb-prick smile and said, "Funny, Charlie. Fun-ny. Har-de-har-har. See? I'm laughing. You'll slay 'em at Eddie Carroll's on the Sunset Strip."

He blew smoke at me—literally, for once. I lit an Old Gold in self-defense. Then he said, "What *are* you doing here? They didn't haul you in with the paddy wagon this time."

"That got straightened out," I answered, which was more or less true. "I'm trying to track a missing person—um, individual."

Charlie raised one tufted eyebrow, all I needed to see to remember he didn't like vampires … or zombies or ghosts or goblins or merfolk … or, for that matter, Negroes or Jews or Japanese or Chinese … or anybody else who didn't wear the blue uniform. Chances are he didn't like himself. Well, I didn't like him, either. But I had to deal with him.

"Gimme the gory details," he said.

"Vampire name of Rudolf Sebestyen," I spelled the last name, same as Dora Urban had. "Last seen Sunday night—said he was on the way to Deacon's."

Up went that eyebrow again. "He was heading for Deacon's, anything that happened to him he musta deserved."

Can't say the same thing hadn't crossed my beady little mind. Even so, I kinda shrugged and said, "If it was anything bad, it's still police business. Got anything on him?"

"Lemme see. Spell me the name again, willya?" Not like he'd bothered to write it down or anything. I spelled it. He flipped through the logbooks. "Nah, nothin' about nobody by that name Sunday or afterwards." He stuffed the rest of the jelly doughnut into his face. It filled his cheeks so full, he looked like a hamster—an ugly hamster, but he did. After one hell of a gulp, he went on, "No reports of any bloodsuckers catchin' fire when the sun came up, neither, case you was wondering."

I was, but not very much. That would have made the news. I might have heard about it. Dora Urban probably would have.

"No missing-individual report?" I asked.

"Not about one of them things, not in here." He smacked the logbooks with a scarred-knuckled fist.

"Mind if I go up and talk to the Missing Individuals folks?"

"It's a free country, 'cept for sales tax. You wanna waste your time, be my guest."

He waved me toward the stairs, so I took the elevator. Stairs would have been quicker; I had to wait for the damn thing to come down. The cage creaked open. "Third floor," I told the operator.

"Third floor. You got it." He started to whistle. Like anybody with half an ounce of sense, I left him alone while he was on the job. Modern elevators have safety catches. This cage was as old as the rest of the station. If he fubar'd the Indian Rope Trick, down would come baby, elevator and all.

When we got to the third floor, the cage's front door opened again. I hopped out, glad to have solid floor under my feet again. The cage groaned closed. The operator stood there whistling, holding the damn thing up while he waited for his next call.

I knew the way to Missing Individuals. Not like I'd never been there before. When I opened the door, three clerks—one a frump, one cute, one chubby but dressed nice—were typing away. For a second, I thought they were the only ones in there. I do that every single time. Sure, soon as the second's passed I feel like a jerk, but Missing Individuals always seems to be run by, well, missing individuals.

It isn't, of course. Bit by bit, you notice that. A manila folder moving from here to there under what looks like its own power. Something that reminds you of curdled air going down the aisle between two rows of steel shelves. A voice you think you hear. And then, when you concentrate, you realize you do, even if it's more inside your head than with your ears.

Ectoplasm is like that. What can I tell you? Who better to investigate individuals who disappear than ghosts? They've almost disappeared themselves, you might say. And they can get into and out of places that give even vampires trouble, and without getting noticed unless their luck's out.

More curdled air across the counter from me. When I looked at it out of the corner of my eye, the way you look for Titan when you're looking at Saturn, it curdled in a familiar way. "What do you know, Eb?"

Ebenezer had been a Pinkerton man during the Civil War till a Confederate Minié ball ended that. But he'd hung around in the

TWICE AS DEAD

same general line of work, you might say. "I'm here," he answered in an echo of a whisper.

So he was. Don't ask me why some people who die turn into ghosts. I'm no archbishop or rabbi or forensic sorcerer. It does happen, though. "What can you tell me about a vampire named Rudolf Sebestyen?" I asked him.

"That one? He's trouble. Always has been." Charlie might not have known anything, or let on that he knew anything, but Eb did. He went on, "How come? What's he done?"

"He's gone missing. Waddaya think he's done? Think I came in here to get a concealed-carry permit?"

"A joker." He sounded like a disgusted breeze sighing through the branches of a forest a thousand miles away. "But I think that's news. Let me check with my colleagues."

I guess he did. A bunch of air got muddled up, not just one spook's worth. Faces I couldn't quite make out wore expressions I wasn't sure I wanted to see. After a while, Eb—I guess it was Eb— came back to me. "And?" I said.

"Nobody's heard anything. Nobody's seen anything."

"Awright. My lucky day." I started to turn around and leave, then stopped. If they'd already heard of Rudolf the dead-nosed vampire .... "You tell me anything about a gal—hey, you know what I mean—name of Dora Urban, connected to Sebestyen?"

Eb didn't need to talk to his pals. "Her?" he said. "Worse than him, by plenty. You mess with her, you'll end up twice as dead as she is."

I didn't know what that meant. I didn't think I wanted to find out, either. But twelve troy ounces of gold argued even louder the other way. You do what you gotta do, that's all. "Thanks a heap," I said, and this time I did go.

I walked down the stairs. Charlie'd lit a fresh trash-fire cigar. He was telling another sergeant with hairy ears an old, old dirty joke. He paused to give me the finger to send me on the way. I smiled and nodded back, sweet as pumpkin pie. Like I say, if they know they've got to you, they win.

Downtown is City Hall and the Federal building and the Hall of Records and the Biltmore and the Central Library and Pershing Square and Bullock's and all that fancy stuff. And it's a bunch of brick and stucco piles run up too fast and jammed too close together. Some are full of people. Others hold the crap people want to buy.

I know a guy who runs a shop up there. Al Harris is a fat old sweaty Jew, as pretty as an unmade bed, but he hears things. All kinds of characters wander into his place. He keeps his mouth shut and his ears open.

The shop's at 131-3/4 Hill St., half a block down and a little bit over from the police station. It's just as big as the address would make you guess, too. Blink when you're walking by and you'll miss it. The faded sign in the dusty window says BOOKS. In smaller letters underneath, MAGAZINES.

I was two steps from the door when a cop came out. I almost kept going. If they were giving Al a hard time again, I was the last guy he wanted to see. But the cop had a fixed, kind of embarrassed look on his Irish mug and a flat paper bag under his arm. He wasn't shaking Al down. He was a customer. All kinds, like I told you.

He didn't look at me. I didn't look at him, either, not so he could see. These joints have their rules, same as any others. I went in. The bell over the door let out a soft ring, almost more of a cough. It sounded embarrassed, too.

Al Harris stood behind the counter. He has more chins than the Hong Kong phone book and a Samsonite bag under each eye. A cigar almost as smelly as Charlie's back at the station and the loud— hell, the noisy—sports shirt he always wears only add to the effect. If you want sleaze, Al's book and magazine shop is the place to come.

His stock in trade also lives up to, or down to, that. Cheaply printed classics with titles like *Super Young Lust* and *Beat Me, Baby, Eight to the Bar* crowded the shelves (which I'd guess he'd made himself, to hold as much as they could). A magazine was called *Vampires in Furs*. The photo on the cover showed a lot more vampire than fur. She wasn't half bad, but she didn't come close to Dora Urban. Zombies … goblins … people, even. Al runs a dirty-book place for folks with, um, varied tastes.

He was going to pretend not to notice me, too. Somebody who steps into a joint like that craves as much privacy as he can get. But then he recognized me. A smile didn't make him any less ugly, but it made him ugly in a different way. "How are ya, Jack?" You could take the boy outa Brooklyn, but you couldn't take Brooklyn outa the boy.

"I've been worse. I've been better," I said. "How about you? And Margie?" Margie's his wife. She's on the porky side, too. She's nice. Nutty as a Christmas fruitcake, but nice. "And Skeeter?" Skeeter's the dog. They have him instead of kids. He's as round as both of them put together.

"We're awright." His gaze sharpened. He isn't pretty, but he's nobody's dummy. "So what can I do for ya?" He figured I wasn't there to ogle. I don't come in for that. And he owed me one or two more than I owed him right then.

"You know anything about a couple of vampires who go by Dora Urban and Rudolf Sebestyen?" I was getting used to spelling the funny last name.

"Heard of the gal. Never ran into her, though. The guy … I know who he is. I heard stuff about him, and none of it good. I wouldn't want nothin' to do with him if I was you. Strictly bad news."

"I'm getting paid to want something to do with him," I said.

He nodded. Everything jiggled when he did. He didn't need me to draw him a picture. He already had plenty in the shop. "He's in some kinda trouble again," he said. It wasn't a question.

I nodded. "Would I be sniffing around after him if he wasn't?"

But Al wasn't listening to me. He was trying to remember what kind of trouble had found Rudolf Sebestyen now. "Something to do with … blood banks, I think maybe."

"Aii!" I said. Transfusions save lives, people's lives. And when people donate blood, they keep vampires going without the need to sink fangs into somebody's throat. They do unless some greedy chucklehead starts making his own withdrawals, anyhow. Was Sebestyen one of those? If he was, didn't he deserve whatever happened to him?

II

Old Man Mose looked up from polishing his balls with his tongue. Cats are limber enough to have fun people can only dream about. You do, don't you? Then again, it works both ways. He has to use that tongue for toilet paper.

"You really going to call that dead-smelling bitch again?" he asked. For him, *bitch* was nastier than *dead-smelling*. He didn't like Dora Urban, not even a little bit.

"I've got to," I said. I wasn't even slightly sure I liked her myself. I thought she was stunning. I wanted to jump on her elegant bones. Like her? That was harder. She looked at me at least partly the way a farmer looked at a pig, imagining ribs and chops and ham sandwiches.

"People!" Mose flipped his nictitating membranes across his eyes. I'd roll mine to get that message across.

"Yeah, well, just remember who keeps you in cat food, buddy," I said. He did that membrane-flip thing one more time. Now it meant he could go out and kill things whenever he felt like it. Which I guess he could, once he worked off some of the lard he'd picked up hanging around with the likes of me.

No noise from Wrigley Field tonight. The Angels had gone on the road. Just me in the office with the spinning fan, with my cigarettes and the Wild Turkey, with my smart-aleck tomcat.

TWICE AS DEAD

I dialed MUtual 8273. That phone number'd been around for a while. It was two letters and four digits. All the newer ones have five digits. Of course, I couldn't begin to guess how long she'd been around. She looked maybe twenty-eight, yeah, but that proved nothing. She might have hired a gumsandal in Nero's day who had to dial his phone with Roman numerals.

Ring … Ring … A clunk as someone picked it up, not too gracefully. "*Halló?*" A man's voice, saying something that didn't sound quite like your usual *Hello?*

"Dora Urban, please," I said, wondering if I was talking to Rudolf Sebestyen. I figured not. She would've let me know if he showed up. She would've tried to get her double eagles back, too.

"Who calls?" This guy spoke English, but not real well.

"I'm Jack Mitchell."

"Oh, yes. Your name I hear. One moment, please." That last came out closer to *Vahn moment, plizz.*

It wasn't what you'd call a short moment. But eventually I heard Dora Urban's precise contralto: "Good evening, Mister Mitchell. What can I do for you?"

"For starters, you can let me know how come you didn't tell me Sebestyen wanted to knock over a blood bank," I said.

This silence lasted longer than the one while she was coming to the phone. "Where did you hear that?" she asked at last.

"Never you mind." If I answered that one, Al Harris would show just how immortal he wasn't, and in jig time, too. "Is it true or isn't it?"

Another pause. She had time to burn. I didn't. In overdue course, she said, "I am not completely certain."

"Awright, it's true," I said. She didn't try and call me a liar. I almost wished she would have. After a Wild Turkey-punctuated pause of my own, I went on, "Listen, if I'm gonna work for you, you gotta tell me the stuff I need to know. If your, uh, half brother sets his sights on a blood bank, that bumps up the number of people— folks—who wanna see him dead … undead—undeader … whatever the devil the right word is, doesn't it?"

"We use the term *finished*, Mister Mitchell," Dora Urban said quietly.

"Finished. Terrific. I've learned something. But you didn't answer my question. If Rudolf Sebestyen was after a blood bank, line to

17

finish him forms on the left, right?" Christ! I reminded myself of my old drill sergeant. "So why'd you keep me in the dark?"

She kept taking her time fishing around for words. Her voice stayed soft when she turned the next few loose: "It is not something I am proud of, Mister Mitchell."

And maybe that was true, and maybe she was in it with Sebestyen up to her well-turned thighs. "Now that I do know, shouldn't you maybe level with me?"

Don't get me wrong. I didn't expect her to. The racket I'm in, they lie to you as natural as they breathe ... if they breathe. But you gotta try. And sometimes you can pull stuff you can use even out of the lies. It's like pulling double eagles out of dog turds, but you can do it. Sometimes. If you put up with the stink and steam clean your fingers afterwards.

"I am sorry," she said. Another lie, unless she meant she was sorry I'd caught her out. "I did not believe—I do not believe—that has anything to do with his current absence."

"You're paying me to worry about that," I said. "Which blood bank is it?"

"The one at County General." Dora Urban sounded as happy admitting it as a debutante would admitting she had a social disease.

"Jes—!" I bit that off sharp. Vampires and holy names don't mix. "Jeepers!" Which didn't do as much for me as the other would have, but I had more consideration for her than I figured she ever would for me. "Sebestyen, he doesn't think small, does he?"

"Anything worth doing is worth doing properly," she said. That wasn't the exact word I would've used. County General is the shining hospital that is set on a hill, and cannot be hid. Well, it damn well *is*. It's a big white building northeast of City Hall. You can see it for miles and miles. You can when the smog lets you, anyhow. They even light it up at night.

"Who was helping him with this little scheme?" I asked. The next obvious question, sure, but you gotta ask 'em even when they're obvious. Sometimes especially when they're obvious. The answers aren't always.

"That, I cannot tell you."

TWICE AS DEAD

"Can't tell me or don't know?" I asked. She didn't say anything, so I drew my own conclusions—drew 'em and didn't like 'em. I said, "How am I supposed to help you if you don't help me?"

"I am paying you for your services, Mister Mitchell. As long as you accept my payment, I expect you to provide them. If you fail to do so, I will take whatever steps seem fitting. Good night." She hung up on me.

I put the handset back in the cradle and shook my head. "You're right," I told Old Man Mose. "She is a bitch."

Mose was biting his toenails, one more thing people aren't equipped for but not one I particularly miss, even asleep. He kept at it for a while. He's a cat. Annoying me is part of his job. Then he said, "What are you going to do now?"

"If the folks who don't like Sebestyen haven't *finished* him, I ought to let him pull it off," I said. "Robbing a blood bank! If that doesn't send people charging into Vampire Village with stakes and torches, nothing ever will." But I knew I was lying. I've seen folk riots, pogroms, call 'em whatever you please. You don't want to wish anything like that on the town where you live, even when it's as rotten a town as this one.

"Go ahead," Mose said. They don't issue consciences to cats, either.

"Nah." I took another slug of bourbon, then held up my index finger as if I were a genius. Uh-huh. As if. "Other thing I'll do is stay away from Al Harris for a while."

"Good. Whenever you come back from that place, you always stink like a dog," Old Man Mose said.

"Anything else to complain about?" I asked. The cat, for a wonder, kept quiet. "Okey-doke," I went on. "I'm going home." I turned out the light and shut off the fan, and I did.

Next morning, after three aspirins, I chose a different joint for break-fast: El Toro Verde. I don't go there all the time, but often enough so the waiter nodded when I walked in. He was a short, stocky guy with copper skin, a coffin-shaped head, and cheekbones to be proud of. He raised a bristly black eyebrow in a silent question.

"Coffee, José," I said. "Black coffee and *menudo*." *Menudo* is tripe soup. Mexicans swear it cures hangovers. I'm no Mexican, but I've tried it a few times, and it works ... as well as anything else. Or as badly.

"*Sí, Señor*," he said. I sat down at the counter. Three stools over from me, a swarthy fellow with greasy black hair and a lounge-lizard mustache was plowing through his own bowl. By the red veins in his eyes, he'd hurt himself worse the night before than I had.

The food and coffee came fast, thank God. A slug of java. A spoonful of *menudo* (which had enough chilies in it to make me sweat in case I wasn't already). Another spoonful. More coffee. By the time I finished the tripe soup and two cups of joe, I felt better. Well, the aspirins didn't hurt, either.

I'll tell you how much better I felt. The phone rang right after I stepped into the office, and I didn't scream. My head didn't fall off. Progress. And whoever it was, it wouldn't be Dora Urban. That felt like progress, too.

"Mitchell Investigating." I sounded almost like myself.

"I'd like to speak to Mister Mitchell, please." A Negro man's voice, but educated, so you had to think twice to be sure.

"You're doing it." No, I wasn't at my sunshiny best, or I would have been more polite.

"Mister Mitchell, my name is Lamont Smalls. I have the honor and the privilege of editing *The Los Angeles Lookout*," he said. The *Lookout* is the biggest Negro newspaper in town. Up along Central, it's a very loud noise. Nobody in Hollywood or Westwood's ever seen it, unless a housemaid happens to lose a copy there.

But I was only a couple of blocks from Central, so I knew damn well who Lamont Smalls was. In that pond, he was one heavyweight frog. "What can I do for you?" I asked, hoping I seemed smoother than I had before.

"I have some business I would like to talk about with you, but not over the telephone," he said. "I can be at your establishment in half an hour. Is that all right?"

"Make it forty-five minutes," I said. I wanted him to believe I had other daytime clients coming in. I wished I could believe it, too.

He strode in right on the dot, a parade of one. He was a small, neat, elegant man, nearly as handsome as he thought he was. His pin-striped suit cost as much as I made in a month; the charcoal fedora he hung on my old hat tree added a week. His skin was coffee with cream. Just the first hint of gray frosted his close-cut hair.

"Pleased to meet you," I said as we shook hands. I meant it for more than the usual mercenary reasons. The *Lookout* does more good than otherwise. Too many papers in this burg you can't say that about. "What's on your mind?"

"This stays between us?"

"Whatever you tell me now, it'll be in the gossip columns and all over the radio by this time tomorrow."

For a split second, he took me seriously. He stiffened, then relaxed. He even grinned, pretty much as if he meant it. "Oh," he said. "You're a wise guy."

Old Man Mose chose that moment to come out from under the sofa. "You don't know the half of it," he said, hopping up.

Smalls sensibly ignored the cat. He took a gold-plated—or maybe it was solid gold—cigarette case out of his inside jacket pocket. He showed his manners: he eyed me before lighting up. As soon as I nodded, he did. So did I, from my not gold-plated pack of Old Golds.

After a couple of drags, he said, "It's the oldest story in the world, Mister Mitchell. I'm afraid my wife is running around on me."

He was right. It is the oldest story in the world. Wives run around on husbands, and husbands run around on wives. They keep people in my line of work working, if you know what I mean. "What do you want me to do about it?" I asked carefully. I won't say I've never been a strongarm, but I don't like it. My price goes up.

But he said, "Get the goods on her. That way, I can cut her loose without getting skinned. Get me stuff that will hold up in court. If I can show it to her lawyer beforehand, maybe I won't have to go there."

"All right." That seemed sensible enough. In his Florsheims, I might do the same thing. I got down to brass tacks: "What's her name? Do you have a picture you can give me? Do you know who she's running around with?"

"She's Marianne Smalls." He shifted in the chair on the other side of my desk to get at the billfold in his hip pocket. The chair made noise when he moved in it, even if it didn't for Dora Urban.

He pulled out a photo of the two of them and slid it over to me. "Here you are."

She was a nice-looking woman, a shade or two lighter than he was. "Thanks," I said. "I asked you before—do you know who her friend is?"

"His name is Schmitt, Mister Mitchell, Jonas Schmitt." He pronounced the J like a Y. He must've done Deutsch in college. He sounded as if he wanted to throw up when he said the name, too. "He is in the piano business. He buys them, he sells them, he fixes them, he gives lessons or arranges for lessons. Sometimes he plays at clubs." He ground out his cigarette as if it were Schmitt's face on a rough file. Then, in a low, hopeless, defeated voice, he finished, "He is a white man, Mister Mitchell."

"With a name like that, he would be, yeah," I said.

No wonder Lamont Smalls felt like change for two cents. Being a Negro in Los Angeles is hard enough any old time. There are only so many places you can live, so many places you can work, so many places you can show your face. Step out of line, the cops and the rich folks the cops work for, they make you sorry.

That's all bad enough. Worse than bad enough, you ask me. A black man, or even a coffee-and-cream man like Smalls, he better know his place and stay there. But at least he's got a place. Or he does till his wife starts sleeping with the enemy, anyway.

That's how it would look to him. How it looked to Marianne Smalls .... Married to Lamont, she was a big frog in the little Negro pond, too. But that *was* a little pond. It always would be. She was even lighter than her husband. On the arm of somebody like Jonas Schmitt, she might be able to pass. Then she could see how big a frog she was in the wide old lake.

Or maybe I was reading too much into it. Maybe Lamont came upside her head whenever he felt ornery. Maybe he was a stingy son of a bitch. Maybe he was just a dud in the sack. I didn't know. All I could do sitting there across from him was guess.

And he was doing some guessing or calculating or whatever you want to call it of his own. Eyeing me, he said, "You, ah, do understand what I'm talking about, don't you?"

"Oh, you bet I do. I understand you real well," I said.

TWICE AS DEAD

Maybe he'd believe me, maybe not. I'm lighter than Marianne Smalls. My hair isn't kinky. It isn't konked, either, but that doesn't have to prove anything. My nose isn't flat, but it also isn't beaky. My mouth looks like, well, a mouth. I can go one place and seem like one thing. I can go another place and seem like something else.

Some of the places the Army sent me, I wouldn't have minded if they thought I looked more colored. They wouldn't have wanted me at the front if I did. Fool that I am, I didn't say anything about it at the time. Way too late to get hot and bothered about it now.

Smalls sat there gnawing on the inside of his underlip for close to half a minute. If he'd got up and walked out the door, how could I have blamed him? (Except for my finances, I mean.) But he'd already told me enough so he must have felt like he had to go through with it. Still looking sour, he said, "Let's talk turkey."

I'll say this about him—he didn't make the *Lookout* as loud a noise as it is by paying too much for anything. *Stingy son of a bitch* came to mind again. But why dear Marianne was doing the dirty with Jonas Schmitt wasn't my concern. Lamont and I dickered till we were about equally unhappy. He pulled five sawbucks out of his wallet to get me started, and I was on my merry way.

Schmitt lived downtown. Lamont Smalls gave me his address. After he left, I discovered I could have found it in the phone book. For all I know, Smalls did. But what the hell? Now I had it.

I headed downtown on the Red Line to scout the place. It was early afternoon. I figured Schmitt would be away pianoing. I had on dungarees, a white work shirt with a name that wasn't mine embroidered above the pocket, and a cap that could have said either railroad or baseball. Not my usual style, which was the point.

I got off the streetcar not far from Al Harris's smut emporium, and without stopping in walked past it to the corner of Third and Hill. The piano man's place was up on Bunker Hill, the one that gave the street its name. Third goes through Bunker Hill, but that didn't do me any good. I mean, Third goes *through* Bunker Hill, in a tunnel. To get to the top, you have to take Angel's Flight.

No, I don't know if he's really an angel. I don't know if he's what made Junipero Serra call this place Los Angeles. No, and I don't know how long he's been at what's the corner of Third and Hill nowadays. Forever, or close enough—although in this town, *forever* can be anything longer than a year and a half. Nobody else knows any of that stuff, either.

I do know he was there when Father Serra arrived. The Indians took Serra to see him. They might have thought the friar and the angel already knew each other. If they did, they thought wrong. The angel surprised the bejesus out of Father Serra. Whether Father Serra surprised the angel—that, I can't tell you. The angel, he was there then. He's there now. If a big old quake ever knocks downtown into the ocean, I bet he can fly mermaids underwater.

He's about twenty feet tall. Here. Wait. He's nineteen feet, six and five-eighths inches tall, by surveyor's measurement. That's what the WPA guide to Los Angeles says, anyhow, and God forbid it should lie. I keep a copy in the office, for the maps and for what it can tell me about parts of town I don't often get to. Parts I do get to, it doesn't talk about much. It's never heard of any nightclubs or hotels along Central, for instance.

Nobody's ever seen the angel, if he is an angel, eat or drink. Nobody's ever seen him leave Bunker Hill, either. He takes people from the bottom to the top, or from the top to the bottom, when they give him something that's worth something. That's what he does. That's all he does.

The Romans had a god like that. His name was Aius Locutius, which means "Up and Spoke." His one job was to sing out a warning in case the Gauls attacked Rome. When the Gauls did, he gave the warning and then went back to sleep. If the Gauls ever come again, maybe he'll sing out some more.

Anyway, I dug in the right front pocket of those dungarees and pulled out a nickel. I held it on my open palm so the angel could see it. I guess he could see it, anyway; his face shows no more in the way of features than an Oscar's does. His right hand moved. His fingers were as thick as a Louisville Slugger, but deft. He took the nickel and made it disappear. I don't know what he did with it, but that wasn't my worry. I paid the fare and I got my ride.

24

He took me in his arms. His wings unfolded from his shoulders. The WPA guide says his wingspan is sixty-three feet, two inches. It only seems like a mile. He flew up to the top of Bunker Hill. No one waited at his stop there to go down, so he flew back by himself.

You always wonder if yours will be the time he decides to drop somebody. He never has, but you wonder just the same, or I do. If Angel's Flight turns into Angel's Drop, it's a long way down.

Back before the first war, Bunker Hill was a ritzy part of town, with big, fancy, expensive houses. They're still there, but they aren't so ritzy any more. What they put me in mind of is a bunch of forty-year-old hookers trying to hide the wrinkles with powder and paint. You can see how they used to be hot stuff—and you can see they aren't any more.

Hookers don't get subdivided, though. The houses on Bunker Hill did. They're nearly all apartment buildings now. All of the signs on the front gates said NO VACANCY. I didn't see any with FOR RENT up instead. Places to live are damned hard to come by these days.

I kind of ambled along, not going anywhere in a hurry. I could have been a handyman looking for work. I was too clean to be a bum, too open to be a burglar—or an obvious burglar, I should say.

Jonas Schmitt's building was kept up better than a lot of the others. It had a NO VACANCY sign out front. I opened the gate and walked in anyway. I was coming up the front steps when a gal with a housecoat and a dyed-blond bob straight out of 1924 opened the door and barked, "Waddaya want?" A cop rousting a drunk doesn't sound any nastier.

"Schmitt, Apartment 4-B," I said. "Gotta check the wiring. The lights in the bedroom keep going on and off."

"Says who?" Her voice was as deep as your usual cop's, too. The coffin nail in her mouth was about her millionth, if the yellow stains on her fingers gave any clue.

"Says Schmitt," I answered. "He wouldn't've called me if he wasn't having trouble."

She muttered, coughed, and muttered some more. Then she said, "He shoulda talked to me first. I'll give him a piece of my mind, I will."

I didn't want her doing that. It didn't worry me much, though. Next time I came around, I'd look like somebody else. When you don't look like any one particular thing, that's easy enough. I folded my arms across my chest and said, "You gonna let me in or not? You don't, I gotta use your phone, let the boss know there's a snafu."

She crushed out the cigarette under the sole of her carpet slipper and lit another one right away. A Camel. Why was I not surprised? She gave me the fishy stare. She had a good one, too. But I just looked back at her from under the bill of my cap. "Okay," she said at last, "but I'm comin' in witcha, make sure you don't promote nothin'."

"Fine by me," I said, and it was. I hadn't figured it was even money she'd let me in at all. What the hell, though? I wasn't any worse off if she did tell me no. Still playing the electrician, or someone like him, I went on, "Lemme look at the fuse box first."

"C'mon through. It's around the back."

The hallway had some of that old-cabbage-and-rat-piss smell that marks a place on the way down, but not too much. You could see the yard out back had been nice once upon a time. Now it was junk and weeds. I opened up the fuse box and unscrewed the one marked 4-B BACK. And I caught a break. There was a penny behind the fuse. "Well, Jesus God!" I said. "No wonder he's got trouble with the lights!"

"I don't know nothin' about that," the manager lady said. A half-witted poodle would've known she was lying. She brightened. "Now you don't hafta go into his apartment."

"Like fun I don't. Who knows what else is messed up?"

She sent me a look that shoulda knocked me over. When I stayed standing, she started to sigh, coughed, and then finished it. "Well, come on, then, if you gotta."

Around the corner and down another hall to the left. The door there had a brass 4 and a B screwed onto it. She reached into her housecoat pocket and extracted a key ring. The master key went into the lock. She jiggled it a little and the door opened. The key ring clinked as she put it back in her pocket.

If I were a private eye in a book, I'd've lifted it without her ever noticing. But if I were a private eye in a book, I'd be better-looking than I am. And richer. And I'd get laid a lot more often than I do. I wouldn't need to sop up *menudo* after too much Wild Turkey the night before, either.

So instead of playing pickpocket, I walked into Jonas Schmitt's apartment. It was severely neat: neat the way a veteran would keep it, not the way a woman would. An upright piano had pride of place next to the window. Beside it, under the panes of glass, sat a wooden crate filled with three piles of sheet music. He brought his work home. Or what he did for work, he did for fun, too. Most people aren't that lucky.

No photo of Marianne Smalls on the piano or the coffee table. No photos anywhere in the front room I could see. A couple of Rembrandt prints on the walls, some ashtrays, a cut-glass bowl with mints wrapped in cellophane, and that was about it.

I went into the bedroom. A bed made the way they teach you in boot camp. A nightstand. A dresser. A photo on the dresser: a blond woman and two short-pants boys in a town square that looked like Europe. I wondered what Marianne Smalls thought of that. Then I noticed the frame had a black border. It was a past-tense photo.

I shoved the dresser away from the wall and bent down to look at the plug behind it. Sure as hell, it was a plug. So was the one near the nightstand.

"They okay?" the manager lady asked.

"I *think* so." I didn't sound like I believed it. "Put a real working fuse in the box and maybe it'll be all right. Schmitt'll spit rivets when I tell him about the penny. You can start a fire with a stunt like that, y'know?"

"Yeah, yeah," she said, which meant *Shut up*. Then she went on, "How's about this? You keep quiet about the penny, I won't say nothin' about him callin' you before he talked to me. Izzat a deal?"

I scrunched up my face to show I didn't like it—and to hide a grin. "I shouldn't oughta," I said, lying through my teeth, "but okay." We were both happy when I left.

I hadn't been back in the office longer than five minutes before Old Man Mose came in. He said something to me, but I couldn't make out what it was. He was trying to talk with his mouth full. He had his pointy little teeth clamped at the nape of a dead rat's neck.

He brought it over to my desk, walking spraddle-legged because the rat's body was between his front legs. The rat bled on the rug as he dragged it along. He'd ripped its guts out with the claws on his hind feet, the way they do. Oh, well. That rug was already pretty ratty.

He dropped the rat at my feet. I moved them in a hurry. I didn't want blood on my shoes. He peered up into my eyes, as proud as if he'd just given me a fancy gold watch. "Are you going to eat it?" he asked.

"That's all right, Mose," I said quickly. "Be my guest." Cats don't get people's eating habits. You should see the faces he pulls when I eat an orange. He hates those even worse than cigarettes.

Now he stared at me as if I were even dumber than he'd given me credit for, which was really saying something. "*I* don't want it," he said. "It's got that undead *bleah* to it." He stuck out his rough little pink tongue to make the disgusted noise, and didn't quite reel it all back in. He looked silly, is what I'm telling you. Then he went on, "I figured you wouldn't care, what with your sorry excuse for a nose and taster."

"Palming the shoddy merchandise off on me, huh?" When he jabs, I always jab back—gotta keep him in his place. But after a second, I actually heard what he'd said ahead of the jab. "What do you mean, that undead *bleah*?"

"See? I knew you couldn't tell. That's why I gave the thing to you," Mose said. "But the *bleah*, it's there, all right."

I believed him. Even if I couldn't tell, he could. And no matter how dumb the cat thinks I am, I can add two and two if you hit me over the head often enough. You don't have to be Bram Stoker to know rats and vampires go together like ham and eggs.

"It was spying for Dora Urban!" I said.

"Sure smells that way to me." Old Man Mose leaned over and started to lick the inside of his leg. I was afraid he'd got nipped—cornered rats fight like, well, cornered rats—but no. He was just neatening up ruffled fur.

"Did it say anything before you killed it?" I asked. Even if rats get along with vampires, they don't talk so people can follow. But Mose is no people. If I weren't, he'd be the first one to tell you that.

"It's a rat," he said dismissively. "Stupid rat, too. Smart rats don't hang around with vampires. But yeah, it was supposed to listen and to go poking around with its ratty little paws."

He sniffed again. I didn't. Rats have clever front paws, more clever if less pincushiony than cats'. I wasn't sure what all it could have stolen or got a look at, especially if it gnawed its way into my desk. I looked down at it. Its beady little black eyes stared blankly up at the ceiling.

"Any chance you can get the other cats in the neighborhood to look out for rats for a while?" I asked. It was worth a shot. Mose is the toughest kitty in Dodge, even if his Dodge is only a block or two wide.

But he curled that thing he has instead of an upper lip, whatever it's called. "They don't do what I tell 'em. They just run away from me." He sounded proud of that. It goes with being the toughest kitty in Dodge. Then he added, "Besides, even if they did listen, you'd have to feed 'em to pay 'em off, and you ain't feedin' anybody but me, Jack."

"You know I don't do that," I said. I scritched him under the chin and by the side of his jaw to remind him he's the A-number-one cat as far as I'm concerned. He's always nervous about that, nervous like a dame who worries her old man is stepping out on her. After a minute or two, though, he started to purr. He believed me … this time. Sooner or later—probably sooner—we'd have to go through the same rigmarole again.

Cats. What can I tell you?

I went on scritching Mose while my little gray cells—if that Belgian with the hairnet doesn't swish, I've never seen anybody who does—rubbed against each other and tried to make fire. All right, Marianne Smalls was doing the dirty with Schmitt. But was Lamont getting some on the side, too? Plenty of broads'd be interested in what he could do for them, and he wasn't ugly even if he could've dropped a few pounds. So was sweet Marianne getting even, or what?

Lamont didn't say anything about a girlfriend. Which proved what? Nothing? Yeah, nothing, or maybe less. You pile what your clients don't tell you alongside of what they do, guess which makes a taller stack. A big part of my job is finding out what the folks who pay me don't want me to know.

Old Man Mose turned his head and kinda nipped at my fingers. "If I'm the one you feed, why don't you feed me?" he said.

So I opened a can of cat food. It smelled too much like fish to me, but not to Mose. Since it was for him, that was fine. He sure thought so. He buried his nose in it.

I took the front page of the *Times* and grabbed the rat with it. I carried the little carcass out to the alley and dropped it there along with the newspaper page. Picking up dead rodents and lining birdcages, that's about what the *Times* is good for. Horrible rag. The *Times* doesn't like anybody but rich white people, and even then only if they vote the right way. But it's the biggest paper in town, and that's not even close. I don't know what that says. Nothing good, for sure.

After I came back in, I paid a few more bills. Having money again was nice. I'd turned the double eagles Dora Urban gave me into cash. Chances are I got gypped doing it, but so it goes. And I had Lamont Smalls' first payment. I felt flush, which I seriously wasn't used to. All the same, watching money go out was even less fun than disposing of a dead rat.

I didn't even notice it get dark outside. It did, though, whether I noticed or not. Shows how much the universe cares about one Jack Mitchell. The telephone rang. I picked it up. "Mitchell here."

"This is Dora Urban," said the voice on the other end of the line. "Do you have anything new to tell me?"

"Only that it's not nice to set spies on somebody you hire to do a job for you," I answered. "But you already knew that, huh?"

"As a matter of fact, yes, just as you must know how pointless discussing niceties with a vampire is." She was a cool customer. I expect she would have been even if she were still alive.

"I was doing some other stuff today," I said. "I'll be back on your business tomorrow."

"Do not let the trail fade," was all she said. A human woman would have pitched a bigger fit. But the undead do have time on their side—till they *finish*, anyhow. Then it's all over for them. People go on … or at least we hope we do.

30

III

What I needed to do was go to Deacon's. I could have done it that night, but I didn't feel like watching the sun come up through the smog the next morning. I went home instead, and slept. I was even a good boy. I didn't get toasted before I left the office.

When I say I slept, I mean I slept. I didn't get back to the office till almost eleven. I called my answering service to see if anybody new had a problem only I could fix.

"No new messages, Mister Mitchell," the operator said.

"Thanks, Hilda." I hung up, thinking *Thanks for nothing*. The world is full of trouble. My trouble was, other folks didn't want me to take care of theirs.

Well, I did have a couple of clients. Old Man Mose had already curled up on the sofa and gone to sleep. That meant I couldn't, not unless I felt like booting him off. It was tempting. I was gonna be up all night. But he looked too comfortable, with his tail draped over his nose. So I twiddled my thumbs at my desk for a little while, then went out with the notion that I'd do something useful.

I walked around to the alley in back of the building where the office is. No rats scurrying around, not where I could see them. Hadn't really expected any, not out in plain sight, but you never can tell. Daylight doesn't *finish* rats the way it does vampires. You need somebody like Mose for that, Mose or .... I told myself to put down some traps by the trash cans. Might not do any good, but it couldn't hurt.

Then I took the trolley up to County General. I wouldn't run into Rudolf Sebestyen, not at that time of day, but I might come across his buddies who could go out in the noonday sun. They'd have to be crazy, as crazy as I was. It was one of those end-of-summer days we get where being out in the open dries up your eyeballs and breathing scorches your lungs worse than a pack of Camels. The sun blazes down on your noggin as if it's no more than six inches away; everything looks all washed out, like overexposed color film.

I had to change from the Red Line to the Yellow Line to get to the hospital. The Pacific Railway station where you do that has air conditioning. All of a sudden, I wasn't sweating any more. I was freezing. Air conditioning is always too damn cold. One of these days, they say they'll get the ice elementals properly trained. They sure haven't done it yet.

And when we set out again, the heat just felt more brutal. I wasn't the only one in the car who made a noise halfway between a sigh and a sizzle when the sun smacked us again.

I saw the hospital on the hill through the trolley's front window— and through shimmering heat. It really does tower as you get close. It's up there, and it's something like twenty stories tall. That has to make it the second-highest building in town, after City Hall. The earth elementals here are so bouncy, most places have to top out at thirteen stories (even if the elevators say fourteen) or 150 feet. Eventually, we may have more skyscrapers. People have been making journeys to the center of the earth to talk—or bribe—the elementals into behaving themselves. So far, nobody's come back from any of those journeys, and we've still got earthquakes.

You don't realize how big the County General complex is till you've got to go somewhere in it. Sweat poured off me as soon as I got down from the Yellow Car and started walking. *It's a dry heat,* people say. *It's not so bad.* And when it's in the nineties, say, that may even be true. Get over the century mark and it just means you roast instead of stewing. Had to be 103, 104 that afternoon.

The blood bank was in a two-story building away from the big, towering tower. It stood right next to another two-story building with bars on the windows and the label PSYCHOPATHIC AND ACCURSED WARD. Somebody in there let out a shriek as I walked by. He sounded like hell, whether his own demons or some from outside drove him there.

A nurse in starched whites looked up from a crossword puzzle when I came in. "Yes?" she said.

"I'd like to donate blood," I told her. As soon as the door closed behind me, I couldn't hear the moonstruck guy howling any more. They had themselves some good soundproofing there.

She brightened. Till then, she'd been at least as starchy as her uniform. "That's wonderful!" she said. "I have some papers for you to fill out, and you'll need a quick, simple blood test before we can draw a pint from you." If I had VD, they didn't want my warm muscatel. But she wouldn't have come out and said that if I'd put her on the rack.

I filled out the papers. Yes, I was doing this of my own free will. Yes, I was over twenty-one. No, to the best of my knowledge I had no infectious diseases. The blood test was in case the best of my knowledge wasn't good enough. I gave them my name and address—I used the office's—and my autograph.

I wasn't thrilled about doing this. I don't like needles. But it gave me an in, and I could talk easier while I was getting stuck than if I just strolled in and started grilling folks.

In a few minutes, the medical wizard said I'd been a good boy, or at least a careful one. They put me in a reclining chair and reclined it. The doc who aimed the needle at my vein was a cheery redhead with a name badge that said BERKOWITZ. "Just look away," he told me. "It'll hardly hurt a bit."

I didn't want to watch anyway. I've lost blood before a time or three, but not on purpose. It makes a difference. Not looking at him, I said, "Go ahead. You're the vampire."

"Not me." He laughed. While he was laughing, he jabbed the needle home, the sneaky so-and-so. I felt it, but it wasn't ... too ... bad. He went on, "I wouldn't have these hours if I were."

"Yeah, you'd be a regular fly-by-night," I said. He laughed some more. Why not? *He* wasn't getting stuck. But I'd made myself an opening, or I hoped I had. I asked him, "How much of what you collect goes to people who get hurt or need operations and how much to vampires?"

"It's about seventy-thirty," Berkowitz answered. "Sometimes the vampires get a little more. We don't *fargin* them ..."

"You don't what?"

He thought about what he'd just said and laughed one more time. "We don't begrudge 'em, I mean. Sorry. Sometimes the *mamaloshen* comes out and I don't even notice. We don't, though, 'cause if they're not getting their blood here they'll be out biting people and doing real harm."

I filed *fargin* away. I could hardly wait to see Al Harris' face when I trotted it out. I'd never heard him use it, but I figured he'd understand it if somebody, even a goy like me, threw it his way. Meanwhile, still eyes left, I asked Berkowitz, "Ever have vampires try to make, um, unauthorized withdrawals?"

"It happened once, right after we opened. It was during the war, when everybody was kinda *meshuggeh* ...." He broke off, but I nodded. I know that one, even if Al says *meshiggeh*. Berkowitz picked up again: "Crazy times, uh-huh. Zoot suits and sailors duking it out, the demon that tore up a mile of Broadway before they could exorcise it, the fun and games the Negroes went through so they could work at war plants ..."

Uncle Sam was already paying my wages when the demon manifested. I read about that in the papers. The other stuff he was talking about, I knew firsthand. I said, "If the war was about anything, it was about treating people like human beings."

"Hey, you get no beef from me," Berkowitz said. "My old man was a kid when his father got him out of Russia. The stories Pop and Grandpa told me .... And they'd be dead for sure, and me with 'em, if they'd stuck around till the New Order came through."

"There is that, yeah," I said. Some things are even harder than being a Negro in America. Some people don't wanna hear it, but it's true. They screw you here, but most of the time they don't just go ahead and kill you. Places the New Order overran .... If the fylfot boys didn't make a clean sweep, it wasn't 'cause they didn't try. I didn't want to think about that, so I asked something else: "Can I smoke a cigarette while you're bleeding me?"

TWICE AS DEAD

"No. Sorry. Oxygen equipment." He shook his head.

"Oh, well." I circled back toward what I was donating this pint to find out. "Ever have trouble with rats? Or with bats?"

"We've got cats prowling the grounds, we've got traps, we've got the best ratproofing the building can buy—and we still have some, but not so much," Berkowitz said, more proudly than not. "Bats .... You don't see it like you do with the bars on the windows next door, but we've got wire mesh over them all, and on the vents to the attic. We try not to take chances. Your blood's safe with us till it gets used. You don't need to worry about that."

"Well, I won't, then." I was glad he thought I was having the vapors for personal reasons, not that I was pumping him.

"Good. And we're about done here." He pulled out the needle and slapped a cotton ball and some adhesive tape on the inside of my elbow. When I looked at my watch, I was amazed. It only took fifteen minutes. He went on, "Stay here another little bit. Then we'll take you out to the anteroom and feed you some cookies and orange juice to pep you up for when you head out."

"I feel all right," I said. But I was shaky walking out to the anteroom. They made me sit down for the snack. The cookies were chocolate chip—good, but they didn't go with the juice. I started getting woozy. Next thing I knew, my face was on the table.

A nurse shoved smelling salts under my nose. "Don't worry, sweetie," she said as I coughed and pulled my head away. "Happens all the time."

They took me back to the chairs that reclined. After a while, another nurse brought me a mug of hot, salty chicken broth. That did the trick where the juice and cookies hadn't. I felt like my old self, or at least like a pretty fresh carbon of me.

"You sure you're good to go?" Dr. Berkowitz asked when I got up again.

"I'm fine." I even meant it. I stuck my fedora on my head at what I hoped was a jaunty angle. "Thanks for everything." Off I went, out into the heat.

I got back to the office just as the sun was going down. After almost drowning myself in my orange juice, I was running late. But I wasn't

35

fretting about it, not on account of I had to get to Deacon's early. Only early Deacon knows about is the wee smalls. His joint doesn't even start to cook till after midnight. So I had time to kill.

Grabbed myself some short-rib hash at a place up the street. You never had short-rib hash, I'm sorry for you. You don't know what you're missing, and that's a fact. It was full dark by the time I came out, and already twenty, twenty-five degrees cooler than when I went to County General.

I grinned. I purely did. Get a hot day back East, you suffer all night long, too. In LA, doesn't matter how hot it is in the daytime. Triple digits, like today? Fine, triple digits. It'll still drop into the sixties at night. You can sleep. You don't stick to your pj's and swelter under your sheet.

If you aim to sleep at night, I mean. I didn't, not that night. After supper, I strolled over to the office again to put on some glad rags for Central Avenue. Before I went in, I checked the alley behind the place, on the off chance I'd spot another snoop with a long, naked tail.

Damned if something didn't move back there. My hand started toward the .38 I wasn't packing before I realized it wasn't that kind of motion. Too big. Too slow. Too not afraid of me.

Not a rat. Just the new zombie janitor from two doors down policing up the alleyway with a push broom. He not only wasn't scared of me, chances were he had no idea I was there; he was deader than a vampire for the time being. His dark hair hadn't been combed in what might have been months. It stuck out from his head like tufts of steel wool. But he was very light if he was a Negro—lighter than I am, even. His nose and chin said he probably wasn't. Whatever he was, he looked like hell.

I wondered how desperate he'd been, and over what, to unsoul himself on purpose. I didn't ask. He wouldn't know why he'd done it himself, not right now. He wouldn't know where he had, either. Somebody behind a desk somewhere would have charge of his file and know the answers to questions like that.

If he'd done it on purpose. You know those stories about shanghaiing people and zombifying them? Some of 'em are true, take it from me. Easier to fall through the cracks if you're colored. But it can happen to a white man, too. They raise a bigger stink when it does.

Sweep. Pause. Step. Sweep. Pause. Step .... Everything happened in slow motion. You can make a zombie work, but you can't make him hustle. Whatever makes somebody hustle, that's what goes away when you drop the spell on him.

The zombie paid me no attention. He wouldn't unless I stood there till he tried sweeping my feet. I had better things to do. As for him, he'd keep on until he finished what he was ordered to take care of. Then he'd go back in the lightless, airless closet with the broom. He wouldn't notice, either, any more than it did. He'd just stand there till the boss man needed him again.

I have a closet of my own in the office. No zombies inside. I don't care to deal with the people you get 'em from. Not the licensed ones who say they're legit, and especially not the others, the scary ones. No, thanks! I was talking about glad rags? That closet's where they live.

You want to go strutting on Central, you can't just throw on your $23.95 Sears suit. Well, you can, if you want to scream *chump!* to the world. You put on a zoot suit now, you're a different kind of chump, one who doesn't know the dragon already pulled that train out of the station. Central's about *now*, not day before yesterday.

Maroon silk shirt. Pale blue tie that lights up against a maroon silk shirt. The jacket with the stripe that's barely there and with the lapels just so. My shoes shined till I could shave in 'em. The good fedora—near as good as Lamont Smalls's—with the brim rolled down. Pimps roll theirs up. I didn't want that look.

Buying those clothes was one reason I couldn't pay my bills before Dora Urban walked in. Gotta have 'em, though. You show up on Central, you gotta look like you belong on Central. I do a lot of work there. I have a lot of fun there, too. When I'm lucky, it's both at once. I'm not lucky often enough. Who is?

Old Man Mose came in and jumped up onto the sofa while I was getting the knot on my tie exactly how I wanted it. He was as impressed as you'd expect a cat to be. "If you had fur, you wouldn't need to mess with all that stupid crap," he said.

"If I had fur, I'd look the same all the time. It's boring," I said.

Mose's sharp-toothed yawn said people didn't know much about what boring was all about. He has a little black spot on his tongue.

I don't know if he's ever seen it; cats don't do much with mirrors. I gave him fresh water and a can of mackerel, so he stayed happy. Then I headed for the avenue where they plug Los Angeles in.

Explaining Central's like explaining jazz. If you don't already dig it, you never will.

The lights are brighter on Central. Damn right they are. Everybody wants to suck you into whatever place he's running. The lights are the lure. Once you get inside, he sets the hook. You go out again with all the cash you came in with, he's doing something wrong.

Music pours out of open doorways. Some of it's jukebox hits from the cheap saloons. Some of it's house combos, guys who're good enough to eat with their music but won't ever strike it rich. Don't waste your time on 'em. You can find the best in the world on Central. All the colored jazzmen who come to town and the hottest, hippest white guys play there, with the house combos or with their own sidemen or by their lonesome. And sometimes they face off against each other, to see who's best of the best. Run across one of those shows, whatever you spend is cheap. You'll keep talking about it till they shovel dirt on you.

Central when the sun's up, that's where the Negroes do their business. Real estate, insurance, the dentist, a scryer, a secondhand car .... You know what I mean. But Central's a different story when the sun goes down. Oh, is it ever. Everybody comes to Central when the sun goes down.

Still more Negroes than anybody else. Hey, it's their—our—part of town. Not like they're—we're—allergic to a good time. But white men who wouldn't be caught dead on Central in the daytime show up when it gets dark. Some are looking for easy women. With money in your pocket, you can find 'em. Pick what you're after. Pick your price.

But some come for the scene, for the music. I saw myself a natty Jew strolling along the avenue. I touched the brim of my hat to him as we passed. He nodded back and smiled. Mickey kills people ... but not on Central. On Central, he's a nice guy and a big spender.

And every once in a while, one goes native. There's this Greek who plays drums .... Look at him, you figure he's light-skinned, light enough so he could pass if he wanted to, and if he didn't talk like he does. But he *is* passing, passing the other way. I know Negroes who'll call you a liar if you say Johnny's anything but colored. Believe 'em if you want to. I know better.

You'll see Mexicans going from a bar to a club to another bar like anybody else. You'll see vampires up from VV. Some aren't out for anything more than a drink, same as some of the whites aren't there for anything more than a whore. But some of them have rhythm and blues in their blood, too, even if you don't want to think about how it got there.

Two cops with faces like clenched fists clumped by me. I didn't tip my hat to them. I looked down at the sidewalk and made like I wasn't there. LA cops, not getting rousted is the most you can hope for. The colored ones are worse than the others. I'd say they sold their souls to get where they're at, but I don't think they were issued any to begin with.

Half a minute later, a black-and-white cruised slowly down the street. The red lights on the bar on top told the world what it was. The world, or the part of the world that's Central, ignored it. Cops don't like getting ignored. Two blocks farther along, the clowns in this car squealed their siren and pulled somebody over. Did he do anything? They said he did. Nothing else mattered.

I walked along. I was almost to Eddie's, which is a bar I'm known to visit, when sweet reefer smoke thick enough to slice poured out of a doorway. I could smell it even with an Old Gold in my mouth. If I could, the flatfoots who'd gone by must've smelled it, too.

Why didn't they charge in and cuff every hophead in the place? You know why, same as I do. Somebody'd paid them off, that's why. That's how things get done here.

When I went into Eddie's, I slid onto a stool somebody else'd just slid off of. "Hey, Jack," the barkeep said. "What'll it be?"

"The usual, Gus. Wild Turkey, coupla rocks. Make it a double." I wanted to wash the taste of crooked cops out of my mouth.

"Comin' up." Gus has one of those double-ended shot glasses, all shiny chrome. Ordinary jigger on one side; flipped over, it's a double. He gave full measure—I watched. I'm regular enough there, they treat me right.

I drank that one fast, the next one slow. Bourbon makes you not care so much what the cops on Central are like. It'd be worth drinking if it didn't do anything else at all.

Soon as I got off the barstool, someone else got on. If a bar ever goes out of business, either the people running it are really dumb or they aren't lining the right pockets.

Three doors down from Eddie's is the Blue Lobster Club. The sign on the sidewalk out front said Bird was there. Two bucks cover, two-drink minimum. For Bird, I paid. Or I tried to. The guy sighed and said, "Don't know if I can squeeze you in. The fire marshal ...." So I greased his palm, and he squeezed me in. And to hell with the fire marshal.

I bet he made plenty with that *Don't know if I can.* The room was packed. The fire marshal would've spit rivets. He wasn't there, though. They kept squeezing in. I wound up at a table with two blond guys from South Gate and the girl who was with one of 'em, or maybe with both.

They gave you little drinks at big prices, and I swear they watered the booze. Soon as Bird came out, everybody stopped caring. It had been noisy and smoky and hot. It stayed hot and smoky, but as soon as he took the stage with his sax you could've heard a pin drop in there. A pin, nothing. A pinfeather.

He started to play. If you don't know, I can't tell you. I'm sorry for you—I'll tell you that. He does things with a sax you didn't know anyone could do. And he must have got just enough junk just enough long ago, because he was on fire. Not herky-jerky-gotta-get-a-fix; not nodding off, either. On fire. If he sold Satan his soul for licks like those, Old Scratch gave better than he got.

After a while, he put down the saxophone and gestured. A pretty girl wearing not much brought him a drink while the crowd went nuts. I'll tell you how good he was. The place he sent me to, I hardly noticed her. *That* good.

I turned to one of the guys from South Gate and said, "Way he blows, he makes me think I grew wings outa my back and flew straight on up to heaven."

Maybe it came out like that because I'd taken Angel's Flight not long before. Any which way, both blond fellas busted up. So did their lady friend. Her name was Babs. She probably had other stuff wrong with her, too.

I must've looked sore. Cripes, I *was* sore. One of them held up his hand. Calluses with ground-in grease on the palms; he worked hard, whatever he did. And he told me what: "Sorry, ace. Don't get torqued. No offense, honest. But all three of us work at the United Rubber plant south of here, the one with the old-time guys with the beards and the wings on the walls."

"Only some of 'em're bulls with men's heads and wings," Babs put in.

"Gotcha." I nodded. I had to. I knew the factory he was talking about. You go past it once, you never forget it. I almost drove off the road the first time I saw it, I was rubbernecking so hard. It's like a palace from Assyria or Babylonia or one of those ancient places dropped down ten miles or so from LA City Hall. Only they don't send out gleaming cohorts from there. They make tires. People who say all the romance has leaked out of the modern world know what they're talking about.

Or I think so most of the time. Anybody who fought in Italy would. But as soon as Bird finished that drink—he didn't take long—and picked up the sax again, everybody in the Blue Lobster Club breathed in together. He started to blow some more. Long as he played, the world not only made sense, it made beautiful sense.

When he finally stopped, the room stayed quiet a second or two. We still heard the music, even after it was gone. *Then* we blistered our palms for the man. He dipped his head. That silence seemed to touch him. You don't win it every day.

I give the club credit. They waited till things died down. Then a fellow said, "People, we got to clear the hall. I'm sorry, but we do. Bird has another show, startin' a quarter to one. It's a new cover, a new minimum. You can see him again, but you gotta go on out now—and there's already a pretty fair crowd out front, waitin' to be as lucky as you were."

Out we went. Sure enough, we waded through people trying to crowd in. Babs and the South Gate blonds headed home. They had to work in the morning. I was already working, so I went back to Eddie's.

Gus was off by then. Well, Vic knew me, too. He held up a fifth of Wild Turkey. I nodded. He poured. The small jigger, not the big one. That was fine. After Bird, I might like a drink, but I didn't need one. Even without wings sprouting from my shoulders, he put me on a higher plane.

For a little while, anyhow.

Other people came in gabbing about the music. I let them. Why not? But I didn't join in. I'd heard it. That was plenty. For once in my life, I'd got better than I deserved, not worse.

At five to two, Vic said, "Last call, everybody!" Whoever needed one more drink bought it and gulped it. Bars close from two to six. Oh, there are after-hours clubs, but they aren't exactly legal. The police give them grief when they find them—and when the fix isn't in.

Deacon's is a place like that. Well, Deacon's isn't a place *like* anything. But it stays open after two. It's just warming up when other joints shut down. You can get a drink there. You can get anything you think you want there.

Of course, somebody who's already there might think he wants you. He can get you, too. Chance you take. It's one of the things that make going to Deacon's ... interesting.

I tossed back the last of the bourbon in my glass. I set it on the bar. The ice cubes sparkled. I walked out onto Central. I didn't look back. You never look back. It doesn't do any damn good.

I hadn't gone far before a beautiful blonde fell into step with me and said, "Would you like some company?"

"Not especially," I said. It was Dora Urban.

"You are going to Deacon's," she said. It wasn't a question.

"And so?"

"I would like to come with you. Someone with my abilities may prove valuable."

"You can come if you want. I can't stop you. But how long can you stay? Don't you have to be somewhere safe before sunup?"

"I intend to go back to my own apartment. But at need they also have arrangements for my kind there. So I am told by those who have used them."

TWICE AS DEAD

"Terrific. Did Sebestyen use them, too?"

That made her miss a stride. She could be rattled. I wouldn't've believed it if I didn't see it. She said, "I presume he did at one visit or another. Whether he did the last time he was at Deacon's, I do not know."

If he did, his movie didn't have a happy ending. You lie down in your coffin, you've got to trust the people who can move around during the daylight. If somebody's got a grudge or just a nasty sense of humor, he's liable to drag you out into the back yard and let the sun shine in. Then you're *finished*, all right.

Most of the watchmen, guards, whatever you want to call 'em, who patrol Vampire Village in the daytime are Jews from Boyle Heights. I mean Jews from, or Jews with parents from, places like Poland and Hungary and Russia and Romania. Almost joking, they call themselves Shabbas goys. They know what getting it in the neck on account of who you are is all about. They don't like it no matter who's on the receiving end, and they stop it when they can.

Of course, that dapper Jew who walked past me, the one who rubs people out when he isn't on Central, he's from the east side of town, too. They aren't all saints—not even close. Still and all, Jewish doctors and lawyers and writers have also done Negroes quite a bit of good. Like I say, they know what the shitty end of the stick smells like.

As we walked along, I asked Dora Urban, "Do you know where Deacon's is?"

"I have never been there myself," she said.

I took a couple of steps before I realized she hadn't answered me. "Yeah, but do you know where it is?" I persisted.

She smiled wide enough so the tips of her fangs showed against her lips for a split second. Then they disappeared again. "It is good to know that you actually listen, Mister Mitchell," she said. "As a matter of fact, I do have some idea, yes."

I didn't have a cigarette going. I sniffed. If she noticed, she'd chalk it up to hay fever or something. Old Man Mose can say whatever he wants—my nose isn't half bad for a person's. I couldn't smell anything undead about Dora Urban. She was wearing perfume, not a lot, with a sweet, musky scent. That was all my snoot picked up. Didn't seem enough to mask anything.

43

But what do I know? This skinny orange-and-white stray trotted up to me, stropped my ankles, and went into her spiel: "Hey, buddy, spare some chow for a hungry kitty? I—" Then her nose caught whatever it was mine couldn't. Her back arched. Her tail puffed out. She bared her own fangs and skittered away.

Dora Urban curled her lip. Did vampires learn that aristocratic sneer from the old-time Hapsburg nobility or the other way around? "Nasty creature," she said.

"What have you got against cats?" I asked her.

"Their blood tastes like piss," she answered.

I opened my mouth. I closed it again. Second try, I managed, "Oh." After a couple of coughs, I said, "I have a cat, you know. Or he has me."

"Oh, yes." Her elegant head bobbed once, to show she did indeed know. "I do not hold it against you … too much."

"Thanks a bunch," I muttered. Mose would have had more to say about that. Good thing he wasn't there.

We walked north up Central. It was the time it was, but life still filled the street. Just because the bars closed didn't mean Central shut down. Even daybreak wouldn't shut it down. The avenue might go from crystal carriage to pumpkin when the sun came up, but it'd still be one busy pumpkin.

A guy across the street whistled at Dora. Her back got stiffer and straighter. I didn't think it could. The fool was lucky—he only did it once. If he'd really annoyed her, he might have found out more about what she was like than he wanted to know.

I counted myself lucky nobody yelled anything my way for walking along with her. If I were even a shade darker …. Colored man out strolling with a gorgeous blond woman? That's trouble waiting to happen. And in the City of Angels plenty of guys are ready to make it stop waiting and start happening.

Never mind that I'm not exactly a colored man and Dora Urban isn't exactly a gorgeous blond woman. The numbskulls and hotheads who start trouble like that, they don't exactly care about those details.

But I am what I am, whatever that is. I can be one thing; I can be the other. Sometimes I wonder if I'm anything at all, to tell you the truth. Nobody on Central that early morning figured I was other enough to be worth taking a swing at, not even the boys with the blue suits and the badges. You take what you can get in this old world.

"Ask you something?" I said.

Dora Urban nodded. "You may always ask. I may not always answer."

"Sounds good." I nodded, too. "All right—how come you call Rudolf Sebestyen your half brother?"

"Ah. That I can answer. There is no better term in English. The one who made Rudolf what he is also made me what I am. We have … a family obligation, I think you would say. We do not always honor those, but people do not always honor theirs, either."

"Boy, you got that right." If people did, I'd have less work than I do. "But you're a good half sister?"

"*Good* is a word with very murky meaning, especially to one like me. I am a dutiful half sister. I understand dutiful. I hope Rudolf would do as much for me, but I am not sure he would."

"Happy day." I'd been watching the cross streets. "We turn here."

Central has streetlights. The cops and the shops both like 'em. The little streets that run into Central, the ones where ordinary—and not so ordinary—Negroes live? Nope. It'd cost too much money. In most of that part of town, any money counts for too much.

I waited a minute to let my eyes get used to the dark. Dora Urban waited with me, even if hers were fine right away. We went half a block, then turned down an alley. It stank of garbage. You had to be careful where you put your feet. Not easy, when it was darker than dark.

If you didn't already know they were there, you'd never find the wooden stairs that went up from the alley. I did know, and I was still groping for them when Dora Urban started up. I followed her toward Deacon's.

IV

Up at the top of the stairs, a boardwalk leads you to Deacon's. The joint has other ways in and out; I've used some of them, anyhow. My guess is, the Deacon's got one for himself nobody else knows about. Or more than one. But the boardwalk's the one for the paying customers, so that's the one Dora and I took.

People make jokes about that boardwalk. The guys who built it, they learned what they thought they knew about carpentry from one of those courses you find out about on the inside of a matchbook cover. Some of the boards are higher than others. If you run your hand along the plank on top of the guardrails, it'll get full of splinters in nothing flat. I'd learned better, so I didn't.

And, without lights up there, you can trip and break your neck if you aren't careful. I am careful, or I try to be, but I damn near killed myself anyway. The front of my right heel caught the edge of a board that stuck up a quarter of an inch higher than the ones to either side of it, and I started to go forward on my face.

Dora grabbed my arm and hauled me upright again. I'm a good bit bigger than she is; she turned out to be a good bit stronger than I am. And a good bit quicker—anybody on the Angels would kill for reflexes like that. She could see in the dark like Old Man Mose, too, because it was as black as the inside of an LA cop's soul up there.

"Thanks," I managed. I've had my nose rearranged once. I wasn't eager for those pine planks to do it again.

"You are all right?" she asked.

"I am now, yeah," I said, and we went on toward the entrance.

She kept her hand in mine, which I hadn't expected. It might have been to keep me from falling over my own two feet again, or it might not. I squeezed her hand a little, in an experimental way. If she didn't fancy that, I figured she'd let me know. She didn't seem to mind. She might even have squeezed back, though I wouldn't have sworn to it.

I noticed she didn't feel cold, the way vampires usually do. That was ... interesting. Had she fed just before we met up? Was that the warmth I was feeling? Or was she just strange for her kind, the way some humans are strange?

Me? I didn't say anything about me. Not a word.

No, I didn't ask her. For one thing, it was none of my business. Far as I'm concerned, long as you don't hurt anybody else, you can live your life—um, go on with your existence—however you want. For another thing, she might tell me, and I didn't want to know that bad.

Dora and I shoved our way through what felt like the thickest, most clinging spiderwebs in the world. I know of one fellow—a tough guy, too, or he thought he was—who didn't expect that, and ran away screaming when soft stuff seemed to stick to his face.

Only they weren't spiderwebs. They were blackout curtains. Who's cared about blackout curtains since the war ended? Who in the States has cared about blackout curtains since six months after we got into the war? The Deacon, that's who.

After we made it past the curtains, we could see again. Well, I could; Dora, I guess she'd been able to all along. I blinked a couple of times. The lights weren't bright, but they felt that way. And there in front of us, big as life, stood the Deacon.

When you talk about Deacon Washington, *big as life* says a lot. He's got to be six eight, maybe six nine, and he's damn near, I mean *damn* near, as wide as he is tall. He's one of the blackest black men you'll ever see anywhere. Only makes his teeth look whiter when he grins (he's had them capped).

He grinned when he saw me. "Hey, Jack. Been a while," he said. His voice is smooth as cream, deep as a well.

I nodded. "It has been."

He held out his hand. He didn't want to shake mine, he wanted his cover charge. I set two engraved portraits of Andrew Jackson on his palm. The hand closed, engulfing them.

"Obliged," he said, and then, "Shall I stop by later on?"

I nodded again. "If you want to, sure. We might talk a bit."

"Okay. I will, then." His eyes slid to Dora, then back to me. "You have a, a … curious choice in friends."

My eyes slid to Acolyte Adams, who was hovering in the background the way he always does. "You know what? I'm not the only one."

If you get the Deacon sore at you, you're in more trouble than you know what to do with. But he threw back his head and laughed and laughed. "Not me, Jack. What I have is, I have a queer choice in friends." He laughed some more.

Acolyte Adams looked pained, as if he wished the Deacon wouldn't say things like that. He's a prissy little guy, as short and skinny as Deacon Washington is big and round. They've been together for, I don't know, twenty years now? Something like that, anyway.

Most men who go for men, they try and hide it. For starters, it's against the law. Even if it weren't, other people look down their noses at men like that (at women who like women, too) because they're the way they are. Of course, when you're a Negro, other people look down their noses at you for that first. When you're a Negro and you're queer—a lot of the time, it's just too much.

Acolyte Adams, he felt that weight all the time, sometimes heavy enough to squash him. He was what he was, but part of him wished he were something else.

The Deacon? The Deacon didn't care. He liked what he was. More than that—he reveled in it, wallowed in it, threw it in people's faces. More fun than a barrel of monkeys? Deacon Washington had more fun than a Barnum and Bailey three-ring circus. He was a three-ring circus all by himself.

"Go on in," he told Dora and me. "Have yourselves a time. That's what we're here for." He laughed again. Then he forgot about us, because more people were coming in and he had to get his big old hands on their covers, too.

We went on in. Deacon's is a funny place. Somebody who knows what she's talking about said one time that it's bigger on the inside than it is on the outside. It feels that way to me, too. No, I can't tell you how it's done. Maybe he owns more of those upstairses than even the law knows about. Or maybe it's wizardry. Those are my two best guesses. I can't prove a thing. You pays your money and you takes your choice.

For that matter, it could be the lights, too. Windows? You're kidding me. The lamps all have shades of one funny green or gold or blue or red or another. Some of 'em are cut peculiar, so the glow that goes out through 'em gets peculiar. And they mix and they mingle and they go on and go off till you don't know what's real and what's your brain getting shell-shocked.

Wherever you are when you're in Deacon's, you aren't on Central in South Central. Which I guess is the point.

No clocks anywhere in there, either. They do the same thing in Reno and Vegas. You need to know what time it is, you better wear a watch. I do, so I mostly don't have to worry about that. That night, that morning, whatever you want to call it, I turned to Dora and asked, "You'll know when the sun's gonna come up?"

What I saw on her face for half a split second, I don't know for sure whether it was a trick of those crazy lights or raw fear. Whatever it was, it was there and then gone. When she answered, "Believe me, I will know," she sure sounded calm through and through.

"Okay," I said, hoping it was.

We flopped down on a couple of big cushions and waited for somebody to notice us. You've never been to Deacon's if you're wondering *cushions*? If a Hollywood designer went nuts halfway through designing the wildest *Arabian Nights* set ever, you'd have Deacon's. Hell, for all I can prove, that's just what happened.

Carpeting thick enough so you can flop on that, too. Cushions, big, small, and in-between. You can build yourself whatever kind of seat or bed you want. Curtains, some see-through, some spangled, some near as thick as the blackout jobs at the entrance.

Everything in bright colors, or else in brighter ones. Mix all that in with the wild and crazy lights and it's quite a place.

Waiters and waitresses wove through the joint, bringing the customers what they wanted. Whatever you want at Deacon's you can get it. Including the waiters and waitresses? Sure. They're all young. They're all good-looking. Some of them don't wear much. Some wear less than that. There are little dark alcoves off the main space. Anything can happen in those. Everything probably has.

Whatever you want. All you have to do is pay. The joke is, everything comes at Deacon's, but nothing comes cheap.

A waitress stopped in front of Dora and me. She was pretty enough so a lot of the time I would've wished I were with her instead of the company I was keeping. Most of the time, but not that early morning. Interesting.

She noticed, too. It annoyed her. "What'll it be?" she asked, spitting out the words.

"Wild Turkey on the rocks," I said.

"A Bloody Mary," Dora said.

"I might've known," the girl said. Dora ... looked at her. You don't want to get a vampire sore at you. Believe me, you don't. The girl flinched. Me, I would've run. Quickly, she told me, "That's twenty-five."

I paid her. Prices like those, you see why Deacon's doesn't go broke. She got the hell out of there.

Dora said, "It must be hard to get good help now." I had the sense not to laugh. She sounded like every aristocrat ever born, pining for the Good Old Days.

The drinks came back fast, I will say that. The waitress didn't get cute more than once. She disappeared as soon as we had them. I bet she wished she could've disappeared for real.

"Here's to you," I told Dora.

"Your health," she said.

We touched glasses. We drank. It was Wild Turkey—a good slug of it, too. What I ordered. Fine. Dora took one sip of hers. She said something that wasn't English and was mostly consonants.

50

TWICE AS DEAD

"Something wrong?" I asked. Was the Deacon's girl trying to get payback for that look? Could you poison the undead?

"It's … a Bloody Mary," she said.

"That's what you ordered, right?" I knew damn well it was.

She gave me a look. Not the kind she'd aimed at the waitress. This one said, *You dumb jackass.* She held out the glass to me. "It's a *bloody* Mary. Taste it."

Warily, I did. Not tomato juice, nope. You ever get hit in the mouth, or even bite the inside of your own cheek, you know that taste right away. I'd never had it mixed with vodka before, though. "Is that … human blood?" I asked, gulping. I think I would've hurled if she'd nodded.

But she shook her elegant head. "No. Horse, I think—the vodka confuses me a little. I never dreamed the Deacon could do, would do, *that.*"

"He takes care of everybody," I said, and then, "What do you usually drink?"

"Scotch, of course." She seemed surprised I had to ask. Playing the aristocrat again. Or not playing, for all I knew of what she'd been before she met the vampire who made her.

A little combo started playing. We could hear them but not see them. Good clarinet, outstanding bass, pretty good piano. He might've sounded better in other company, but he was the weak link here.

They went on for fifteen or twenty minutes. You could listen to them. You didn't have to. That was how you knew they were a house combo. The next step up, an outfit grabs you by the ears and won't let go.

Then they finished whatever number they were playing and clammed up. A buzz went through the Arabian Nights, a buzz that rose to a roar: "Bird is in the house!"

The lights came up—some, anyhow. All the way from murky to dim, you might say. Curtains pulled back, so you could see more of the place. There was the stage where the combo'd played. The clarinetist and the bass man had already got down. The guy at the piano—a white cat—still sat there.

I sighed. "Why's *he* hanging around?" I said to Dora. Not loud, because he wasn't terrible. But I said it just the same.

"Because we're lucky." She didn't keep her voice down. Vampires are like cats. They don't give a damn.

I don't *think* the pianist heard. He didn't make like he did. Before I could worry about it, the Deacon's big, deep voice boomed out: "Ladies and gentlemen and whatever else paid the cover, here he is, the one, the only, *Bird!*"

He walked by me, no more than three or four feet away. He was heading for the bar, only he had trouble getting there. Folks were hanging on to him: women, men, whatever else paid the cover. Some of them wanted the fame to rub off. Some wanted the power, the mana, the juju, the thing that made him what he was, to rub off. And you can bet they all wanted the money to rub off. Oh, yeah. They wanted that.

He worked his way forward, one step at a time. He took it slow, but he kept going. Not like he hadn't done this before. He's been famous a while now. He knows how. He doesn't let it swamp him, the way so many do.

I felt Dora's eyes on me. When I turned away from watching Bird, I found I was right. "You are not going up to him?" she asked.

"Not me." I shook my head. "I'm not stupid. Not that kind of stupid, I mean. Not that kind of greedy, either. Or I hope like hell I'm not."

"Well." She made a complete sentence out of one word. Maybe it was the Wild Turkey, but I felt proud of myself.

Then Acolyte Adams started clearing a path for Bird. It didn't work as well as he would've wanted. The Acolyte, he's the kind of guy who can piss you off saying hello. The most I can give him is, he didn't get punched. And that might've disappointed him.

Bird finally got his drink. He poured it down like he needed it and like he enjoyed it. Why wouldn't he enjoy it? He wasn't paying the Deacon's prices, or I didn't figure he was. The Deacon knows how to keep the talent wanting to come back.

Soon as Bird set the empty glass on the bar, he had a full one in his hand. It didn't stay full long. He waved away whatever the barkeep tried to give him then. Booze is like dope. A little can help. Too much and you think you're great when you stink.

He made his way to the stage and took his sax out of its silver case. Before he started to blow, he leaned over the piano and talked to the guy on the stool for a minute or so. The piano player nodded, nodded again, nodded some more. When Bird lays down the law for a sideman, what's that cat gonna do but nod?

Then the sax wailed, and even at a place like that people paid attention. You can't ask for more. You go to Deacon's to get swept away from the regular world. If Bird can sweep you away from the Arabian Nights ... then that man can play a little bit. Yeah, just a little.

He swept me away. You'd best believe he did. He did, and then after a bit he didn't. It wasn't him. It was the fellow behind the piano. No, not the way he tickled the ivories. He wasn't bad enough or up front enough to be annoying. He rode along behind Bird, which was what he should've done.

Call me stupid. Plenty of people have. A lot of 'em've been right, too. Stupid. Tired. Worn out. Bourboned. In company I was enjoying. So I took way too long to realize the piano player looked familiar.

He should have. I'd seen him, or his picture, just the day before. Jonas Schmitt could brag till the end of his days that he'd backed up Bird.

Bird even turned and gave him a wave and a nod and let him solo for a little bit. He did it with the air of the boss handing the hired help a Christmas bonus, yeah. That he did it at all, though, showed his class. And Jonas, he played okay, and he had the smarts to cut it short.

Crazy. I'd come here for, with, one of my clients, and then all of a sudden I found I was working for another one. A writer with any sense wouldn't stick in a bit like that. It's not, y'know, believable. But the world doesn't have to be believable. The world only has to happen.

"Something is wrong?" Dora asked. No, I don't know how she knew. Did I smell different? Could she sense my heartbeat change? Any which way, she knew.

"Not wrong. I don't think so, anyway. But strange," I said. More than anything else, I was sore at Schmitt for bringing me back from where Bird had taken me. You don't get to go to those places often enough.

But there I was, washed up on reality's rocky shore, or as close to it as you can get at Deacon's. I started thinking like a private dick again. A stupid, tired, worn out, bourboned private dick, but that's part of the job description.

If Schmitt was at the dive, was Marianne Smalls there, too? If I was playing with Bird, I'd sure as hell want my ladylove to watch me do it. I started looking around. I didn't want to be too obvious, and the waitress came by with a fresh round, but I was doing what I could.

Seek and ye shall find. If that wasn't the Deacon's motto, I don't know what would be. If I'd been paying attention, I would've spotted her a lot quicker. She sprawled on a mound of cushions between Dora and me and the stage. Bird had walked between her and us on his way to get something cold and strong.

Now I saw her, not a photo. She could pass if she wanted to, you bet. Folks have reasons not to want to. Throwing away everything you and your people ever were, for instance. Of course, if everybody else had been spitting on everything you and your people ever were for lifetime after lifetime, you might think twice about wanting to keep it. Yeah, you just might.

You might if you'd moved to our fair when it wasn't smoggy city, too. People come to California to be what they want to be, not to keep on being what they were. If you'd had it up to there with all the crap that comes with being Negro—and it's more than anybody who isn't will ever understand—and you can get away with acting white, maybe you will.

Looked like Marianne Smalls aimed for that. She wouldn't be the first. I could name some names that'd surprise you. She wouldn't be the last, either. Not a chance. Not even close.

I wanted to write down what I was seeing. I didn't, though. Nothing would've got me kicked out faster. Kicked out, roughed up, and on the never-get-in-again list. The Deacon's bouncers don't stand around looking mean. That spoils the vibe. But they're there. Oh, yeah.

So I remembered. I'm good at remembering. I remember too much I wish I could forget. Don't we all, friend? Don't we all?

Then Bird started blowing again. That made me want to forget everything else, but I couldn't, dammit. I was working. I kept half an eye on Marianne, the other half on Jonas Schmitt. He did what a backup man needed to do. He rolled with the guy out front and didn't try to upstage him.

He was okay. He was good enough. But what Bird had a whole great big jug of, he had two or three drops.

Bird gave him another little solo. He's a gent, Bird is. Jonas did what he did, did what he could. Marianne Smalls ate it up. She was proud of her new man. The rest of us waited for Bird to put down his glass and pick up the sax again.

After he finished the set, you could hear the shouts of "More!" all the way to City Hall. He gave us an encore, but only a short one. Then he put the sax back in the case, set the case on its side, and mimed using it for a pillow. I'm sure Bird's not poor, but he works for his money.

"That was the man, Bird his own self!" the Deacon roared. The *was* let Bird make his getaway. Meanwhile, the Deacon added, "And on piano, our own Mister Jonas!" Marianne squealed and clapped. A few other people clapped, too. Schmitt's face said he hadn't expected anything more.

The lights dimmed. The curtains slid back into place. I thought I saw a clump of curdled air glide through one as it moved forward. So ghosts made the scene at Deacon's, too? How did he get cover and minimum out of them? If anybody knew a way, he'd be the one.

"What did you think?" I asked Dora.

"Bird is gifted. Remarkably gifted. The piano player? Much less," she answered. The house combo started up again right then, as if to prove her right. Then she asked, "Since this is so, why did you note him more?"

No, she didn't miss a thing. "Business," I said, and not another word.

"Ah." She respected that; she didn't ask me any more. She didn't ask about Marianne Smalls, either. If she'd spied me eyeing Schmitt, she would've seen I'd noticed his ladylove, too. But she didn't ask. I admired her for that.

A few minutes later, the Deacon rolled up to us. As usual, Acolyte Adams was a couple of paces behind the big man. "So what's going on, my friend?" the Deacon asked. I didn't know that I was his friend, or that I wanted to be, but I liked it better than some of the other things he might've called me.

Dora answered before I could: "Can we speak under the rose? And privately?"

He didn't fail to understand her. He didn't misunderstand her on purpose, either. "What I can hear, the Acolyte can hear. You don't fancy that, no talk," he told her. "But we can find somewhere more out of the way."

"Agreed." She wasted no words.

Deacon Washington led us to one of those dark nooks. I don't know how he knew it didn't already have people in it, but he knew. It had had people in it not long before; the air smelled of reefer and sweat and French perfume. You couldn't see much in there. We found ways to make ourselves comfortable anyhow.

"Now then ..." the Deacon rumbled.

"What do you know about the last time Rudolf Sebestyen came here?" No, Dora didn't beat around the bush.

Acolyte Adams sucked in a sharp breath of that crowded atmosphere. He knew something, sure as the devil. Deacon Washington answered a question with a question: "Whatever I know, why should I tell you?"

"I am his half sister," she said. She didn't say, *I'll find out what you taste like if you hold out on me*, but you could smell that in the air, too.

Where I'd had to ask, the Deacon got what that meant. "Are you, now?" he said.

"I am." She waited. So did I. Was the Deacon going to ask her to prove it? How would she do that? By showing that she and Sebestyen had the same fang marks on their necks?

But he didn't ask. He said, "Yeah, he'd come by here every so often. He punched somebody once, laid him out flat, but I didn't even ask him to leave for that. Guy called him a goddamn lugosi, pardon my French, ma'am."

"I am surprised Rudolf did not kill him," Dora said. Call a black man a nigger, whatever happens to you after that's your own damn fault. Call a Jew a kike, same deal. Call a vampire a lugosi .... Vampires are a lot stronger than people. I'd seen that on the boardwalk coming to Deacon's. I was surprised Rudolf Sebestyen didn't kill the son of a bitch, too.

"I thought he did," Acolyte Adams said. "Good thing he didn't, though. Disposing of a body is such a nuisance." His fussy exasperation convinced me he knew what he was talking about.

"The last time," Dora persisted.

"Right," Deacon Washington said. "He was looking for somethin'. That's why he came here, he said. He heard you could get anything here. I always thought he heard right, too." He sounded more proud than anything else.

"What was he after?" I asked the obvious question.

"He called it vepratoga. You know what that is, either one of you? I never heard of it before then."

"I never did, either," I said.

"Nor did I." Dora sounded troubled. "It is not a word I know, not in English and not in Magyar, either."

"Whatever it is, Sebestyen wanted it bad. He didn't stick around real long after I told him I didn't have it or know where to get it. It was like all the juice leaked out of him at once," the Deacon said.

"Before he left, he talked to a couple of people who could get their hands on this and that," Acolyte Adams added. People who sold dope, he meant, but he was too careful not to say that. "They couldn't help him, either, if getting him what he craved counts for helping."

Dora Urban set a hand on my wrist. Her fingers were cold now, whether from fear or because she'd been drinking her iced Bloody Marys I can't tell you. "We'd best go," she said. So we did.

And I awoke and found me here, in the cold alley off of Central Avenue. That's what it feels like, coming out of Deacon's. You have to shake yourself, because it seems like a dream in there. First thing I did was look east. I didn't see anything past the gray beginning of twilight. We were at that season where you notice how much earlier the sun sets and how much later it rises every day. It worked for Dora.

Yes, she was still there, reminding me that place was real. "You truly don't know about this vepratoga, whatever it is?" she asked, sounding worried.

"Not me." I shook my head. "I was hoping you did."

"No. I wonder if the Deacon knew then. If he did not, I wonder if he does now."

"My guess is no. He sounded like it was something he thought he should've known."

"He did not smell false. The other one, his lover, he was harder to read. He holds everything corked tight inside," Dora Urban said, and if that didn't sum up the Acolyte in a sentence, what would?

"I wish we would've found out more," I said.

"We found some things we need to learn more about. This has value," Dora said. "And now I had better go. The other thing I can smell is the coming of the White Fire. Not here yet, but on the way."

She leaned toward me for a moment and brushed her lips against mine. Not a kiss. A ghost of a kiss. Then she was gone.

Or not. Bats don't fly the way birds do. They go more like moths. Now this way, now that, now the other. No curves in the air, just one straight line after another, each different from the one before in length and direction. Seems that way to me, anyhow. I saw her for a heartbeat or two against the sky—yes, it was starting to lighten—but then I couldn't any more.

I walked out to Central. Bright as day there. It always is. I looked at some expensive shoes in a shop window—in a shop window behind steel accordion bars. Those shoes wouldn't have stayed in the window long without the ironmongery.

Then I blinked a couple-three times, on account of the shoes seemed to blur, as if the air in front of 'em'd curdled. I didn't hear somebody say something. After a little no-time, I did, only inside my head, not through my ears. "Vepratoga?"

"What do you know, Eb? Thought I spotted you inside Deacon's." I didn't need to answer loud to make the ghost understand me, either. Moving my lips and thinking about what I was saying, that was plenty. A good thing, too, because Central still had lots of people on it. Even there, they notice if you go around talking to yourself.

"Vepratoga," Ebenezer said again, only this time it wasn't a question.

"What *do* you know?" My attention sharpened. "You know something, sure as I'm standing here."

"I know something, sure as *I'm* standing here," Eb said. And how sure was that? Heisenberg's Uncertainty Principle runs home in tears when it tries to cope with ghosts. "I've heard the word before."

"That puts you one up on me. And on the Deacon. And on a vampire," I said.

"It could be. Or else not. I don't know what it refers to. I don't know anyone who does know," the ghost replied.

"Somebody does. Words point back to things. Rudolf Sebestyen knew, or thought he did."

"I wouldn't trust Rudolf Sebestyen as far as I could throw him," the ghost said. I had to admit, that wasn't far.

"Can I find out about it?" I asked. You'd be surprised how handy the library can be to a private dick.

"I wish you luck," he said. "No one in Narcotics has written anything about it. Don't tell anyone, but I've looked through the files. No references to vepratoga. Other things, yes, but not that."

"Other things, huh?" What could the LAPD do about a ghost who poked his ectoplasmic snoot in where it didn't belong? Anything at all? I had my doubts. And what "other things" had Ebenezer seen? Enough for him to blackmail a pile of lieutenants and captains if they tried anything he didn't care for? Wouldn't surprise me one bit.

But if the Narcotics Department wasn't talking about vepratoga, even the big downtown library was unlikely to have heard of it. Still, you never know till you try. When I got around to it, I would.

As long as he'd decided to manifest here, I asked him, "Know anything about Jonas Schmitt or Marianne Smalls?"

"Not a thing," he said. "I don't believe either one has ever had anything to do with Missing Individuals."

"Ah, well," I said. "If they're lucky, it'll stay that way."

"This is a question connected with what you do?" Eb asked. Well, back before he stopped a Minié ball, his line of work wasn't a whole lot different from mine.

"That's right." When I nodded, I could feel how tired I was. A long day. A long night's journey into day, because now it was nearing sunrise by the minute.

"I see." The curdled air may have nodded back. "If I run across anything interesting, shall I pass it on to you?"

"If you would. Listen, Eb, I've got to grab some shut-eye."

"Ah. Sleep. I remember that. All right, since you need it." All of a sudden, Eb wasn't there any more. Or wasn't manifesting, anyway. Who knows anything for sure with ghosts?

I went back to the office. That was faster than going home. The zombie sweeper was in the alley again, getting started with his slow-motion cleanup. Or maybe he never stopped, just went up and down, back and forth, all day and all night. They could build a machine to do that, but it'd cost more than a zombie.

I walked right past him. He didn't look at me. He didn't notice I was there. The only way he would've noticed me was if I stood where he was trying to sweep. Then, after he noticed he wasn't getting anywhere, he would've gone around me. It would've taken a while.

I could have punched him, knocked him down. He would've got up—slowly, again—and gone back to work. People do that sometimes, for what they call the fun of it. Some fun. It's a little like playing Russian roulette. Every once in a while, you do something like that to a zombie, he'll smash in your skull and feast on your brains. Chance you take.

Machines aren't the only things that go haywire. Oh, no.

Old Man Mose was sleeping on the beat-up couch when I walked into the office. His top lip curled up when he got a whiff of me, the way it would have if I'd been swimming in orange juice. "You smell disgusting," he said needlessly.

"I love you, too," I said. "How about I give you some extra cat food?"

"You can do that!" As long as I was feeding him, he didn't care how I smelled. He hopped down off the sofa, which was part of my cunning plan. If he was on there, I'd have trouble sleeping there myself, and it was getting to the sleep-or-die point.

I hung my hat on the hat tree. I shed my shoes, my belt, my coat, and my tie. That would do. I lay down on the couch. I'm not one of those sissies who need it to be pitch black to sleep. I closed my eyes. Old Man Mose's little smacking noises as he committed gluttony there on the floor soothed me like a lullaby.

TWICE AS DEAD

Next thing I remember, I had thirteen pounds of fluffy red tabby on my stomach. "Do you have to?" I mumbled.

"Damn right I do," he answered. "I'll eat on the floor, but I don't want to sleep there."

Maybe that makes sense if you're a cat. I was too worn to care. I moved him a little, so his sharp back foot wasn't digging into my crotch. Then I closed my eyes again. He might've kept me awake for a minute and a half.

The phone rang. I jumped. Old Man Mose jumped off me. He didn't draw much blood, but some. As I stumbled to the desk, I looked at my watch. I'd had three and a half hours of sleep to stagger through the day on.

"Hello?" I said, and then, remembering where I was, "Mitchell Investigating."

Wrong number. I hung up, thrilled as you'd expect. A perfect start to another perfect day. I love LA.

V

I did go home after that. Little studio apartment, a few blocks from the office. For once, the landlady wouldn't complain my rent was late. I showered. I shaved. I put on clean clothes. I took three aspirins. Home is where the aspirins are. So is the office.

On the way back, I had coffee and *menudo* and more coffee. Old Man Mose was curled up on the sofa when I came in again, his tail over his nose, looking for all the world as if he'd never heard of original sin. Cats have it rough. I shook my head. If you wanted some original sinning, Deacon's was the place. Or some not so original sinning.

After I looked at the bottle of Wild Turkey in my desk, I put it back. That made me feel like a good boy. I knew the feeling wouldn't last. While it did, I called the number Lamont Smalls'd given me.

It turned out to be the switchboard at the *Los Angeles Lookout*. "Can you put me through to Mister Smalls, please?" I said to the operator.

"Who shall I say is calling?" She didn't quite say *Why would the editor want to talk to the likes of you?* but that was what she meant.

"My name's Mitchell, Jack Mitchell."

"And what is this about?"

"He'll know."

TWICE AS DEAD

No, she didn't think I deserved to speak to The Man at all. "Hold on," she said, clearly expecting to hang up on me and enjoy doing it. I heard some clicks and pops. Then she came back on the line. "I'll connect you," she told me. She had the grace to sound surprised.

"This is Lamont Smalls. How are you today, Mister Mitchell?"

How was I? Better not to think about that. "I'll do," I answered. "I have some news that'll maybe interest you. Do you want to hear it on the phone?" *Is that snooty switchboard girl listening in?*

"Why don't I pay you a call? If I come in an hour, will that be convenient for you?"

"Let me check," I said, for all the world as if I might have something else going on. Five seconds later, I told him, "That will work."

"See you then," he said. The line went dead.

Fifty-eight and a half minutes later, he knocked on my door. Old Man Mose dove under the couch. I opened the door. There he stood, as natty as the first time he'd visited. We shook hands. "Come in. Sit down. Good to see you," I told him.

"I'm not nearly so sure it's good to see you," he said, which was understandable enough. I could see him bracing himself for what was liable to come next. "You ... know something about Marianne?"

"I saw her last night." *I saw her this morning* would have been truer, but I came close enough. Then I gave him the other barrel: "At Deacon's."

Whatever Smalls had braced for, that wasn't it. He flinched as if I'd slapped him. "At Deacon's? Good God, what was she doing there?" He didn't ask what I'd been doing there. Either he thought I was working or he thought Deacon's suited me, which it (mostly) doesn't. Nice place to visit, but I wouldn't want to live there.

"She was there with Jonas Schmitt. He plays in the house combo."

"He would," Lamont Smalls muttered darkly. After a few seconds digesting that, the editor added, "You'd think Deacon Washington could hire better."

I had to nod. "Yeah, you would. Don't get me wrong—he isn't terrible, not even close. He can do the job, but he's about as exciting as Cream of Wheat with skim milk." I didn't tell him his wife thought otherwise. Why rub it in? Besides, it's not as if he couldn't work that out for himself.

63

He did some more muttering, this time mostly to himself. I thought I heard *ofay bastard*. He stared down at his elegantly manicured hands. After a bit, he looked up to me again. "I don't suppose you have photos?"

"Sorry. No. I was there on other business." I didn't tell him taking pictures in Deacon's was another good way to get yourself killed. He was bound to know that himself. I went on, "I didn't even know he was the cat on piano till they reeled in the curtains and he backed up Bird."

Smalls looked as if I hadn't just stuck in the knife—I'd twisted it, too. "Jonas Schmitt ... backed up Bird?" Sure as hell, by the way he sounded, that hurt worse than Schmitt doing the nasty with his wife.

" 'Fraid so," I said.

"How was that? Do I want to know?"

"It could have been worse. He's a born sideman. He didn't get pushy—he knew better than that."

"With Bird? God wouldn't get pushy with Bird. Chick Webb might not've got pushy with Bird." Dwarfed and crippled, poor Chick Webb died young, before the war. But what he couldn't do with a drum kit, nobody ever will. And did he know it? Oh, he might have. Yeah, he just might.

"If I try, I may be able to get pictures of them coming out of the place," I said. "Have to buy some superfast film—you better believe I'm not gonna use flashbulbs around there."

"That will help ... I suppose." Lamont Smalls shook his head. "That may end up saving me money in divorce court, I should say. Nothing will help." I didn't need to be Einstein to work out what he meant. He still wanted Marianne back—still loved her, if you'd rather call it that. He wanted some sorcery to make it as if things'd never gone wrong between 'em.

Sorcery can do all kinds of things. The wizards learn more about what it can do every single day. But I'm here to tell you, it can't do that. Whoever says different's no wizard, only a grifter. Lots of grifters running around loose, bleeding suckers dryer'n a vampire would.

"Mister Smalls, you pick up the pieces and you go on the best way you know how. What else can you do?"

When he eyed me this time, I wasn't just a hired gumshoe in his eyes. I was a human being. I think it caught him by surprise. "You know what you're talking about, don't you?" he said slowly.

"Uh-huh." Not another word after that.

"Not so easy when you're in the middle of it, though."

"No. It isn't. You're crazy, only you don't realize you're crazy. Lasted a couple of years for me. I think I'm over it, but the guys with the butterfly nets still may pop me in a straitjacket and cart me off to a rubber room."

"Get your fast film. Take the photos if you have the chance. Expenses, of course, and good photos should be worth a bonus," Smalls said.

"Gotcha." I nodded. And he might remember when the time came, and then again he might not.

"If … If Jonas Schmitt had an accident, that would be worth a bigger bonus," he said.

I think I told you before, I don't like strongarm work. If I do it at all, I have to figure the fella on the receiving end's got it coming to him. Which I didn't here. Schmitt didn't need to stick an ether cone over sweet Marianne's face before he jumped on her bones. He didn't clout her with a caveman club and drag her into the bushes. She was looking for it at least as much as he was.

When I didn't rise to the bait, Lamont Smalls sighed. "Well, it was a thought," he said.

Old Man Mose chose that moment to come out from under the couch. "It was a dumb thought," he said.

For the first time since he stepped into the office, Smalls cracked a smile. "Another county heard from!" he said. "Why is it a dumb thought?"

"Because if they throw Jack in the jug, who's gonna keep me in tuna fish?" Mose said, as if the editor were an idiot. To my furry Falstaff, no doubt he was.

Smalls's smile got wider. "You're right, of course. I should have worked it through."

"Yeah, you should have." The cat submerged again.

Before Smalls left, I said, "Just on the off chance, have you ever heard of something called vepratoga?" Newspapermen hear about all kinds of strange things.

But he shook his head. "No. What is it?"

65

"I'm trying to find out. If you hear the name, give me a call, will you? Vepratoga."

"Vepratoga," he repeated, and wrote it down in a little notebook he pulled from an inside jacket pocket. Then he did leave. Okay. I tried.

Just after sundown, I called Dora Urban's number again. She'd be out of her coffin, I figured, but maybe not going anywhere yet. The guy or vampire or whatever he was who barely spoke English answered the phone. When I told him I needed to talk to her, he said, "Pliz vait," same as he had the last time.

So I vaited. Before too long, she came on the line. "Good evening, Jack. What do you want from me?"

No beating around the bush. She was a vampire. Wanting, she understood. Anything else? Maybe not so well. I said, "I need the answer to a question I should've asked you sooner."

"Go ahead." No promise she'd answer or anything. Well, I wouldn't've made a promise like that or anything, either.

"I remember you said you and your half brother were having permit problems with City Hall. What kind of permit problems? It may have something to do with whatever happened to him, you know."

"Ah." Pause. "It is ... not impossible, I suppose." She conceded as little as she could, then paused again. "We ... have been running a small import-export business, Rudolf and I."

What did vampires import and export? Did I want to know? I decided I didn't, at least not right then. Instead, I asked, "Import-export? Did you have any problems with Federal officials, too?"

One more pause. Then she repeated, "It is ... not impossible, I suppose."

If she'd been human, I would've wanted to kick her. I still did, but I also recalled how much stronger than me she was. Sighing, I said, "How can I do a job for you if you don't tell me things I need to know?"

"Now I have told you. Are you happy?" By the way Dora said it, being happy was a way sicker perversion than being queer. When I didn't answer right away, she hung up.

I listened to the dial tone for a few seconds. Then I hung up, too. And then I said one of those words everybody says all the time and nobody will let you print. She'd paid me in gold. But she was finding ways to make me pay, too.

TWICE AS DEAD

Before I went home, I made sure I put extra food and water in Old Man Mose's bowls. Yes, I know he's a cat. Yes, I know he can find things for himself. But I don't want him doing it. I want him thinking I'm the gravy train. Cats are practical beasts. They remember who feeds 'em better'n most people do.

Of course he noticed. "What's this?" he said. "You fattening me up for dinner?" He might've been kidding, or he might not.

"No, chowderhead. I've got to go downtown in the morning. I don't know if I'll be back here at all. In case I'm not, I don't want you starving."

"That's good. I don't want me starving, either." To make sure he didn't, Mose stuck his nose in the cat food.

I rode the Red Line up to downtown, however little sense that makes. City Hall, then the Federal building across Temple from it. Joy. Rapture. Almost as much fun as visiting police headquarters.

City Hall, at least, has signs that tell you where to go, not cops who do. I found the Business Permits room without any trouble. Then it was hurry up and wait. I hadn't seen anything like it since I got out of the Army. After what only seemed like forever, I worked my way to the head of a line.

"I represent Dora Urban and Rudolf Sebestyen," I told the clerk. If she wanted to think I was a lawyer, I didn't mind a bit. I was thinking I should've brought mine along. Wally Baker is way more patient than I am. Smarter, too. I went on, "I'm trying to get to the bottom of the permit troubles they're having."

She yawned in my face. "Let me have the names again, please." I wrote them on a sheet of scratch paper and shoved it across the counter to her. She looked at it without pleasure. "I have to go look in the files." She stood up and walked into a back room.

For all I can prove, she had a couple of Chesterfields in there, or a plate of bacon and eggs. Eventually, very eventually, she came out again. The look on her face said she didn't understand *happy* any better than Dora did.

"We haven't been able to issue those permits because your clients haven't given us the required Federal authorization forms. I can't imagine how they will, either, because they're seeking to deal with Hungary." She eyed me as if wondering whether to call the FBI.

I felt like an idiot. With those names, with that background, where else would they be dealing with? Hungary'd been on the other side in the war, but that wasn't the problem. The war hasn't been over for five years yet, but it might as well be ancient history. A lot of things have turned upside down and inside out since then.

No, the problem was the Red tide rising in Hungary—and in a lot of other places close by, and in still others not close by at all. You try dealing with Hungary, somebody's going to ask you *Are you now or have you ever been?* Somebody's going to ask if you have red blood or Red blood. That'd go double or triple if you're a vampire. The HUAC doesn't think vampires make proper Americans anyway.

And vampires who might be Red? Lord have mercy! They might as well be colored. Almost.

"I'd better go talk to the Federal people, then," I said, and I must have sounded as thrilled as I felt.

"You do that." The clerk sounded as if she hoped they'd grab me and ship me off to Alcatraz on the spot.

Across the street I went. City Hall's the only building in town more than 150 feet high, for fear of what the earth elementals do every so often. The Federal building comes real close to the limit itself. But, where City Hall's an asparagus spear, the Federal building looks more like an oversized white toaster.

The directory in the lobby admitted there were people who dealt with things that involved international commerce. I popped up to the room they inhabited. I had to wait in line again, but not for so long this time. "Yes?" said the man at the counter. He seemed more interested in the cardboard cup of coffee at his elbow than he was in me.

"I represent Dora Urban," I said. "She and her business partner, Rudolf Sebestyen, seem to be having some difficulties in getting the paperwork they need for their import-export business. I'm trying to get to the bottom of that."

After one more longing look at the coffee, he said, "Spell the names, please." I did. He wrote them down himself. Then he asked, "And which country or area will the business be involved with?"

"Mostly Hungary," I answered.

It wasn't hot in there to begin with. As soon as he heard that, it got ten degrees colder. "I see," he said. "That presents certain intrinsic

TWICE AS DEAD

problems, you understand." By the way he said it, he could see the Red tide swirling around me, too.

"Not if they've kept their noses clean. As far as I know, they have," I said, hoping like hell I knew far enough. And I hoped that *As far as I know* gave me a foxhole in case I was wrong.

"Let me see what the status on their documents is," he said, and rose from his chair. He didn't have to go into a back room, the way the gal at City Hall had. The file cabinet he needed stood only a few feet behind him. When he came back, he looked as if somebody'd died and he wished it were me.

He didn't say anything. He just kept looking at me like that. Okay, my move. "What's the trouble?" I asked, 'cause I knew damn well there was some. More than some.

He clicked his tongue the way your mama did when you were naughty. As sadly as your mama would have, he said, "You didn't tell me these ... individuals were PAFs. You are familiar with this term, PAFs?" He would've asked me if I knew about cooties the same way. Well, to him there wouldn't be much difference.

Since I did happen to be familiar with that term, I said, "Yeah." Then I waited. I can be difficult, too. I've even known people who claim I'm good at it.

He tried to wait me out. It didn't work. Now he looked irked. Irked I could deal with. "Since you are familiar with it, you are also familiar with what it means?"

"I sure am. It means they didn't like the fylfot boys and their slimy pals before the politicians here got around to deciding not liking 'em was okay. Before I put in a year fighting 'em, too." I threw in that last bit to head him off from asking if I'd done my hitch in the service.

The way he closed his mouth told me he'd been about to ask me just that. I do know how to forestall 'em. Sometimes. When the wind is southerly. "Your attitude could be better," he said.

"That's nice," I said cheerfully. At least he didn't get to question my patriotism, which is dangerous these days. Instead, I questioned his: "Doesn't the government have better things to do than punishing people for being right?"

"People." How he said it told me he knew Dora Urban and Rudolf Sebestyen lived in, inhabited, however you want to put it,

69

Vampire Village. You aren't supposed to discriminate against vampires. You aren't supposed to discriminate against Negroes or Jews, either. Theory's wonderful, ain't it?

"Should I talk with your supervisor?" I asked him. No guarantee. If his supervisor was as warm and caring as he was, I'd be up the well-known creek without a paddle. Worth a shot, though.

He scowled, so I figured his boss might be guilty, or at least accused, of humanity. "With things the way they are, I can't promise you anything even if you talk with the Secretary of State," he said.

"Do what you can," I told him. "My client will be happy to see we mean it when we say everybody's welcome in this country." I'd be happy if I saw that, too. We say a lot of things we don't mean, starting with *All men are created equal* and rolling downhill from there.

"I'll see what I can manage. You understand that I can't promise when I'll be in touch, or what—if anything—I'll accomplish." He didn't like my making him live up to what I say we are, not what we really are.

I knew I'd got as much out of him as I was going to get—more than I'd expected, really. "Thanks very much, Mister Timmons. I'll be here." I read his name from the plaque on the counter. Broderick Timmons. Some handle, huh? I added, "I know Miss Urban will be glad to learn how conscientious you are."

"Is there anything else?" he asked, in lieu of telling me, *Get the hell out of here.* Since there wasn't anything else, I got the hell out of there. I wondered if I'd ever hear from him. I kinda doubted it, but you never can tell.

It was still pretty early. Old Man Mose wouldn't starve, or start imagining he was starving, for a while yet, not with the extra chow I'd given him. I didn't need to go straight back to the office. So I didn't. I wandered down toward Hill Street instead.

A guy leaning against a wall that didn't really need bracing took a step out toward me as I walked by. "Got any spare change, pal?"

A few years younger than me. Nasty scar on one cheek; just missed his eye. Khaki jacket that'd seen a lot of wear. Toes leaking out from boots even more battered than the jacket. We say nothing's too good for dogfaces when they come home. The parades've been over for a while now, and you never could eat 'em.

70

I dug in my pocket and found half a buck. I put it in his dirty palm. With only a little less luck, I could've been him. One of these days, I may be.

He gaped at the silver. He gaped at me. Panhandling doesn't pay off much. "Thanks, Mister!" he managed.

"It's okay. Next time you can give somebody a hand, do it, that's all." I got going again. I'm no preacher. We're all bound to be lucky.

When I got to Hill, I turned right. A few minutes later, I ambled into the little shop at 231-3/4. From behind the counter, Al Harris said, "Hey! How ya doin'?" A couple of other guys were in the place, looking over the ... merchandise. Al is a gentleman, of sorts. He didn't use my name where anybody who didn't already know it could hear.

"Could be worse," I said. I gave his stock in trade a quick once-over. Now, don't get me wrong. I like looking at pretty women as much as the next guy, maybe more than the next guy. The less they're wearing, the better, too. But enough is enough and too much is too much, if you know what I mean.

Or I think so, anyhow. Enough guys don't to keep Al in business, at least when the cops don't try and shut him down. They have a time or three, but never for long. Al looks like an unmade bed, sure. Some of what he sells'd make a zombie puke. He knows people, though, and he knows about people.

I didn't eyeball the customers. In a place like that, you don't. I picked up a magazine. It was called *Bound to Please*. It was what it said it was. If that was what got you going, you could give Al a fin and take it home in a paper sack. If it wasn't, he had stuff for other tastes, too. Variety is the life of spice, right?

I put it back on the rack and looked at another magazine. I put that one down again in a hurry. Other tastes, uh-huh.

One fellow bought something. The other guy just left, his eyes on the ground, trying to tell himself and the world he'd never been in there to begin with. When we had the place to ourselves, Al said, "Nu, what's going on?"

"Got a question for you," I said.

He chuckled. "Didn't figure you came in to browse, like. Go ahead, shoot." He pulled out the latest pack of Camels he was killing and started to light a new one.

"Ever hear of something called vepratoga?"

The hand with the lit match stopped halfway to his mouth. He stood there frozen for a couple of seconds, till he felt the heat on his thumb and first finger. If he'd dropped the match, we both would've roasted. But he blew it out. "Didn't expect that one," he said around the unlit coffin nail in his mouth. My best guess is, he forgot he had it in there.

"Life is full of surprises," I said. My surprise was that he'd heard of the stuff. Even Deacon Washington hadn't, and the Deacon knows a thing or two about junk.

"You don't want to mess with it. Live people don't want to mess with it. They better not mess with it, or they ain't live people no more." Al shuddered. All his chins did the shimmy and the shake. "I tell you what. People say I run a dirty bookstore. That stuff, that stuff makes all my *shmutz* look clean."

I tried to add two and two and not get twenty-two. "Who does mess with it? Somebody must. Is it—?"

A man a few years older than I am walked into the place. I shut up and made like a customer again. I grabbed another … educational magazine. One of the girls in it was definitely worth looking at. If I met her somewhere and didn't know how she paid the rent on her place, I might've tried to buy her a drink and see what happened next.

That other guy didn't case the magazines. He went for the books instead. A reader! He bought something, stuck it in an inside pocket, and beat it. No, he left. He'd probably beat it later.

After he took off, Al remembered that cigarette. This time, he managed to get it going. He took the first drag as though he needed it bad.

I'd done some remembering of my own. I tried my question a different way: "What does the stuff do for a vampire?"

Al coughed when he blew out smoke. "You don't know as much as you think you do."

"You can't say that. You aren't even married to me."

I made him wheeze laughter. Then he coughed some more. "You don't know what you're talking about, there or with the other shit. No vampire in the world would touch it."

"I know of at least one who wanted to," I said.

TWICE AS DEAD

"That Sebestyen item." It wasn't a question. I nodded. Al muttered under his breath, not in English. Then he came back to talk I could follow: "I knew he was a bad one. I never figured he was that far out of his tree."

Which made sense, as much as anything made sense. Dora was as much a vampire as her half brother, and she'd never heard of vepratoga. Not never used it or never wanted to use it, but never heard of it. I asked, "You know of anybody who deals in it?"

"Not me. Don't want to, neither. You think I don't got enough *tsuris* already?"

He sounded like somebody who meant it. Which proved nothing, or two cents less than that. People I hang around with, they're mostly good at sounding like they mean it. They'd be doing honest work if they didn't.

"Thanks," I told him.

"Any time."

"I'll see you around, like a doughnut," I said. He laughed some more. I left. I didn't have to try very hard to look embarrassed when I did, the way you're supposed to. I didn't have to try at all, in fact. I damn well *was* embarrassed.

When I got to the office after lunch, the zombie sweeper wasn't manicuring the back alley. I pictured him standing in a closet with his broom, or maybe leaning against a wall like that beggar downtown. Only he wouldn't have leaned there himself. The guy who was paying for him would've leaned him there, with the push broom next to him at the same angle.

I spat. I don't like those pictures. I make 'em anyway. Lucky me.

As soon as I walked in, I saw the food dish was about empty. "Mose, you're a pig, a furry pig," I said.

He came out from under the sofa—I might've been a burglar or a bill collector, after all. "It was there," he said.

Which makes sense if you're a cat. Makes sense if you're a good many people, too. Tomorrow? What's tomorrow? Anyhow, arguing with a cat is a losing proposition to begin with. I called my answering service. "Any messages for me?" I asked.

73

Usually, Hilda just says no. If I didn't scuffle for business, I wouldn't have any at all. That afternoon, though, she surprised me. "A Missus Jethroe called. Her husband is missing, and she wants you to help find him."

"Did she? Does she? What did you tell her?"

"That you were out, and that I expected you back late this afternoon. She said she'd try then and hung up."

"Okay. Thanks." I hung up, too, and sat there waiting for the phone to ring. Most of the time I'm in my office, I'm sitting there waiting for the phone to ring. This was different, though. This time, it might even happen.

Only it didn't. Somebody knocked on the door instead.

"Come in," I called. A split second later, I wondered if I should have. That was how I got mixed up with Dora. But the sun was still up. Whatever I'd just invited in, it wasn't a vampire. Not the kind that sleeps in a coffin, anyway.

The door opened. In walked a woman five or ten years older than I am, and three shades darker. She gave me an uncertain look, and who could blame her? "Are you Mister Mitchell?" she asked, as if she didn't want to believe it.

"Afraid so," I answered—I have days when I don't want to believe it, either. I thought I knew who she was, but I could have been wrong, so I went on, "And you are …?"

"My name is Jethroe, Clarice Jethroe," she said. "I gave it to your secretary." She looked around my crappy little office. No secretary. No place for a secretary.

"My answering service." This time, I sounded resigned. "They said you told them your husband is missing." As I talked, I sized her up. She was from down South, but she spoke better than she dressed. Her blouse and skirt weren't cheap or flashy; she'd had them both a long time, though. She didn't just look worried about her husband, either—she looked worn down. More education than luck, was my first guess. Well, a lot of people the color she was could sing that song. Or even lighter. Me, for instance.

"That's right." She nodded.

"What's his name? How long has he been missing? How old is he? What does he do for a living? Where does he work? Does he

TWICE AS DEAD

have any enemies you know about?" All the obvious questions. I took a notebook and a pencil out of the top left desk drawer to write down the answers.

"He's Frank Jethroe. He didn't come home five days ago. I went to the police yesterday, but—" She brushed the first two fingers of her right hand against the top of her left wrist. This part of town, you see that gesture a lot. It means *I'm this color, so what are you gonna do?*

She eyed me again. Looking the way I do, there was a chance I wouldn't follow that. I nodded to show I did. "You're not the first person who's told me that kind of story," I said. "Okay, he's Frank Jethroe. How old is he? What does he do?"

"He's forty-three, four years older'n me," she answered. "He makes tires down at the big US Rubber factory on Scrying Crystal Road. You know the place I'm talkin' about?"

"I sure do," I said. Funny that I'd been listening to Bird at the Blue Lobster Club with three people who worked there. Coincidence? Or somebody (or Somebody) pulling strings? You never know till later. Half the time, you don't know even then. "Anybody there who doesn't like him? Anybody there he's running around with?"

"One o' those silver fox jacket hussies? I don't *think* so, Mister Mitchell." Clarice Jethroe knew what I was driving at, sure enough. She didn't get mad. She thought it was funny. For a few seconds, she did. Then her face clouded over again. "Somebody who doesn't like him, though .... He saw the way they were doin' some things down there, an' he spoke up to his boss about it, an' to his boss's boss. They weren't real happy about that, let me tell you."

"Do you know their names? Do you know what Frank didn't like?"

"He never gave me details. The way he talked, the less I knew about it, the better off I was," she said: interesting enough so I wrote it down, anyhow. "His boss down there is a fella called Pat Brannegan. Frank used to like him—said he was a good guy for an ofay. But he sure soured on him on account of this mess, whatever it was."

I wrote that down, too. "Have you got a picture of your husband?" I asked.

"I do." She pulled her wallet out of her handbag and extracted a photo from it. Setting the picture on my desk, she said, "You can keep this. I've got me another print."

75

"Thank you." I looked at the black-and-white photograph. Well, a lot of what goes on in Los Angeles is about black and white, isn't it? Frank Jethroe grinned up at me from the palm of my hand. He wore a coat and tie, but not with the air of somebody who did that a lot. "How big is he? What does he weigh?"

"He's a big man. He's six one, goes about two-ten. Strong, too. But gentle. He never smacked me around or anything like that." Clarice Jethroe's mouth turned down. "I don't put up with that kind o' nonsense. He ever tried it with me, he would've gone missing a long time ago."

"I understand," I said. "I don't know how much I'll be able to do, Missus Jethroe, but I'll see what I can find. Now we come to the nasty part."

"The money." Her mouth turned down even farther. "We were gettin' by, Mister Mitchell, but nobody who works on a line making tires is rich. We have two girls, too. So how much are you gonna hit me for?"

"I wish I could say I'd do it just to be doing it. But—" My wave took in my banged-up desk, the rumpsprung sofa she was sitting on (and Old Man Mose was hiding under), and the rest of the cramped office. "A hundred up front to get me started, and we'll go from there."

She sighed, but nodded. "I can do that. I can just about do that, anyways." She took out her wallet again, and gave me eight tens and a twenty. "Here y'are. Tell you the truth, I thought you'd put the bite on me harder."

Which of course made me think I should have. I've always been a jerk about money; if I weren't, I'd have more of it. "Let's see how it goes," I told her.

"I hope it goes good. I hope that whatever's happened to him, it's somethin' somebody can fix. I hope—" Clarice Jethroe broke off short. Hardly anybody ever says *I hope he isn't dead*. If you have to hope that, you already know there's a pretty fair chance whoever you're hoping about *is* dead, and no one wants to think about that. Mrs. Jethroe sighed. "I do love that man."

"I'm sorry," I said. "I'll do what I can."

She nodded now. "Thank you," she said, and got up to go. I stood, too. Chances were she didn't realize how little I probably could do.

76

TWICE AS DEAD

Private eyes do all kinds of exciting things in books and in the movies. They have plenty of dough there. Pretty girls fall all over them.

If I'm not living proof it doesn't work that way in real life, I don't know who the hell would be.

After Clarice Jethroe left, Old Man Mose came out and started washing himself. Halfway through, he looked up at me and said, "I don't like the smell of this."

"Maybe Frank Jethroe brought the rubber stink home with him," I said.

"Rubber? Who's talking about rubber?" Mose went back to washing.

VI

I gave myself plenty of time to get down to the tire factory the next morning. I had to change cars at the Slauson Tower (all two stories of it), and then take a bus over to Scrying Crystal Road. That part of the county isn't incorporated. It's full of factories. They make more autos around there than anywhere but Detroit. Lots of train lines, too, to haul away what the factories turn out.

That part of the county's full of factories, yeah, but the US Rubber plant stands out. Oh, a little bit. Most of the places around there look like overgrown shoeboxes, sometimes with smokestacks, sometimes without. The tire factory's more like a castle built from blocks of stone, complete with waddayacallems—crenelations—up top. Better to crenel late than never, I guess.

And the decorations. Assyrian kings. Assyrian gods, I suppose they are, with wings so they look like Assyrian angels. Fierce hawk faces. Big curled beards. I don't know who carved them, but whoever it was knew what he was doing.

As I came up to the entrance, I checked my watch. It was half past nine. I'd got there sooner than I expected. The Red Line *works*. And the bus hadn't been more than a couple of minutes late.

Out of the corner of my eye, I thought I saw one of the god-things flanking the doorway roll its eyeball at me. I shook my head.

78

I hadn't started my day with Wild Turkey for breakfast. I shouldn't be seeing things now.

I took off my charcoal gray fedora when I went in. My suit was charcoal gray, too—no Central Avenue glad rags today. There's a season for everything, the Good Book says. White shirt. Maroon tie. Black shoes. Not quite an undertaker's outfit, but leaning that way.

A receptionist in a little booth in the lobby sized me up. A blonde, decorative enough but not gorgeous. Would she decide I was one thing or the other? I purely do envy people who don't have to worry about that.

"Yes, sir?" she said, so she figured I was one thing.

"My name is Mitchell, Jack Mitchell. I'm looking into the disappearance of a man who works here. His name is Frank Jethroe. He didn't come home six days ago—that'd be last Wednesday. His wife hasn't seen him since. As far as she knows, nobody else has, either."

She gave me a funny look. It wasn't the kind you'd give before you asked, *Are you a cop?* That was what I expected next, but I didn't get it. Instead, she said, "Don't I know you from somewhere?"

"I don't think ...." Then I noticed her name plaque. It said she was Barbara Woodson. Babs. I grinned my number one friendly grin. "Yeah, as a matter of fact, you do. We were at the same table at the Blue Lobster Club Saturday night, listening to Bird."

"That's right! Isn't that funny?" she said. I wouldn't have recognized her. She wasn't dressed to hit the clubs on Central now, either. But the coincidence distracted her enough so she never did get around to asking me if I was a cop. "What did you say his name was?"

"Frank Jethroe."

Plainly, it didn't ring a bell. "I'm sorry, Mister Mitchell, but you can see this is a big place. Can you tell me what department or unit he works in?"

Something I didn't think to ask his wife. Always the stuff you don't think of that ups and bites you. "I'm afraid I don't know. I can tell you his boss is Pat Brannegan, though, if that helps."

Her face lit up. "It does! That'd be Molding and Treads. Do you want me to call him and ask him if he'll talk to you?"

She had a switchboard, there in her booth. She put on a headset with earphones and a mike that went in front of her mouth, pulled a couple of cables out from where they were and connected them somewhere else, then waited a few seconds. She spoke too quietly for me to follow. After another small wait, she spoke again. She listened. I could see her mouth *Thanks*. She took off the headset and turned up her volume for me: "He'll be here in a couple of minutes. Uh, you can smoke if you want to."

"Don't mind if I do." I took out my Old Golds. Before I lit up, I offered her the pack, but she shook her head. I sucked in smoke. I'd feel a little smarter, a little more relaxed, for a little while. Damned if I knew whether I'd be either, but I'd feel that way.

I had time to finish the cigarette before Pat Brannegan walked out into the lobby. Well, Babs had it right; it was a hell of a big building. Red hair, freckles, broad forehead, pointed chin. Irish as they came—no doubt who he was. He wore chinos, a neat blue shirt with *Brannegan* embroidered by machine or magic over the pocket, and crepe-soled shoes. Not a suit; not what a guy on the line'd put on, either. A foreman type.

I told him my name, in case the receptionist hadn't. We shook hands. I said, "I'm looking into the disappearance of Frank Jethroe. He didn't come home from work last Wednesday, and his wife hasn't seen or heard from him since."

"Are you with the police or with the County Sheriffs?" Brannegan asked the question Babs should have.

Not without reluctance, I shook my head. Impersonating a law-enforcement officer lands you in so much trouble, you've got to be desperate to think about it, much less try it. "No, I'm not," I said. "I'm a licensed private investigator, working for Missus Jethroe."

"I've been wondering what the devil happened to Frank myself. I thought he was a pretty reliable, uh, fella till he stopped showing up all of a sudden." Brannegan didn't say *a pretty reliable boy* or anything like that. I couldn't prove he almost did, either. He went on, "Why aren't the police looking into it?"

"His wife reported it to them day before yesterday. You'd have to ask them about that." Somebody Pat Brannegan's color grows up sure the police are there to catch crooks and help ordinary people. Somebody like Clarice Jethroe knows better.

Sure as hell, he said, "That's … peculiar."

TWICE AS DEAD

"Isn't it?" Was I dry? Oh, I might've been.

He spread his hands. "I don't know what to tell you."

"His wife says you and Jethroe had some kind of disagreement over something that had to do with the way the production line was going. I don't know any of the details," I said.

Pat Brannegan's smile would've made a used-car salesman jealous. It was that wide, that sincere, and, if I was any judge at all, that phony. "Line workers come up to the people above them all the time with ideas about how to make things go smoother or faster or better. The company wants 'em to. When we use an idea like that, the guy who suggested it gets a bonus or a raise or a promotion. But we only use a few—most of 'em don't work out for one reason or another. Frank's was like that, I'm sorry to say. I was the guy who had to tell him so. He didn't take it real well, I'm afraid."

He sounded smooth. He sounded reasonable. So does the guy in the plaid jacket who swears the rusted-out '35 Hupmobile he's trying to unload will get forty miles a gallon doing 110. But I'm just a private eye. I couldn't haul him down to the station and bust him in the head three or four times to see if he'd change his tune.

Instead, I fished out my wallet and gave him a card. "If you remember anything else, if you get any news, please let me know. His wife and his little girls are worried to death about him."

He looked at it before he stuck it in the pocket under his name. Told you he was smooth. "I'll do that," he said, and then, after exactly the right pause, "You want anything else?"

Before I could answer, a janitor came by with a push broom, a dustpan, and one of those trash cans on wheels. He was a little darker than Frank Jethroe, and old enough so his hair was gray. They'd pay him more than they'd give for a zombie, but you can bet not much more. The glance he gave me said he knew what I was, whether Pat Brannegan did or not. But he didn't say nothin'. Like Old Man River, he just kept rolling along.

Which brought me back to Brannegan. "No," I said. "Thanks very much for your time." We shook hands again. I nodded to Babs and headed for the door.

I didn't catch the god-thing looking me over when I got outside, but that doesn't prove it didn't. Instead of going back to the bus stop,

81

I looked across Scrying Crystal Road. Factories as big as the US Rubber plant and some of the others in the neighborhood spawn saloons and diners and all kinds of little shops that help the working stiff unload some cash even before he goes back to where he lives.

I jaywalked to the other side. Got honked at once, but it wasn't close. The place I went into had EAT in red neon letters in the front window. But it was empty except for me and the guy behind the counter. Still a while till the lunch crowd.

"What can I getcha?" the counterman asked.

"Coffee, please." I put a dime down in front of me.

He poured from a percolator sitting on a hot plate. Corrosive as battery acid, even with cream and sugar. Strong, though. Strong was good.

Halfway down the cup, I set my picture of Frank Jethroe where the dime had been. "This guy ever come in here?"

"You a cop?" The guy gave me a once-over before he answered his own question: "Nah, you ain't a cop. Why do you wanna know?"

"He's missing. His wife's worried about him. They've got two kids."

"Ahhh, that's a bastard. Yeah, Frank'd come in two, three times a week."

I'd figured he might, if he didn't carry a lunch pail. It was the closest place to grab something quick and then get back to work. I took back Jethroe's picture and set a dollar bill in its place. "If some of the guys he works with show up today, will you tip me a wink?"

The counterman didn't say anything. I put another dollar on top of the first one. My turn to wait. He made the money disappear. "I can do that."

"Thanks." I finished that vicious joe and said, "Let me have another cup." The things you have to do in my racket!

I nursed this cup. The guy didn't bang his gums at me. He made like I wasn't there, in fact, which suited me fine. When it got close to twelve, I ordered a hot pastrami on rye. I didn't expect much, but it turned out good. The pastrami was laid on thick, and it wasn't all fat.

While I ate, the place filled up. For a while, the counterman was as bouncy as a flea circus on a hot griddle. Then, when he slid by me with a plate in one hand and two in the other, he muttered, "Them guys under the sign."

TWICE AS DEAD

"Thanks."

I went over to them, fighting the tide of customers coming in. Four men sat at that table, three white, one about the color of Frank Jethroe. I stood right close to the table, trying not to block anybody heading toward the counter.

One of the white fellows said, "You need something, Mister?" It wasn't exactly unfriendly, but it sounded as if it could get that way in a hurry.

"A man you work with—his name's Frank Jethroe—hasn't been home since last Wednesday. I'm trying to find him."

That got their attention, all right. Before any of the white men could say anything, the Negro asked, "You with the police?" The way he asked made me guess he wouldn't like it if I said yes.

But I said, "No. I'm a private investigator. I'm working for his wife. She went to the police first. They didn't want to listen to her."

All the white fellows seemed surprised, the way Pat Brannegan had. The colored workman didn't. It was one of the white guys, though, who said, "Grab a chair. Talk to us."

I didn't think I'd be able to grab a chair, but I got lucky. Somebody at the table behind me got up and left. I snagged his before anybody else could. Making the fifth seat at a table barely big enough for four isn't easy, but the men who were already there scooched around enough so I didn't stick out too much.

"Got any proof you are what you say you are?" the black man asked.

I took out the photo of Frank Jethroe. "His wife gave this to me. Her name's Clarice."

He nodded. "I'm sold. They got a big print o' this one in their front room." Dollars to doughnuts none of the white guys had ever been anywhere near the Jethroes' front room, but they went along with him.

One of them, a tough-looking fellow in his forties, said, "Okay. What do you wanna know?" He was missing the ring finger on his left hand. War wound? Job accident? Chances were I'd never find out.

"Was he acting different than usual before he disappeared? Was he having trouble at work? His wife said something about an argument with his boss, but she couldn't tell me any more about it."

83

They all looked at one another. The youngest, a blond guy a year or two younger than me, said, "Buddy, if you don't have trouble with Pat Brannegan, you ain't half trying." Their heads bobbed up and down in pretty good unison.

"That's a fact," the colored man agreed. "Don't help if you look like Frank or me, neither."

"Oh, yeah?" I said. They nodded again, raggedly this time. The way I said it made the Negro give me a second look. He hadn't suspected. Now he wondered, at least. I went on, "What was Frank's beef with this Brannegan?"

"How fast the line runs. How come the machines don't have more shields and guards on 'em. How come we don't get more breaks. We all bitch about that stuff, but not too much, 'cause the pay's good. Frank didn't care. He said he didn't want to come home in chunks." That was the last white fellow. He looked as Irish as Brannegan, only with black hair, cat-green eyes, and skin so white it might've been phosphorescent.

"It can happen. That's how I got this." The older man held up his left hand, so I learned how he got hurt after all.

"What did Brannegan tell him?" I asked.

"To shut his damn mouth and do the damn work," the Irishman said.

"Brannegan, he didn't used to be so bad," the Negro said. "Past few months, though, he's turned hincty as all get-out."

"He jumps at his own shadow, too," the guy with nine fingers put in, proving he didn't know what hincty meant.

"Was he arguing with Frank at quitting time Wednesday?" I asked.

"Not then, but earlier in the day," the young blond fellow said.

"Frank and me, we headed for the bus stop, 'cause we ride the same one to the trolley line," the Negro said. "He stopped to take a leak, though. The bus came up right when I got there. He wasn't there yet. I reckoned he took the next one. Guess not, though. That was the last time I seen him." He sadly shook his head.

I got their names—well, the names of three of them. They weren't senior enough to have them on their shirts. The colored man was Alonzo Horton. The guy with the missing finger was Carl Angeletti.

TWICE AS DEAD

The Irish looking fellow was Bob McGraw. And the young blond man didn't want to tell me. "I'm me. No offense or anything," he said.

"Whatever you feel like," I said. Not as if I could make him do anything. People in my line of work don't get to do that.

Angeletti looked at his watch. "We better head back. You know we'll catch it if we're late."

They stood up. So did I. The diner was emptying out. Lunch looked like the place's big moneymaker. Some people would come in for supper—bachelors who didn't want to cook for themselves or eat close to where they lived—but fewer.

I went to the bus stop. I knew more than I had before, but not nearly enough. I'd gone ten or fifteen miles in less than an hour. Same county. Different world.

I stopped at the office to change clothes and say hello to Old Man Mose, then went on up to Bunker Hill. When I got there, I gave the angel a penny. He spread his wings, took me in his enormous hands, and flew me up to the top. He's never dropped anybody. I know I told you that before. All the same, I couldn't help thinking, *Always a first time.*

What I had on said I was a workman. God knows the places up on Bunker Hill need work these days. I carried a metal case in my left hand. It might've held tools. In fact, it did, but some were the tools of my trade, not the kind a plumber or dowser or carpenter would use.

Walk around like that and you might as well wear a tarncape. You're as good as invisible. No one pays any attention to somebody who looks like a repairman on his way to do a job. What does he look like? A guy. What's he wearing? Clothes. Is he holding anything? Who notices? Who cares?

A beat cop galumphed right past me without looking my way. Beat cops get paid to be suspicious. They're good at it. But they aren't as good as they think they are. As long as you don't do anything out of the ordinary, you don't register on their crystal.

I stopped at a light pole across the street from the place where Jonas Schmitt lived. It was an iron tube, painted the same color as

85

the uniform I'd worn. A little iron door, about head high, let somebody who needed to fix something get inside. One of the tools in my case was an adjustable wrench. I undid the nuts that held on the door and reached in for all the world as if I were supposed to.

I fiddled around. I shook my head, as if the job were giving me more trouble than I'd expected. I sat down on the curb and smoked an Old Gold. If a workman grabs a smoke, so what? I ground out the butt under my heel and kicked it into the gutter. It had company there. I went back to work.

Nobody who did happen to watch me would have been able to say I was eyeballing the place across the street. I looked as if I were looking into the hole, which was on the sidewalk side of the light pole.

A woman walking a wirehaired terrier came by. The dog wanted to stop. The woman didn't want to listen to his reasons. "Get moving, Vernon," she said, and rolled her eyes at me. I grinned, the way you would. Vernon got moving, even if he didn't much want to. Hell of a name to slap on a poor mutt.

Thirty feet farther along, the terrier lifted his leg against a telephone pole. Now the other dogs'd know he'd passed through. If he was lucky, they wouldn't know he was called Vernon.

After he and his person turned a corner, I sat down on the curb for another smoke. Detective work is gambling. You show up where you think something may happen. Once in a while, it does. Mostly, you waste a couple of hours. If you aren't patient, you'll never make a snoop.

I figured I'd stick around another forty-five minutes, maybe another hour, then give it up and try again some other time. An hour and ten minutes later, I parked on the curb with one more Old Gold. Anybody who knows me will tell you I'm a stubborn so-and-so. That was *it*, though. I'd finish this one and call it a day.

And I got lucky. Out of the place that had seen better years came not just Schmitt but Schmitt and Marianne Smalls. A so-long scene if I'd ever watched one.

Quick as a snake, I grabbed a miniature camera from my case. Half the size of the palm of my hand, but it uses 35mm film and takes good pictures. I got it off one of the fylfot boys, a major, a few

86

miles south of Milan a week before the war ended. He'd never need it again, that was for sure.

Schmitt and Marianne were too wrapped up in each other to give a damn about the fellow across the street goofing off on the job. They wouldn't hear the clicks the camera made; I could barely hear 'em myself. At last, Marianne tore herself loose from the piano man and headed off towards Angel's Flight. Schmitt stood watching her backfield in motion for a few seconds, then went inside again.

Me? I was in no hurry now. I had what Lamont Smalls wanted—some of it, anyhow. Not in a hotel room or through Schmitt's window, but if he wasn't busy alienating her affections, nobody ever was.

Before I left, I put the little access door back on the light pole and made sure I fastened it good and tight. You don't want to do any damage while you're out there looking busy. That taken care of, I stuck the wrench in my case. I used the lid as a shield so nobody could watch me unloading the camera, then put the film in my pocket. I went back to the angel myself.

Most of the time, he gets pennies or nickels. He's not a businessangel, always out for profit. What he makes for flying somebody up to the top of Bunker Hill or down to the bottom has to be worth something, but it doesn't have to be worth much. I pulled a quarter out of my pocket and gave him that. If I had money, I was going to enjoy it.

For a while. Till I was broke again. That's how things go.

He didn't care that I crossed his palm with silver. I have no idea how he knows what coins are, but he does. He took me down to the bottom of the hill, then waited for the next person who wanted to fly up.

Before I went back to the office, I stopped at Allums Drugs on Central. The cat who does their photo developing lived down the street from me when we were kids. "Hey, Terence," I said. "I've got six or eight on this roll. Can you give me prints by to-morrow morning?"

"Could be. Afternoon for sure," he answered.

"Morning'd be better." Which meant I'd slip him something when I got 'em. You have to keep the wheels greased.

"I'll see what I can do," he said. Which meant he'd take care of it.

"Nine o'clock?"

"Half past."

"Thanks, man. That'll work." I headed out. You know the folks who say it's not what you know, it's who you know? They're so right. I wouldn't have to shell out as much cumshaw as a stranger who needed rush prints would, either. If a stranger could've got Terence to do the job at all.

When I finally did get back to the office, daylight was leaking out of the sky. Where? Down into the Pacific, probably. Old Man Mose sniffed when I walked in. Literally, I mean: he said, "You smell happier than you did before."

"I took care of something that needed doing," I said. He thought all the complications between men and women were stupid. If a lady cat wasn't interested, he knew. He knew if she was, too. If some other tomcat also knew, Mose tore him up before he jumped on her. Life's simple when you're a cat.

When you're my kind of animal, though .... I didn't have to know why Marianne Smalls was running around on Lamont, not to do my job, but I wanted to. You like it when the puzzle pieces fit together in your head. Did she aim to set sail in the big white world? Was that it? Was that all of it? Or any of it? Was Lamont a stingy bastard? Was he just a Sad Sack in the sack?

I didn't know what had happened to Frank Jethroe yet, either. All I did know was that Pat Brannegan had told me some lies. That was interesting, anyway. You don't lie for the sake of hearing yourself lie. You lie because the truth's bad. I wondered whether Clarice Jethroe or anybody else would ever see Frank alive again.

The chair behind my desk creaked and squeaked when I sat down in it. I opened the drawer with the Wild Turkey in it and took a slug. If I got soused, I wouldn't have to wonder about things. I liked that idea.

"Why do you drink that stuff?" Old Man Mose said. "It stinks. So do your cigarettes. Your nose must not work right."

"I wouldn't be surprised," I said, and took another slug. The bourbon punched like Sugar Ray. I didn't want it to KO me, just to leave me loopy. Not caring whether I wondered or not, that was what I was aiming for.

TWICE AS DEAD

I missed. Like most of us, I've spent a lot of my life missing. I wondered what had happened to Rudolf Sebestyen, too.

There was the bottle. One more good glug and I wouldn't be able to wonder any more for a while. Or walk. A big chunk of me thought that'd be great. But still I persisted in wondering.

So instead of opening up the bottle, I opened my address book. There was the number I wanted. I spun the chair around and peered through the closed slats on the venetian blinds. Not much light leaked in. What there was, was gray. The sun would be down. I dialed the number.

It rang three or four times. Then somebody picked it up. "Hallo?"

A woman's voice. "That you, Miss Urban?" I said.

"It is, yes, Mister Mitchell," she answered, so I didn't have to tell her who I was. "You have learned something of importance?"

"No. I wish I had. I just wanted to ask more questions, that's all."

"This is not a bad thing. You are at your office?"

"That's right."

"I will see you soon." She hung up. So did I. I looked over to the sofa, wanting to tell Old Man Mose she was coming. He knew; cats' ears are better than people's, too. He'd either dived under or got the hell out of there. I shut the bourbon drawer. Dora would know I'd been drinking anyway, but that didn't mean I had to advertise it.

A knock on the door: formal, precise. "Come in," I said, formal myself. I didn't know whether she needed a new invitation for a place she'd already visited. In case she did, I gave her one.

The door opened. She could do that. I'd already seen she didn't have to. She wore something elegant and expensive looking and a few years out of style. That didn't matter. Whatever she wore, it looked good on her and she looked good in it.

She sat down on the sofa. What she sat on was as much cat hair as cloth, but she didn't care. I suspected the fluff wouldn't dare cling to her dress.

Those green eyes focused on my face like searchlight beams. "Ask your questions," she said. She didn't tack on *if you still remember them*, but I heard it anyway.

89

"What kind of things have you and your half brother been moving in and out of Hungary?" I said. "Does that have anything to do with why he's disappeared?"

"I don't think so," she said carefully. "We've brought in a few packing cases from the old country, and also a bit of soil."

"Packing cases," I echoed. Wild Turkey or not, I could still think after all. Maybe it even freed up what passes for my brain. "Do you mean coffins? And the dirt from where they'd been buried?"

"That's right." Her voice sounded as calm as if she was undead. Which she was, even if I had to remind myself every so often.

"Did these coffins have anybody in them?"

She looked amused. "No one living."

Well, I believed that. "The government of Hungary doesn't have any worries about what you're doing?"

Dora still looked amused. "The government of Hungary, no matter what it may be, listens to the concerns of everyone inhabiting the country."

She wasn't just amused. Her word choice seemed as precise as her knock. She didn't say *living in*. Oh, no. I said, "Even after everything that's happened?"

"Of course. This regime is more Red than the one before, but you may take that in more than one way."

How many vampires were running things in Budapest? I didn't have the nerve to come out and ask. Instead, I tried, "What does Uncle Joe think of that?"

"It is not of great concern." She couldn't have been more indifferent.

I doubted whether Uncle Joe would agree. But that had nothing to do with me. I said, "You told me your little business was having trouble with the city. Till I poked you about it, you didn't tell me it was having trouble with the Feds."

"They do not understand the situation. If they did, they would realize it is to their advantage to let us proceed. Our business roots folk like us more securely here. How could anyone in Washington think that a bad thing?"

"Those people wonder whom you're dealing with," I said. *Are you now or have you ever been?* rolled through my head again. I had no idea how old Dora Urban was or what all she'd ever been. Okay, she looked somewhere not far from my age. And what did that prove? She might have talked shop like this with some Greek snoop who was working with Aristotle, too.

"We deal with familiar folk," she said. "Politics come and go, as people come and go. We endure. We are the true Reds. The ones who use the name now? Only another ripple on the lake. The wind that pushes it up will blow by, and it will flatten out again."

She seemed to believe it. The House Un-American Activities Committee didn't. Me? I have to tell you, I didn't know what to think. I still don't. The Reds—the Reds who take their marching orders from Moscow—don't look as though they're going away by next Tuesday. As far as I can see, they'll last at least as long as I do.

For me, that's all that really matters. I won't worry about what happens after I'm not around to see it. To Dora, I had to seem like Old Man Mose, or maybe more like a mayfly, worrying it was getting old because afternoon had come.

"What are you thinking?" she asked. "Whatever it is, it grips you."

She'd done things like that before. I wondered how she could tell. Smell, like Mose? I didn't know, and didn't care to ask. Instead, I told her. Why not?

"People come and go, yes, but they are not cats"—her nostrils flared—"or insects. They do not endure, but they pass memories down through the years, down through the centuries. They bind time, as we do. They would be more dangerous if they did it better."

A more serious answer than I'd looked for. She was gorgeous, and she had brains—or enough experience to do duty for brains. Yes, I knew she was a vampire. She'd been around a lot longer than I had. I'd thought that a couple of minutes earlier. I didn't know how much longer, but *a lot* came close enough.

And I'd seen she was a heck of a lot stronger than I was. Just the two of us in the office, unless Old Man Mose was under the sofa. She could do whatever she wanted with—to—me. Somehow, I didn't care. A beautiful blonde with brains? I could do worse, even if I was more interested in the brains than what color the hair on top was.

She laughed. "Now I know what is on your mind." Sure as hell, she smelled it on me. She and Old Man Mose had more in common than either one of them cared to admit.

I felt as if I could have lit an Old Gold on my ears. "Yeah, well …" I mumbled. If I'd been standing up, I would've scuffed one foot against the rug.

"It is a compliment," Dora said. "It is a compliment unless you get stupid about it, anyway. I do not expect that from you. For one who has not lived even a single lifetime, you are wise." She winked at me. I couldn't've been more surprised if she'd jumped up and turned a cartwheel. While I picked my jaw back up off the floor, she went on, "Yes, I saw the stupid film. How do you feel about movies that show Negroes as clowns or apes?"

"They make enough of 'em. They make too damn many of 'em." I can pass at least as well as Marianne Smalls can. Sometimes I do, for work or because I don't want to waste time on all the trouble that comes with being born what and where I was. The difference between her and me is, I don't want to do it all the time. I can't lie to myself that way.

"I understand. Some of us were finished on account of that film," she said. I nodded; I believed her. Musingly, she went on, "There was talk of … calling on the star. It came to nothing. We decided that would bring more hatred down upon us. I wonder whether we reckoned wrong."

"Chances are you were right. What you would've got afterwards …." If half the country were Negro or Jewish or vampire, it wouldn't work the way it does. But half the country isn't, and it does work that way.

"So it seemed to us, too. All the same, I wonder. Revenge is a pleasure we can enjoy." Dora paused, considering. "Sometimes, under the right circumstances, we can still enjoy some of the others as well, among our own kind or with yours. Sometimes. Not often."

"Is that a fact?" I said. If I'd been wearing a tie, I would've wanted to run a finger under my collar to loosen it up. I still had my work shirt on, and my top button wasn't buttoned. I felt the urge just the same.

"It is." She stood up. I did, too, bracing for whatever came next. Whatever it was, bracing myself wouldn't stop it. I knew that, and did it anyhow. What came next was her saying, "Now you must excuse me. I have other engagements for this time when I may have engagements."

As she did the first time she visited me, she walked out through the door without bothering to open it. It didn't blindside me now. It did remind me the laws of nature aren't nailed down as tight as we think most of the time.

Old Man Mose came out and hopped up onto the couch, taking care to stay as far as he could from where she'd sat.

"How big an idiot are you, exactly?" he asked.

I shrugged. "Big enough, I'd say." He didn't try to tell me I was wrong. Unlike people, cats don't waste time talking nonsense.

VII

I bopped into Allums at a quarter past nine the next morning and headed straight back to the camera and film counter. Terence nodded from behind it. "Hey, Jack! What do you know for sure?" he said.

"I know I want to see those pictures," I said.

He pulled an envelope from a drawer on his side. "Here you go. Negatives are in here, too. Comes to a buck eighty-five."

I gave him a five and waved away change. He'd worked late for me, or else early. Then I opened the envelope. That little camera was the real deal, you bet. The photos were just what I'd hoped they'd be. "Thanks, man!" I said. I took out the negatives and gave them back to him. "Hang on to these, okay? If I need 'em, I'll ask for 'em."

He looked at me. "Like that, huh?"

"Well, it could be. I try not to take chances I don't have to."

"You old soldier, you." Terence had fought in the Low Countries and good old Fylfotland. The war was winding down by then, but it wasn't over. The limp he walked with proved that.

"Old soldiers. Bold soldiers. Ain't no old bold soldiers," I said. He chuckled as if I were joking.

After I thanked him again and promised to take him to Deacon's—he'd heard of the joint but never been there—I went back

TWICE AS DEAD

to the office and called Lamont Smalls. I don't know if I got the same operator or a different one, but, whoever she was, she put me straight through without any back talk.

"Good morning, Mister Mitchell," he said when he picked up the phone. "What's the good news?"

"Well, I've got a couple of things you may want to see," I answered.

"I can be there by ten forty-five, if that's all right with you."

"See you then," I told him. We said our goodbyes and hung up.

I'd got to Allums early. Smalls knocked on my door a couple of minutes after ten thirty. I called for him to come on in; it wasn't as if I had clients lined up ahead of him in a waiting room or anything.

"What do you have?" he asked, direct as a hungry hound hoping for a hunk of ground round.

An envelope lay on my desk, one that didn't show where the pictures inside came from. I didn't open it yet. "Before I show you these, you've got to know you won't like what you're gonna see. I don't want you blowing up, you understand me?"

He gnawed at that scrawny mustache of his. "I hear you."

I still didn't pass him the envelope. "That's not what I asked you."

"Okay, okay. I'll be good." He gave me a sarcastic two-fingered salute. "Scout's honor."

Somebody like Lamont Smalls really might've been a Boy Scout when he was a kid. I sure hadn't, or wanted to. But he'd done what he could do. I passed him the envelope. He opened it, took out the pictures, and looked at them one by one. "This is in front of Schmitt's place," I said.

For a few seconds, I don't think he heard me. The photos hit him hard; I could see that. Knowing what you know and seeing what you know, they're two different critters. I was glad I'd got as much of a promise out of him as I had.

After he pulled himself partway back together, he neatly put the prints back in the envelope and remarked, "I don't see any negatives here." He sounded almost like his regular self.

"That's right. I can give them to you eventually."

He made a face, but he didn't make a fuss. "All right," he said, even if we both knew it wasn't.

"I've got some bourbon, if you need it," I said.

95

He shook his head and smiled. It was pretty ghastly, but he made the effort. "Appreciate it. No thanks, though. They'd smell it on me when I got back. Or they'd smell the Sen-Sen." He tapped the envelope with the manicured nail of his right index finger. "These are good, Mister Mitchell. They're very good—don't get me wrong. But they aren't enough."

"What do you mean?" I asked, though I feared I already knew the answer.

"She's going to leave me. She's going to divorce me. For that stinking white son of a bitch, she's going to divorce me." No, Lamont Smalls didn't blow up. He hissed like a venomous snake instead. He was scarier that way, let me tell you. He went on, "She thinks she's going to take me to the cleaners, too. If you're a man in Los Angeles, alimony is a four-letter word."

He wasn't the first fellow who ever told me that. I knew he wouldn't be the last, either. "Those pictures ought to throw a monkey wrench into that little plan," I said.

"They aren't enough," he repeated. "I want—I need—pictures of her and the goddamn piano man in the sack together. I want to see her lawyer's face when he gets a look at them. I really want to see *her* face when he tells her she won't get one thin dime out of me, but that's probably too much to ask for."

Did he want those pictures for dear Marianne's mouthpiece or for himself? There are people who cut themselves for the fun of it, for the thrill of it. I don't get that; pain hurts, dammit. But it happens. I wondered if Smalls was that way. I wondered if he was after the sick kick of lacerating himself with photos of his wife in Jonas Schmitt's arms. And yes, to a black man the cut would go even deeper, draw even more blood, because her lover was white.

I couldn't ask him. Even when a man's paying you, you don't get the right to ask questions like that. Slowly, I said, "That kind of picture isn't as easy to get as you'd think from the stories."

"How much do you need?" he asked. "I don't want Marianne getting her filthy fingers on my loot, but I'm glad to give some to you."

He hit me in my greed. That's a bad place. He ran the *Lookout*, which had to make him one of the richer Negroes in our unfair city. I still didn't want to do it but, but …. *I'll set my price real high, so high*

TWICE AS DEAD

he'll tell me to forget about it. That'll take care of that, I thought. What was going on down in the bottom of my mind? Pretty much what you'd guess, only the top part didn't realize it.

"Half a grand for me," I said. "Another couple of hundred for his landlady. If she's not in on the deal, it's DOA."

Smalls didn't even blink. "I can do that," he said, and it came to me that I could have asked for twice as much and he would've answered the same way. I've been broke so long, what's a little to a guy with money looks like a hell of a lot to me. He went on, "When will you need it? How do you want it?"

And then I had to go ahead. I was in too deep to back down. Oh, I could have, but it was curtains for my job if I did. He'd blacken my name on the street, and nobody but nobody'd want anything to do with me after that. Some things, you don't live down.

Ever get stuck doing something that makes you hate yourself? Of course you have; everybody has. There I was, up that old, stinking creek without a paddle. I sighed. I lit an Old Gold to stall. "I'm not real thrilled about busting down the door and popping off flash-bulbs," I said.

That worked as well as I might have known it would. Lamont Smalls knew he had me on the hook. He reeled me in: "I don't care how you do it. It's your trade; you work that out. All I care about is results."

"I'll see what I can do. I'll need some of the money up front." I kept trying to spit out the hook.

It kept not working. "I'll bring you the payoff for the landlady tomorrow, and a hundred for yourself," Smalls said. "You get the rest after you deliver."

"I'll try."

"You've done fine so far. I'm sure you'll take care of this, too." Smalls didn't want the hook to hurt any more than it had to. He just didn't want it coming loose. I bet he was fun to work for at the paper. He'd fire you and have you nodding along and going, *Yeah, I sure do deserve that.*

Out he went, with the photos I'd already taken for him. And since I'd taken those, why *wouldn't* I take these? No sensible reason. *I don't wanna* is what a short-pants kid says. It wasn't even noon yet. Lamont Smalls didn't want his people smelling bourbon on his breath. I didn't care. I took the bottle out of the drawer and hurt it some more.

That afternoon was nothing but a waste of time. I put my feet up on the desk and dozed for a while. I had some whiskey in me, I wasn't sleeping much at night, so why not? Old Man Mose on the couch gave me company. A couple of brainless, useless lumps, that was the two of us.

Not as if the phone rang to bother him or me. I had more dough than I'd got my hands on in a while, but I still wasn't drowning in business. I wasn't working as hard as I should've on the business I did have, either. I might've gone down to the US Rubber factory to try to learn what had happened to Frank Jethroe. I might've tried harder to see what vepratoga was and why Rudolf Sebestyen wanted it.

I might have, but I didn't. I slacked off, the way dogfaces would when nobody was shooting at them right then. Tomorrow would be tomorrow. For now, I had my hat down over my eyes to keep the light out. Mose used his tail the same way.

Wild Turkey doesn't make a filling lunch. My growling belly was what got me moving again. An awful lot of places'll sell you a bad dinner in that part of town. I got a hamburger and a plate of French fries at one of them. I'd had worse overseas, hardly ever since I came home. I got out of there as fast as I could.

As soon as I was on the sidewalk again, I wondered, *Okay, now what?* I could have gone home, but I didn't see the point. I'd just rattle around inside the apartment by myself. And I wouldn't sleep, not for a long time. I could feel that. I'd bought it by napping before.

So I mooched back to the office. The sun was down; it set earlier by the day. *Something may happen*, I told myself. What happened was, I fed Old Man Mose, gave him fresh water, and put clean sand in the catbox. That made him happy. Me? I was rolling along, running on cigarettes and greasy food. Sooner or later, I'd run down, maybe grab a little more shuteye the way I had earlier.

If I put another dent in the Wild Turkey, that might make me sleepy. I tried it. Didn't work. It made me stupid, though, the way

TWICE AS DEAD

whiskey does—stupid without knowing you're stupid. Why else would I have called Dora Urban's number then?

She answered the phone herself, and recognized my voice right away. "Ah, Mister Mitchell!" she said. "You have news?"

"No, not really." I shook my head, as if she could see me through the telephone. "I want to talk to you, that's all." *Talk* was what I said. What I meant. What I thought I meant.

"I am ... not particularly hungry at the moment. I can come to your office, if you like."

I'd been in the office all day. Enough was too much. "Can I come see you?" I heard myself say. "In Vampire Village, I mean. I've got your number, but I don't even have your address."

"I will give it to you," she said after a brief pause, and did. I wrote it down. No more than a fifteen-minute walk from where I was. But she hadn't finished. "Not many ... living people would ask this. Coming here now means a certain amount of risk for you, you understand."

"Risk anywhere in LA after sunset," I said. Oh, maybe not on the Westside or up in the Valley, or not so much. But in my part of town. Risk while the sun was shining, too. I'd been in VV after dark a few times. I was still breathing, still warm.

"If you care to come, I shall not try to stop you," she said. "I will see you. I hope I will see you."

Old Man Mose encouraged me as I put on my hat: "I knew you were nuts, but I didn't think you were this nuts."

"Never can tell, can you?" I went out into the night. Mose could take care of himself. I tried to convince myself I could, too.

You know right away when you walk into Vampire Village. It's quiet there. Real quiet. Not many cars go by. The ones that do are all closed up tight, tight, tight. The live people who drive them don't want anything asking them if it can come in. They're afraid they might say yes.

Another difference is, where I live there are as many churches as there are night clubs, and that's saying something. One on every corner, half the time another one in the middle of the block. Not in VV. They don't want to hear the Lord's name there, not even a little bit.

99

A punk with slicked-back hair walked past me. I couldn't tell whether he had fangs or not. As long as he left me alone, I didn't care. Something flittered past a streetlight. A real bat? A not so real bat? Whatever it was, it didn't bother me.

I found the street. The numbers got bigger as I walked down it, so I was going in the right direction. Some houses, some apartment buildings. I didn't know what I was looking for. And then I did, because there stood Dora, in front of one of the apartment buildings.

"It is good to see you," she said seriously. "Did you have any trouble getting here?"

"Nah." I shook my head. The streetlights weren't any brighter than they had to be, but they were bright enough. "You look nice."

"Thank you." The way she said it told me how many, many times she'd heard it before. No doubt every guy who said it to her meant it. I know I did it.

"What do folks do for fun around here?" I asked.

"We can walk for a while, if you like," she answered. "Nothing— no one—will trouble you as long as you are with me."

"That sounds all right," I said, thinking, *Finders keepers. Honor among thieves* occurred to me, too, but that wasn't right. She hadn't stolen me. I was there because I wanted to be.

A guy in one of the few cars going by tapped his horn when he got an eyeful of Dora. Well, I might have myself, if I were stupid and horny. The look she sent back …. He hit the gas so hard, his Plymouth farted smoke out the tailpipe as he sped up and got the hell out of there.

I just got the side effects from that look, and it froze my marrow, too. Then she was all charming and old-world again, telling me, "You have more sense than that."

"I hope so!" I said, and added, "It would be hard to have less."

"Yes, it would," she agreed. A moment later, she went on, "Something is troubling you? You said you wanted to talk."

I had said that, hadn't I? I found I'd meant it. I told her about Lamont Smalls and Marianne Smalls and Jonas Schmitt. I didn't name names, but I knew she'd realize who I was talking about. She'd been in Deacon's with me, after all. She knew which people I'd been paying attention to.

When I got to the part about the photos I'd already taken and the ones Lamont Smalls wanted me to take, she stopped short in front of a hedge full of white flowers that smelled kind of nasty, if you want to know the truth. "You intend to do this?" she asked. *I thought better of you* hung in the air, the same way that unpleasant scent did.

"I'm not happy about it, either, but yeah, I guess I do." Saying that showed me how not happy about it I was. All the same, I said, "I need the dough, and the guy needs the pictures so he can hang on to his own dough and not give it to his cheating wife."

"I understand how these things work," she said. I bet she did! Before she became a vampire, in how many triangles had she been the hypotenuse? How much more would she have seen in all the years since, however many those were? She clicked her tongue between her teeth. I got a glimpse, a bare glimpse, of pointed canines. "I would not have thought you cared to involve yourself in them, though. It seems ... none of your business."

"Divorce cases are always part of a detective's business," I said. "Not like I've never worked any before. I haven't taken photos like that up till now, though. It's ... part of the filthy side of things."

"It is indeed. The ways live people find to steal one another's small store of happiness never stop amazing me," she said.

I felt like an even bigger heel than I had when I told Lamont Smalls I'd do his dirty work for him. Then I remembered that her half brother'd been working out a way to rob the blood bank at County General before he went missing. Live people weren't the only ones whose hands needed washing.

That made me feel better, the way you do when you rush out the door without a shower and everybody on the Red Line smells bad. But you don't feel better for long. They may be dirty, too, but that doesn't make you clean.

"Perhaps we should go back the way we came," Dora said, which made me feel even better than I did before.

"Whatever you want," I said. "If you don't want a rotten son of a gun like me looking for Sebestyen any more, either, all you've gotta do is say the word."

I brought her up short. I suppose I should've been proud of myself; that's not easy for a live man to do with one of the undead.

The way I was then, I hardly even cared. She started to answer, stopped, then started again: "No, thank you. I think you are doing as well as anyone is likely to." She paused again. "I may have spoken too quickly. Do please forgive me."

And how often did a vampire say anything like *that* to a warm one? Once in a month of blue moons of Sundays. I waved her words aside. "Don't worry about it. If I were happy with what I was doing, I wouldn't have bent your ear about it. Thanks for listening."

"We do what we do, what we think we must do, not always what we know we should do," she said. "This does not change, whether alive or undead." She started walking again—ahead, not back. Something lifted inside me as I went with her. It wasn't absolution, but maybe you could see that from there.

A bigger street had shops mixed in with the houses. In most neighborhoods, they would've been closed and locked by that time. Not in Vampire Village. Clothing store, jeweler's, second-hand bookshop, another secondhand bookshop (this one with a rack of out-of-town papers out front)—they all looked to be doing a brisk business.

"Finding something new and worth reading is a rare joy for us, for whom time stretches long," Dora said, seeing me peer at the second bookshop's front window.

"Sure. Makes sense," I replied. But that wasn't why I'd been looking there. I could see my own dim reflection in the plate glass. But hers? Nope. I might have been walking by myself.

To remind myself she was really there, I took her hand. She felt cool—not cold, but cool. A live woman with cold hands would have seemed warmer. Well, Dora was what she was, the same way I was what I was. Sometimes, some ways, she could make like she was something else. So could I ... up to that point.

She didn't pull away. "The further you go, the harder it gets to turn around," she said.

"That's how things work, all right," I said. We walked on.

Pretty soon, we came to a bar. "Closing time at two a.m. is a nuisance for us. We are trying to get it changed, but we have not managed yet," she said. "Still early, though. Do you want to go in?"

I nodded. "Sure."

TWICE AS DEAD

"Bend forward a little," she said. When I did, she leaned toward me and kissed me on the forehead. Her lips were cool, too. "I have marked you. Not so one of your kind can see—you don't have lipstick on your skin. But my folk will know you are friends with me. They should not trouble you for a few days, till the sign wears off."

"Thanks." She hadn't said *they will not trouble you*, only *they should not*. I already knew vampires were no more reliable than anybody else. Nobody's any more reliable than anybody else. That's what's wrong with the goddamn world. A big part of what's wrong with it, anyway.

I held the door open for her. She inclined her head as she went in before me, a countess acknowledging a courteous commoner. The joint smelled cleaner than most places: not much sour sweat, no puke at all. Another odor was in the air, though, one that made the hair on the back of my neck prickle up. With Dora by herself, I'd never noticed that smell, even if Old Man Mose had. But a bunch of vampires smelled like a bunch of vampires.

They noticed me, too, the way people at a restaurant would notice if a giant medium-rare T-bone walked in. They didn't try to take a bite out of me, you understand. Just the same, a few of 'em sure looked as if they wanted to. Maybe that was her protection working.

We sat down at the bar. I'm pretty sure the guy behind it was another live one. He looked like a Jew. He was skinny and sallow, with haunted eyes. I wondered how long he'd been in the States, and what the fylfot boys had put him through before he got here. A good many Jews help keep an eye on Vampire Village while the sun's up. Like black folks, they know what getting kicked in the teeth for what you are is all about.

"What'll it be?" he asked. Sure enough, his accent was thicker than Dora's.

"Bikavér," she said. I didn't know what that was, but it didn't faze the bartender. After nodding, he looked a question at me.

"Wild Turkey over ice," I told him. He nodded again.

The Bikavér turned out to be a deep red wine. As we touched glasses, Dora said, "In English, the name means 'bull's blood.' " I must have looked startled, because she smiled a little and added, "No, not like the Bloody Mary at Deacon's. It is called that from the way it looks."

103

"Okay." I wouldn't have been surprised if it were the real stuff. I wouldn't have been bothered, either, unless whoever'd had the blood before hadn't wanted to lose it.

Speaking of which .... Whether I had her protection, charm, whatever you want to call it, or not, I wasn't going to get blotto in the middle of VV. I couldn't think of a better way, well, to spring a leak.

A fellow came up, looked at me, looked at Dora, and asked her, "Fattening him up? Or just slumming?" He had an accent, too, one that said he'd spent a long time in Atlanta or Birmingham or somewhere like that.

"Get lost, Bedford," she said. When he didn't shove off right away, she tacked on something that sounded fierce even if it was consonants I couldn't understand all mashed together. And she bared her teeth at Malachi. Even by vampire standards, they seemed longer and sharper than usual.

He must've thought so, too, because he made himself scarce. Nobody else decided to bother us. I was impressed. "You have some clout around here, don't you?" I said.

"It could be. A little," she answered. I didn't push her, but I know sandbagging when I hear it.

We had another drink. She let me sip the Bikavér. I don't know anything about wine, but it tasted good to me. "From Hungary?" I asked. When she nodded, I went on, "You and your half brother should bring in more of that. You'd do better business than with, uh, the other stuff."

"We might, but that line of trade is tightly controlled. Very tightly." Her slim, elegant fingers closed on the wineglass stem in a strangler's grip.

"Okay. You'll know better than I do." Since I'd never heard of Bikavér till we went in there, that had to be true.

"Another?" she asked when we'd got to the bottom of our second ones.

"Probably not a good idea," I said. I hadn't had enough to drink myself stupid, and I wanted to keep it that way. "I'd better head on back. Thanks for the company, though, and thanks for letting me talk before."

"What a friend does for a friend," she said, which made me feel pretty damn good. I settled with the barman, and then we got up and left.

When we stopped in front of her building, I kissed her. For a split second, when she put a hand on the back of my neck, I got reminded how strong she was. But only for that split second. She felt like a woman in my arms; not a real warm woman, but a woman, yes indeed.

"One of these times, I may invite you in. I don't think either one of us is ready for that yet, though," she said after we separated.

Part of me was: the dumb part, the trouser snake. Another couple of drinks and I might've listened to it, which would've meant all of me was dumb. The way things were, I nodded. "You're bound to be right," I said, and kicked at the sidewalk. "Dammit."

I made her smile a big smile, which I had the feeling wasn't so easy to do. "Take care of yourself," she said. "My benison should see you safe from the Village, but not everything that troubles you is confined to darkness."

"Sweetheart, you sure got that right." It came out of the side of my mouth, and made me sound so much like a tough-guy private eye in a bad movie, I had all I could do not to fall down laughing.

Dora stood watching me till I almost got to the corner. When I turned back toward her again as I rounded it, she wasn't there any more. Had she gone up the stairs or turned bat? I didn't know then; I still don't know now.

Somebody who may have been a vampire took a couple of steps toward me before I got out of VV. That was all he did, though. He sheered off in a hurry, like a ship that spots the sea breaking on offshore rocks. So the benison was worth something, all right. No one else gave me any trouble till I got back to the warm-blooded part of town.

Next morning, I went down to the US Rubber factory again. I got the feeling the god-things on either side of the entrance gave me the onceover when I walked in, same as I had the first time I did. A feeling proves nothing, of course. I wondered what a visiting wizard would say. I made a note of that; I might need to find out.

As I'd hoped, Babs was sitting in the little receptionist's booth again. She smiled at me as I came up. "Good morning, Mister Mitchell! What can I do for you today?" Yeah, now she knew who I was.

"Got a favor to ask you," I said, and put a fin on the narrow counter between us. Quickly, I added, "Not *that* kind of favor."

She looked at me. She looked at the bill. She made it disappear. "Go on," she said.

"The two guys from South Gate you were with at the Blue Lobster Club, I want to buy 'em lunch, see if they know anything about the missing man I'm looking for."

"Ray and Mickey? I don't know why they would," she said. I stood there and waited. She thought. "I can ask 'em if they want to, I guess. Where d'you want to meet 'em?"

"That place right across the street, the one with EAT in the front window."

"Okay. I'll ask 'em. If they don't want to come, though, it's not my fault."

"That's fine. Thank you," I said. Always smart to be extra polite after someone's done what you want.

I made it across Scrying Crystal Road without getting flattened. The way the counterman's eyes flickered across me said he remembered me, too. I ordered coffee and nursed it. The lunch crowd wouldn't materialize for another hour. I hoped I'd recognize Babs's friends. At least I had names for them now.

They were blonds like her. I did remember that. That meant I only had to worry about half the guys who came in. Some relief, huh?

But as things worked out, I had no trouble at all. They came in together, paused in the doorway to see who was there, and spotted me about the same time I spotted them. I got up and shook hands with them, and we grabbed a table.

Mickey was shorter and chunkier and liked to hear himself talk. Ray, taller and skinnier, kept watching his words. I ordered the pastrami again. Ray got fried chicken; Mickey, a hamburger.

TWICE AS DEAD

Neither of them knew Frank Jethroe. That disappointed but didn't surprise me; the factory took up several city blocks. I tried a different angle: "Anything funny been going on here lately? Strange, I mean."

They looked at each other. After a pause, Ray said, "Whatever you hear, you didn't hear it from us."

"You never even heard of us," Mickey added.

"Heard of who?" I said, deadpan. Mickey snickered. Ray gave me a sober nod, as if to show he liked the answer. After a beat, I went on, "What didn't I hear from you, then?"

"Nothing you can put your finger on, anyway, not for sure," Mickey said. Ray nodded again. The stocky fellow continued, "Past few months, maybe the past year, the lights've been flickering sometimes, and they never used to."

"I worked graveyard a coupla months, and it's especially bad then," Ray put in.

"You know what the place smells like, too, right? You've been inside," Mickey said to me.

I nodded and mimed holding my nose. "Rubber. Burnt rubber. Fried rubber."

"Kinda like my burger here," Mickey said. That had to be slander. The hamburger looked juicy. My pastrami was fine, and Ray marched through his chicken like Sherman through Georgia. I didn't worry about it; Mickey hadn't stopped. "Yeah, like that. It's not too bad most of the time—they keep the blowers blowing all day and all night. But sometimes it gets worse, usually right when the lights are peculiar, too. It can be pretty nasty then, like, like ...." He scowled, looking for a word.

I suggested the first one that popped into my head: "Brimstone?"

"Brimstone!" He gave me a grateful look. "There you go! Just like that! Like something from Down There's on vacation up here."

"I didn't connect the way the lights and the smell matched up, but he's right." Something in Ray's voice said he wasn't used to Mickey being right, but had to admit it anyway.

"That's interesting," I said, and it was, even if I had no idea what it meant. "Did you notice it Wednesday, when Jethroe disappeared? It would've been just after the end of the day shift."

107

"Can't help you. We would've been heading out ourselves then," Mickey said.

"Ahh, you're right." I'm always mad at myself when I'm stupid. That doesn't mean I'm stupid any less often, only that I'm mad at myself a lot of the time. You, too, probably.

"I hope you find the guy you're looking for. He didn't just quit and light out?" Ray said.

"His wife doesn't think so. They've got two kids. She says he likes them, too. I don't have any reason not to believe her," I said.

"Gotcha. Okay. Sometimes a fella'll just skip, though, know what I mean?" Ray said. "We've had some o' those lately, haven't we?" He looked at Mickey.

"Yeah, we have," his friend agreed. "One on our tread line, one in the next one over. Makes you wonder. Pay here's pretty decent, and I've sure worked at places where they drove you a lot harder."

"I've got a question for both of you," I said. Mickey nodded. Ray made a go-ahead gesture. So I did: "When you're coming into the plant, do those gods or angels or whatever they are on the wall give you funny looks?"

They both started to laugh. Mickey said, "They sure as hell did when we were new hires. Now, not as much. It's like they're used to us, like they know they're supposed to see us."

"Security system, that's what I think it is," Ray said.

"Makes sense," I said, nodding myself. "Kind of creepy, though."

"It is if you think about it," Mickey said. "But when you've been here a while, you don't think about it much, any more than you think about which stop you go to to catch your trolley."

"Like another cigarette," Ray added. "You don't notice lighting it or putting it out. You only notice if you have to do without it for some reason."

He made me want another Old Gold. But the counterman laid the bill on the table just then. I settled up at the register and left a quarter and a dime for a tip. Mickey and Ray stood up. "Back to our exciting lives," Mickey said. "This is the stuff I forget about when I hit the clubs on Central."

"You got that right," Ray said. He swung back to me. "Thanks for lunch, pal. Maybe we'll run into each other again up there."

TWICE AS DEAD

"Could happen," I said. "I make that scene when I can." We shook hands again. They hurried back to the factory; they didn't want to be late. I went to the bus stop. I had plenty to think about, but no idea what it all meant, or whether it meant anything.

I was the only one waiting for the bus. I lit that Old Gold. Two drags later, it came.

VIII

Up to the top of Bunker Hill. Again. I don't like Angel's Flight. Have I mentioned that? I think I may have. I didn't like any of what I was doing. I was doing it anyway. Money's a terrible thing, you know? You do all kinds of things you don't like if there's money in 'em.

I'm sure Ray and Mickey would've said I was right. They didn't like their jobs any more than they had to. I wasn't sorry they didn't know what I was doing up on Bunker Hill, though.

This isn't any of your damn business, I told myself as I neared the old house where Jonas Schmitt was staying. And it wasn't. I knew that. But I had Lamont Smalls's money in my wallet. It weighed me down and kept me on course, even if most of what I had so far would go to the landlady.

Up the stairs to the front porch I went. I rang the bell. After a while, the door opened. There she stood, narrow-faced, wattle-chinned, disapproving. Of me. Of everything. "Yeah? Waddaya want?" Her voice mixed anger, fear, and wariness.

"Good morning, Missus Parrott," I said. That was her name, Carlotta Parrott. So help me. I'd checked this time. As far as I could find out, there was no current Mr. Parrott. Widowed? Divorced? Can't tell you; I didn't look that hard.

110

"Waddaya want?" she repeated. "I don't buy from no door-to-door salesmen."

I'd wondered if she'd make me. No sign of it. I was in my gray suit now, not an electrician's duds. That makes a difference. And I've already told you, I've got one of those faces that can look like almost anything. I can look like I belong in your neighborhood, for instance, no matter where your neighborhood is.

"I'm not trying to sell you anything. I'm investigating a case here." I handed her my card. For good measure, I unfolded my wallet and flashed a fancy badge, all chrome and polished brass, that looked like one a cop would carry but said PRIVATE INVESTIGATOR instead.

The card was the real deal. It had my license number and everything. The badge? It cost me sixty-nine cents plus postage from a costume company in Fond du Lac, Wisconsin. It always impresses people more, though.

It sure did with Carlotta Parrott. She made as if to shove the card back into my hand. "I didn't do nothin'!" she gabbled.

"I'm sure you didn't," I said. *I'm sure you did*, I thought, but whatever she'd done wasn't anything that had to do with me. "I want your help, though. I'm willing to pay for it."

"*Pay* for it? How much? What do I gotta do?" She understood the key point, all right, and got down to brass tacks in a hurry.

"One of the people who lives here is involved in a divorce proceeding," I said, which wasn't true yet but would be soon.

And I didn't have to go any further. "I bet it's that Schmitt critter," she said. "You never can trust a musician to keep it in his pants." Then she cocked her head to one side and looked at me like a chicken sizing up a bug. "That gal he's pumpin', she really white or just high yaller?"

"I can't tell you that," I said. She took it the way I hoped she would, that I didn't know or the work I was doing wouldn't let me pass on what I knew. But I wouldn't have said boo to save my life. It was the first time in the whole nasty business that I sympathized with Marianne Smalls.

"So what do I gotta do? Tip you off when they're rollin' in the hay so's you can get your dirty pictures?" She'd seen too many movies or read too many spicy-detective magazines. The hell of it was, she was right. I didn't like getting sucked into one like this, but here I was.

"That's about the size of it," I said.

Carlotta Parrott didn't mess around: "How much'll you gimme?"

"A hundred." I knew she'd raise me. That came with the territory. No matter what I said first, it wouldn't be enough. This way, I had room to maneuver without cutting into my own take.

Sure enough, she looked at me as if I'd told her a dirty joke that wasn't even funny. "You gotta do better'n *that*, pal." Her voice dripped even more scorn than it had when she asked about Marianne Smalls's bloodlines. "You'll never hear from me again for less'n a yard and a half."

If I said yes to that, she'd jack it up again. Have I ever played these games before? Oh, once or twice. I screwed my face up. "I'm not made out of greenbacks, you know. I could maybe go a yard and a quarter, but that's pushing it."

"Yeah, an' rain makes applesauce, too," she said. "You ain't gonna get nothin' without me, an' you know it. A yard and a half or you can go peddle your papers."

"You're costing me money," I whined. Unlike the rest of this deal, the lie didn't hurt my conscience one little bit. Mrs. Parrott folded her arms, waiting for my next move. I made it: "A hundred and forty, and that's it."

She swatted that away like John Ostrowski swatting one over the left-field wall at Wrigley for the Angels. "The whole yard and a half, or I don't play. I can always tell Schmitt somebody's on his tail, y'know."

"Yeah, go ahead," I jeered. I was ready for her there. "Wait till he finds out you've already let me into his place."

"I never—" She broke off. She looked at *me*, not my clothes. It took her a while, but she added two and two. "You were that guy!" she said in dismay.

"I sure was," I agreed. "Tell you what I'll do, though. I'll give you the yard and a half. But you're gonna earn it fair and square, understand me? You let me know when I can do what I've gotta do, and no more stupid talk about blabbing to Schmitt." I peeled one of Lamont Smalls's C-notes out of my wallet. "Here. This now, the rest after I get my pictures."

TWICE AS DEAD

The way she grabbed the bill was a sight to behold. "That tramp, she usually shows up Wednesday nights, okay? She's around other times, too, but that's the regular one. So all you gotta do is come over then, an' I'll let you know when she goes in."

"I can do that." It made things a lot simpler, in fact. If I could be waiting, we wouldn't have to work out getting hold of me at short notice. I added, "I know she stops by other times. I saw her here one afternoon."

That was a mistake. Her narrow eyes narrowed some more. "You was the fella messin' with the light pole!"

So she did notice things when she set her mind to it. I needed to remember that. "How do you know?" I asked.

"On account of it still didn't work after you went away," she said. Now, I would've figured the city repairman didn't know what the hell he was doing. For that matter, I would've been surprised if a city repairman showed up at all in the part of town where I live. But Carlotta Parrott had it right this time.

"What time does she usually come?" I asked.

"Prob'ly about fifteen minutes after they start." She cackled. I managed something that might have been a laugh. She went on, "She's mostly here about half past eight, a quarter to nine sometimes."

"I'll be here at eight on Wednesday, then," I said. "You have some-place close where she won't see me when she's going to his room?"

"You betcha. Broom closet right across the hall," she said.

I hadn't noticed it when I went to Schmitt's place before, but what does that prove? You don't notice broom closets most of the time. I nodded. "That should do it."

"You'll gimme the other fifty then?" Mars. Parrott knew what was important to her. You bet she did.

"If I can. If things don't go nuts. If I can't, I'll get it to you. I don't stiff people for the fun of it." I wasn't lying. I'd stiffed plenty when I couldn't pay 'em, though. Little by little, I was catching up. Getting all the way there would take a while.

"You better," she said.

"If you aren't happy, give me back my hundred and we'll forget the whole thing," I answered. Give back money? The way she looked at me, I might've asked her for some other kind of unnatural act. I touched the brim of my fedora. "See you Wednesday at eight." I got the hell out of there.

I breathed the usual sigh of relief after I lived through Angel's Flight one more time. Then, as long as I was up near downtown anyway, I went to Al Harris's dirty-book emporium. Nobody ever admits to reading or looking at any of the stuff he peddles. He makes a good enough living to stay fat just the same.

When I walked into the little shop, that same old rush of dull embarrassment made my cheeks flame. I wasn't even a customer. All I wanted to do was talk with Al. I'm not saying I never saw anything like his stock in trade; anybody who says something like that is probably out to snow you. But if somebody who knew me spotted me there, or if I saw somebody I knew ...

Guys were looking at whatever they were looking at. Nobody paid any attention to anybody else. Somebody bought a magazine with a gal showing off how limber she was on the cover. Al took his money and put the magazine in a paper bag without showing he had any idea what the fellow'd chosen or why he might want it.

We're all animals. Most of us don't like to admit it.

After a while, I got a chance to sidle up to the counter. "Waddaya know for sure?" I said.

Al's eyes darted back and forth behind his narrow bifocals. "I know I been shaken down twice since the last time I seen ya."

"Shaken down? By who? The mob?" I wouldn't've thought a little place like his was important enough for them to notice, but you never can tell. They try not to leave any money on the table if they can grab it.

But he shook his head in disgust. "I wish it was the goddamn mob. I can deal with those boys, and they don't try and put ya out of business. They're like vampires—they want ya nice and fat so they can keep bleeding ya. No, it was the vice squad, a sergeant named Jackson. Elmer V. Jackson. Said he was gonna shut me down and chuck me in the calaboose unless I paid up."

"Elmer ... Jackson." The name rang a bell. I hadn't run across him myself, but he'd been in the papers. "Wasn't he the guy they said was screwing that fancy madam up in Hollywood?"

TWICE AS DEAD

In our lovely City of Angles, the cops who go after whores and gamblers and drugs are dirtier than most, and that's saying something. They rub up against a lot of pussy and loot and dope, and sometimes they don't just rub up against it. Sometimes it sticks. You get in right with 'em, you can do damn near anything you want. You don't …

"Wouldn't surprise me," Al said. "First time he showed up, I told him he could grow like an onion, with his head in the ground. I've been paying this other Vice cop for years. He's okay—he stays bought. I even write him off my taxes, call him an incidental expense. So Jackson went away. But he came back. Said the old deal didn't include suspicion of selling drugs."

"You don't, though." I would've known if he did. He's had the same kind of stuff in his shop as long as I've known him. If somebody'd walked out of there with reefers or coke instead of filthy pictures, I would have noticed.

"Tell me about it," Al answered. "He said I was dealing in—" He stopped. He printed VEPRATOGA on a scrap of paper, turned it around so I could read it, then crumpled it up, dropped it in an ashtray, lit a match, and burned it up. "That's a bunch of crap, but proving it's a bunch of crap wouldn't be easy or cheap. So I gave him a hundred bucks an' he went away."

"Interesting," I said. "Interesting he showed up right after we were talking about it, too." Al had held up a pudgy hand as soon as he saw which way my sentence was heading. He didn't need to, though. I'd noticed how he handled that name, so I wasn't gonna come out with it myself.

"Uh-huh." He nodded, smiling at the way I finessed that. "I made the connection my very own self, 'cause I sure as hell haven't talked about it with anybody else. I mean, why would I?"

"Don't ask me. I don't even know what it does." Me, I was wondering how the LAPD knew we'd been talking about vepratoga. I figured they had to; otherwise, the coincidence was just too big. Some kind of spell over all of downtown—or maybe over the whole city—that made a light go off inside a crystal ball when somebody said the magic word?

It might happen. You couldn't run a spell like that to listen for talk about broads or dice or even mary jane. Too much of it. All the

115

lights'd go on all the time. But for something as specialized as that? Possible. Or I thought so, though I'm a long way from a wizard.

Al, meanwhile, screwed up his face so he looked like a bad-tempered baby. A bad-tempered baby who needed a shave, I should say. "With that garbage, you don't want to know," he said.

Did he know for himself? Or had he just heard this and that? Had he heard it here in the bookstore? If he had, why hadn't the Vice cops given him a hard time about it before?

I tried to ask him. He waved me away. "You came for that, you can get lost," he said. "I talked too much once, and look what it got me. I ain't got nothin' more to tell nobody about the shit. Beat it."

Beat it I did. I went down to Central Avenue, down past Vernon. Central bops day and night, but it's a different place when the sun's up. It's more like the rest of LA. I found the boardwalk off of Central that takes you to Deacon's. In the daytime, I was the only cat on it. That sure felt different. So did not paying a cover charge. I rang the bell by the door.

I didn't hear anything inside, but it opened soon enough. There stood Acolyte Adams. He looked sleepy, and less neat than usual. He also looked unhappy to see me. "What do you want at this time of day?" he growled.

"I need to talk to the Deacon. About this." I wrote VEPRATOGA on the back of a card, the way Al Harris had on his bit of paper, and gave it to the Acolyte.

He eyed it. "I don't even know what this is," he said sourly.

I looked at him. "That's how come I need to talk to the Deacon."

His expression said he wanted to spit in my eye, but he didn't. He turned around and went inside. He shut the door but didn't slam it. I lit an Old Gold. My thought was, if I finished it before the Deacon showed up, I'd leave, 'cause he wasn't coming.

The door opened pretty fast, though. The Deacon loomed over me. I'm not small, but Deacon Washington looms over everybody, near enough. "First you, then the Vice Squad, now you again," he rumbled in a voice like a rockslide. "You part of their games, or what?"

"No, but you're the second fella who's told me that in the past hour," I answered. "How much did Jackson pry out of you?" I was guessing, but it felt like a good guess.

"Elmer? Two-fifty. I still don't know jack diddly about—"

Now I was the one who held up my hand. "Don't name it," I said quickly.

He hoisted an eyebrow like a signal flag. "Like that, is it?" I nodded. The Deacon went on, "Okay, that clears up some things. I *don't* know anything about that stuff, but he could've written me up for all kinds of other things, too, so I gave him the money. Hope to God he doesn't get greedy and start showing up twice a week. He's got that look, you know?"

"I never set eyes on him, but it doesn't surprise me. He got his name in the papers not so long ago, remember?"

Washington shook his big head. "No. About what?"

"Keeping the cops off his girlfriend in exchange for a cut from what she made off the string of fancy hookers she was running."

"Oh. I *do* remember that. Same guy? Jackson's such an ordinary name, it didn't register with me."

"Same guy. And now he's buzzing around this stuff. I've got no idea what it means, but I don't think it's good news, either," I said.

"I know all kinds of folks, but I'm not sure I know folks with enough mojo to go up against a police sergeant," Deacon Washington said.

He understood how the deck was stacked. You'd best believe he did. Cops are supposed to put crooks away, not to be crooks. When they go bad, juries hardly ever want to see it.

"Be careful how you talk about the stuff from now on. Don't use the word. I'm pretty sure saying it isn't safe. They focus in on people who do," I said.

"How about that?" Deacon Washington sketched a salute. Any Army top sergeant who saw it would've wanted to kill himself. It didn't bother me. I got the message he wanted to send.

I did some thinking of my own on the way back to the office. Whatever vepratoga was, some high-powered people were interested in it. Not nice people, not if Elmer V. Jackson was one of them, but people with connections that had to run way high up. The mayor always brags about how he's kept the rackets out of LA. That bragging got him elected. It keeps getting him reelected, too. Which doesn't mean it's true.

The zombie sweeper was pushing his broom in the alley behind the building. He didn't pay any attention to me. If I'd stood in his path, he would have kept pushing the broom till it bumped up against my shoes. Then he would've tried to shove me out of the way. He might have gone around me eventually, or he might not. If shoving me took an hour, a week, a year …. None of that mattered to him. He had all the time in the world. Yeah, some people think zombies are funny. Not me. They scare me—not to death, but past death. Vampires aren't alive, but you can understand why they do what they do. Zombies do it because somebody with authority orders them to. They don't care themselves. Not caring, that's the essence. It's an emptying out of everything that makes people human. No, thanks.

Old Man Mose wasn't curled up on the couch when I walked into that little place I call mine. Doing cat things, I guess. If cats had thumbs, they'd be the ones with offices, and we'd yowl on fencetops.

I picked up the phone and called my answering service. "Anything interesting, Hilda?" I asked.

"You have a message from a law firm. Dewey, Beagle, & Howe. They want you to call 'em back." She gave me the number. "What kind of trouble are you in now?"

"Beats me. I guess I'll find out." I hung up and called the number she'd given me.

One ring, two …. "Dewey, Beagle, & Howe," a woman said. Most actresses would have envied her diction. It was almost as good as the Deacon's.

"My name is Jack Mitchell. I'm returning a call from your firm."

"Oh, yes, Mister Mitchell. I'll put you through to Mister Howe."

Only she didn't put me through to Mr. Howe, of course. She put me through to Mr. Howe's secretary. That exalted personage put me through to Howe himself. "This is Victor Howe," he said. "You are Jack Mitchell?"

"That's right," I said. "What's this all about?"

Well, he told me. "This firm, of which I have the honor to be a senior partner, has the privilege of representing, among others,

TWICE AS DEAD

the US Rubber Company. I am given to understand that you are looking into the alleged disappearance of Frank Jethroe, a US Rubber employee."

"It's not alleged. He's missing, all right. I'm trying to find out what happened to him, yes."

"Very well. You are hereby informed that neither the US Rubber Company nor anyone affiliated with it in any capacity is involved in the alleged Jethroe disappearance. Any further encroachments on US Rubber property will be construed as trespassing and illegal entry, and will be prosecuted to the fullest extent of the law. Is that clear, Mister Mitchell?"

"I understand what you're saying, if that's what you mean. But you can 'inform' me of anything you want, Mister Howe." Staying polite when you're threatening or insulting somebody is an art. Victor Howe was good at it. I worked to keep up. "Until you inform me about what evidence you have to back up what you're saying, though, I'm not going to take you seriously."

I could hear him breathing out through his nose. I'd irked him. "I had hoped you might be persuaded to take a more reasonable attitude."

"Oh, yeah, that seems fair. Right. I'd hoped the US Rubber Company might care about what happened to somebody who works for it. Frank Jethroe's got a wife and two little girls who love him. You can replace him. You probably have. They can't."

"The US Rubber Company does care. It is simply unconnected to this alleged incident." Howe wasn't about to admit anything. People paid him stacks of dough not to admit things.

"If it cares, if it's not involved, why are you telling me you'll have me arrested if I walk into the lobby?"

"If you need to ask, Mister Mitchell .... What did the old geometry books say? 'The proof is left to the student,' that's it. Good afternoon." He hung up on me.

I fumed for a minute or two. Then I had a wicked thought. I walked a few blocks before I ducked into a telephone booth. From there, I called Dewey, Beagle, & Howe again. This time, Victor Howe's secretary said, "I'm sorry, sir, but he doesn't care to speak with you at this time."

"Tell him it's important, please," I said—I'd expected that.

"Hold on," she said doubtfully. I did. I had to throw in another dime before she came back on the line: "I'm putting you through."

After switchboard noises, I heard Howe's gruff voice: "Had some second thoughts, Mister Mitchell?"

"As a matter of fact, I have," I answered. "There's talk on the street that US Rubber is messing around with vepratoga. Do you want your outfit associated with anything like that?"

Of course I was bluffing, bluffing without even a pair of deuces. I didn't know what vepratoga was, or whether the US Rubber Company had ever heard of it. If Howe had gone *What the hell is vepratoga?*, that would've been the end of that and I would've been out some pocket change.

He didn't say anything at all for fifteen or twenty seconds. Then he breathed, "Where did you hear that?" in tones nothing like the ones he'd used before.

"I told you, it's on the street. Why haven't you heard about it yourself?"

"You've just slandered our client. If you think we'll let that pass unchallenged—" He blustered, but without any power behind it.

I'd hit him harder than I'd guessed I could. "Oh, crap," I answered. "I didn't even say I believed it. I just said it was out there. And it is. I don't think you're surprised, either. So long." I hung up on him this time.

I half turned to open the booth's door. Then I stopped. I grabbed my handkerchief and wiped prints off the phone and the door handles, inside and out-. That done, I walked down the street and pretended to be fascinated by the hats in a haberdasher's window.

Not a minute after I left the phone booth, a woman stepped into it. I smiled; some fingerprints would be there after all. Then I walked over to the next shop down. Like those places I'd seen in Vampire Village, it sold secondhand books. I'd spent money in there a few times.

Had things been different, I might've stepped in. But I was waiting for something to happen. I didn't know whether anything would, or exactly what it would be. But I had a pretty good notion I'd recognize it when I saw it.

That woman kept feeding money into the phone every three minutes. I don't know if she was talking to her mama or to some company that didn't want to give her what she thought she deserved. Her back was to me, so I couldn't see her expression.

Not quite fifteen minutes after I left the telephone booth, two Newton Division police cars roared up, the lights on top blazing red, the tires screeching as drivers slammed on the brakes. Two cops jumped out of each car. Newton Division rides herd on what the LAPD frankly calls the Negro Belt. When those cops do anything, they do it in force. They've made themselves so loved, they know what's liable to happen to them if they don't.

One of them yanked the phone-booth door open. Another one grabbed the woman in there and hauled her out. "What the hell you doin'?" she shouted. "I didn't do nothin'!" They took no notice. All four of them hustled her into the back of one of the cars. "I didn't do nothin', damn you!" she yelled again. A cop slammed the door—not on her leg, but almost. They all piled in and zoomed away.

They couldn't have been there longer than a minute. If they'd hung around, odds were good they would have had trouble on their hands. The bastards understood that. Bastards, yeah, but bastards who knew what they were doing.

The next shop down, the Madras Trading Company, sold thaumaturgical supplies. I don't suppose an uptown wizard would have had any idea what to do with half of them, but nobody ever said Central Avenue was uptown. I pretended vials of dried chicken blood and goofer dust and mummified rat tails fascinated me.

Twenty minutes later, another car stopped by the booth. Two men in suits got out, one white, the other a Negro. They started giving the booth and especially the telephone a going over. Detectives? Forensic sorcerers? I didn't know. I didn't stick around to find out, either. I was glad I'd cleaned up after myself, though, and hoped like hell I'd done a good job.

I must have. They didn't come for me. I knew I'd been stupid calling Howe again, but I'd learned something doing it. I'd really have to watch myself from then on.

121

And I hoped they'd turn that poor woman loose when they figured out she didn't have anything to do with vepratoga.

When I went back up to the top of Bunker Hill, I had two cameras with me. Terence had told me he didn't have film fast enough for shooting in a pitch-black room, which I was liable to have to do. So they were both loaded with flashbulbs. I wouldn't have time to change bulbs. I might not have time for a second shot, either, but you never know. If I did, I'd use it.

A couple of punks appraised me as I walked to the place where Jonas Schmitt lived. They decided against it. I'm good sized, and the way I walked said I'd come across worse things than punks. I had, too.

I knocked on the door. Carlotta Parrott opened it as if she'd been standing by it waiting for me to show up. She probably had. "Here. I got this for you," she said in a low voice, and pressed a key into my hand. "Now you won't make a racket gettin' in, an' I won't hafta pay for fixin' the door if you smash it."

"Thanks," I said, sure the second counted more with her than the first. But it *was* a help. This way, I'd have a better chance of catching Schmitt and Marianne in the act, as it were.

She led me to the broom closet. When she closed the door, it was as black as Victor Howe's heart in there, and even dustier. I'm glad I don't get the horrors in tight spaces, let me tell you.

It was really dusty in there. I hoped I didn't pick the moment when Marianne was walking down the hall toward Schmitt's arms to sneeze. That wouldn't be so good. Along with the dust, the closet smelled faintly of floor wax. Faintly, I guess, because Mrs. Parrott didn't do all the cleaning she might have.

As my eyes got used to blackness, I noticed a tiny bit of light leaking in from around the door—and, eventually, an even tinier glow from my watch dial. I'm hardly ever anywhere dark enough to notice that; I'd almost forgotten the watch had a glowing dial. If I raised my wrist in front of my face, I could see what time it was.

I didn't. I just stood there, as quietly as I could. For all the moving I did, I might as well have been the zombie janitor who swept up the alley. The only difference between us was, I knew I was standing there and where *there* was. The zombie didn't know; he wouldn't have given a damn if he did. Not knowing. Not caring. That's what being a zombie is all about. Ever so slightly, I shook my head. Nope.

I stood there and stood there. Not looking at my watch turned into a game. I tried to guess how much time was passing outside this black little stuffy chamber where nothing had ever happened or ever would. Then I heard footsteps in the hallway. They weren't Carlotta Parrott's; she'd worn soft-soled slippers. With these, I could hear heel and toe thumping on the floorboards.

They stopped in front of me. If Carlotta'd sold me out, I was in deeper than I wanted. But the person who'd made them knocked on the door across the hall. Shave-and-a-haircut-six-bits: a soft, familiar knock, the kind you'd make if you'd been there lots of times and the person inside expected you again.

The door opened. "Sweetheart!" a man said. I'd never heard Jonas Schmitt before, but who else was this likely to be?

"Hello, darling." Marianne Smalls sounded educated, the same way the husband she was discarding did. There were other noises that weren't words. Then Marianne giggled and said, "For heaven's sake, shut the door before you start with that!"

"Can't keep my hands off you, baby," the guy answered. She giggled again. The door closed. I wouldn't have to break it down with my shoulder, anyway. I hadn't been looking forward to that. Now I'd have a straight run to the bedroom door, as long as I didn't trip over the coffee table or the piano bench and fall on my stupid face.

Next question was, how long should I wait before I went in? I knew how long I'd planned to. Now I revised that down. They hadn't seemed as if they'd take real long to start doing what came naturally.

"Crap," I muttered, there where nobody could hear me. I still hated what I was going to do, and I still knew I was going to do it anyway. *Part of the business*, I thought, the way I had when Lamont Smalls told me the photos I'd got weren't juicy enough for him. It hadn't made me feel much better then. It didn't now, either.

I had the key. I had the cameras loaded up and ready to go. I waited till I reckoned the time was ripe. Then I shoved the closet door open. It didn't have a knob inside, only a flange that pushed against the jamb and held it closed. That made a faint click when I shoved, but I didn't think Schmitt and Marianne would notice. They'd damn well better not.

Into the keyhole went the key. I did it as cautiously as I could. He might not be as gentle unlocking her. Another small click and I was inside.

They'd left a lamp on in the living room. That made things easier. I hotfooted it toward the dark bedroom.

"Somebody's in here!" Marianne Smalls exclaimed, just as I got to the door. I fired off the first flashbulb.

Marianne and Schmitt both screamed. The blaze of light showed me I'd have what I needed. It'd also leave them with green and purple smears that wouldn't let them see what they were doing for a few seconds. In case the first photo didn't turn out, I took the second one. Marianne screamed again. I ran like hell. Schmitt wasn't wearing enough clothes to chase me.

Implacable as Cerberus, Carlotta Parrott barred the way out. But I had the sorcery I needed to defeat her. The key and a Grant turned the trick just fine. She stood aside. I trotted off towards Angel's Flight.

I gave the angel a quarter, the way I had the last time I played shutterbug. I'd been exhilarated then. Now, it felt more as if I were expiating a sin. I thought I saw—imagined I saw—reproach in his eyes as he took hold of me and spread his great wings. All the time we were in the air, I kept thinking he'd drop me … and that I'd have it coming.

But he didn't. He never does. He's flown murderers and kidnappers and rapists up and down. Judging people isn't his job—and a good thing, too, says I. Most of the time, people need mercy way more than they need justice.

He looked at me again when he set me on the sidewalk. I didn't have to meet his eyes, and I didn't. A man and woman stepped forward together and gave him a penny apiece. He took them in his arms. The downdraft from his wings staggered me. I straightened up and headed for the Red Line stop at the corner of Third and Broadway.

When I got back to the office, Old Man Mose was curled up on the sofa. "You again," he said.

TWICE AS DEAD

"Yeah, me again. I just brought in enough loot to keep you in cat food a while longer."

His yawn showed off needle teeth. "That's important! You should be happy!" Mose's world centers on Mose, nowhere else. Yours is bound to center on you, too. I hope you're less blatant about it than he is.

The desk chair creaked when I sat down in it. I yanked a drawer open and pulled out the latest fifth of Wild Turkey. I didn't bother with a glass. I just swigged, trying to get the taste of what I'd done out of my mouth.

"You don't pour that smelly stuff down like this when you're happy," Old Man Mose said suspiciously.

"How about that?" I said, and drank some more.

IX

Allums was still open by the time I got back to the neighborhood, but Terence would have gone home hours earlier. So I didn't take in my film till the next morning. Late the next morning, in fact, because I woke up feeling as happy as a vampire five minutes before sunrise. Aspirins, coffee, and *menudo* helped, but I still wasn't at my best when I walked into the drugstore.

"Hey, ace. Waddaya know for sure?" Terence said as I came back to the photography counter.

"I know there's something extra in it for you with these. I know you'd better not let anybody else get a look at the prints or the negatives. I know you'd better make like you never saw 'em, too." Unless I'd messed up, Al Harris could have sold these photos—especially the first one—from under the counter at his place.

"Like that, huh?"

"'Fraid so. All part of the job." I kept saying that to myself, and to anyone else who would listen. Myself kept not believing me. I hoped Terence would.

He pursed his lips. "How many exposures are there? When will you want 'em by?"

Exposures was the word, all right. "Just two. How soon can you do them?"

"If I start now, I can give 'em to you after lunch. Two o'clock okay? I'm guessing these have something to do with the last set you gave me?"

"Don't guess. You never saw nothin', remember? But you're a lifesaver." I reached over the glass case that separated us to punch him on the shoulder.

More aspirins, more java, and more time left me amazingly lifelike when the afternoon rolled around. Terence greeted me with, "You weren't kidding, man. I oughta give you these in a plain brown wrapper, not one of our envelopes."

"Did they both turn out?" I asked. He nodded. I handed him five bucks over the change they cost.

He tried to give the fin back. "Too much!"

"Don't worry about it. I'm playing with house money." You'd best believe I was going to put that five on my expenses report for Lamont Smalls. If the photos were what Terence said they were, they'd make the editor happy—and make him unhappy a different way. They'd save him a pile of money, but who'd want to see his wife doing that with a man who wasn't him?

Back to the office I went. I didn't look till then. Somebody might've seen me if I had. Nobody's supposed to see you when you look at pictures like that. And Smalls, I found, wouldn't have anything to grouse about this time.

Forty-five minutes later, he walked into the office. I gave him the photographs: again, not in an envelope that showed where they'd been developed—Terence's plain brown wrapper would have been fine. He stared at them for a long time, first one, then the other. I watched him bite down on the inside of his lower lip, trying not to let out what he was feeling.

He couldn't do it. "That goddamn needle-dicked ofay son of a bitch!"

He wasn't quite fair to Jonas Schmitt, who hadn't been caught at his best. I didn't say so. I also didn't tell him it wasn't what you had but what you did with it. He wouldn't have been in a mood to listen. I did say, "These *are* what you were after?"—the kind of question that means, *If they are, pay me the rest of what you owe me.*

"What?" Smalls needed a few seconds to come back to the here-and-now from whatever dark place the photos had taken him to.

Who could blame him for that? Then he nodded—jerkily, but he did. "Oh, yes, Mister Mitchell. These are *exactly* what I was looking for." He took out his wallet and gave me my balance. No fuss, no muss, no bother, not about that. I wish it were always so easy. "Have you written up your expenses yet?" he asked. Yeah, he was working hard to stay professional.

"Not yet. Sorry," I said. "Shall I mail them to you?"

"Do you have an idea of what they'll come to?"

"Nothing real big. Twenty-five or thirty bucks."

He nodded again, more smoothly this time. "That seems reasonable." He laid one more twenty and a ten on my desk. Then he left. Every line of his body said he hoped he never laid eyes on me again as long as he lived.

One more time, who could blame him? I just hoped he wouldn't go out and kill his unloving wife or her white lover or himself. When somebody who holds stuff in breaks, he's liable to break all the way.

I wasn't doing anything he didn't want me to do. I wasn't doing anything he hadn't paid me to do. I wasn't doing anything I didn't wish like hell I weren't doing. Whatever Lamont Smalls did on account of what I'd done, it wouldn't be my fault.

I said that to myself several times, too. Myself didn't believe me any more than he had before.

After I put the expenses money in with the rest, my wallet felt nice and fat and sleek. I wasn't used to a wallet that felt like that. I could pay some more bills, keep climbing out of the hole I'd dug for myself. One of these days, I might not owe anybody anything. Not so long ago, I would've told myself I was nuts to imagine such a thing. Myself would have believed me then, by God!

It got dark early. Daylight Savings Time had ended the Sunday before, so it got dark even earlier than it would have otherwise. It couldn't have been much past five when somebody knocked on the door.

"Come on in. It's not locked," I said.

It wouldn't have mattered if the door had been locked, or it might not have, anyway. Dora Urban did open it, though we both knew she didn't have to. "Good evening," she said, sounding not a bit like the fellow in the movie vampires love so much.

"Hi." I can't say *Good evening* without sounding pompous, so I don't. I smiled, though. I was glad to see her.

She was all business. "Do you have anything new to tell me about what may have happened to my half brother?"

"Not much," I answered, but then I caught myself. "Or maybe I do." I told her about the sorcerous dragnet trawling for the word *vepratoga*, and about how the cops were shaking down people who used it—or sometimes people who happened to be where somebody else had just used it. I did all my explaining without once using the word myself.

She listened intently. Not many things more flattering than an attractive woman hanging on your every word. When I finished, she said, "But you may have made a mistake by calling that lawyer a second time. If he talks with the police, he can cause you trouble you do not want."

Dora wasn't only an attractive woman. She was a damn smart attractive woman. That would've been plenty to scare off a lot of men even if she weren't a vampire. A lot of high-powered women hide their brains so they don't alarm the so-called stronger sex. I liked her better because she didn't waste time on those games.

"That crossed my mind about ten seconds after I hung up," I said ruefully. "Too late is too late, though. And it *really* crossed my mind when the cops pulled up and hauled that poor woman out of the phone booth. I hope they finally realized she didn't do anything." After a moment, I added, "I hope they care."

"She was a Negro, this woman?" Dora asked.

"Sure she was. They wouldn't have treated her like that if she were white." Was I bitter or simply stating the obvious? Is there a difference?

Her nod was somber. "Before I crossed the ocean, I saw only a handful of Negroes. No one over there hated them—they were too few to hate. People over there hated Jews instead. They treated them the way Americans treat Negroes. People always need someone to hate. Who the someone is will change. How they treat the someone is always the same."

"What do vampires do about it?" I asked.

She didn't misunderstand what I meant. Her eyes flashed, the way a cat's will when light hits them right. Human eyes don't do that, but then she wasn't exactly human herself. "We hate the living, of course. You always hate what you depend on. But we cannot do to them what the police did to that woman or the fylfot followers did to the Jews they could catch. There are not enough of us."

"You've got that right," I said. Jews in Europe and Negroes right here at home can hate their oppressors till everything turns blue, but they'll never be able to take revenge. There aren't enough of them.

Do Jews hate themselves because so many outsiders do? Wouldn't surprise me at all. Some Negroes sure do. In different ways, Lamont Smalls and Marianne both might've had a dose of that.

With all those cheerful thoughts in my head, I felt like killing the latest bottle of Wild Turkey. It wasn't as if I had no reasons to hate myself, either.

And Dora picked that precise moment to ask me, "The thing you did not want to do, did you do it?"

My arm started to go to the drawer pull where the bourbon lived. I had to yank it back. I lit a cigarette instead. That's poison, too—they don't call 'em coffin nails for nothing—but it's slow poison. "Yeah, I did," I said, staring down at the worn, ink-stained green blotter on my desk. "I got paid for it, too. I'm closer to not being broke than I have been since before the war."

"This does not make you happy." It could have been a question. It wasn't, not the way she said it.

"Too damn right it doesn't. I did it anyway, and I got the money."

She didn't say anything for a minute or two. Then, slowly, she did: "You may, in a very small way, begin to understand what vampires feel, looking back on the moment that made them what they are. I would not say this to many of the living, but I think it is so with you."

"What ... do you do about that?" I asked.

"Nothing. Nothing is to be done. It is forever there, till the moment of finishing." She shrugged.

I wanted to ask her how she lived with that. But she didn't, or not exactly. Instead, I recited, " 'Between the idea / And the reality / Between the motion / And the act / Falls the Shadow.' "

TWICE AS DEAD

"Just so. Just so, Jack." I think that was the first time she ever used my first—my Christian, if you'll forgive me—name. She went on, "For one who has not lived even a single lifetime, he is a wise man, Eliot." Her nose wrinkled. It made her look like a kid, no matter how many years she carried. She'd done that before, dammit. She knew it, too. "That horrible film! I hate it, and I cannot escape it."

I laughed. I couldn't help myself. So did she. Whatever was funny could only be superficial to her. I understood that, in my head if not in my gut. But even superficial relief might help a little. And, speaking of superficial relief, I hauled out the Wild Turkey after all, now without oblivion on my mind.

"Want some with me?" I asked. "I remember you had those Bloody Marys at Deacon's."

"Yes, give me some, please," she said. "It does not do for me what it does for the living, but I will drink it anyhow."

I had to rummage around for glasses. Most of the time, I don't bother with one. I just drink straight from the bottle. I didn't tell her that. The bourbon'd kill germs, and vampires probably don't need to worry about them anyway. Damned if I didn't find a couple of cocktail glasses, too, in a file cabinet top drawer. They'd been there so long, I'd forgotten about 'em. I poured for her and for me.

Instead of going back behind my desk, I parked on the couch beside her. Raising my glass, I asked her, "What shall we drink to?"

"To learning the truth about my half brother," she said.

We clinked. We drank. I could see why she made that toast, but it wasn't what I'd hoped for. Well, she had her ... not her own life to live, but her existence to continue. To her, I was nothing but a buzzing bug.

And what do bugs do when they're buzzing? They find a mate, and then pretty soon they die. Here I was, next to this gorgeous dame who seemed to like me well enough. If I made a pass at her, I might find as much heaven on earth as people are ever likely to. Or, if she happened not to care for it, I'd discover what going in the other direction was all about. I wasn't the big strong man here. If I wasn't welcome, I'd find out about it.

As experimentally as I ever had since I started shaving, I put an arm around her. Then I waited to see if the sky would fall. Sounding dryly amused, she said, "I know what is on your mind."

131

"Do you?" I said.

"Of course I do. For one thing, I would have to be an idiot not to. For another, even if I were an idiot, your odor would tell me."

"Oh. Sure." I'd used my Mitchum that morning. If I wrote to the company to complain, what would they tell me? That it wasn't made for situations like this. They'd be right, too. So I said, "And?"

"We can see what happens," she answered. "You have the sense to ask, not to try to take. And—" She said a few words that weren't English. Before I could ask what they meant, she leaned toward me, and I quit worrying about it.

First times are always strange. You don't know just what your partner wants or likes. With Dora, there was an added strangeness. She was warmer than room temperature, but she wasn't people-warm. It put me off a bit the first few times I touched her, no matter how perfectly shaped she was. Then I quit worrying about that, too. She might be chilly, but she sure didn't act cold.

She did act as if I were the big strong man. Maybe she thought I needed that, and maybe she was right. Or maybe it sprang from what vampires use for a sense of humor. But if she was laughing at me, she had the manners not to let on.

When things were getting pretty frantic, she nuzzled at my neck. I thought she did more than nuzzle, but I wasn't paying much attention right then. A few seconds later, I stopped paying attention to anything but my own joy. It was …. It certainly was, wasn't it?

I'd got all hot and sweaty. She hadn't. I didn't know whether that was the way vampires worked or a comment on my technique. Not asking seemed like a good idea.

Of itself, my hand went to my neck. When I took it away, my first and second fingers had blood on them. Not a lot of blood— I've seen more when my Gillette Blue Blade slipped—but blood. I looked at her. "Did you—?"

She nodded. I would say shamelessly, but shame is one of the things the undead don't bother with. "Yes, naturally," she said. "I always do. I need to find out what my lovers taste like. It is part of what knowing the living means to folk like me."

I always do. If your lady friend is who knows how many times older than you are, you have to be dumb in a way I'm not to imagine you're her first. The matter-of-factness did jar a little, though. I couldn't help asking, "Do I pass the test?"

"Oh, yes. In that way among others," she answered. It could have been polite, or it could have been praise higher than saying I might barely start to understand what being a vampire was all about. I chose to take it for a compliment. Go ahead. Call me vain. I don't care. Then Dora tilted her head to one side and asked, "And do I please you?"

Some people say vampires are vain to begin with, or they wouldn't try and cheat death the way they do. Was *she* fishing for compliments? Or was it a woman's question, not a vampire's? Because she was still a hell of a lot of woman, as I was in a position to know. "What do you think?" I said. With her sense of smell, she was bound to know already.

"We seem well suited," she said. She walked into the tiny bathroom stuck on to my office and did whatever female things she needed to do to clean up. I don't suppose she had to use it for anything else, being what she was.

When she came out, I went in. She was getting dressed when I opened the door again. I'd hoped for a second round, but after that first one it wasn't urgent.

"There is cat hair all over my skirt," she said, as if it were my fault.

"You sit down on that sofa, there will be," I said. Since we'd done other things on that sofa besides sitting, there was bound to be cat hair on her elegant backside, too, but I didn't point that out. Old Man Mose, he gets around. I also started dressing.

She got ready to go. Then she paused and came over to kiss me, as if she'd just reminded herself she needed to do that now. "Be careful, Jack."

"Yeah, you, too." Romantic parting, huh? But it was good advice to both of us, and we both knew it.

She went out through the door without bothering to open it. That seemed even stranger now than the first few times I'd seen her do it. I knew that body felt like flesh: lively, squirmy flesh. And how did she make her outfit go through the door along with her?

Don't ask me. I'm nothing but a private eye. I'd bet War Department wizards in a thaumaturgical lab somewhere near Washington are trying to duplicate the effect so live people can use it. So are Red wizards in a thaumaturgical lab somewhere near Moscow.

Old Man Mose came in through the cat door. He stopped, sniffed, and made a horrible cat face. "You have disgusting habits," he said, and hoisted one leg in the air while he licked his behind.

"Shut up," I explained.

I'd just walked into the office the next morning when the phone rang. I picked it up anyway. "Mitchell Investigating."

"Hello, Mister Mitchell. This is Isidore Berkowitz," said the guy on the other end of the line. The name and the bright, cheery tenor both seemed familiar, but I couldn't place either one. He took care of that: "I'm the doctor who drew your blood at County General. I'd like to talk with you about something that has to do with your line of work."

"Okay," I said slowly, not sure whether it was or not. "Uh, how do you know what my line of work is? I don't remember putting it down on any of the paperwork I filled out."

"You were talking about robbing the blood bank. That doesn't happen every day. I had your number, of course, but before I called it I looked in the phone book. It said you were what I thought you might be."

I chewed on that for a few seconds. "Oh. I wouldn't want to do your job, Doctor Berkowitz, but it sure sounds like you could do mine."

"Don't be silly." He sounded pleased. "But there's something I really would like to discuss with you."

"Professionally? Professionally for you or professionally for the hospital?" If he wanted to get my ideas on something simple over the phone, I'd give them to him. Why not? I wasn't doing anything else right then. If he wanted something bigger than that, though, it would cost him money. I wanted to be real clear about things from the start.

"Professionally, of course," he said. "I understand that you don't work for nothing." He was an optimist, but I didn't tell him so. At least he got the point without my needing to bang it home for him.

"I'm listening," I said. "When I hear what's going on, I'll tell you where the tariff starts."

TWICE AS DEAD

"That sounds fair. I had an unusual visitor yesterday afternoon, so unusual that he made me remember you. He was a police sergeant, and he was asking about how the blood bank stored drugs and how we made sure pushers and dope fiends couldn't get their hands on them. He was also wondering whether the blood bank was secure against drug thefts by vampires."

"I do see why you remember me, all right," I admitted. I played with the puzzle pieces inside my head, and damned if some of them didn't fit together. "By any chance, was this sergeant named Elmer V. Jackson?"

"How in the world did you know that?" Berkowitz's laughed sounded nervous. "When you said I could do your job, you had no idea what you were talking about."

"People say that about me all the time. Look, Doctor Berkowitz—"

"Izzy, please."

"Izzy, okay. I'm going to ask you about a particular drug—I think it's a drug, anyway. I'm not going to name it. I'll spell it out. When you answer me, don't you name it, either. It's important. You with me?"

"I sure am," he said.

"Fine." I thought I'd figured out a way to beat the listening spell. Now I'd find out if I was right. And I'd find out how big a mess I'd made of things if I was wrong. "Did Jackson ask you about V-E-P-R-A-T-O-G-A?"

"One of these days, I'll have to find out how you could possibly know that. But yes, he did. I think he wanted to shake me down, or shake the blood bank down, on account of it. I explained to him that we did not have any, had never had any, and never would have any. I may have explained rather firmly. He didn't seem happy, but he went away."

My guess was that Dr. Berkowitz explaining things rather firmly could peel paint off steel bulkheads, and probably set it on fire, too. That didn't matter, though. "You know about this stuff, then?" I asked.

His laugh was so empty of mirth, it might've come from a vampire's throat. "For my sins, I do. I say that, and I'm not even slightly Catholic. You never would have guessed, would you?"

"Don't need to put on my deerstalker cap to deduce that one, no."

This time, he really laughed. "Okay, you got me there."

135

"The stuff you shouldn't name, it's involved in some other things I'm working on," I said. "If I come up there, will you have lunch with me? You can talk about it and around it with me, if that's all right."

"That's great. We may both learn some things we didn't know before."

"I'd love to learn some things I don't know. The people I've talked to about this stuff, most of them've never heard of it, and I mean people who know about these things. The ones who have heard of it, it scares them to death."

"Worse than that," Berkowitz said.

"Huh?" I said. He sounded as if he meant it.

"We'll talk about it at lunch. I have to pretend to earn my living now. So long." Without waiting for me to say goodbye back, Berkowitz hung up.

I rode the trolley up to Country General. Since I'd been there before, I more or less remembered how to find my way to the blood bank. Dr. Berkowitz waited for me outside the door. As we shook hands, I asked, "Where do you want to go?"

"We could eat at the cafeteria. It's right here and it's cheap, but it's the cafeteria, if you know what I mean. Or …. Do you like Mexican food?"

"I'm your man. I don't know how many hangovers I've killed with *menudo*."

"I've done that myself. C'mon. This is the Mexican part of town. You can get all kinds of goodies here. The place I go to most often is about ten minutes' walk."

It was called El Burro Loco. It was a hole in the wall, not even as big as Al Harris's shop. You miss a lot of great food if you get snooty about joints like that. I ordered tongue stewed with peppers and sliced cactus leaves. So did Berkowitz. It came in a hurry.

"They'd never seen a white fellow get that till I did," he said. "I love tongue. Now they know I've got crazy friends, too."

"I love it, too." I'm not exactly a white fellow, but I'm not exactly not, either, so we could talk about that later if we had to. "It's poor-people food, whatever color you are. Those are my people."

"Mine right along with you," Berkowitz said. We ate for a while. He was right. The cook at El Burro Loco knew what he was doing and then some. When we were most of the way through what they'd

136

given us—which was a lot—the doc put down his fork and asked, "You were in the war, right?"

I nodded. Most people our age were. "Yeah. Italy."

"I was in Gaul. I had red crosses on my arm and my helmet, not that spells or bullets cared. But if you worked your way up the boot, there's a chance you ran up against some of the fylfot boys' LR units."

"The Lightning Rune troops? Uh-huh, a few times. Very bad news." I nodded again, and clicked my tongue between my teeth while I did. Those were the Leader's elite outfits. They got the best men, the best wizards, the best equipment. They were tough, mean, and nasty. They didn't want to retreat, and they really didn't want to surrender. Half the time, they'd kill themselves instead. Not quite so fanatical as the Knights of Bushido on the other side of the world, but getting there.

Oh. The LR ran the fylfot boys' murder factories, too. Some of them hanged for that afterwards. Not enough, but some.

"All right. You'll know what I'm talking about, then," Izzy Berkowitz said. "When you fought them, what did you notice most?"

"They wouldn't wear down," I answered at once. "I took some pills to stay awake myself—who didn't? But I don't think they ever slept. I'm exaggerating, but not a lot."

"No, not a lot," Berkowitz agreed. "The Leader's biggest trouble was, he didn't have enough of anything. He sure didn't have enough soldiers, not when he was fighting us and the Reds and Albion all at once. So he had to get the most out of the ones he did have. You're right. The Lightning Rune soldiers had more different chemicals in them than a fancy Gilbert chemistry set. And it still wasn't enough. His doctors and his wizards got together, and they did some experiments."

"Experiments?" I didn't like the sound of that. You didn't want the fylfot boys experimenting on you.

"That's right. It's possible some of my relatives who didn't make it out of the old country were guinea pigs. I don't know if that's true, thank God, but it's possible. If they were lucky, they just got killed."

I took another bite of my stewed tongue. For some reason, it didn't seem so savory any more. "You're going somewhere with this," I said.

"Afraid so. They came up with something that killed the need for sleep, sure enough. They liked that, so they tried it on some LR soldiers. But it killed too many other parts of you along with needing to sleep. You took it, you stopped caring. If you were a Lightning Rune man, you didn't care about the Leader any more, or the holy fylfot, or your country, or much of anything else."

"They made a zombie drug? Zombie soldiers aren't especially dangerous, even if you can't kill 'em. Too slow, too stupid, no good at following orders." I'd run into some of them, too. The fylfot boys tried everything they could as their dreams crashed down on their heads.

But Dr. Berkowitz shook his head. "No. With what they made, you're still as quick as ever and as smart as ever, but you don't care about anything. What's the use of a fighting man who doesn't care about fighting?"

"And the name they gave this stuff was …?" I didn't say it.

"That's right." Berkowitz didn't, either. We both knew what we were talking about, but the LAPD's listening spell wouldn't. "They didn't use it in the war. It was no damn good for fighting. But they kept careful records about what they did and how they did it. The fylfot boys have always been good at that. And they didn't have the chance to burn all of them when they realized they might have to pay for what they'd done."

"This is how we found out about it, huh?"

"Right the first time," Berkowitz said.

"I can see how it might be a problem," I said. "Not caring about anything …. A lot of the drugs they cook from poppy juice make you feel that way. Some people would want it. How long does the high or kick or whatever you want to call it last?"

"You *are* a smart fellow," Berkowitz said, peering down at his plate as if he could find answers on it. "There's the rub. You take it once. It always lasts for weeks or months. Sometimes it's permanent. Depends on how it hits you. You don't know till you try."

"Permanent." I echoed the word as if I'd never heard it before. I imagined hundreds, thousands, tens of thousands of people not giving a damn about whatever had mattered to them before they swallowed vepratoga or injected it or did whatever you had to do to get it inside you. "No wonder they're trying to keep it under wraps."

TWICE AS DEAD

"No wonder at all," Izzy Berkowitz said. "But you know Poor Richard's proverb, don't you? Three can keep a secret, as long as two of them are dead. This kind of thing always leaks out. Always. And it's starting to."

"Why did Elmer V. think you had some at the blood bank?" I asked.

"If I knew, I'd tell you. He said he had reason to believe we were involved with the stuff. I told him he was welcome to search ... after I called a couple of County General lawyers and a sorcerer to make sure nobody planted anything that wasn't there before. He didn't like that."

"Good for you!" I said. A lot of white people who make decent money honest to God believe the police are there to protect and to serve, and not for any other reason. If you watch things like that luckless woman dragged out of the phone booth and taken away, if you see them over and over again, you know better. I can't tell you how Dr. Isidore Berkowitz came to see he couldn't trust cops any farther than he could throw them. But he had.

He chuckled now. "After Jackson went away, I did talk with a lawyer, to let him know what had happened. He said one bad apple could ruin a whole barrel, and the longer Jackson stayed on the police force, the worse off it would be."

"He got his name in the paper not so long ago, remember?" I answered. "He had a madam for a girlfriend, or that's what they said, and he was taking money from her so the cops wouldn't close down her operation."

"Was that him? I didn't make the connection." Berkowitz said that with the air of a man who hates to miss anything. Come to think of it, Deacon Washington sounded the same way. Then Izzy added, "A madam for a girlfriend, *and* taking kickbacks from her? A regular snatch purser, that guy."

I looked at him. I didn't say anything. What could I say?

"Sorry. I do that once in a while." He had the grace to seem shamefaced.

"You might have warned me first."

He spread his hands. I've seen Al Harris make exactly the same gesture. "It catches me by surprise sometimes, too," he said.

139

"Whatever you say." But then I thought of something else. "And your lawyer was right. The LAPD isn't even close to clean, in case you didn't know."

"You can judge that better than I can," he answered. Did he mean I was a private eye and had to deal with cops, or had he realized I was the other thing and not the one, and so I had to worry about cops dealing with me? I couldn't very well ask. One more mystery being betwixt and between left me with.

Before I could, he paid for lunch. It wasn't a big check, but I meant to grab it. He beat me to the punch. "Thanks," I said. "Thanks twice, in fact. The food here *is* good. And I learned some things I didn't know before, and God only knows where I would've found out about 'em if not for you."

"Glad to help. It works both ways," Berkowitz said. "I'd never heard of anything like that sorcerous dragnet the police are using. I'm going to talk to the lawyer again. Something like that has to violate people's freedom of speech. I bet you can call it an illegal search, too."

Even if he didn't trust cops, we came from different worlds. He thought laws and courts could solve problems. Oh, sometimes they can. But don't they prop some people up and hold other people down a hell of a lot more often?

I tried to spell it out for him. "Be careful what you stick your nose into. You're liable to be fighting way out of your weight. Remember, Jackson isn't still a sergeant by accident."

"He knows where the bodies are buried, you mean?"

"More than that. He knows the people who put 'em in the ground. Odds are he's put some there himself. You want to be careful yours isn't one of 'em."

Slowly, Berkowitz got to his feet and pushed his chair under the rickety table. I did the same. We went outside. It was gray and gloomy, about the way I felt. As we headed back to the blood bank, he said, "County General isn't a small outfit, you know."

"Is it bigger than the LAPD? Is it bigger than City Hall? Is it bigger than the gangsters who run things behind the scenes? You need to make sure you know what you're playing with."

140

He looked at me the way I'd looked at him when he made his horrible pun. "We don't see things the same way, do we?" he said after a few steps.

"I was thinking that a little while ago."

"Which of us sees the truth?"

"What is truth?" I asked, just like Pilate. Like Pilate, I knew the question was easier to ask than to answer.

X

There was a fog upon LA the next time I went down to the US Rubber factory. I know, I know, San Francisco has the reputation for fog, but we get it here, too. Every once in a while, we get a really thick one, so people who live in neighborhoods without streetlights (more of those than the city fathers want you to know, believe me) come home late from work because they literally can't see where they're going.

The Red Cars I took south and east had their lights on and their bells clanging. Even so, they went slower than usual because the motorman saw through a glass, foggily. We passed a car that had run up on the curb, and two more that had smashed together. I got a glimpse of cops through swirling mist. That was the kind of thing cops were supposed to take care of. All the same, I wasn't sorry when I couldn't see them any more. Too often, they protected and served … themselves.

It had thinned out some by the time I got where I was going. The day had worn along, and I was farther inland. I still breathed damply, but I didn't feel as if I had a wet cotton veil over my face as I walked along.

Now, I didn't try to go right into the plant. Howe of Dewey, Beagle, & had warned me I'd get arrested if I did. I believed him. The way the god-things eyed me made me believe him.

TWICE AS DEAD

No, I went to the diner on the other side of Scrying Crystal Road. I figured I'd nurse some coffee till the lunch crowd came in.

I figured wrong. The counterman looked up from whatever not much he was doing and jerked as if he'd got stung by a yellowjacket. "You!" he said.

"Me," I agreed. "How about some joe?"

He shook his head. "I can't. It's worth my ass if I do. They told me they'd make this place off-limits if I let you snoop around here. That's most o' the business we do. We'd go bust without it. So get lost."

"They? Who's they?"

"You know damn well who. The big boys across the street. I ain't gonna piss them off, not for nothin'. Beat it. Amscray. I'll call the sheriffs if you try an' stick around."

So I left. What was I gonna do? He meant what he was saying. I don't know how they found out I'd been there. Squeezed it out of Babs or her friends? Sicced a sorcerer on me? However they'd done it, they'd done it.

Scrying Crystal Road runs from northwest to southeast. I crossed over to the northerly side, the one where the castle, uh, factory sits. I didn't try to go in, mind you. I just mooched along the sidewalk, then turned around and mooched back the other way. My vague thought was that I might spot somebody I knew and take him to an eatery whose owner wouldn't get in trouble for letting me sit down.

Every time I went by, I felt the Assyrian god-things' eyes on me. They knew who I was, and they didn't like me one damn bit. Whenever I looked back at 'em, they were nothing but carved stone. When I wasn't looking at them, though, I swear they were looking at me.

You can call that nerves or runaway imagination or whatever you want. But tell me what you call this. Not ten minutes after I started going back and forth in front of the US Rubber plant, a couple of big guys who'd been around the block a few times came out of the place and made for me. In a bar or a Central Avenue club, they would've been bouncers. I don't know what the US Rubber job title is.

"You want to move along now, pal," one of them told me.

"Don't you?" the other one added.

"I dunno," I said. "It's a public sidewalk. I'm not on private property or anything. As long as I don't make trouble, I've got as much right to be here as you do."

"You bein' here, that's trouble," the first one said. He wore an old Army jacket. One hand was in a pocket. Whatever he pulled out, I probably wouldn't like it.

"Are you sure? Have you checked with Sergeant Jackson?" I said.

He spat on the sidewalk, not quite straight at me but pretty close. "This is the county, not the city. Elmer, he don't got no clout here." He knew who I was talking about, but he didn't care.

His sidekick did, though. He set a hand on the first bruiser's arm. "Maybe we better find out, Louie," he said.

"Go find out if you want to." Louie lumbered toward me.

And I trotted toward him. That made him slow up. He thought I'd run away. You don't want to do what they expect. He had a wrench in that pocket. I'd guessed a shiv, but a wrench would be easier to explain to cops. By the way he drew his arm back, he was gonna rearrange my phrenology with it.

I kicked him in the balls. Anybody who wastes time fighting fair never saw combat, and that's a natural fact. He folded up like an accordion, clutching at himself. The wrench hit the cement with a clank. After I kicked him in the head, he quit wriggling.

I looked at his chum. "You want some, too?" I asked pleasantly.

His eyes were as big as gumdrops. "I told him not to mess with you. Honest to God, I did," he said.

And he had. But .... "You told me I couldn't walk on the sidewalk here," I said.

He hopped off the sidewalk and onto US Rubber property as if standing there were some sorcerous charm. "Go on, beat it," he said. "I don't want no trouble."

I could have done for him. We both understood that. He didn't even have Louie's stupid tough-guy confidence. What was the point, though? "Whatever you want, sweetheart," I said, and turned and headed for the bus stop. I didn't waste time telling him not to come after me. He wasn't going to.

On the way back up to my usual part of town, I did some thinking. They could try to tag me with a battery rap, though they wouldn't have a happy time telling their story under oath and truth geas. *We went out there to beat him up, only he got one of us instead,* was what it amounted to.

But I'd made a mistake mentioning Elmer V. Jackson. I'd told them some of what I knew. You never want to show a card when you don't have to. Word would get back to him, which might not be so good.

Once you've done something, you can't undo it. Old Omar Khayyam and his moving finger got that right. Whatever happened because I opened my big fat mouth, I'd have to deal with it.

When I walked into the office, a dead rat lay on my desk. It was giving the blotter some new stains. Old Man Mose had been sleeping on the sofa. He looked up at me and said, "I got another spy."

"I never would have guessed." I picked the rat up by the tail and dropped it in the wastebasket. Then I took the wastebasket out to the alley behind the place and dumped it into one of the big galvanized-iron trash cans there. And *then* I scrubbed my hands in the tiny little bathroom.

"Eating it would have been simpler. That's why I left it there for you," the cat said after I finished all that. He had the feline *humans-are-so-stupid* tone down pat.

I didn't feel like arguing with him. Life is too short sometimes. Instead, I asked, "Who was this one snooping for?"

"Somebody called Lappid," Old Man Mose said. "Whoever that is." His attitude was, if he didn't know, it wasn't worth knowing.

I'd never run across anyone called Lappid, either, so I was inclined to agree with him. For about a minute, I was. But I'm not always a jerk, only most of the time. "Do you mean LAPD?" I asked.

"That's what I said. Lappid." He yawned to show how interested he wasn't.

Well, he would have got it from the rat. Who can say how much rats really understand? Too much, sometimes. Not nearly enough, more often. "You know what the police are, don't you?" I said.

"Humans. Noisy humans." Mose yawned again. No, he didn't care much. Not that he was wrong. I remembered the squad cars screaming up to that phone booth. And cats have better ears than we do. They must love sirens to pieces.

If the LAPD was spying on me, I had a problem, all right. "Did you catch the rat in the office?" I asked.

"No, out in the alley. Couldn't you smell that?"

"Sorry, old boy. My nose wasn't all that great to begin with, and then I started doing this to it." I lit an Old Gold.

Old Man Mose showed his teeth. "Don't you know doing that makes you smell like a trash fire?"

"Most people smell the same way, so it doesn't bother us. We don't even notice."

"If I could work a can opener, I wouldn't come around here any more," the cat said.

"Nice to know I'm loved for myself alone."

"Wish for the moon while you're at it." Mose snarled again. "And if you think that doesn't go double for the refugee from a graveyard you're spearing, you'd better think again."

He was trying to make me mad. He did it, too. I made as if to throw a paperweight at him. He beat it, even if he knew I wouldn't really pitch the thing. That suited me fine. I knew he'd come back. He always did. That suited me, too, even if I didn't care to admit it to myself.

The night after I threw out the dirty rat Mose had assassinated, I was getting ready to give it up and go home when somebody knocked on my door. "Come in," I said, hoping it was Dora.

But it wasn't. It was Clarice Jethroe, looking tired and worried. "Hello, Mister Mitchell," she said, "What can you tell me about Frank?"

"Not a whole lot," I answered, waving her to the sofa. I gave her what little I knew. Then I went on, "I hit a nerve, anyway. US Rubber won't let me into the factory any more, or even into the diner where people who worked with your husband eat lunch."

"That doesn't do me any good. I want to know what happened to him," she said. In the books and the movies, the detective always works out exactly what happened, and inside two hundred pages or two hours, too. I wish real life were that neat.

TWICE AS DEAD

Then I remembered how Victor Howe had hung up on me. I wrote VEPRATOGA on a scrap of paper and handed it to her. "Did your husband ever mention this stuff? Don't name it, but did he? Naming it's dangerous for you and for me."

"He sure did," she said, sounding surprised. "He said he'd heard they had some in the plant, and they shouldn't ought to. It didn't mean anything to me. It still doesn't. What is it, anyways? Some kind of dope?"

"Something like that. When did he talk about it? How long before he disappeared?"

"Just a few days." Mrs. Jethroe had a lot on her mind wearing her down, but she was nobody's fool. "You reckon it had something to do with whatever happened to him?"

"That's what I'm looking at right now," I said, in place of screaming *Yes!* as loud as I could.

"All right." By the way she said it, it wasn't. She wanted answers, she wanted them yesterday, and who could blame her for that? After a sigh, she went on, "Well, I'm sure you're doing the best you can. Do you need more money?"

"No, ma'am," I answered.

"You aren't tryin' to leech off me. That's somethin'." *Not much*, her tone implied. She rose to her feet and tried to get cat hair off her dress. People who sat on the sofa did that a lot.

I stood up, too. "I'm doing what I can. There's only one of me, and I can't do things the police can. Have you talked to them again?"

"Those people!" She rolled her eyes and shook her head at the same time. "They don't give a damn. They don't even hardly pretend to give a damn. What's Frank to them? Just another stinkin' ...." She didn't say it, or need to. I knew what she meant.

"Remember, don't name the stuff. You can talk about it, the way we were, but don't call it by its name. You do, you'll see how fast trouble comes down on your head. If it takes even half an hour, I'd be amazed."

"You aren't kidding, are you?" she said.

"Not even a little bit."

"Okay. I won't forget. I already got me plenty o' trouble. Don't need more." Out she went, heading off to take care of whatever she

147

needed to take care of next. People like that, the ones who carry on no matter what lands on them, never get any credit. There aren't enough of them, either.

I thought about going home. I thought about eating my own cooking or something out of a can. I can cook a little, but only a little. Everything I make ends up tasting like K-rations. You can live on K-rations a long time. Pretty soon, though, you wonder why you want to.

So I went to a hamburger stand around the corner. K-rats would've been better for me. Sid's burger and french fries tasted good. That counted for more. If he sold beer to wash down the grease, he'd be a millionaire.

I still didn't go home after I ate. I could've read a book. I could've listened to the radio. I could've sat there wishing I had the dough to buy a TV set. The wild, exciting life of a bachelor on the town. The same way detectives are smarter in the movies, bachelors have more fun.

Or I could've gone to a bar. I don't mind drinking. You never would have guessed, would you? I don't mind seeing who I might meet up with, either, though I seemed to be taken at the moment. I do mind paying those prices when I don't have to. So I headed back to the office instead.

Old Man Mose sprawled on the sofa. "Oh, it's you," he said, not bothering to roll onto his stomach. As far as he was concerned, what had happened yesterday might've been a million years ago. Cats are smarter than people.

I sat down and pulled out the Wild Turkey. Good for what ails you. Forgetfulness in a bottle. What does the distiller buy that's half so precious as what he sells? Another one old Omar nailed.

I took a slug. Fire flowed down my throat and exploded in my stomach like a bursting 105. Bourbon is a Sugar Ray right; it hits hard and fast. That was why I wanted it. The lines needed some blurring.

Another swig followed hard on the heels of the first. It was almost as if I had nothing to do with the actual drinking. The *I* in there was just a target for what my gullet sent to my belly. Almost like that, but not quite. I knew how much I wanted the stuff. Most

TWICE AS DEAD

of the time, I'm holding the bottle. It isn't holding me. Most of the time, but not always. Not that night.

Two jolts just got me started, of course. The way it looked to me was, I'd spend the night in the desk chair, if I didn't spend it on the sofa or on the floor. I'd wake up in the morning feeling like hell, too. Not as if I hadn't done it before. Not as if I wouldn't do it again.

But I didn't do it then, because somebody came in while I was about to pick up the Wild Turkey bottle again. No, nobody knocked. The office door didn't open. It wasn't Dora, either. I'd seen her leave that way, but never what it looked like on the other side. I still haven't.

What I did see was Old Man Mose all of a sudden sit up and look very alert. I wasn't sure what that proved. He looked that way when a tiny gnat or moth I'd never spot in a hundred years fluttered around the office.

A moment later, though, following his gaze, I saw what looked like a patch of curdled air between the door and the desk. It was about the size and shape of a human being—if I wasn't starting to see things, I mean. A ghost. The LAPD had tried a rat, but that didn't work so well, thanks to Mose. Were they using a spook to snoop on me now?

I eyed the ghost as best I could. If I wasn't imagining things (and I knew there was no guarantee I wasn't), the beaky-nosed, long-chinned profile I could almost make out looked familiar. "That you, Eb?" I asked.

The ectoplasm that probably formed the defunct Pinkerton's head may have bobbed up and down. "Who were you expecting, Rudolf Sebestyen?" he said. I could just about make out his words, even if I wasn't exactly hearing them.

"That'd be nice," I said. Then, remembering my hospitality, I held out the Wild Turkey to him. "Here. Have a snort."

He flowed forward. "Don't mind if I do," a breeze might have whispered. He didn't drink. He couldn't. But *something* happened. Soaking up essence? Don't ask me. I've never been a ghost, not yet. He sighed a ghostly sigh. Then he said, "That's a better grade o' corn-mule than we made in my day, yes it is." He seemed louder all of a sudden. Maybe he was, maybe not.

"And what can I do for you?" I asked grandly. "Are you here to lend the grand and glorious Sergeant Elmer V. Jackson a helping hand?"

149

He said something about the grand and glorious Sergeant El-mer V. Jackson and an elephant turd. After another sniff at my spir-its' spirituous essence, he added, "You've gone and got people mad at you again, Jack. Some of them haven't twigged yet to its being you they're mad at, and you'd best hope they don't."

"Including the grand and glorious Sergeant Elmer V. Jackson?" I liked the grand and glorious sound of that, which proved I'd had a bit to drink.

"He's a sergeant," Eb said patiently. "He's no big thing." *Big thing* was Civil War slang, the kind of lingo that would've been in Eb's mouth back in the days when he had a mouth. It meant anything worth paying attention to. A pretty girl could be a big thing. So could the Battle of Gettysburg.

"Big enough for somebody like me."

"That business goes up from him, remember, not down."

Now I wished I hadn't put down enough to slow my wits. I needed to think straight. "Does it have to do with this stuff?" I asked, and wrote VEPRATOGA on some scratch paper one more time. I didn't even know if I was spelling it right; I'd only heard it. Hastily, I added, "Don't say it when you answer."

"Yes, I can feel the spiderweb they put out for it," he said. "You've almost got gummed up a few times."

"Oh, that," Old Man Mose said. "I wondered what that was. But I can't eat it, so it isn't very important."

The way cats look at the world will drive you crazy if you let it. I told myself not to let it, and gave my attention back to Eb. "Are they in the business of moving that stuff?"

"I don't know. They're being careful. I guess that's why there's nothing in the files, the way I told you before," the ghost answered. "They sure know people who know about it, though."

"Like the ones down at the US Rubber plant?" I asked.

"It's possible," he said, and then, "Are you guilty of assault down there?"

"Hell, no," I said, not without pride. "I'm guilty of battery. And I'd be guilty of landing in the hospital if I hadn't flattened one plug-ugly and scared off the other one."

TWICE AS DEAD

Technically, Eb was part of the LAPD. I couldn't prove he wouldn't give whatever I told him to the big wheels he'd been warning me about. But you have to trust *somebody* in this old life, know what I mean? He'd never done me wrong yet. I could hope he wouldn't.

"You know about the fylfot boys, don't you?" I said, less at random than you might think.

"Oh, yes," he answered right away. "Slaveholders wearing a different shade of gray."

"You're aces in my book, Eb," I said. Yeah, I felt happier trusting him than most live people I know. "This stuff, it comes from their wizards and doctors."

"One more strike against it," he said. I hadn't been sure he knew about baseball, either, but he did. "Those who make money from it wouldn't care if it came from Satan's druggist, of course."

He wasn't wrong, either. We've been picking the fylfot boys' brains since we beat 'em. They say the Reds have, too. Makes you wonder if anyone in the world has clean hands these days.

"Doesn't it just?" Eb said, answering a comment I hadn't made. He'd never shown me he could read minds before. He added, "You watch yourself, you hear?" and left the same way he'd come in.

Sometimes I wonder why I bother having a door at all.

Next morning, feeling more chipper than I would have if Eb hadn't come by, I found out why I had a door. Somebody banged on it, loud enough to make Old Man Mose vanish under the sofa. Nobody I know knocks like that, not even the landlord when I'm behind on the rent. Which probably meant .... "Who's there?" I asked, on the off chance I was wrong.

But I wasn't. "LAPD!" that somebody growled, as loud as he'd knocked. "Open up!"

"Have you got a warrant?" I asked.

A pause. They always hate when you make them play by the rules. As far as they're concerned, there shouldn't be any rules. Not for them, anyway. "No," the voice admitted. "But you better open up irregardless."

151

"Forget it," I said. Before the cop could start whacking the door again or knocking it down, I went on, "But I'll come out and talk. You still don't have permission to come in."

I opened the door. Outside stood a cop in a suit, not a uniform. More a suit you'd—or I'd—wear to a club than to an office, but a suit. His mug had *look how smart I am* written all over it. "You're a cute boy, Mitchell," he said, sounding like a cop on a radio show—and like he'd practiced sounding that way.

"Thanks," I answered. He scowled; that wasn't the line I was supposed to feed him. I looked him up and down, as if he were the one under suspicion. "Who are you, anyway?"

"Jackson. Sergeant Elmer V. Jackson." He preened like a peacock.

I might've known. I guess I had. I kept on being difficult all the same. "Let me see your badge, please. And something with your name and a picture."

He fumed, but I wasn't doing anything I didn't have a right to do. He flashed the tin. I wrote down the number: 714. Instead of anything with a photo, he handed me an LAPD card with his name and telephone number on it. "This okay, your Majesty?"

"It'll do." I stuck it in my inside breast pocket with my notebook. Then I said, "C'mon. Let's go for a walk. We can talk outside."

He fumed some more. He had to think I was trying to pull him away from the office, which I was. But I wasn't asking anything too unreasonable, and I look white enough so he couldn't casually black-jack me or stick a .45 in my face. So we went for a walk.

The zombie was doing his slow-motion alley sweep. Jackson looked at him the way you would if you stepped in warm cat puke in your socks. "Those damn things give me the heebie-jeebies," he muttered.

Since I felt the same way, I didn't answer. He lit a cigarette. He didn't offer me one, so I fired up one of my own. I wasn't paying special attention to where I wanted to go, but my feet took us down toward Vampire Village. "What's on your mind?" I asked him, blowing smoke up to the indifferent sky.

"Vepratoga."

I almost asked him whether he was afraid a couple of squad cars would pull up and take him away. Almost. But I didn't. I said it before: the fewer cards you show, the better. In that vein, I answered, "What? Never heard of it."

"Don't screw around with me," he said. "You're looking for a lugosi name of Sebestyen, right?"

Now I knew what he called black people most of the time, too. "What if I am?"

"Don't screw around," he repeated. "It's known he was after that shit. And you asked a high-powered mouthpiece if his high-powered client knew anything about it, which of course the high-powered client don't."

"Yeah, of course," I said, walking along when I wanted to stop and kick at the sidewalk. Dora was right—I'd been a jerk to yank Victor Howe's chain the way I had. Wasn't the first time. Won't be the last.

"So you know more'n you're letting on," Jackson said. "Quit playing coy with me, awright? Vepratoga, that's filthy stuff. You have any at all, it's a Federal crime. You do hard time, plenty of it."

"If it's a Federal crime, how come the FBI isn't questioning me?" I asked. The FBI would be more honest than Elmer V. Jackson. It couldn't very well be less honest.

"Because I am," he answered. And that just about sums up the way our fair city works.

Vampire Village by sunlight is a creepy place. It feels so empty, you'd think nobody lived there. You wouldn't be far wrong, either. At night, the undead come out, and it's lively if not alive. Not at this time of day, though.

A tall, skinny fellow with a bushy gray beard and sidecurls watched us from a corner. He wore a long black coat and a wide-brimmed shtreimel: one of the Shabbas-goy Jews who kept an eye on VV when most of the folks who resided there couldn't. I nodded to him. Soberly, he nodded back. As long as Jackson and I kept walking, we weren't a problem.

"Big-nosed bastard," the sergeant said under his breath. As if lugosi hadn't, that told me everything I needed to know about what he'd think of me if he ever realized I wasn't everything he assumed I was.

We hadn't got out of sight of that first watcher before we came into sight of another—a woman, this time. "What can you tell me about Sebestyen?" I asked.

"Only that I don't know what happened to him, an' I wish I did. Some higher-ups wanna know, too," Jackson said. That explained why he was interested. If he was telling the truth, it did.

"I haven't found anything," I said: only too true.

"You're messing in places where people with clout don't want you messing. Don't you know what happens to fools who keep doin' that?"

"I'm doing my job."

"Uh-huh. Right. If things happen to you, don't act all surprised, though. Then you'll think, *I shoulda been smarter*."

"I think that all the time anyway," I said, and God knows I meant it. "How much would it cost to get you to help me, or even just to leave me the hell alone?"

Sergeant Elmer V. Jackson laughed in my face. He laughed so hard, he had trouble stopping. "You ain't got enough for that, Mitchell," he said when he finally did. "You ain't within miles of having enough for that."

Since we seemed to have said everything we had to say to each other then, I turned around and started back to the office. Jackson came along with me, so I guess he thought the same thing. He slid into one of those new Studebakers with the rocket nose and drove away. I made damn sure he was out of sight before I went back inside.

Central Avenue, Saturday night. It was chilly, with the air holding the wet-dust smell that promised rain. The avenue was packed anyway. It always is, of a Saturday night. A few worrywarts carried umbrellas. Most folks looked willing to take their chances.

Like me, for instance. And Dora. Of course, if it came down hard enough to annoy her, she could always ditch me and fly away. I wouldn't have bet against her dodging all the raindrops when she did it, either.

"I went up to the blood bank before I came to meet you. I needed to be filled," she said, talking about herself as if she were Elmer V. Jackson's Studebaker.

"Did you see a doctor named Berkowitz?" I asked.

She shook her head, setting golden curls flying around it. "Doctors are for taking blood out—when one does not do it oneself, I

TWICE AS DEAD

mean. All I need is a nurse or a clerk to give me the volume I pay for." I wondered whether she used gold coins or paper money (and whether handling silver certificates would pain her).

Before I could ask, somebody behind us whistled at her. Well, any guy who saw that shape from behind would be tempted to whistle, too. She turned around and drew back her lips enough to give him a glimpse of her fangs. He was a Negro, but he damn near turned white when she did. He found some other direction to go in as quick as he could.

"And I am not even hungry," she said. I laughed, but she sounded wistful. You ask me, blood banks are great. They let the undead hang with the living and not feel the need to treat them the way people treat cattle. But Dora Urban sounded as if she missed the chase.

She paused in front of the windows of the Madras Trading Company, where I'd been, less happily, a few days before. I happen to know Los Angeles is as close to India as the fellow who runs it has ever been; he's from Puerto Rico. If you want to hex somebody but you don't care to pay a wizard, he'll sell you what you need. Or if someone's doing that to you, you'd better believe he has wards for sale, too.

Charms, rosaries, sacred oil, John the Conqueror root, lodestones (which sound ever so much more mystical than magnets), floor wash to clean up evil along with the usual grime … and if none of that fills your bill, you can play the numbers in the back room. I can't tell you whether Señor Javier pays off the cops or the mob, but nobody gives him any trouble.

That thought made me ask, "Is any of what he sells any good? Or is he just another con man fleecing the marks?"

She frowned, pointing to a sign. "I don't know what goes into goofer dust—"

"I do," I said. Dora looked a question at me, so I had to explain: "Graveyard dirt, snakeskins, whatever else the hexer making it up decides to throw in to give it an extra jolt." My family never messed around with magic like that, which doesn't mean they pretended it wasn't there. I wouldn't carry it if I were silly enough to think that.

"Ah," she said. "For my kind, graveyard earth helps; it does not harm. But I can see how it might be used against live people. I am not really familiar with this sorcerous tradition, so I should not speak about it. Dwelling here, I ought to know more. What is this John the Conqueror root, for instance?"

"Well ...." We were lovers, but she'd embarrassed me anyway. A proper John the Conqueror root looks something like a dark-skinned fella's ball. You can use them to help your getalong if it needs help. Or you can do bad things to one of those roots and aim them at a man you don't like. Then his getalong *will* need help. That's what I hear, anyhow; I never tried it myself.

The way I didn't answer told her most of what she needed to know. "Men are strange creatures," she observed.

"We think the same thing about women," I replied.

"Women are complex. Men are very simple, and they are also strange. I suppose complexity may seem strange to someone simple."

So there, I thought. I didn't try to tell her she was wrong; she was way too likely to be right. She looked smug—complex maybe, but smug. On her, it looked good.

Music poured out of open doorways. None of it made me want to pay a cover charge and buy a couple of rounds of overpriced drinks to hear it better. I did wonder whether Jonas Schmitt was pounding on a piano in one of those clubs. A moment later, I wondered whether he was still pounding on Marianne Smalls. If I was lucky, I was all done with them.

"Do you want to go to Deacon's when it opens?" Dora asked, which paralleled my thoughts without quite following them.

If we went to Deacon's, we wouldn't go back to my office or my apartment. Yeah, men are very simple. But she'd hired me to help her find her half brother, so not all of what she wanted was the same as what I wanted. "We can do that," I said with as much grace as I could.

She smiled. Had she been a live woman, she likely would have fallen down on the sidewalk laughing. "Deacon's is an interesting place," she reminded me.

I remembered all the dark little nooks and hideaways in there. "Not exactly the kind of place I'd pick for something like that, but there are worse ones," I said. She smiled again.

TWICE AS DEAD

A police car went by. It wasn't after anybody in particular, just patrolling. The red light on top wasn't spinning around; its siren didn't scream. Both cops inside were darker than I am. But still, a police car. Nobody in a police car meant well for people who enjoyed places like Central.

When I was in Italy, my company chased the fylfot boys and the local axes-and-rods fellows out of a village south of Milan. The guy who ran a café there had lived in the States for years, then gone back to the old country. Back home, he passed for rich; that was how he'd bought the eatery to begin with.

He spoke better English than some fellas who wore the same uniform I did. *Youse guys don't know what it's like when they come down the street every day, checking everybody*, he said.

I nodded along with all the other dogfaces in the place. He was feeding us. What he could do with some noodles, olive oil, and a little garlic made the miracle of the loaves and fishes seem like an exercise from basic training next to a real battle. Yeah, I nodded.

But I knew what that was like, all right.

XI

When things on Central slowed down as much as things on Central ever slow down, we went to that dark little side street and worked our way along the boardwalk till we got up to Acolyte Adams. He stiffened when he recognized me. That didn't stop him from taking my money, though.

After he had it, he said, "You aren't going to make trouble, are you?"

"Not that kind," I answered. It seemed to satisfy him—he waved Dora and me into the place.

You never know beforehand what will happen at Deacon's. You aren't always sure afterwards what did happen, either. The only thing you can be sure of is that you'll have bought at least two massively overpriced drinks before you get out. I had a Wild Turkey and Dora chose a Bloody Mary, same as we had the first time we went in.

Before the drinks came back, a tall white man in top hat and white tie who was working his way through the crowd plucked a silver dollar from my nose and a quarter from Dora's ear. "That is strong sorcery, considering what I am," she said, baring her teeth to show him exactly what she was.

He didn't panic, the way the guy on the street had. He swept off the topper and bowed, though how he found the room to do it

I can't tell you. His scalp shone in the strange lights; he shaved his head. "I beg your pardon," he said. "I hope the silver didn't alarm you or endanger you."

"It surprised me," she answered, "and I am not easily surprised. As I told you, strong sorcery."

He bowed again. I wondered if I should be jealous. "The strongest sorcery there is," he said: "No sorcery at all."

Dora frowned. For once, though, I knew what he was talking about where she didn't. "Oh!" I said. "You're from the Magic Castle!"

"At your service, sir," he said, and I got a bow of my own. "Have you visited us?"

"Afraid not, but I have heard of you. It's a wonderful idea," I said. The Magic Castle sits up in the Hollywood Hills. It is what it says it is: they put on magic shows, most of them much fancier than the kind of thing he was doing at Deacon's. The joke is, there's no magic in them. It's all sleight of hand and hidden wires and whatever else they can think of. Some of it, a real wizard would have trouble matching.

He pulled a card case out of thin air, the way he'd pulled the dollar out of my nose. With a flourish, he opened it and handed me one. I took it warily, half expecting it to burst into flames or something. But it didn't. It said he was Thomas Rivers, Prestidigitator Extraordinaire. Extraordinaire he was.

"Use my name if you want to watch what we do," he told me.

"Obliged. Much obliged." I gave him my card, too.

He did me the courtesy of looking at it before he stowed it away. "I make illusions. You pierce them," he said.

"Sometimes," I answered. "When I'm lucky."

"You strike me as lucky enough," he said, looking from me to Dora and back again. "And now, if you'll excuse me ...." Off he went. Pretty soon, he'd startle somebody else at Deacon's.

"The magic of ... no magic?" Dora said.

"That's about the size of it," I agreed.

Our drinks showed up then. The Deacon brought them himself, which didn't happen every day. Taller than Tom Rivers and twice as wide, he plowed through the crush in the club like an icebreaker pushing floes aside. "I heard you were here," he rumbled.

159

"Not yet. I expect to get here pretty soon, though," I answered.

He eyed me as if wondering whether to break me in half. After a moment, he contented himself with saying, "You aren't funny enough for me to put you up on stage."

"I guess not." I raised my glass in salute and drank. He didn't water the bourbon, anyhow. At his prices, he could afford not to.

Dora drank, too. "Where do you get the blood for the Bloody Marys you serve to folk like me?" she asked the Deacon.

Deacon Washington looked sheepish, an expression I'd never seen on his face before. "I know a man who makes dog food," he said. "He sells me some."

"You may thank him for his hospitality," she said. "And, of course, I thank you for yours."

"I appreciate that," he said gravely. "Have you had any luck finding your half brother?"

"No," she said, and not another word.

"I had the good luck to meet Elmer V. Jackson, though," I said.

Deacon Washington hoisted an eyebrow. Everything he did was theatrical. For him, life wasn't to be lived; it was to be performed. That would wear me to a nub in nothing flat, but he couldn't act any other way. "With good luck like that, who needs bad?" he said.

"I'm going to steal that line," I told him.

"Fair enough. I did," he said. "Was he trying to shake you down on account of the stuff Master Sebestyen was looking for?" He remembered not to name vepratoga. He might have overacted—or that's how it seemed to me—but there were no flies on him.

I made as if to clap my hands. "Right the first time!"

"Do you know yet what it is? Do you know what it does?"

I thought for a moment. Then I told him. Izzy Berkowitz hadn't told me to keep it under my hat or anything. And stuff that acted the way the blood-bank doc said vepratoga did wasn't likely to be up the Deacon's alley. Benzedrine, now, he might use that so he didn't miss anything.

He listened gravely. When I got done, he asked Dora, "Why would your half brother want stuff like that?"

"You would have to ask him to know for certain. At the moment, no one can do that," she replied. "I will say, though, that he often felt the world was too much with him. He might have been looking for something that made it seem to press in on him less unbearably."

"An interesting thing for a vampire to feel," the Deacon remarked. I didn't know whether Dora heard the words behind the words. Deacon Washington was a black man. If he walked down the street, the world—or at least the LAPD—was liable to press in on him. And he was a queer black man who threw being queer in people's faces instead of hiding it. When the world pressed in on him, he pushed right back.

"We are all of us different, live people and vampires alike," she said, so she did understand him, sure enough. "With us, I imagine you can blame our once having been live people ourselves."

"That might do it." The Deacon wasn't about to let anybody out-sangfroid him, even if vampires have a natural edge when it comes to cold blood.

The lights dimmed, not that they'd been any too bright to begin with. Curtains whisked this way and that. A spot hit the stage. The house combo started playing. I didn't need to look to know they'd found themselves a new piano player. Sure enough, a broad-shouldered black fella with a konked pompadour was tickling the ivories. He was good, too. He played boogie-woogie like nobody's business.

"What happened to Schmitt?" I asked.

Washington shrugged a massive shrug. "I can't tell you. He said he had some kind of trouble, but he didn't say what." His gaze sharpened. No, no flies on the Deacon. "Why do you even know who he is?"

"Because I do," I said. If he wanted to make something of it, he could. But he just shrugged again. I didn't see Marianne Smalls, either. It might not have proved anything, of course. You can't see far at Deacon's any old time.

Dora and I found hassocks to perch on and listened to the music for a while. Tom Rivers drifted through the crowd, doing magic that wasn't sorcery. I could half track him by the startled squeaks that followed in his wake.

When he came by us, he winked and said, "I've already annoyed you folks." With a flourish of that topper, he went on to presti his digits at someone else.

161

"He has a finely honed skill that is of no use whatever," Dora said once he was out of earshot.

If that's not a metaphor for mankind in general, I don't know what would be. But I said, "Don't be too sure. I bet he's the best pickpocket you never saw."

She started to say something, then stopped. When she resumed, what came out was, "I do admire your turn of phrase."

That made me feel so good, my cheeks got hot. All the same, I answered, "Another finely honed, useless skill." I wasn't wrong, either. Even in the movies, a wisecracking gumshoe gets killed in the second reel.

After a while, the combo took a break. A girl wearing more than she'd been born in but not a whole lot more brought them drinks. The piano man's tumbler was full of what had to be either straight scotch or straight bourbon. The way he tossed it back reminded me there were people who drank more than I did. It also probably told me why I didn't know who he was when anybody who could play like that should've had a name from coast to coast.

I whispered something in Dora's ear. She nodded. We stood up and stretched and walked around. Somebody giggled when I bent down to peer into the first dark little nook we found. I backed away in a hurry. Everything was quiet at the next one, though. When we slipped into it, we had it to ourselves.

What happened after that's none of your damn business.

Downtown is pretty quiet on Sunday. City Hall is closed, and the Federal building and the county offices, too. Most businesses also shut down for the Sabbath. They give the people who work in them a chance to rest, a chance to go to church, or a chance to listen to football or baseball on the radio.

Of course, some places stay open. Bars, for instance. And Al Harris's little bookstore. For one thing, since Al's Jewish, his Sabbath is Saturday. For another, odds are he does half his business from good Christians who're remembering their Sabbath and keeping it holy.

The place smelled of tobacco smoke and of old paper getting older, the way it always does. A blond young man was glancing at a

TWICE AS DEAD

deathless piece of literature called *Cruising Sailors*. The book might have appealed to Deacon Washington. The young man might have, too, though the Deacon and Acolyte Adams have been a couple for years and years.

You notice such things out of the corner of your eye, of course. I found a magazine to look at while I waited for a chance to talk to Al. It was educational, but I don't expect it to show up at the library down the block from your house.

Guys kept coming in and looking over Al's stock, or whichever part of it interested them most. Sunday was the only free day a lot of them had, of course. Every so often, somebody would leave after getting an eyeful or would go up to the counter, buy something, and then leave. Al wasn't going to get rich, but I didn't think he and Margie and Skeeter would be out on the street any time soon, either.

After a while, there was a lull. I made my way over to him. "How ya doin'?" he said. "See anything you like?"

"One of the brunettes," I answered honestly, and he laughed. I asked him, "How much do you look at what you sell?"

"Not a whole lot," he said. "I been doin' this a while now, y'know. Ain't like I never seen it before. Y'ask me, it's like using a picture of a steak dinner to make somebody hungry. But nobody asked me."

Right after I got out of the service, I did something—never mind what—for a gynecologist. I asked him if he got tired of looking at pussy all the damn time. He rolled his eyes and went *Do I ever!* Of course, he'd already been divorced twice, and he was in hot water with number three. He wasn't even forty, either. So don't believe everything people tell you, which is a good rule most of the time.

Al's mind went somewhere else. "What's with your neck? Looks like you got yourself shaving, only twice."

"Yeah, I'm practicing for when I finally cut my own throat," I answered, straight-faced. He laughed some more. Because I didn't make a fuss over it, he forgot about it. I did wish Dora wouldn't do that every time we messed around, but she seemed to need to. Things I hadn't known before I found myself with a vampire girlfriend …

A guy who wanted to spend money came up with a magazine called *Werewolf Women—Wild in Las Vegas*. Not what floats my boat,

163

but I wasn't laying down a fin for it. "Plus another thirteen cents," Al told him. "Sales tax."

The fellow rummaged in his pocket for change, then took off. "Sales tax," I said.

"I mind my P's and Q's," Al said. "They've jugged me for what I sell a couple-three times, but I always beat the rap. Taxes, though, they get you for taxes and you're screwed. They sent Scarface Al up the river for dodging taxes."

"You going to deduct what Elmer V. shook you down for?" I asked.

"Him? He can go take a crap on the ocean, that one. I'd like to deduct *him*, not what he squeezed outa me. Lousy shmuck." He lit a cigar.

"He's a piece of work, all right," I agreed.

"Jackson? He's a piece o' somethin' else," Al said.

I couldn't argue with that, either. "He sure is," I said. "I've met him now, over the same stuff he was interested in with you."

"Oh, yeah? How much did he wanna steal from you?"

"He didn't get anything. He didn't have enough on me to make that work. But he was in there swinging."

"He should *alevai* swing—by the neck. He won't, though. Bastards like him never do. In a clean city, he wouldn't get away with the *dreck* he pulls."

"A clean city? What kind funny foreign language you talk, Meester?" I put on a silly accent, the way comics used to. It worked for them then, and it worked for me now. I chuckled myself; it was chuckle or bang my head against the wall. Then I asked him, "You ever have vampires come in here?"

"This time of year, every now and then. In the summer, the sun's still up when I go home. I don't think I ever saw that Sebestyen item you're looking for, though. I just heard about him." By the way his mouth twisted, he liked none of what he'd heard.

I also didn't like what I knew about Dora's half brother. But that wasn't quite where I was going. "What gets a vampire all excited?" I asked.

Al Harris's mouth twisted again, in a different way this time. "Whips. Switches like the one your old man used to smack you with when you were bad."

TWICE AS DEAD

"My old man just used his belt," I said.

"Lucky you. But you're younger'n I am. They don't switch kids so much any more, huh? Anyway, that stuff, on account of the blood. Oh!" He looked to be reminding himself of something—something he wished he could go on forgetting. When he lowered his voice, he explained why: "And girls with their monthlies."

I said, "Oh," myself, and then, "They print that kind of stuff?"

"They print *everything*," he said with great conviction. "You gotta be careful who you sell it to, though. Vampires, they're pretty safe."

He didn't bother hiding he'd gone to the hoosegow a few times. I knew he'd always got out fast, too. Now more than ever, I wondered how. Some of the things in there, you might make a case they were art. Not great art, but plenty of art that isn't dirty also isn't great. Still, how would you go about making a case for *that*?

How? I wondered what Victor Howe would say. Probably something like, *Pay me a stack of cash and I'll see what I can do*. There are times when lawyers make crooked cops seem honest.

My face must've shown some of what I was thinking—one reason I didn't come home rich from Army poker games. Al snorted. "Remember, you asked me."

"I know, but why did you have to go and tell me?" I answered. He thought that was the funniest thing I'd come out with yet. Then I asked him, "Where do you have ... those? I've been in here enough to know they aren't on your racks."

"What, you think I'm *meshiggeh*? They're put away. You want 'em bad enough to ask for 'em, I'll scratch your itch. Unless you smell like a Vice cop, I mean. I got a decent nose for them."

Him talking about decent after something like that? You never know. I wondered who made those magazines, and why. For money? You wouldn't make much, off vampires or live people. Because it got *them* excited? Somebody could write a novel about that. Some strange fish crazy enough to want to, I mean.

"Listen," I said, "you hear anything about Sebestyen, pass it along to me. Anything about the other stuff, too. If it's important enough for Jackson to be interested, it's important."

"I'll do it. And anything else I run across," Al said. "You play straight. One o' these days, you'll pay me back some kinda way."

165

"Thanks." I don't always operate like that. I wish I did, but I don't. I do try, though. Nice to see somebody notice once in a while.

We said our goodbyes. I got out of there. Most of the time, I don't think about walking out of Al's emporium any more than I think about walking out of, say, Allums. Although lately I haven't been sorry to escape the drugstore, either. Dirty pictures both ways.

Dora and I lay in each other's arms—all tangled up with each other, if you want to know the truth. We pretty much had to: the bed in my apartment unfolds from the sofa, and it's narrow for one, let alone two. It was dark in there, darker than dark. I couldn't see much of anything. She could, I'm sure—one more way vampires differ from live people.

I wiggled my left hand till I could touch my neck. Had she got me again? I thought so, though saying I'd been distracted when it happened is putting things mildly. I tasted my fingertips. Yes, blood. Enough to notice, not enough to worry about.

"Why do you do that?" I whispered. Our heads were no farther away from each other than any other parts.

"Because I do," she said, as if that were all the answer I deserved. For a second or two, I thought it was all the answer I'd get. But then she added, "Why do you do this?" She slid her smooth leg along mine so I'd know just what she meant by *this*.

"Why? Because you're fascinating. And because you're beautiful." I hadn't known which of those I'd put first till I heard myself talk. I got it right, though. She was smart to begin with, and she'd got more experience (take that how you will) than any live person could.

"I thank you," she said, and I think she meant it, but she shook her head at the same time. "I thank you, yes, but it is not enough. Nothing that lasts can come of this. I will not bear your children." She laughed; that was the kind of thing that struck a vampire funny. "I have not needed to concern myself over such things for many long years now."

How many long years? I didn't know then. I don't know now. I shrugged. "I wasn't worrying about anything that lasts. I'm enjoying it now, that's all." I squeezed her to me, as if I were the strong one, not she. And I hoped I'd be able to enjoy it again in a little while.

TWICE AS DEAD

She let me pretend I could master her. She knew how live men worked, sure as hell. But she said, "Your *now* is so sadly short. It flickers like a guttering candle and, like a guttering candle, it is gone. How can you afford to waste time when you have so little of it?"

If I looked at it straight on, that had no answer. Well, it had one: me looking down into my waiting grave and watching the wiggling worms the diggers had cut in half. You can't do that for very long and keep your marbles.

"We'll last as long as we do, the two of us," I said roughly. "I don't know what to tell you. One of these days, they'll figure out how to go to the moon or to Mars. Where live people go, vampires will, too. It may even be easier for you folk. Maybe you'll look up at the Earth in the sky and remember me."

"That is very pretty," she said. "What happens six months from now, though, when you meet a live woman you might want to spend some of your handful of years with? Will you tell her about your vampire lover? Will you tell her all about me? Will you tell her about *this?*" Her teeth touched my neck again. She didn't draw blood this time, but I knew she could have.

I stared, not that that did me any good. "Are you jealous?" I asked. In another tone of voice, it would have been disbelief. In another one yet, it would have fired a lovers' quarrel. But I only wanted to know; I hadn't imagined anything like that.

Dora must have heard as much, because she answered seriously: "Of course I am jealous. The undead know pleasure, but not love. Never love. I remember love, from the days before I became what I am. I remember it, but as if it happened to someone else. In every way that matters, it did."

"Oh." I paused. "Should I tell you I'm sorry?"

"I know you are. I can smell it. I am not insulted or angry to know. We are different, though. We would both do well to remember it."

"Most of the time, sure. Not now," I said. We started again. I didn't know if I'd get where I wanted to go. I didn't know if I'd get her where she wanted to go, either. There are ways to do that even if you don't get there yourself. Some people call them perversions. The ones who don't, though, they have happier lady friends.

167

Happy? Is that a word you can use about vampires, any more than you can use a word like *love*? What do I know? I'm only a live guy. I did the best I could. If it wasn't good enough, she was gentlewoman enough not to let me know it.

They make jokes about men who roll over and go to sleep afterwards. I've made them myself. I didn't quite this time. I didn't have the energy to roll over, you see.

Next thing I knew, it was morning. The window has blinds and curtains, but light slips in anyway. I lay alone in the bedraggled bed. Of course Dora wouldn't stick around to watch the sun rise with me.

I got up and started setting the place to rights. Yes, I remembered what we'd talked about. I shrugged one more time. Happy? Is that a word you can use about private eyes?

When I walked into the office, one more dead rat lay bleeding on my desktop blotter. All things considered, I was going to have to get a new one. There's a place on Avalon called the We Ain't Moving Stationary Store that sells me such things when I need them.

Old Man Mose looked up at me from the couch. "This one got inside," he said. "I found it trying to open one of your drawers there." His copper-gold eyes swung towards a filing cabinet.

"Was it? Did you?" That was bound to make it another spy. I could have done without the honor of so many people interested in what I was up to. "Could you find out who sent it before you killed it?" After my unsatisfactory encounter with Sergeant Elmer V. Jackson, my money was on the LAPD.

Good thing I don't gamble much; I would've lost. Mose answered, "Something or somebody called Usrubber." Since he didn't know what Usrubber was, he was sure it couldn't be important to him. That's how cats' minds work. A good many people's minds, too.

I'd had my coffee, so I didn't need long to work out what Usrubber meant. That might not be important to Old Man Mose, but it was to me. If they were anxious enough to try to spy like that, I must've poked a nerve.

I phoned Dewey, Beagle, & Howe. Victor Howe didn't take my call at first. "If I don't talk to him, I'll talk to the newspapers,"

TWICE AS DEAD

I told his secretary. "I mean it. He'll like that less than he will getting his ear dirty from listening to me for a few minutes. Let him know, okay?"

"Please hold," she said. It was a toll call and costing me money, but I held.

A click, and then Victor Howe: "Blackmail is a nasty game, Mister Mitchell," he said in a voice like the last winter of the war.

"So is breaking and entering. I've got the snoop on my desk, dead. She wasn't good enough," I answered. The rat was female.

"You ... what?" he said.

"A rat. Before she died, she told me Usrubber sent her here. Asking what Usrubber is wouldn't be the sixty-four dollar question— more like the two cent question, I'd say."

"No reputable firm would stoop to such a thing," he intoned.

"Yeah? How about your client?"

He didn't hang up on me, not quite. "I deny the imputation. On behalf of my client, I deny the accusation."

"That's nice. You aren't under oath now. Would you still deny it if you were?"

"Haven't you wasted enough of my time by now?"

"Not yet. Maybe you want to think about why US Rubber is working so hard to keep me from finding out what happened to Frank Jethroe. They don't want me in their factory. They don't even want me in the diner across the street. And now they're trying to find out what I know even if I can't go into those places. What are they so scared of?"

"You're inventing things, spinning them up out of whole cloth," Howe said.

"Not me. Maybe you should look in a mirror instead. Who told me not to go into the US Rubber factory or they'd arrest me for trespassing? If that wasn't you, somebody could win a prize for impersonating you well enough to fool your own secretary. I can prove it, too. I was taking notes while we talked." Yeah, I lied to him. That's what I should have done, not what I did. But he didn't know I hadn't. And contemporaneous notes are worth their weight in diamonds in court.

"Is this more blackmail?"

169

I laughed. "There's a saying that goes something like, 'This animal is treacherous. When it gets attacked, it defends itself.' Oh, and just so you know, I don't keep everything at the office, or at my apartment, either." I didn't want anybody tossing either place to find the notes that weren't there.

"No wrongdoing on my part has occurred," Howe said starchily.

"Now tell me another one. I bet I think it's funny, too." This time, I hung up on him. You take the small pleasures when you can find them. Sometimes they'll come back and bite you later. You mostly take them anyway.

I wrapped the rat in the blotter and took the whole mess out to the trash cans in the alley. Then I came back and washed my hands. Twice. And then I walked over to We Ain't Moving Stationary and bought myself a new blotter for Old Man Mose to mess up. I'd like the place less if the dark brown widow who ran it didn't spell it wrong on purpose.

"How do you wear out a blotter?" She eyed me. "You don't look like a writin' man, either." She didn't say *Aren't you too light to hang around in this part of town?* She didn't say it, but her expression did whenever I went in. You look like me, you can get it coming and going. Sometimes you aren't white enough, sometimes you're too white.

I scooped up my change and went back to the office feeling like a toad. Toads aren't as good as fish in the water, and they aren't as good as ferrets on land. They're stuck in the middle, not all the way at home in the one world or the other. This old amphibian heard those blues in his head going along the sidewalk.

"Why do you bother with that stuff?" Mose asked as I fitted the blotter into its frame. "What good is it?"

"It helps me write smoother," I said. The widow wasn't wrong. I'm not a writin' man, not the way she meant it. Reports for clients? Letters? I can do those all right. Anything that takes style, though? Not likely. Look at this if you don't believe me.

What good is it? was a bigger question, though. What good was anything? When you aren't exactly one thing or the other, when you don't exactly belong anywhere, you ask yourself questions like that more often than you wish you did.

170

TWICE AS DEAD

That might've been why Dora took up with me. She didn't fit in Los Angeles any better than I did. For one thing, she was what she was. Live people have hated vampires and feared them since the beginning of time. Blood banks don't wipe that away, only paper it over a little. You think white people are going to admit—admit to themselves, where it counts—black people are as good as they are any time soon? Don't hold your breath.

For another, if Los Angeles is about anything, it's about tomorrow. And if vampires are about anything, they're about yesterday. Seeing everything she'd seen over however many years she'd seen it, how strange did right this minute seem to her? As strange as it did to me, I'm sure, but not strange the same way.

Old Man Mose distracted me again, which was bound to be just as well. He asked, "Why does it matter whether you're smooth or not? You're scratching either way." Cats don't understand writing any better than they understand reading. They'd keep us for pets if they did, same as if they had thumbs.

But the way he'd asked the question told me how to answer it. "You know how you sharpen your claws on things to get them just the way you want them?" The things he sharpened them on included the back of the sofa where he lay sprawling, but that was an argument for another time.

"Of course." He seemed surprised I made so much sense. Well, plenty of others would have been, too.

"Writing is the same kind of thing with people. It feels better when everything's smooth and sharp."

He thought about that for a few seconds, shot the claws on his front feet, looked them over, and gnawed at one before letting them go back in. "These are for killing things, though," he said. "Writing's only a waste of time."

I could have told him words on paper, on parchment, on papyrus, on clay tablets, and on stone had done more killing than all the cats since the start of time. I could have told him, but I couldn't have made him believe me.

Luckily, I didn't have to try. The phone chose that moment to ring. I picked it up with something approaching relief. "Mitchell Investigating."

"Mister Mitchell, this is Victor Howe's secretary. I'm putting him through to you now." Something clicked in the bowels of the switchboard.

Victor Howe came through. "You there, Mitchell?" he growled, loud as life and twice as rude.

Since I didn't have time to think, I gave him a different take on the line I'd used with Deacon Washington: "Afraid not. I'm out getting a sandwich. I'll probably be back in fifteen or twenty minutes."

Some silent seconds followed while he worked through that. Then he said, as much to himself as to me, "It's a joke." He was slow, but he got there in the end. When he did, he focused again: "Funny, Mitchell. Very funny. You should go on the radio."

"Is that what you called to tell me? You want to read through my contracts when I do? How much would you charge for that?"

I didn't distract him for so long this time. "I called to tell you that not only does US Rubber deny ever having refused you access to their factory or any adjacent properties, they are removing that refusal and state through me that you are welcome in that area."

I thought about that. Then I thought about it some more. Then I scratched my head, even if Howe couldn't see me do it. "Now you're the one who's joking, right?" I managed at last.

"Excuse me?" he said.

"They're taking back a refusal to let me on their property that they say they never made to begin with?"

"That is correct," Howe replied.

"How can they take back something they say was never there in the first place?"

"They are being thorough," he told me, as if convinced he was speaking to an idiot. To him, I was one. I should have realized right away that Dewey, Beagle, & Howe was talking, not US Rubber.

"Okay," I said. "And if I come out of their factory as a spare tire for a new Nash, that's one of those unfortunate accidents nobody could expect, right?"

TWICE AS DEAD

"Heh," he said. "Good day, Mister Mitchell." All of a sudden, I heard the dial tone instead of his mellifluous voice. Let me tell you, it sounded one hell of a lot warmer and friendlier.

As I hung up, my first thought was that I might want to go back to the diner across the street, but I never wanted to poke my snoot into the US Rubber plant again as long as I lived. Getting turned into a spare tire for a Nash was liable to be the least of my worries in there.

I was wrong, and then again I was right.

XII

When I went out to get some lunch, there was the zombie sweeper, slowly pushing his broom along the alley. I didn't want to look at him, even; he gave me the creeps, same as he did with Elmer V. Five minutes later, I almost choked on my hamburger. "Jumping Jesus on a pogo stick, but I'm a jerk," I said once I managed to swallow after all.

Nobody wants to look at zombies. They give everyone the creeps. They're worse than undead. The undead at least still have free will. Zombies have no will at all. Oh, they go off the rails once in a while—who doesn't remember the Denver Zombie Riots of 1934? Most of the time, though, you use them the way you'd use a piece of sandpaper or a pickaxe. They're tools with feet.

If Frank Jethroe hadn't got killed, if he'd got turned into a zombie instead, he could be pushing a broom somewhere like the one in the alleyway. That zombie'd been a white man, so he wasn't Frank Jethroe, but still …

After that occurred to me, the burger and fries didn't taste so good any more. Neither did my after-lunch cigarette. I was going to have to visit zombie dealers. All things considered, I would've been happier if the angel dropped me to the bottom of Angel's

TWICE AS DEAD

Flight. Zombie dealers made taking those photos for Lamont Smalls seem clean by comparison.

There are dealers on Avalon, and some on Central, too. A couple have their places up in Bronzeville, but those could wait. Zombie dealers in the Negro Belt? What a surprise! Anybody'd think people who spent their whole lives getting kicked in the teeth by the world might want to quit worrying about what it'd do to them next. Surprising notion, yeah, but there you are.

And here the zombie dealers are.

I didn't have to walk very far to find the closest one. It's on Avalon, just a couple of blocks from Wrigley Field. I wondered if they got extra business from poor bastards who lost their last dime betting on the hometown heroes.

The season was over, but the zombie place stayed open the year around. The gold letters on the front window said PERSONAL AID AND ASSURANCE. Even zombie dealers—maybe especially zombie dealers—don't like to call zombies by their name.

I walked past the place twice, once heading north, once south, before I could make myself go in. I hadn't felt that way since my squad had to take one of those Italian stone barns with a machine gun chattering from the doorway.

The man standing behind the counter was short and dapper. He was a shade or so darker than Lamont Smalls. Another, bigger, fellow sat on a chair tilted back against the wall. He glanced up from the Racing Form when I came in, then went back to it. If he wasn't a bodyguard or bouncer, I'd never seen one.

"What can I do for you today, sir?" the dapper man asked with a broad smile. How many of the poor jerks who opened that door had never been called *sir* in their lives, even once? He knew how to draw 'em in, all right.

"I hope you can give me some help," I said.

"That's what we're here for, sir." That damn word again. He sized me up as if he had a sorcerer's crystal ball to help. He didn't need one to know what I was. White folks don't always, but he wasn't white. Chances are he thought I'd tried passing and got burned bad. Voice syrupy and sympathetic, he said, "Whatever's troubling you, we can ease your mind."

175

Ease it forever. Yeah.

I stepped up to the counter and set a card on it. Then I laid Frank Jethroe's photo next to it. "I'm a private detective. I'm looking for this man. I have reason to think he may have been made into a zombie against his will."

Fwup! The Racing Form hit the floor about the same time as the front legs of the bouncer's chair came down on the worn linoleum. He'd seen plenty of sorry losers walk in to throw away their lives. He was used to that. It didn't mean anything to him, one way or the other. It was just business. I was different, though, and different might mean dangerous.

I made the dapper fellow stiffen, too, but only for a second. He picked up my card, read it, and set it down again. "We're an ethical outfit, Mister Mitchell. We don't deal in individuals who aren't here of their own free will."

"That's right," the bouncer agreed. His voice sounded like boulders rolling downhill. Everything he said would be a threat.

As best I could, I ignored him. "You swap back and forth with other dealers, though, right, depending on what you need? You wouldn't have to know somebody you got didn't want to turn zombie?" I said to the dapper man.

His mouth went down at the corners. No, he didn't care to hear zombies called zombies. "That's highly unlikely," he said. "We don't deal with fly-by-night places that might make those mistakes."

As long as the paperwork they got with a new shambler looked halfway legit, they wouldn't ask any questions. I knew that. He knew I knew. It didn't matter. Making sure he didn't land in trouble was also part of his job.

"Yeah, yeah," I said wearily. "But would you check your files anyway, on the off chance somebody did pull a fast one on you? The man's name is Frank Jethroe. He's got a wife and two girls worried sick about him."

He sighed a martyred sigh. "If you insist. How far back do you need me to go?"

"A month should do it. And could I look at the zombies in your back room, in case they changed his name on you?"

176

TWICE AS DEAD

The big man started to heave himself to his feet. "You're pushin' it, buddy," he said, hands folding into fists.

I think the dapper guy would've told me to go chase myself if the bouncer hadn't gone into his act. As things were, he said, "Take it easy, Oscar. We've got nothing to hide. I think we can accommodate Mister Mitchell."

Accommodate went clean over Oscar's head, but he got *Take it easy*. Muttering, "Okay, Mister Renfroe," he sat down again. The chair creaked under his weight.

To me, Renfroe said, "I'll check the files. If I don't find anything— and I don't expect to—I'll take you back to the lounge and let you see our current workforce for yourself."

Lounge. Workforce. What you call something shapes how you think about it. Or lets you not think about it. I didn't throw up on my shoes. I don't know how I didn't, but I didn't. I really am a tough guy sometimes. "Thank you, Mister Renfroe," I answered. See? I proved it.

Renfroe went into a back room. Oscar glared at me like a mean dog on a chain too short to let him bite. The dapper little man came back a few minutes later. He spread his hands so I could see his paler palms. "I'm sorry, Mister Mitchell, but no one named Frank Jethroe has paused on our premises in that period of time. Do you want to come back to the lounge now?"

Did I want to? Are you out of your ever-lovin' mind? I shook myself, the way I did when a round from that machine gun cracked over my head. Sometimes you've got to keep going whether you want to or not. "Let's do it," I said, and walked around the counter and past Oscar.

"This does bother some people," Renfroe said as we walked down a short hallway. We went past a couple of preparation rooms, one on either side of the hall. They had a particular smell, half spicy, half like dry dirt. I'd talked about goofer dust with Dora; now I wondered if it was one of the ingredients in the spells that robbed zombies of whatever part of the soul it is that makes people people.

A wizard in a wrinkled robe sat in the room on the left. I might have asked him, but I was sure he wouldn't tell me. Wizards are as coy about how they do what they do as actresses are about their

177

age. And he was smoking a cigarette and reading a paperback with a cover so lewd, he might've bought it from Al Harris. He was relaxing till he had to turn the next desperate fool into something less than human.

Mr. Renfroe opened the door at the end of the hallway. A different odor wafted out. Some of it was from sour, unwashed bodies. I'd smelled that stink around here and more in Italy, where it often came from me. I'd smelled fear in Italy, too, also often from myself. But even the odor of fear wasn't what made the hair on the back of my neck stand up. I'd never known before what dissolution smells like. I wish I still didn't.

That dreadful reek didn't bother the dapper man one bit. Why would it? He made his living off it. By his suit and his pinkie ring, a good living it was, too.

He waved me forward. "Here we are, Mister Mitchell. If you find this Jethroe among the workforce, we'll talk. But you won't."

Yes, I would sooner have been back on that farm south of the Po, trying to crawl close enough to that damn barn to chuck in a grenade without getting my spleen vented first. The fylfot boys only wanted to kill me. What was in that storeroom had had worse happen.

A lot of courage is not wanting other people to see you're scared green. I can't imagine what else made me go in there. The other thing I was scared of was that Renfroe would close the door behind me and I'd never get out.

An old-fashioned dim orange bulb that hung naked in a ceiling fixture gave the only light there was. People—well, things that had been people—stood close together, waiting till somebody wanted to use them. Mm, not *waiting*. They would have stood there forever and it wouldn't have mattered to them.

Tall. Short. Fat. Thin. (Mostly thin.) Men. Women. Black. White. (Mostly black.) A couple of Mexican-looking men. A woman who might have been Japanese or Chinese. Just enough room between the rows for a customer to pick out the merchandise he wanted.

I liked being surrounded by zombies even less than I liked everything else about the whole deal. But I had to push along, making sure each blank face didn't belong to Frank Jethroe. None of them did. Before I finished, though, I smelled my own fear along with theirs.

178

TWICE AS DEAD

After I'd checked the last one, I got out of there. Renfroe raised a questioning eyebrow. "You were right. He's not there," I said.

"I didn't think he would be," the dapper man said. We went back to the room that opened on to the street. The bored wizard in the prep room didn't look at me this time, either. The dirty book was a lot more interesting than I was.

"Nothin'?" Oscar asked.

"Nothing," Mr. Renfroe and I said at the same time. That's what zombies are, especially before the person using them charges them with a task. Nothings that used to be people.

The worst of it was, I wasn't done after I made my escape from that place. I knew of two more outfits on Avalon and another couple on Central. I visited them all that afternoon. One of the ones on Central wouldn't let me past the front room. "Come back with a warrant if you want to snoop," said the hatchet-faced woman in charge of that one. She knew I couldn't. So did I.

But the rest didn't care. I had to wait at one place while a sad-faced, fortyish woman finished signing her papers. "There's got to be a better way than this," I told her.

"Mind your own damn business," she answered. "My people, they need the money they'll get for me." I shut up.

Nobody'd ever heard of Frank Jethroe. Nobody recognized him from the photo I showed. He wasn't in any of the workforce lounges (people who worked in the zombie dealerships all talked the same way—people in any business will).

Okay. It was a smart idea. It didn't pan out, that's all. When I got back to the office, Old Man Mose pulled a face worse than the one he makes when I peel an orange at my desk. His tail bottlebrushed. "Wherever you've been, don't go there again!" he said.

"Good plan," I answered. "Don't let anybody ever call you a dumb animal again."

"As if I would!" he said indignantly.

I drank dinner that night. You don't approve, go to hell.

I've hurt myself worse. I had a headache the next morning, but not the whole set of jimjams. I didn't need to worry about the sun

179

seeming too bright: no sun. Rain pattered down out of a sky as gray and gloomy as the thoughts that chased one another through what passed for my mind.

After *menudo* and coffee, I rode the Red Line and the connecting bus down to the US Rubber factory. Victor Howe'd told me I could go in, but I didn't. After all, what's a lawyer's word worth? Its weight in gold, nothing more.

I did stick my head into the diner across the street. When the counterman saw who I was, he shook his head. "What is it with you that drives the fat cats nuts?" he asked.

"Must be my good looks," I said. He made as if to spit.

But he didn't grouse when I parked my behind on a stool at the counter. He sold me more coffee. He shoved an ashtray at me when I lit up. And he said, "What is it this time?"

"Same as the last. Can I ask you something?"

"Yeah, go ahead. But that's how you pissed 'em off before."

"It's what I do."

"Piss off the fat cats?"

I grinned. "I was thinking more about asking questions, but I try with the other one, too." The counterman chuckled. I went on, "There any zombie dealers around here?"

His face slammed shut as if he were closing a book, hard. "How come you wanna know about shit like that?" He had enough sense to be scared of zombies.

"Because I do," I answered. I laid a couple of singles on the counter. He left 'em there and didn't say a word. I put them back in my wallet and took out a five instead.

I thought he'd ignore the fin, too, but after a few seconds he made it disappear. "You never heard nothin' from me," he said. "You was never in here today. You ain't comin' back in here any time soon, neither."

"Deal," I said.

"It better be. One o' them places over on Jillson, the west side o' Eastland. You gotta be nuts, you wanna go near it."

"Of course I'm nuts. Where the hell is Jillson?"

He pointed south and west. "That way, a few blocks over. It's the last street this side o' Washington."

"Thanks." I finished the coffee and walked out. I could feel his eyes on my back even after I closed the door. I went southwest. Most places in the county, streets run north and south or east and west. I think I already said it's turned forty-five degrees around the rubber plant. Jillson was easy enough to find. It was one of those streets that start out with houses on 'em but sprout little businesses as more people move into the neighborhood.

Next question was, which way was Eastland? The counterman hadn't said. But he had said it was on the west side of Eastland, so I went west—northwest, really. The rain drummed its fingers on my umbrella. I was glad I'd had my shoes half-soled not so long before; my feet didn't get wet.

I guessed right. After I crossed Eastland, I looked for the zombie dealer's place. It didn't say ZOMBIES FOR SALE OR RENT or anything like that. Zombie dealerships never do, any more than Al Harris's place says DIRTY BOOKS AND FILTHY PICTURES. When I spotted a window across the street that read PERSONAL ASSISTANCE, PERSONAL ASSISTANTS, I figured I'd found it.

After waiting for a couple of cars to splash by, I jaywalked across Jillson. Washington, I knew, was the more important street. In my part of town, dealers set up on the big streets. This place was more out of the way, maybe because rents on Jillson were lower, maybe because important people here didn't want it on a main drag.

I opened the door and went in, closing the umbrella as I did. Out of the way or not, this place did more business than any of the ones I'd seen on Avalon and Central. The out-front waiting room was bigger and cleaner. The smart guy behind the counter had not one but two tough guys for backup.

The smart guy behind the counter …. He was about my age, tall and blond and fit. If I'd met him in Italy and he'd had the Lightning Runes on his helmet, I wouldn't've been surprised. That would have disposed me not to love him on sight even if he'd found some other line of work.

He was sizing me up, too. A tiny something changed on his face. He got the right answer, and showed what he thought of it: not much. If he'd been born over there and not over here, he probably would have been proud to wear the runes.

"Yes, sir? What can I do for you today?" he asked. His voice held a salesman's hammy good cheer, nothing more. He would have sounded the same if I'd had green and purple stripes.

I set my card and the photo of Frank Jethroe in front of him. "I'm a private investigator. I'm looking for this man. He works for US Rubber. His wife is concerned that he may have been made into a zombie against his will."

Both bully boys had been standing there looking bored. They came alert as soon as they heard what came out of my mouth. So did the fellow who didn't care for my face. "That wouldn't happen here. It can't happen here," he said. Now his voice sounded flat, take-it-or-leave-it. The good cheer was gone.

"Would you check your files, please? His name's Frank Jethroe. You might have got him from somewhere else, not knowing there was a problem with him." I didn't think that was likely, not with what I'd heard about how he'd disappeared and not with how close to the US Rubber factory this place was, but I tried to stay polite.

The blond man shook his head. "I don't see any point. I told you, that kind of thing is impossible here."

"Maybe so. But I'll tell you, the older I get, the fewer things look impossible to me. Unlikely, sure, but that's different."

"I'm sorry"—his tone and the way he stood shouted he was lying—"but I don't have to waste my time shuffling through papers because somebody with a card and a photo he got from God knows where tells me some stupid story. I'm going to ask you to leave. This is private property, and you aren't welcome here."

"But—" I said.

One of the guys with broad shoulders interrupted me: "Better listen to Dolf, pal. If you go out by yourself, you get to open the door first. We help you out, we won't bother with none o' that."

So I left. One against two or three isn't betting odds. I wished I'd shown him a card that didn't have my real name and address on it. I've got some, but I didn't expect that from him. With luck, he wouldn't remember my handle. With luck.

What would Blond Boy have done if I'd asked him about vepratoga? He might've given me a blank look and gone *Huh?* Or

TWICE AS DEAD

he might have sicced the bouncers on me right then. Keeping my mouth shut could've been one of the smartest things I'd done, even if I did it by accident.

"Oh, hell," I muttered as I started back to the bus stop. When people act as though they've got something to hide, it's usually because they do. Which meant I'd have to come back to try to find out what it was. The idea thrilled me as much as a root canal without novocaine would have. Maybe even more.

That evening, I called Clarice Jethroe and let her know what I'd been up to. "The nerve of those people down there!" she said. "They wouldn't even check for you?"

"I'm afraid not, ma'am," I answered.

"They're like the Pharisee in the Good Book, turning a blind eye to the poor robbed man and passing by on the other side of the road." She sounded ready to go down there and give them a good piece of her mind.

I didn't want her doing that. If she did, I was afraid she wouldn't come back. "They may be worse than the Pharisee," I said.

"How do you mean?"

"He didn't rob the man he walked past and leave him lying in the dirt. He just pretended the fellow wasn't there."

"Oh!" She got the point right away. "You reckon these folks did?"

"I don't know, but I'll try to find out." I hesitated. "There's something else we should talk about, too."

Clarice Jethroe also got that right away. She sighed. "You're gonna want more money from me, aren't you?"

"Afraid I am. I wish I could do this for nothing, but I'd be on a radio show if I did. I'm real. I've got to eat and pay the rent and the phone bill and things like that."

She sighed again. "I understand. I don't much like it—I don't much like any o' this—but I understand. How much you have to have?"

"Another hundred." Considering how much time and aggravation I'd put into poking around after her husband, I should've asked for two or three times that much. I didn't have the crust. If I were tougher over money, I wouldn't have to worry about it so much. I tell myself so a lot. But if I were like that, I wouldn't want to look at myself in the mirror any more than a vampire does.

"I'll bring it to you tomorrow. Thank you, Mister Mitchell." Clarice Jethroe hung up. I believed her. She struck me as one of those people who'd sooner walk through dragonfire than lie about something like that.

I was about to go home when somebody knocked on the door. "It's not locked. Come in," I said.

It wouldn't have mattered if the door were locked. Dora Urban came in without bothering to open it. I'd just been thinking about vampires; now I had one in my office. I was glad it was this particular one.

"I went to your apartment, but you were not there," she said. "I thought you might still be here, then, and turned out to be right."

Had she knocked on my door and got no answer? Or flittered outside my window and seen the place was empty? It didn't matter. "I was going to have a drink," I said. "Want to have one with me?"

"*A* drink, spelled with an *i* and not with a *u*," she said. I hadn't seen booze get to her much, but then I realized she was talking more about me than herself. And sure enough, she went on, "I was lonely. We mostly are, but I am less lonely with you than without you, especially at certain times."

She didn't come right out and say what those certain times were, but I had a fair notion. I took the Wild Turkey out of the desk drawer and offered it to her. She drank, then gave it back to me. I drank, too. It tasted good. It felt fine. Bourbon always does to me.

I went around the desk and sat on the sofa beside her. When I put my arm around her, she slid closer. I laughed a little. "What strikes you funny?" she asked, her lips maybe six inches from mine.

"I was just thinking that if I did that and you didn't want me to, it would be the last stupid thing I ever did."

"Oh." She thought about that. She didn't need long. "Yes. It would. But since I do want you to ..."

Things went on from there. Yes, I got nipped again; that did seem to be something she needed to do. If you want more details, you can find them in one book or another at Al Harris's place.

Afterwards, we untangled from each other and had another nip of Wild Turkey. "I feel less lonely when I'm with you, too," I said.

TWICE AS DEAD

"It is not the same thing." Her tone was as pointed as her canines. "You are lonely because you drink too much and you know too much about what brutes most people are to want anything to do with them. I am lonely because loneliness is an essential part of what a vampire is."

"The feeling is the same no matter how you get there," I said.

"Live people can cure it. They do not always, but they can. We are able to ease it a bit, but no more than a bit."

I started to say something, but sirens in the not too distant distance made me stop and listen. Fire engines, not police cars—the tone was deeper than the cops use. Rain or no rain, something was going up in smoke.

"Do you want to see if you can ease it again?" I asked. Maybe the whiskey made me overconfident. I looked forward to finding out.

I managed. Believe me, I had good help. What Dora felt …. Ah, how can a live man know what the undead feel or don't feel? I know what she showed. How much what she showed had to do with what she felt and how much with what she wanted me to think she felt, I can't tell you.

After I came back from the bathroom, she asked, "Why aren't you married to a live woman and raising a couple of babies?"

We'd been round some of that barn before. Not all of it, though. "I never found one who suited me." But that wasn't the whole answer, was it? *In* Wild Turkey, *veritas.* "I never suited one of them, either. Not even close."

"They must not know what they are missing. Either that, or you do not know what you have missed."

"Maybe I know some of it." I set a hand on her bare shoulder. She wasn't as warm as a live woman would have been, but I was getting used to that.

She shook me off. I'd annoyed her. "This is play. As long as you remember that, it can be enjoyable play. If you try to make it more than play, you will only wound yourself. I am as I am. I can be no other way, however much you might wish I could. You had best understand as much."

It wasn't quite the Lord Jehovah's *I am that I am,* but close enough. In my head, between my ears, I knew she was right. But

185

I knew something else, too. Live people don't always do things because of what they think. A lot of times, they should, but they don't. Damned nuisanceful feelings ...

I'd made one glancing approach to talking about love, and she'd swatted me like a fly. Fool that I am, I was about to try another one when the world outside the office distracted me again. Since they pinned a Ruptured Duck on me and sent me back to civilian life, I'd heard the Emergency Thaumaturgic Response Team's warbling hooter no more than twice. Here it was again.

Dora recognized it, too. "That is not good. That cannot be good. Those people, they do not come out for nothing."

"I was just thinking the same thing," I said. We both started putting on clothes. The emergency wizards, we wanted to see why they'd shown up. She could've turned bat and flown to find out, but she stayed with me instead. I've had smaller compliments.

I grabbed my umbrella. She didn't have one; she huddled close to me, which was nice. After we'd gone half a block, I realized she and her dress hadn't been wet when she came in. I wondered again whether she'd flown from my apartment building to the office. If she hadn't, she really had dodged all the raindrops.

My apartment building .... A pillar of smoke rose into the dark gray sky, lit from below by what must have been one hell of a blaze. The direction was about right. So was the distance. Something in my midsection clenched, as if trying to make a kick in the belly hurt less. I went into a half trot.

Dora kept up without breathing hard. Well, of course she did. I knew she didn't show up in a mirror. I didn't think she'd fog one, either.

"That is not natural fire," she said.

"You're reading my mind again." I hurried on for a few more steps. Then I said the thing I didn't want to say: "I think it's a salamander."

She didn't try to tell me I was wrong, no matter how much I wished she would. I'd run into salamanders in Italy a couple of times—at a good distance, or I wouldn't be here now to spin this yarn. The fylfot boys did everything they knew how to do to hold us back, but even wizards with the Lightning Runes on their collar tabs didn't mess with fire elementals unless they were desperate.

TWICE AS DEAD

They remembered *Do not call up that which you cannot put down* almost till the very end. By that time, some of them didn't care any more.

So I recognized the color lighting up the smoke column, too. Red. Redder than red. Red beyond red. Red so red, you shouldn't be able to see it at all. A lot of filthy things happen in Los Angeles. More of them happen to you if you aren't as rich or as white as you ought to be.

But nobody deserves salamandering. Nobody. Yes, I know what happened to the people in Hiroshima and Nagasaki. Yes, I know it made the Knights of Bushido say uncle at last. Even so.

And I remembered that the people in Hiroshima and Nagasaki hadn't been white, either.

This one wouldn't be anywhere near so big as those city-roasters, of course. One more time, though, even so …

"How much do your clever thaumaturges know about quieting a salamander once it begins to burn?" Dora asked. By then, we were only a block and a half from the blaze. I smelled smoke through the rain.

"Army wizards always said the best thing you could do was stay away. If you couldn't stay away, water wouldn't help. Sand and prayer might do a little something. Not much, but a little."

"That was also my understanding. I wondered if they knew more now."

"If they do, they never told me. I know the ones we used against the Knights of Bushido are still burning. You want hell on earth, there you are."

We rounded the last corner. We couldn't go any farther after that. Jumpy cops, harried-looking firemen, shell-shocked wizards, reporters, people in soggy pajamas who seemed amazed to be alive, I don't know what all.

Yes, my building had got the salamander. Three or four other apartment houses around it were burning, too, but they'd caught fire from mine. I could see the salamander blazing in midair. Even a block away, even through the steady rain, the heat that came off it made me shield my face with my free hand.

They tried spraying the salamander with a stream from a fire hose. I could have told 'em it wouldn't work. Somebody probably had. They tried anyway. They added steam to the smoke. That was all.

187

Something about where the fire elemental hung caught my eye. "You know," I said, "that's about where my apartment would be. If the building were still there, I mean." Which it wasn't. The nearby ones were still on fire. Nothing much was left of mine. As best I could make out, nothing at all was left of my apartment.

Nothing at all would've been left of me, either, if I'd been in there when the salamander started incinerating things. I would've been, too, if Dora hadn't come by and given me something more interesting to do than going home. My knees didn't want to hold me up for a few seconds. You come that close to getting killed, you feel it all the way down.

She gave me the time to pull myself together. Not many live people would have thought to do that. Then she said, "You are right. I noticed it, too, and wondered whether you did. Who wants you dead?"

Who wants you dead? That is the question, and to hell with *To be or not to be?* The list was longer than I wished it would have been. "I can think of a few people," I managed.

The salamander went on blazing as if it had not a care in the world. I'm sure it didn't. It was doing what it wanted to do, doing what salamanders did. And it was doing it twenty-five or thirty feet up in the air. Sand does bother salamanders some—not much, but some. But the cops and firemen would have needed a young mountain of it to make this one notice.

Prayer? In my part of town, you've got storefront churches and storefront preachers on every block. The police might not have understood—the LAPD doesn't understand one hell of a lot about the Negro Belt—but the Emergency Thaumaturgical Response Team did. A disheveled-looking fellow in a bathrobe did his damnedest to pray the salamander down to the infernal regions. An ETRT man held an umbrella over his head to keep off the rain. He didn't look to be having much luck.

Then I stopped caring about him, because Dora said, "Your home is gone. What will you do now?"

I banged into that one head-on. It hadn't crossed my mind till then. It wasn't as if I kept a lot of stuff in the apartment. I didn't have a lot of stuff to keep. I'd miss some books. I'd miss my clothes.

But getting burned out mattered less to me than it would have to most people.

"I'll live in the office for a while, I guess," I said. "I've got some clothes there, and I can buy some more. Buy a hot plate, too, so I can cook a little. That's cheaper than eating out all the time."

"If this were an ordinary fire, I would say yes, do that," she replied. "But if you stay in another known place all the time, how long until the next salamander tries to make your acquaintance?"

"Urk." I hadn't thought about that, either, but she wasn't wrong. The more I stayed away from the office, in fact, the better off I was liable to be. But find another apartment? Comedians've been joking about the housing shortage since right after the war, but it still ain't funny, McGee. I'd been lucky to land one place. Getting another would take something more like a miracle. I spelled that out for her.

"A point," she said when I finished. She thought for a moment. "I would not say this to many, but to you I will. You may stay with me for a time, until you sort out your own troubles."

And that's how I spent a while living in Vampire Village.

XIII

I missed my books less than I thought I would. Dora's place was full of them, in English, Magyar, French, German, Russian, Latin (I may be missing a language or two). Books? Yes. A refrigerator? No. When someone like her wanted a snack, she wanted it warm. No stove, either, for the same kind of reason. I bought a hot plate after all.

Only in VV are you likely to find a coffin in the living room. Existing room? Undead room? What do you call it when a vampire's in the apartment? The coffin was carefully placed and screened so no sunlight could fall on it. If I was in there, too, though, how much did that matter?

"You see? I make myself vulnerable to you. You can betray me," she said as we lay in bed a couple of days after my place went up in fire. Yes, she had a bed along with the coffin. Who'd been in it with her before she knew me … I told myself that was none of my business.

"If you don't trust me, throw me out," I answered. "You know I'll get along some kind of way."

"If I did not trust you, you would not be here," she said. "But it makes me anxious even so. I can do nothing about what happens in the brightness. My kind have many tales of those who were finished because they put their faith in live people. They are not all tales, either. It happened to someone I once knew."

"Oh." I gave her a little squeeze. "This must be love, then."

She made a noise that couldn't have come from a live person's throat. "You keep saying that word. You keep not believing it has no meaning for those like me. What is love, anyhow?" I'd thought of Pontius Pilate when I was talking with Dr. Berkowitz. Now I did again.

Pilate, of course, didn't stay for an answer. I gave Dora one. It wasn't mine, but the fellow who came up with it had his head on pretty straight: "Love is when you care more about someone else's happiness than about your own."

I slowed her up. I made her think. After half a minute or so, she said, "I do not believe we are capable of that."

"No? Then why are you trying to find out what happened to Rudolf Sebestyen?"

This time, she hesitated not a bit. "That has nothing to do with love. That is only an obligation. And we are not happy. We have satisfactions. We have sensual pleasures. When the sun is down, all our senses work. But happiness is for the living, who know no better."

So there, I thought. She wasn't about to admit anything that gave my teasing legs. But was she right not to, or was she only stubborn and proud?

I didn't know then. I still don't.

By that time, stories in the *Times*, the *Herald-Express*, the *Examiner*, and the *Mirror* had all said I was missing. Not presumed dead, but missing. When I bought some razor blades at Allums, Terence waved to me and called, "Good to see you got found, buddy."

"Who, me?" I looked around behind myself, as if I thought he was talking to somebody else. He laughed.

If I stayed missing for other people, it was because they didn't look for me very hard, no different reason. That didn't break my heart. If they presumed I was already dead, they wouldn't try to kill me again. Or they might not.

When I went back to the office, Old Man Mose curled that thing cats have instead of a real upper lip. "You stink like a bloodsucker," he told me.

"Get used to it," I answered. "Otherwise I'd stink like a charcoal briquette. And who'd keep you in cat food then?"

"I'd manage," he said loftily. He sounded the way I did when I told Dora I'd get by if she threw me out. I'd do it somehow. Mose would, too.

I called Hilda to see if there were any messages for me. "You have one," she said. "It's Sergeant Elmer V. Jackson. When I told him you weren't in, he asked you to call him back." She gave me the phone number.

After I'd dialed the two letters and one number after them, I hung up instead of finishing. What better way for Jackson to find out I'd lived through the salamandering than for me to show him myself? I didn't know the cops had had anything to do with that, you understand, but they sure could have.

Of course, so could US Rubber. Or their law firm—anybody who figures lawyers don't know how to play dirty never dealt with any. Or the vampire dealer down by the factory. Or any of the other dealers I'd visited. Or all of them at once, working in cahoots.

A few seconds after I hung up the phone, I looked at it again. By my own logic, I shouldn't answer it at all if it rang. Which was fine in a way: if I didn't answer it, nobody would hear my voice and realize I hadn't got incinerated after all. How much work would I be throwing away if I didn't answer, though?

More than I could afford to. I was sure of that. I wasn't out of the woods when it came to dough, only better off than I had been. If I hadn't paid off people I owed, I'd have more myself. But I had, so I didn't.

Somebody chose that moment to knock on the door. I sat there, trying to decide what to do. Before I could, Old Man Mose called, "Come in. It's not locked." Then he disappeared under the sofa so he wouldn't be the one who got hurt in case he'd made a mistake. Yeah, he was a cat.

Turned out he hadn't goofed. The door opened, and in came Clarice Jethroe. She smiled from ear to ear when she saw me, which is not anything a lot of people do. "Oh, Mister Mitchell, I'm so glad you're all right!" she said. "I saw in the papers you were missin' on account of the fire."

TWICE AS DEAD

"Reports of my death are greatly exaggerated," I answered gravely. As with the line about love, I wasn't smart enough to have said it first, but I sure was smart enough to steal it once I heard it.

It went to waste, because she kept on with what she'd been about to say anyhow: "I've been comin' in every day, hopin' I'd find you—I got the money you said you needed from me." She took an envelope out of her purse and set it on the desk. It had my name on it. "The whole hundred's there. You can look."

"I believe you, Missus Jethroe. And thank you very much. Most people wouldn't have bothered," I said. If I didn't need the cash myself, I would've told her to keep it. She made me want to cry.

And then she drew herself up straight, proud in the way people who don't have much but pride can get. "Don't want to owe nobody nothin'," she said, quietly but with great determination.

"There *are* other people like me!" I blurted. If I hadn't been sitting down, I would have fallen over.

"My mama raised me right. Reckon yours did the same with you," she said. "Now I better go. Got me a white lady's house to clean. Good to see you back." She didn't waste any more time. She had a job to do, and she was going to do it.

My mama .... My mama was maybe even a shade lighter'n I am. Looking back, I have a pretty good notion she would have liked to pass. But she'd married a brown man, so she couldn't even try. They died within a few months of each other right before the war: first her of consumption, then my pa. The doctor called it a heart attack, but I think it was a broken heart. He loved her like you wouldn't believe. She loved him and looked down on him at the same time.

Me? I don't know if I got raised right, but somehow I got raised.

I opened the envelope. Two twenties, some sawbucks, some fins, and a bunch of singles. It came to a hundred bucks. I'd known it would. A hundred bucks the hard way, the way somebody who has a tough time scraping a hundred together finally does.

Old Man Mose came out. "It's all right?" he asked.

"It's all right," I told him. "Hey—how did your mother raise you?"

His pupils widened; I'd surprised him. "She had milk," he said after a beat. "She showed me how to hunt—you know, with bugs

193

and little lizards and things. She smacked me when I bit my brother and sisters too hard."

I thought for a couple of seconds myself. Then I nodded. "Sounds about right."

Pretty soon, I'd met all the Shabbas-goy Jews who kept a daylight eye on things around Dora's building. One of them hardly spoke any English. Rivke hadn't been here long. She had a number and a fylfot branded on her arm. I suspected she watched extra carefully.

That brand ... I'd known the fylfot boys were bad news before I went overseas. Things I saw in Italy sure didn't make me want to change my mind. I didn't know how bad they were, though, till after I came home myself. Even they tried to hide some of what they were doing. Just the idea makes me want to heave.

Rivke was one of the lucky ones, if you want to call it luck. She'd lived. There are still some old folks, darker than me, with whip marks on their backs because their masters got sore at them. People are horrible to people who aren't like them. That's one of the things people who aren't like them are for.

I met some of the other vampires in the building, too. Not all of them knew much English, either. One who did was called Bedford Tyler. I'd met him in that bar. By the way he talked, his family owned slaves once upon a time. For all I knew, he might have himself. With vampires, how can you be sure? Once when he was over at Dora's place, he told me, "It's a good thing you belong to her. You'd get sucked dry in nothin' flat if you didn't."

"Heh," I said. I didn't like to think I belonged to Dora, especially not with slaves already on my mind.

His grin showed off his fangs. He knew he was riding me, poking me. Speaking of blood, he knew I had the one drop, too, the drop that made sure I'd have to pass if I wanted to be white. "You understand what I mean," he said.

I did, too. I not only understood him, I wanted to punch him in the nose because I understood him. That wasn't a good idea. Dora had shown me it wasn't. Breaking into his apartment, now, and setting up his coffin so he could get a nice suntan when morning came ...

No, I didn't do it, regardless of how tempted I was. But whenever he started going on about the good old days and how wonderful things had been when everybody knew his place and stayed in it, I thought, *That's the same kind of nonsense the fylfot boys spouted. No place for it here.*

I never called him on it. I wasn't there to quarrel. Mm, I did once. He kept trying to see how far he could push me. This time I'm talking about, he said, "You'll agree, I'm sure, that the ways history prescribes work better than the ones we have in these sorry times, the ones we make up as we go along." He gave me another one of those fang-filled smiles.

"Well, that depends," I answered.

He blinked, the way a frog might when a grasshopper it was about to snap up twitches an antenna in a way it doesn't expect. "On what?" he said, sure I wouldn't be able to come up with anything.

But I did. "On your point of view, of course." I enjoyed talking to him as if he were an imbecile. When you're on top, you don't even think you have a point of view. You take looking down on everybody else for granted. I went on, "If history prescribes that you're a master, chances are you have yourself a swell old time. If it prescribes that you're a slave, your odds don't look so great."

Bedford Tyler gave me a look that said he could talk himself into forgetting I enjoyed another vampire's benison. But I wouldn't have been so bold if I hadn't been sitting next to Dora. She let out a snort. Vampires don't show they're amused much: they *aren't* amused much. She was this time, though. She let Tyler know it, too.

If he'd been a live man, he would have turned red. Vampires don't work that way. Don't ask me why; I don't know. All I know is, they don't. He made some kind of excuse and went away. I didn't miss him a bit.

"He had that coming," she said.

"Yeah, he did." I nodded. "But how's he going to pay me back for giving it to him?"

"We do play the game of revenge," she said thoughtfully. "Sometimes for years, decades, centuries. Time does not matter to us, and the game helps hold boredom at bay. That alone makes it worth playing."

Time does not matter to us. There it was, out in the open, and it pierced me worse than her teeth did when we made love. Like a polite cat, she knew how to hold back even if she didn't have to. "Time matters to me, though," I said. "If he tries getting back at me in the twenty-third century, I won't be around to worry about it."

"This is the main reason we seldom play the game against living people," she answered. "Seldom, but not never. The Seleucids should have beaten Rome. If the grandfather of the king who left the dynasty his name had not given a vampire to the White Fire, that vampire's half sister would not have worked so hard or so long or so hard to make sure they failed. Or I could speak of the Plantagenets, and of Richard III in particular."

My jaw dropped, and not just because I imagined all my descendants three hundred years from now coming to grief at once and never understanding why. That was part of it, but not all. Oh, no, not all.

"How do you know that?" I asked, trying to sound less mind-boggled than I was. "I don't think any live people who write history do. In fact, some live people say Richard III was a vampire himself."

Dora showed her own pointed teeth in an epic sneer. "They are mistaken. He was not." Her voice brooked no argument. She continued, "We have our own historians and chroniclers. Like reading, writing is a medicament for ennui. Their works do not circulate widely among the living. The reasons for that should be clear enough."

Not as if she were wrong. Live people already had, or imagined they had, plenty of reasons for pogroms against bloodsuckers. If they thought vampires were fiddling with who won and who lost in the live world, they'd want to make sure it never happened again. If they had to finish every last vampire to do that, how much would they care?

I did my best to seem sly when I said, "So you didn't watch this vampire go after the old Greeks yourself? Or the one who had a grudge against the Plantagenets?" I'd never dared ask her, *How old are you?* I was scared she might tell me. This let me nibble around the edges of the question, anyhow.

TWICE AS DEAD

"I never said that." She smiled once more, none too pleasantly. I'd managed to amuse her again, so she'd alarmed me again. The way vampires think, that must have seemed a fair exchange to her.

The longer I stayed in Vampire Village, the more my own habits went vampirish, if that's a word. No, I didn't get a yen for raw blood. But I started sleeping during the day and getting up about the time the sun sank into the Pacific. I liked Dora's company every way you can like it. If she kept those hours, I would, too.

That also meant I wasn't in my office much during the ordinary business day. Old Man Mose didn't care what time of day I fed him, as long as I did. I wasn't so busy on things that I missed a lot of calls. I could take care of the ones that did come in in the early evening.

And staying away from the office during the day made me less likely to get cooked if a salamander torched the place. Or I could hope so. Sergeant Elmer V. Jackson didn't come by to grill me, either.

"You know what zombies are, right?" I asked Mose one night.

"Sure. They're revolting. They're more revolting than vampires, and you *like* vampires." The cat made it sound like a horrible perversion. To him, I guess it was.

I didn't argue with him. Arguing with a cat only wastes your time. I said, "I'm looking for somebody who may have got made into a zombie."

"That Sebestyen thing? You should have found him by now."

"Thanks a lot," I said. Old Man Mose really knew how to hurt a guy. I didn't let him get me mad. I tried not to, anyhow. I went on, "No, not him. The fellow who works at the US Rubber plant."

"Okay. So?" Mose yawned. If it didn't involve food or scritchies, he didn't care what people did.

"So I'm going down to a place near the factory that turns people into zombies." I don't know why I talk to a cat like that. I have to talk to *somebody*. Everybody has to, I guess.

"What happens if they do that to you?"

It was a better question than I wished it were. What I planned on doing had names. Breaking and entering. Burglary. Being a private eye lets me bend the law sometimes. It doesn't let me break it.

I wished I could bring Old Man Mose along. He's a lot smaller and sneakier than I am. He could prowl into storerooms and take files out of drawers for me.

He could ... if he could read. But cats don't. So I'd have to do it myself. You don't always look forward to what you've got to do. If you do it anyhow, the people who know you are glad they do.

I wasn't thrilled, in other words, but I was braced. With a sigh, I answered, "Chance I take. If it goes wrong, you already told me you know about other suckers who'll keep you in chow."

"Yeah, yeah." He waved that aside with a flick of the tail. "If you have to run around with a bloodsucker, you should at least get some use out of her. Why don't you bring her along?"

I opened my mouth. Then I closed it again. That was why I talked with Old Man Mose. He can't read, but he's liable to be smarter than I am anyway. He sure was then. Taking Dora with me hadn't even crossed my mind. That was partly because we were lovers, I know. But it was also partly because her case had nothing to do with Frank Jethroe's.

Only what if it did? Who could say how vepratoga hit vampires? What it did to live people wasn't just like zombifying them, but it wasn't so far away, either. If Sebestyen had got his hands on some and then fallen in with a zombie dealer ...

"I owe you some salmon," I told Mose.

"I'll take it," he answered. Cats don't get gratitude. Pay for services rendered? They understand that just fine.

So instead of heading down to PERSONAL ASSISTANCE, PERSONAL ASSISTANTS, I went back to VV. And that meant I wasted the rest of the night, because Dora wasn't in her apartment or in the building. I waited for a while. I started a book about the Dutch wars against the Spanish Empire. After a chapter or two, I couldn't hold my eyes open any more. I put the book back, lay down, and went to sleep. It would have been about two in the morning— early for me lately.

When I woke up, light was leaking into the bedroom. Daytime, sure as hell. I yawned and got out of bed. The coffin in the front room was closed. Dora wouldn't stir till sunset. I fixed myself some instant coffee. It was the same kind of powdered mud they'd given

TWICE AS DEAD

us in our K-rats. It tasted the way it looked, too. But it'd help me get going.

I had to leave Vampire Village to find a place that served the kind of food a live person craved. Then I went to the zombie dealer on Avalon near Wrigley Field. Sharp-dressed Mr. Renfroe stood behind the counter, same as he had the last time I came in. Oscar's eyes flicked up from the Racing Form. When he recognized me, he went back to it.

"Hello, Mister Mitchell. What is it today?" Renfroe said.

"Do you know of a zombie dealership down on Jellison, near the great big US Rubber factory?"

He just stood there. When I put a portrait of Abe Lincoln down in front of him, though, he pocketed it like a pro. "I have heard of that establishment, yes," he said, his tone precise enough to have made Deacon Washington smile.

"What do you hear about them? Are they ethical?" I asked.

"We stopped dealing with them a few weeks after the war ended. I don't care to talk about why, but the fact speaks for itself, doesn't it?"

Oscar looked up from the horses again. "Them fellas, they'd goofer up their own mamas if they seen fifteen cents in it."

Mr. Renfroe eyed me. "You never heard that here, you understand."

I cupped one hand behind my ear. "Never heard what?" Tipping my hat to Renfroe and to the guard, I left. If other zombie dealers want nothing to do with you, you might not be the salt of the earth.

As long as I was out and about by daylight, I got a little salmon filet at a place called YOU BUY, WE FRY! When I headed out, the gal who sold it to me said, "Bet your life we'll fix it up better'n you can. Only a dime extra. C'mon!"

"It's not for me. It's for an accomplice," I said. I don't know what she made of that. I know what Old Man Mose made of the salmon, though. He liked it.

Then I went back to Dora's apartment and waited for the sun to set. The year had turned, but sunset still came before five. I was try-ing to make headway with the Dutch and the Spaniards again when I heard hinges creak as she pushed up the lid.

"Good evening," she said when she saw me. Yeah, same accent as Bela's, though it sounded better from her. She was just stepping out

199

of the coffin. She looked ready for whatever might happen. I'd never known her not to.

"Hi, honey," I said.

Her eyes told me I'd stepped in it. "Do not call me that," she said in a voice that would have frozen a steam engine solid. "I am not your girlfriend, to be sweetened so."

"If you aren't my girlfriend, what am I doing in your apartment? Why do we use the bed when I'm not sleeping in it?" I thought they were reasonable questions.

She didn't look any happier. She said something in Magyar that should have wilted the flowers on the wallpaper.

"What does that mean?" I asked, more in admiration than anything else.

"A horse's cock up your arse," she translated with clinical precision. A moment later, she added, "Hungarians were a nomad folk. Some of our curses still hark back to the steppe."

"Okay. I learned something today. Now I've got a question for you—did Rudolf Sebestyen ever go down around the tire factory on Scrying Crystal Road? You know the one I mean—the one where the Assyrian kings and god-things on the walls don't look like they're just carved there."

"*That* place." She knew it, all right. "I fly around it, never over it. If I were to go over it, something might catch me. I am not the only one who fears this—I have heard others of my kind say the same thing." Then she seemed to remember what I'd asked her. "As for my half brother … I do not know that he did, but I also do not know how much of his affairs I do not know. Why do you want to know?"

So I told her about Frank Jethroe, and about the zombie dealer on Jellison. "They're hiding something. I was going down there to see if I could find out what it was—"

"You were going to break in," she broke in.

"That's right," I admitted. I couldn't very well deny it. "And somebody said it would be good if I had the kind of help I couldn't get from a live person."

I didn't name Mose. I didn't have to. Dora knew me and my cat too well. "I need to have some words with that furry fleabag," she said.

200

TWICE AS DEAD

"I'll go by myself if you don't want to come along," I said. "I know there's no evidence this place has anything to do with Sebestyen."

"You are brave. You are also less stupid than you make yourself out to be. I am your friend, even if I am not someone you should call *honey*. I will go with you. Have you eaten? Or shall we leave now?"

"I need to grab some food, yeah. Are you all right?"

"I can do what I need to do."

"I want to try later, though. I don't know how late they stay open. I want to go in when everything's quiet and at a low ebb."

"Live people always think that time is the middle of the night," Dora said. "Since you are dealing with live people, you may be right. But do not take it for granted."

I'd long since given up on taking anything for granted. That's part of the reason I still am a live person. And one of the things I didn't take for granted was riding the Red Line with a vampire. Not many folks of any kind riding, not at that time of night.

One tough guy looked at me when he got on, sizing up his chances. He didn't know how bad they really were—I sat by the window, so Dora's not reflecting would be less obvious. But I just looked back at him. He sat down and didn't bother us. That was fine.

She and I were the only ones on the bus that stopped by the factory. We got off one stop before that; I didn't want the god-things noticing me. There were no streetlights. Dora guided me down to Jellison. She saw in the dark at least as well as Old Man Mose.

PERSONAL ASSISTANCE, PERSONAL ASSISTANTS—red neon shone in the window, but the place was closed. "Zombies!" Dora's lip curled so I could see a fang. In the bloody glow from the sign, it looked especially alarming. "Not alive at all but still moving!" She shook her head. Too many people, of course, feel that way about vampires.

"Let's see if there's an alley behind this block," I said. "Nobody's around now, but I don't want to break in right here on the street unless I have to. I should've checked when I was down here before, but I didn't. Sorry."

"We will find out. It will be as it is, and we will do what we must do."

There was an alley. She took the lead as we walked along it. A couple of times, she kept me from stumbling into trash cans I didn't

201

see soon enough. That would've been good, wouldn't it? Nothing like kicking galvanized iron to let the world know you're there.

No neon sign on the back door. I had lockpicks and enough unofficial practice to know what to do with them. Dora put her ear to the door before I started. I knew she heard better than I did, too. "It seems quiet," she said. "Quiet as the tomb."

I got to work. The lock was a good Yale. Two pins were easy, two were hard, and one ... one didn't want to go up for anything. I muttered under my breath, both because I was having trouble and because I was scared to trip an alarm.

"Would you like me to try?" Dora asked.

"You know how?" I whispered back. She nodded. I stepped aside. "Hope you have more luck than I did."

It wasn't luck. It was technique. I don't know where she learned it, but she had it and then some. The door swung open less than a minute later. We slipped inside. I slid a rubber wedge under the door to keep it from closing when we didn't want it to.

"Old blood. Stale blood. Foul blood," she said, and then more in Magyar. We found our way to a door. She read what was written on it: "Assistants." No, people who deal in zombies don't like calling them zombies.

I tried the knob. It turned. We went in. I snapped on a little flashlight. I wished I hadn't. Standing bodies, row on row of them. I'd seen it before, but it was even worse in near darkness.

Faces. Dead faces, white and black. Eyes open. Eyes closed. Eyes halfway in between. Eyes however they'd been when zombification hit. The zombies didn't care, not now they didn't. The ones with closed eyes would be ordered to open them when they went into service so they could see what they needed to see to do what they had to do. They wouldn't care about that, either.

Smells of stale sweat, stale tobacco, stale booze. Some smells nastier than that. I'd smelled those smells in Italy—fear'll make anybody unpucker. Some of these ex-people had been that afraid when they went in to sell their souls and wills. But they'd done it no matter how scared they were.

Pupils in open eyes didn't shrink when my light touched them. Nothing but disconnected numbers on those switchboards. Dora

TWICE AS DEAD

and I went along the rows, she looking for Rudolf Sebestyen, I for Frank Jethroe. When we got to the back, I felt more hemmed in than I had in the tightest foxhole south of Milan. I don't know if she did; I was too nervous to ask.

She sounded calm enough when she asked me, "Did you see the man you were looking for?"

"Unh-unh," I managed. I needed another inhale before I could come out with, "Did you?"

"No. I wish I had, but no," she said. "What now?"

"Now we see what kind of files they've got," I answered. "They have to keep records for the county and for the state." How much truth lay in those records was liable to be a different story, but all you can do is all you can do.

I was never so glad to get out of anywhere as I was to escape that storeroom. If a zombie had reached out a hand and set it on my shoulder, I would have filled my pants and screamed so shrill, only dogs could hear it. No zombie did. They aren't supposed to be able to do anything like that. They mostly don't. But I know a couple of guys who lived through the Denver Zombie Riots. They'll tell you mostly isn't always.

We found two rooms that I figured would hold files. Dora could read the door labels in the darkness. One said CLIENTS—A-T; the other, CLIENTS—U-Z. That was an odd place to break the alphabet. Also, the door with A-T behind it was open, but the one that held U-Z was locked. U, it occurred to me, was the first letter of US Rubber. Maybe that signified, maybe it didn't.

I squatted down and got to work on the lock. Sometimes you have the feel. I did then, the way I did when I was fourteen and knew I was gonna hit one out. I got us into that room as fast as I would have with a key.

Dora touched my arm. "That was nicely done," she said.

"Thanks, babe," I answered, not thinking. She didn't call me on it. Either she didn't mind or she figured we had more important things to worry about. And we did.

The room had no windows. I shone my flashlight around. The file cabinets against the walls had drawers with labels that started at UA and ran to ZY. On a hunch, I tried to open the drawer with the UP records. It was locked.

So I went to work again. Most file-cabinet locks are little cheap ones, nothing next to the ones in doors. Most. Not this one. It was a bastard. A bastard and a half, if you want to be exact.

I was just about to ask Dora for more help when the last pin rose. I muttered, "About time!" as I yanked the drawer open.

Then I checked the names on the manila folders inside. I felt like shouting when the first one, instead of being for somebody with a handle like Upadsky, read *Padden, N.* The next one was for *Padilla, J.* After that came *Paige, L.* Then *Palmisano, G.* And I will be damned if the one after that didn't have *Jethroe, F.* neatly on it, with a file number: 5149.

I yanked it out of the drawer and showed it to Dora. "Got one!" I said. "I bet your half brother is in the next drawer down."

"We had better not take the time to find out," she said. "Something is wrong. I felt it as soon as you took that one out."

Something was wrong about the whole place. I can't tell you how she noticed anything worse all of a sudden, but she did. I didn't argue with her, either. "We beat it?" I asked.

"We beat it," she agreed.

Even when you hurry, you have to watch the details. I closed the drawer, so it wouldn't be obvious what I'd been looking for. I closed and locked the door that said CLIENTS—U-Z. Dora was already heading for the back door. That probably saved my skin, because the zombie came at her instead of me.

As I'd said to Izzy Berkowitz, zombies aren't great fighters. They're stupid and slow. But they don't care what you do to them, or feel it. Once they get hold of somebody, they won't let go for hell. An ordinary live person can't do enough to make them stop. They keep doing things to a live person till he's not a live person any more.

When this one grabbed Dora, she bent his thumb back the way you'd break off a drumstick. I heard the snap. As soon as he didn't have a good grip on her any more, she slammed him against the wall. Something else snapped then. He tried to stand up anyway, but it's harder when one leg doesn't work. She broke one of his arms over her knee, then the other one. He still wanted to keep fighting, but about all he could do was try to bite her kneecaps off.

"Get past him!" she said urgently.

And I did, even though the corridor was narrow. The zombie tried to grab me with the hand with the working thumb, but his ruined arm wouldn't let him. I just hoped the sorcerous alarm wouldn't loose more of them against us. We got out of there as fast as we could. I locked the back door, too.

"They will know they had visitors," Dora observed.

"What? You think a wrecked zombie is a clue?" I said.

"If this is humor, it is not good humor."

"Good humor is ice cream," I said. She looked at me. I gave up. "Let's go home," I told her. And we did.

XIV

We had to wait a while for the bus that took us back to the closest Red Line stop; they don't run so often in the middle of the night. If any more zombies had come after us, we might've been in trouble. But everything behind us stayed quiet. Whoever'd designed their alarm system had figured rousing one would be plenty. He hadn't counted on a burglar having a vampire along for company.

I couldn't look at the folder before the bus pulled up, or after we got on. The lights were down low, and with reason. The only passenger on board with us was a wino snoring while she leaned against the window.

She woke up when we got off, but only to give us an indignant stare: how had we appeared out of nowhere? We hadn't, of course, but her muscatel-muddied mind couldn't work that out before we disappeared again.

Another wait in the dark till the trolley came up. Dora tapped the folder with a fingernail. "What do you hope to learn?" she asked.

"How they got hold of him. Where they unloaded him—they must have, because I'm sure he wasn't in that storeroom." I shuddered. I never wanted to think of that storeroom again as long as I lived. I knew I would, too, of course, want to or not. "Maybe who's in cahoots with them at US Rubber. Somebody is, that's for sure."

TWICE AS DEAD

"What will you do if the papers make it look as though he chose to become a zombie?" she said.

I grimaced. "I don't know. I don't even know what I'll do if it's plain as plain he didn't. I ought to take it to the police, but …"

Dora let out a scornful snort, a noise that a vampire—especially a beautiful lady vampire—shouldn't have been able to make. "But," she agreed, a word that was a paragraph and a half all by itself.

"Yeah." I nodded. If US Rubber wasn't working with the LAPD, Dewey, Beagle, & Howe was. I wondered who Elmer V. Jackson got his marching orders from. And I wondered how long it would be before I found out.

A couple of cars went by. I couldn't see inside them. Whoever was in them probably couldn't see us, either, or anything the headlights didn't paint. Then a solo beam higher off the ground announced the Red Line car. I put a dime in the fare box; Dora used two nickels. "Transfers, please," I told the motorman.

"You got 'em, suh." The way he spoke, the way he eyed me, said he didn't hear *please* every week. He eyed Dora, too, as any man might have. "Y'all're out late."

"We were visiting friends," she said. Her very precise English, and the accent that flavored it, made him start minding his own business again. Kind of a shame; she didn't mean to do that.

Half an hour later, we walked into her apartment. She started running a bath. I understood that; something unclean had laid hands on her. Of course she wanted to scrub it off. I would have, too.

While she washed, I sat down on the sofa and looked at the *Jethroe, F.* folder. A slightly blurry photo said it did have to do with the Frank Jethroe I wanted to find. Somebody'd written a code on the back: 583 USR.

That made my mouth fall open. The US Rubber people who were doing whatever the hell they were doing had sent 582 other people to be made into zombies or people who'd already been made into zombies to PERSONAL ASSISTANCE, PERSONAL ASSISTANTS? At least 582? How much turnover on their production lines did they have? Or were they dragging people in off the streets? That happened all the time in B movies. In real life, it wasn't supposed to.

207

After I reeled my lower jaw back up into place, I went through the papers that backed up the photograph. If I remembered straight, and I was sure I did, the date on the form was the day he'd stopped to take a leak before he got on the bus, then didn't get on. Nobody'd seen him once he walked into the men's room ... nobody except the people who'd got him to the zombie dealership, I should say.

Everything on the forms was neatly printed in block letters, the way a fifth grader might have done it. Did Frank Jethroe fill out paperwork like that? I had my doubts, but Clarice would be able to tell me one way or the other. Where the form asked the reason for seeking the process, Jethroe or whoever'd done the writing answered I OWE TOO MUCH DOUGH. From what his wife said, the family didn't have killing debts. They might have scuffled to get by, but that isn't the same thing.

On the last line of the enrollment form's back page were a thumbprint and a signature. It said *Frank Jethroe*, but no grown-up in the world writes that way. It was clear and legible and utterly without character, soul, personality—you choose the right name. Either somebody else did it on purpose, or he'd already been zombified when they stuck a pen in his hand. I knew how I'd guess.

Except for the dark storeroom full of soulless, spiritless *things*, that signature scared me more than anything else about the whole night. I kept looking at it; I couldn't stop myself. Every time I did, it got worse.

I had to make myself go on to the form that said what happened to him. He'd been leased out to O'Flannery and Muldoon, one of the biggest road-building outfits in the county. He might be anywhere, anywhere at all.

Then Dora walked out into the front room. She had on bedroom slippers, and nothing else from there on up. If that wasn't a distraction, nothing ever would be. She smelled of soap and scented bath oil. "I know what you need," she said.

I slammed the folder closed and tossed it aside. "You bet I do!" I said, instead of *Jesus Christ, do I ever!* Then I asked, "How about you?"

"Yes, some. I do not always think myself lucky for my state, but I do now," she answered. "There are worse ways to be, and that is worth celebrating."

TWICE AS DEAD

So we celebrated. By the time we finished, twilight warned that sunrise wasn't far off. She got out of bed and went to her coffin to wait out the short winter day. Me? I put on pajamas. The apartment was always chilly, not that she cared.

I woke up in the early afternoon, which was moving from strange toward normal. *You work the graveyard shift these days*, I thought as I flipped on the hot plate. I'm not real funny till I've had my coffee. I grabbed breakfast at a little diner on the edge of Vampire Village and went on up to my office.

Old Man Mose gave me a sour stare when I came in. "You really are on cats' time these days," he said, so he couldn't have been at his best, either. Maybe I wasn't the only one who needed coffee.

"Complain, complain, complain," I said. I cleaned out his bowl at the sink in the little bathroom, then opened a can and plopped some fresh mashed tuna in there. He kept slaloming between my legs while I carried it over to where it goes, so I could trip over him and kill myself. I didn't, quite. As soon as I put the food down, he slammed his face into it. I watched him for a few seconds. "How do you like me now?"

"Jush fine," he answered with his mouth full, and went back to making a pig of himself.

I called Lamont Smalls. "What can I do for you today, Mister Mitchell?" he asked when the *Lookout* switchboard put me through. He sounded wary. He was probably wondering if I had something I could use to blackmail him.

"I've come across a story you may want to use in your paper," I answered. "I can show you what I've got if you want to come over and have a look at it."

"Why don't you tell me now?" he said.

"I don't want to talk about it over the phone."

He thought for a little while. "I suppose I can get over there about half past four, if that's all right with you."

"That's fine," I answered, and we said our goodbyes. He'd always been *I'll run right over!* when I was getting him dirt on sweet, unfaithful Marianne. A story for the *Lookout*? That wasn't so important.

209

He knocked on the door when he said he would; I give him that. When he showed up, he looked the way he always did: smart, well dressed, successful, unhappy. I waved him to the sofa. As he sat, he asked, "What's so hot you can't talk about it on the telephone?"

I told him the story of poor Frank Jethroe. After I told him, I showed him the file from the zombie dealership. "Look at these papers," I said. "Are you going to tell me a grown man filled them out?"

He studied them while he pulled at his lower lip and let it go back into place with a wet plop. I don't think he knew he was doing it; it drove me nuts. "This is connected to US Rubber, you say? That big, weird factory where you think the Assyrians came down like the wolf on the fold?"

"Their cohorts were gleaming in silver and gold." Nobody'd out-Byron me.

Only he did. "Purple and gold," he corrected absently, and went on, "Can you nail this down tight?"

"Not yet. I just found out a little while ago. But this was the day he went to the men's room before he caught the next bus toward home. Only he didn't catch it. Either he decided out of the blue, *Hey, I'll turn zombie*, and went off and did it or somebody there did it to him."

Smalls flipped to the last form in the folder. "Not just US Rubber but US Rubber plus O'Flannery and Muldoon? That makes everything even better, doesn't it?"

"You run the *Lookout*. Are you on the lookout for stories or not? I promise you, he's not the only black man this has happened to. People need to know."

"Yes. They do." He touched the manila folder with the *Jethroe, F.* label. "Can I take this with me?"

"No. Not yet. You don't want to know what I went through to get it. But I'm only one guy." I didn't say a word about Dora, and didn't intend to. "You've got reporters you can send out to see if this is real. Five gets you ten they don't have to look real hard."

"That's so." He fished out a little notebook and wrote in it. Of course he would've been a reporter himself before he was an editor. When he finished, the notebook went back into that inside breast pocket. "Is it all right if they talk to you tomorrow?"

"Tomorrow afternoon. I have some things I need to do in the morning." I didn't tell him about the hours I was keeping, either.

"Okay. You'll hear from somebody then." Out he went, doing that thing with his hand and his lip again. I'd given him something to think about, anyhow.

I got to the office early the next day: not much past eleven. The telephone rang at a quarter to two. "Mitchell Investigating," I said.

"Hello, Mister Mitchell. Lamont Smalls here." Not a reporter. The big man himself.

"What's going on?" I asked.

"I ... talked to a few people this morning. It ... doesn't look like we'll be able to go ahead with this story. The risk is just too big."

"What kind of risk?"

"A risk to the newspaper. The owner would not be happy with me if I put her property in jeopardy." The lady who owned the *Lookout* was the widow of a brown man who'd made a fortune in insurance. Harder than winning the Irish Sweepstakes, but he did it. She was brown herself, only not very, and didn't always like getting reminded about it.

"You'd be doing a lot for the folks who read the rag if you let them know what's going on around here," I said.

"I have to weigh the present against the future. You see a lot more crusading newspapermen in the movies than you do for real," Smalls said. I believed him. It sure as hell worked the same way with detectives. He added, "I didn't use your name at all. I just said I'd heard a few things."

"Thanks." I meant it, though I knew his discretion wouldn't do me any good. The people who mattered, the people with money, the people who told other people what to do, they'd know Lamont Smalls wasn't asking about zombies because some hotshot reporter of his had stumbled over the story on his own. They'd know he'd got it from me. And they'd know that salamander hadn't cooked me after all.

I wondered what would do me any good. The only thing I could think of was locking up the whole LAPD, or at least the Vice Squad, and losing the key. That wouldn't happen. I knew it wouldn't, too. The old line, *Who will watch the watchmen?* Nobody watches the watchmen. When they realize nobody does ...

When they realize that, you've got the City of Angels, the way she is today. You can love it or you can hate it. The only way you can get away from it is to move out. I didn't have the jack for that. I didn't have anywhere else to go, either.

I called Clarice Jethroe once I figured she was home. I guessed right. I'd almost rather have guessed wrong. This way, I had to tell her what had happened to her husband.

"They can't do that!" she explained when I got done.

"They aren't supposed to do that," I said. "It's not the same thing. I wish it were."

"What can you do? What can I do?" she asked.

"I'll go to O'Flannery and Muldoon's headquarters tomorrow. I'll see if I can find out where Frank is and whether they'll turn him loose. If they do, the next thing is to find a wizard who can bring him back to being Frank Jethroe instead of a shovel that walks on two legs."

"And if they don't?" Mrs. Jethroe knew the questions that needed asking, sure as hell.

I sighed. "If they don't, two choices I can see. One is just stealing him."

"He's a man. You can't steal a man!"

We both had ancestors whose owners would have told her different. They thought abolitionists stole slaves. They thought slaves who ran away stole themselves. Mentioning that didn't seem likely to make things better, though.

Instead, I said, "I wouldn't try it anyway. They'd have a pretty good idea where to look if he disappeared all of a sudden."

"Yeah, they would," she said, her voice going dull. "What's my other choice, Mister Mitchell?"

"A lawyer," I answered.

She laughed the sour laugh of somebody who'd just heard somebody else say something really stupid. "I barely got the money to pay you. You know it, too. How'm I gonna afford one o' them leeches?"

"Maybe you can get somebody to take it on pro bono." I realized I'd better explain that: "For nothing, because it's the right thing to

TWICE AS DEAD

do and because you can't afford to pay. Somebody who wants to make a splash for himself might want to tackle it." I wondered if my own mouthpiece would do that. I doubted it. Wally Baker was a pretty damn fine lawyer, but he liked the good things in life. He liked them a lot.

"I dunno," Clarice Jethroe muttered, so low I could hardly hear her. I couldn't pump her hopes up very high, because I didn't know, either. She went on, "You go on out there tomorrow, like you said. Maybe the company'll let him go on account of it's the right thing to do."

"Maybe they will," I said. Neither one of us believed it. We told each other goodbye. We were probably both relieved to hang up. I know I was.

After that, I didn't see much point in sticking around the office any more. No, let's talk straight—I wanted to get the devil out of there. So I made sure Old Man Mose wouldn't starve to death or be reduced to brigandage before I came back, and then I headed down to Vampire Village.

The wind snapped at my cheek when I went outside. People go on and on about how wonderful Southern California weather is, and they're right ... most of the time. Everyone knows it can get too hot in the summertime. But nobody talks about how it shows its teeth during the winter. This was one of those times. That breeze was *cold*, and sharp as if it carried a switchblade. I had to grab at my hat to keep it from blowing away, too.

And grabbing at my hat was lucky—it made me jerk my head to one side, which meant I had to look at the copies of the *Mirror* on a rack beside the door to a little grocery. They had a screamer of a headline: "**POLICE SCANDAL!**" I grabbed one, gave the nice lady in the store a nickel, and tried to read and walk at the same time.

Even before I knew anything about the story except those two words in big type, I wanted to lean back against a telephone pole and laugh till I sagged to the sidewalk as if the pole weren't there. What had I been thinking? That it would take arresting every crooked cop in town to keep them off my back. And here they'd gone and done it!

Well, pretty close. And, as with horseshoes and hand grenades, close counted. They'd indicted Sergeant Elmer V. Jackson; and

213

Lieutenant Rudy Wellpott, who was Jackson's boss in the Vice Squad; and Captain Jack Donahoe, who was Wellpott's boss; and Assistant Chief Joe Reed; and Chief C.B. "Cowboy" Horrall his very own self. Horrall had resigned. The charges were bribery and corruption and perjury.

The more I read, the more amazed I got. There was at least one cop on the LAPD who hadn't gone along with picking up extra cash in exchange for looking the other way at this, that, and the other thing. On the LAPD? Whoever'd hired him had to be looking for other work right now. But he'd got hired, he'd seen what was going on, and he'd talked to a grand jury.

Mayor Bowron denied knowing anything. Well, anybody who knew Mayor Bowron even a little could've told you he didn't know anything. But he was running for reelection again, so the timing couldn't've been worse for him.

Dora was up and about when I let myself into her apartment. "Hey, beautiful!" I said, and waved the newspaper at her.

She looked annoyed, as if she didn't already know she was beautiful. But then she noticed the paper. "What is so important there?" she asked. I told her. I hadn't seen her surprised very often, but I did that time. "They arrest police officers?" She sounded as if she'd never dreamed such a thing was possible.

I couldn't blame her; I hadn't dreamed it was possible, either. "All I know is just what I read in the papers," I said.

She knew who I was stealing from. "I listened to him on the radio. Even for a live man, he died too soon," she said.

"He did, yeah." That was half a lifetime ago for me. I mostly remembered my folks being broken up about it. To Dora Urban, it probably seemed like the day before yesterday. The older I get, the more everything seems like the day before yesterday. And she had a big head start on me.

Like any vampire, she also had an eye for the main chance. They are nothing if not self-centered. "What does this do for you?" she asked.

Not as if I weren't wondering about that myself. "I hope it'll get 'em off my back for a while. I don't know that it will, but I hope so. At least till somebody else starts looking through the files ... or until these bastards get off the hook."

TWICE AS DEAD

The grand jury'd done its job. It indicted a bunch of crooked cops. But how often does a regular jury ever convict a cop of anything, no matter how guilty he is? You know the answer to that as well as I do.

We celebrated. No, not like that. We went from one club on Central to another. We left one in a hurry when I saw that Jonas Schmitt was part of the combo backing up a visiting fireman from Chicago. I didn't think he knew who I was, but I didn't want to find out I was wrong.

As we were walking up the street, Dora said, "Jazz was something new to me. It is much less ordered, less put together, than the music I was used to in the land where I grew up."

"I can see how it would be, yeah," I said.

"It is the music of the hunted, not the hunter," she went on, as if I hadn't spoken.

"The underdog, not the top dog," I put in.

Again, I might as well not have bothered. She kept on talking: "Where I come from, the Roma and the Sinti and the Jews made hunted people's music, but no one who mattered paid much attention to it, except to borrow a clever phrase here and there for a proper composition."

When she said *borrow*, she meant *steal*, only she didn't know it. Well, music always steals from other music; that's part of the game. So I couldn't get too upset there. But she did sound like a society lady sniffing at jazz and not quite noticing she's tapping her foot at the same time.

Then I found out I wasn't being fair to her, because she continued, "I have always been a hunter. You will understand this, I think."

"Could be." Of itself, my hand went to those nicks on my neck. As fast as one set healed, I got myself another. They reminded me what she was. She couldn't be anything else.

"After things fell apart, though, I was hunted more terribly than I had ever been before," she said. If she was talking about what I thought she was, that would've been about the time I was born. Quietly, she finished, "I was lucky to come to myself here one day, so lucky. Too many of my kind are but ash on the wind, ash from the White Fire, these days. This music speaks to me now in ways it never would have, never could have, before."

215

"That's … interesting," I said. And damned if it wasn't. I'd wondered now and then what white folks saw in jazz. It wasn't theirs, not till they started lifting it. It was underdogs' music, the way I'd told Dora. And how could white people be underdogs? They were *white*.

But now I saw there were degrees to everything. Sure, white people could look down on the ones who lived in the Negro Belt. The cops' name, not mine. Still, if you had no job or a lousy job and you were broke all the time and your boss wouldn't stop giving you grief, weren't you going to think of yourself as an underdog? Would you be wrong if you did? Especially if you looked at things the way a white person would.

I started to laugh. Oh, not the way I had when I saw those policemen'd landed in hot water, but I did. Dora gave me a quizzical look. "Where is the joke?" she asked. Yes, she was a hunter, or she wouldn't have put it that way.

"You know I'm not quite black and not quite white?" I said. She nodded; she knew, all right. I went on, "I may not be quite one or the other, but the more I think about it, the more I see I'm liable to be a Red."

"Do you *enjoy* being hunted?" To her, the idea had to seem unspeakably perverse. "I will not betray you, but you may not be so lucky with others."

"Uh-huh." *Are you now or have you ever been?* was hunters' music, sure as hell. I looked around. We were in front of the Last Word, across the street from the Club Alabam. Buddy Collette and the Stars of Swing were playing. "Want to?" I asked. Dora nodded again. We went on in.

Next morning, I made myself get moving pretty early. When I left the apartment, I blew the coffin a kiss. I wondered how I would've explained that to my mother. Well, I didn't have to.

I rode the Red Line downtown. O'Flannery and Muldoon had their offices in a building only a block away from City Hall. Anybody surprised at that shouldn't have been. Thieves always get together to split the loot.

The morning *Times* had headlines about the dirty cops, too. That was something. You bet it was. The *Times* was the kind of paper that

TWICE AS DEAD

thought the fylfot boys didn't go far enough half the time. But it couldn't ignore what lay right under its nose, no matter how much it might've wanted to. Lay stinking under its nose, I should say.

A smiling, blue-eyed receptionist at O'Flannery and Muldoon greeted me with, "How can I help you this morning, sir?" The smile and the *sir* told what she thought she was seeing.

I set a card on the counter. This time, I had the sense to use one with a name and address that weren't mine. "I'm a private investigator. I'm looking into the disappearance of a man named Frank Jethroe. I have reason to believe he was made into a zombie against his will, and that your company is using him in a labor gang."

The smile disappeared. "What do you mean, you have reason to believe?" The *sir* vanished, too.

"His file says he was leased to O'Flannery and Muldoon," I answered.

Luckily, she didn't ask how I'd got hold of the file. She stood up. "Wait here," she said. No *please* now, either. She hustled into a back room.

I had time to smoke most of an Old Gold before she came back, followed by a middle-aged man in a quiet tweed suit that cost more than I wanted to think about. "Good morning, Mister Michaels," he said, using the alias on the card. "I'm Gerald Gallagher, assistant chief counsel here. What seems to be the issue?" I told him the same thing I'd said to the receptionist. He frowned. "Why don't you come back to my office? We can talk there."

So I came back to his office. He had a desk that could have landed dragons when we were fighting the Knights of Bushido in the Pacific. When I sat down on the far side of it, he looked about a mile and a half away.

He drummed his fingers on the polished mahogany. "You realize, I'm sure, we don't keep track of unsouled laborers"—he didn't like saying *zombies*, either—"by name, since they have no ability to keep track of their names themselves. So, even assuming everything you told me is true, tracking down your Mister, uh, Jethroe, did you say, will be difficult if not impossible."

Since I'd been thinking of the Pacific a second before, I answered with the motto of the Conjuring Battalions there: " 'The difficult we do at once—the impossible takes a little longer.'" Gallagher frowned

217

again; I hadn't thought he'd appreciate getting the Seabees thrown in his face. I went on, "O'Flannery and Muldoon leased him from the zombie dealership down on Jellison that calls itself Personal Assistance, Personal Assistants."

One more frown. He was good at them, I admit. I wondered if he practiced in front of a mirror. "Jellison?" he asked.

Okay. It isn't an important street. He might not know offhand where it was. I did my best to help him out: "It's not far from the big US Rubber factory on Scrying Crystal Road, where Mister Jethroe worked and where he disappeared. His number at the dealership was 5149. Can you track him down with that?"

He didn't frown when I mentioned US Rubber. He winced—not very much, but he did. He hadn't expected it, or I don't suppose he would have. He rallied fast; he gave O'Flannery and Muldoon their money's worth. "You will understand, Mister Michaels, that even if, hypothetically, things are the way you describe them, that we had no knowledge he became unsouled in any way other than through the prescribed legal process."

Some of the Lightning Rune people said things like that after they got caught. *We didn't know what was going on. We just did what they told us to do.* We could prove they were lying, and they paid for it. Some of them did.

I couldn't prove anything with Gerald Gallagher. Not without subpoenas and truth geases I didn't have and couldn't get, I couldn't. So I answered, "I'm not saying you did. But if he didn't want to become a zombie, you don't have any business profiting from his labor." Sure enough, the more I talked, the Redder I sounded.

Gallagher looked at me. "How will you be able to demonstrate that he became unsouled involuntarily?"

I'd been thinking about that myself. "How's this sound?" I said. "When you find out where you've got him digging and hauling for you, let's go out there and use a sorcerer to bring him back to himself. Then we can ask him. I've got twenty bucks to put on what he says, if you're interested."

"I'm not a gambling man, thanks." He gave me a very thin smile. "But if he is resouled and you prove wrong, he's unlikely to want

TWICE AS DEAD

to return to his previous state, and we would lose the benefits we gained under the lease agreement."

"Will it bankrupt you?"

"No, of course not, not by itself, but—"

He'd given me an opening, and I pushed through it: "Not by itself, huh? Hold on for a second. Why do you think he's not the only zombie who doesn't want to be one you've leased 'by mistake'?" I made sure he could hear the quotation marks. "If you've got dozens of them, what will that do for O'Flannery and Muldoon's good name? Everybody'll love you as much as people love the Los Angeles police right now. You'll have more lawsuits than you know what to do with, too."

He looked as if his stomach pained him. Then he got to his feet. "Make yourself comfortable here. I may be gone a little while. First, though, you're acting only on behalf of this Frank Jethroe?"

"For now, that's right."

"That will do." Out he went. I had time for two or three cigarettes before he came back. In his wake followed a skinny, disheveled-looking fellow with a sorcerer's carpetbag. "Mister Michael, this is Robert Grau, one of our staff wizards. Robert, John Michaels."

"Call me Jack," I said as we shook hands. I didn't want to worry about who the card said I was.

"Then I'm Rob," Grau said. "Not Bob, if you please. A bob is what you use inside a toilet tank."

Gallagher looked impatient at the byplay. "Let's go," he said.

"Where are we going?" I asked.

"Up to where they're pushing the Hollywood Freeway north past the Cahuenga Pass," he answered. "That's where this ... unsouled individual has been working. My car is in the lot next door. I'll drive."

Grau and I followed in his wake as he headed for the elevator. I kept sneaking glances at the wizard. If he was going to bring Frank Jethroe back to his normal self, it would be good if he had at least one drop—to give him a kind of feel for the business, if you know what I mean. He didn't look as if he did, or talk that way, either. Of course, you never can tell. Take me, for instance.

219

Gallagher drove a Cadillac—last year's, not a brand new one. He'd had that suit a while, too. He bought top quality and hung on to it. He and Grau rode up front; I sat in back. No, not like that, or I don't think so. They knew each other. I was the stranger, the nuisance. When Gallagher turned the key, the engine was so quiet, I hardly noticed.

We got on the Hollywood Freeway and zipped northwest up to the Cahuenga Pass. They were pushing the freeway toward the Valley now. Pretty soon, it would go down to downtown, too. Red Line tracks ran between the lanes going one way and those going the other. We went past a trolley as if it were standing still. If you had a car, and if it wasn't rush hour, the freeway was the way to go.

Pretty soon, we passed signs that said things like CONSTRUC-TION AHEAD and PREPARE TO STOP. Most cars got off the road. Gerald Gallagher kept going till a workman in overalls flagged him down, barking, "What the hell you doin'?"

"I'm Gallagher, from the office," the lawyer answered, and the guy waving the red bandanna came to attention as if Gallagher were a colonel or a general. He went on, "Hop in. We need to check on a laborer. Point us at the people who keep track of them."

The man hopped in. I scooted over to give him room. We nodded at each other. He told Gallagher, "That tent about a quarter mile up. Go slow—the paving ends right after it." He pulled out a pack of Luckies. I gave him a light.

We stopped by the tent. The fellow who'd flagged us down beat it. I looked ahead. After the paving ended, they were laying the base for more. Some of it was bulldozers and dump trucks. Some was skilled artisans pouring and grading concrete over steel reinforcing bars. But an awful lot was pick-and-shovel work, digging and hauling, the kind of thing you could train a chimpanzee to do. Or a zombie.

I didn't have long to see if I could spot Jethroe (I couldn't). Gallagher ducked into the tent. Rob Grau and I followed. A guy in a suit who also wore an aluminum hard hat with EDDIE stenciled on it looked up in surprise from whatever he was doing at a card table. "Jerry!" he said. "Who turned you loose from your desk?"

Gallagher jerked a thumb at me. "This fella here. I need you to fetch me Unsouled Number 5149, quick as you can. There seems to

TWICE AS DEAD

be some problem with his recruitment. We'll bring him back to the way he was beforehand, see if we can get to the bottom of it."

"He won't wanna go back after you do," Eddie predicted morosely.

"I know, I know. We'll be down one, that's all," Gallagher said with a resigned wave. "But have somebody fetch him back here, and make it snappy."

Eddie gave me a dirty look, but he nodded. "What was the number again?" he asked. Gallagher told him. He sent a young guy in chinos, a shirt and tie but no jacket, and a hard hat with TAD on it off to do the actual work.

He didn't come back and he didn't come back. I was wondering what had gone wrong when he finally did. And I will be damned if he didn't have what was left of Frank Jethroe with him.

XV

"This the one you're looking for?" Gallagher asked me.

"That's him," I answered, even if I wasn't better than two-thirds sure. Jethroe didn't just look as if he'd been worked like a machine with two legs for too long, though he looked that way, too. But his face …. If you've ever seen a zombie, you know what I mean. If you haven't, I'm not sure I can explain it. Even though he'd shambled in under his own steam, he looked deader than most corpses. His eyes were open, but I don't think they did him much good.

"Okay." The lawyer turned to Rob Grau. "Do what you need to do. We'll find out what's going on with this one." Gallagher didn't want to admit, even to himself, that Frank Jethroe was a person. Admitting that would also mean admitting what had happened to him, and how O'Flannery and Muldoon had taken advantage of it.

Grau had already started rummaging in his carpetbag. I tried to keep from fidgeting as I watched him. The last thing, the very last thing, I wanted was for an ofay who didn't know what he was doing to mess up the revival. Then he pulled out a dried calabash crisscrossed with beads and snake vertebrae and with a little brass bell attached, and I breathed easier. If he had an asson, he wasn't so clueless as I'd feared.

"You a houngan?" I asked him.

TWICE AS DEAD

Now he looked at me. I'd changed my thinking about him; I saw him change his about me. He hadn't supposed I'd know what a houngan was, which is what I get for being how I am. "I've had my head washed," he said shortly.

"Good enough for me," I said. He might not have the one drop—I still didn't believe he did—but he'd been initiated into the priesthood, whether he kept it up or not. He might cope after all. He just might.

He shook the asson at Frank Jethroe. The gravel or beans inside rattled in a rhythm Chick Webb wouldn't have been ashamed of. Then he stepped up to Jethroe (who, I saw, had 5149 marked in indelible ink on his raggedy shirt and dungarees) and sketched a big cross above his head.

And then he made another gesture. Some people will recognize the Grand Hailing Sign of Distress; some will not. Those who do may not describe it, so I won't. I hadn't thought to see it in a ritual like this, but Jethroe sure was in distress, so I suppose it had its place. Like musicians, wizards here borrow from wizards there. They always have. They always will. No use getting stuffy about it.

"I wish I had a chicken to sacrifice," Grau muttered, more to himself than to me. He shrugged; no chicken in that carpetbag. Or I didn't think so, anyway, but he reached into it anyway. No, no chicken. He pulled out a little pair—almost a toy pair—of bongo drums. I jumped when he thrust them into my hands and asked, "Can you play these?"

"Not what you'd call well," I said. Lord knows that's true.

He didn't care. "Follow along with me the best you can, then," he said. "It doesn't need to be perfect, nowhere close. Make noise. Give the asson some bottom, know what I mean? I'm going to summon his soul, his life force, whatever you want to call it, back into his body. I want to make sure it's able to hear me, wherever it's gone now that it isn't with him any more."

I looked down at the tiny bongos. Somebody outside the tent might be able to hear them, but not if he was more than twenty feet away. Yes, I understand. It's sorcery. What goes on Over There isn't the same as what happens Over Here. Things that seem silly aren't. This sure was a thing that seemed silly.

223

Grau shook the asson at Frank Jethroe's husk again. It had a different, more urgent, beat this time. I started working the skins. I didn't think I'd do anything but distract poor Jethroe's life force, not at first. But then I felt myself getting sucked into the sorcery Rob was building. Following along got easier. It was almost as if I was a part of what he was doing. Or maybe not as if; I seemed to know what he'd say with the calabash before he said it.

He began to chant. Out of the corner of my eye, I saw Gallagher start and come on point, like a bird dog. "That's French," he said to Eddie. Then he scratched his head. "No, it isn't. Not quite."

I wanted to tell him to shut up so he wouldn't distract the wizard. But that would have distracted me, and it seemed as though Rob was doing fine. He went right on in Kreyòl. He sure had had his head washed.

No, I didn't know what he was saying. I know of that stuff, but not as much about it as I ought to. My mother didn't hold with the old ways, the ways that came with our folks from Africa, any more than she held with comic books. And so I also didn't, not with either one. Things rub off on you without your even noticing that's what's going on.

"Come back! Come back!" Grau called. Don't ask me what language he was using; I can't tell you. I didn't know what language I was using myself, or whether I was Over Here or Over There. Betwixt and between again. The story of my goddamn life.

I do know *something* didn't want to turn loose of Frank Jethroe's soul. Something old, older, oldest, Something alongside which even the ancient ritual Rob was going through seemed to have been cobbled together day before yesterday. Whatever it was, it didn't want me to get a glimpse of it, if that's the right way to put things.

"Come back! Come back!" Rob called again. This time, I took it to mean the thing that was clinging to Jethroe, not him. Inside my head, I got a brief glimpse of a fierce profile and a curly beard. Only that glance, and then it was gone again.

Letting itself be spotted, if just for an instant, seemed to weaken it. "Summon him one more time!" I said to Rob Grau. I think I used Kreyòl. I already told you I don't know any Kreyòl, but I used it anyway.

224

TWICE AS DEAD

However I said it, he understood me. "Come back! Come back!" he cried, and set the hand that wasn't holding the asson on Frank Jethroe's heart.

Next thing I knew, I was picking myself up off the ground without any idea how I'd got there. I felt as if I'd been blackjacked, only I didn't have a welt or a bruise. Grau didn't look much better off than I was. Ridden hard and put away wet, they say in the B-movie Westerns.

But Frank Jethroe .... He still didn't move. For a horrible moment, I thought the Something had won and Rob had failed. Then I saw Jethroe blink. He hadn't done that at all since the guy in the chinos brought him in. He probably hadn't since they made him into a zombie.

He blinked again, and raised a hand, wonderingly, to touch his own face. "Where the hell am I?" he said in a voice dry as Death Valley. "What the hell happened to me?"

Eddie took a coffeepot off a can of canned heat. He poured a cup full and gave it to Jethroe. As he drank, I said, "Tell me your name."

"I'm Frank Jethroe," he answered. With his whistle wet, he sounded twenty years younger. He drank some more.

"Did you volunteer to become a zombie?" I asked him.

When he shook his head, the mechanism seemed rusty, but he said, "A zombie? Me? You out o' your ever-lovin' mind?"

I turned to Gerald Gallagher. "You see?" I said.

"I see," he said somberly. "We'll need to discuss an equitable settlement." I knew what he meant by that: a settlement that wouldn't cost O'Flannery and Muldoon too much and wouldn't leave them with their backside bare in the chilly breeze of bad publicity.

That could wait a little while. Frank Jethroe asked his plaintive questions again: "Where am I? What the hell happened?"

"What's the last thing you remember before you woke up here?" I answered his questions with one of my own.

"I had to take a leak," he said. "I was gonna go on home after my shift at the tire plant, only I had to take a leak. I went into the head"—five gets you ten he was in the Navy during the war—"an' I did what I needed to do, an' I was gonna go on out to the bus stop, an' this fella says, 'Hey, want a taste o' this?' an' held out a flask to me.

225

I coulda used me a snort. It was one o' *those* days. So I drank, an' it tasted kinda funny, an' ...." His voice trailed off.

"They shanghaied you," I said. "They turned you into a zombie, and you've spent most of the time since working on the Hollywood Freeway."

He looked disbelieving, then furious, then worried. "Is Clarice okay? How about the girls? How long I been doin' this?"

I told him. He gaped at me. I nodded. "I swear," I said, and held up my right hand as if taking an oath.

He was looking at his own hands. The palms weren't blistered; they were worn raw and bloody. The more he came back to himself, the more blood flowed in him and the bloodier they got. The way he screwed up his face said they hurt more and more, too. He had to work to turn his eyes back to me. "I'm so empty inside, reckon you're right," he said.

One of the guys in the tent came up to him with ointment, gauze, and adhesive tape. He bandaged those battered hands. I turned to Gallagher, who looked more than a little green. "Maybe you people shouldn't use zombies at all any more," I said.

"They don't feel it unless they come back, and that doesn't happen very often," he said.

"Does that make it better or worse?" I asked him. This time, he didn't answer.

Somebody in there gave Jethroe a sandwich and a thermos. Even more than the bandaging, that was a genuinely kind thing to do. He ate as if he'd never seen food before. Well, he hadn't, not for a long time.

Rob Grau was staring at him as if he'd invented him. In a way, he had. "I never did that before," he said to me. "I knew how, but it isn't real till you do it."

"You did great," I said. Glancing at Gallagher again, I added, "Maybe you'll be doing it a lot." Gallagher still didn't answer.

He did drive Grau and me and Jethroe back to the O'Flannery and Muldoon offices. When we got there, he found Jethroe a set of work clothes a man with an intact soul might use. They were nothing much, but a thousand times better than the rags he was wearing. Jethroe put them on in a bathroom. His face was damp when

226

TWICE AS DEAD

he came out, so he'd probably washed it with a wet paper towel or something. He might have done more if his hands weren't torn up.

"I can draw up some papers for you to sign …" Gallagher said.

I answered before Jethroe could: "Nobody's signing anything yet. We'll talk with a lawyer. Then we'll be in touch."

Gallagher looked unhappy. "Don't go to the papers till you know what kind of compensation we'll offer, okay?"

"For now," I said, to make him flinch. He didn't know I'd already tried to go to the papers, and they'd been scared to look at it? Good!

"Can I get on home now? That's all I want to do, go home." Frank Jethroe shook his head. "Dunno how I'll get in or what I'll do. Ain't got no wallet or nothin'."

"We'll manage," I said. I walked him over to the closest Red Line stop. A southbound trolley clanged up. We got on. While we rode, I filled him in on who I was and how I'd come looking for him. "Your wife is a pretty special gal," I finished.

"I sure think so." His face clouded. "Wish I could call her, let her know I'm … I'm me again. The cleanin' she does, though, I got no idea where she'll be at. Don't seem right. Kids'll come home from school, they won't expect me, neither."

"Everybody'll be glad to see you. That's what counts," I said.

I had some lockpicks in my pocket, but I turned out not to need them. The longer Jethroe was Jethroe, the better his brains worked. When we got to his house, we went into the back yard. He asked me to lift up one of the flowerpots on the fence between his place and a neighbor's. Then he grabbed the spare key hidden under it.

"We owe you more'n I know how to tell you," he said as he opened the back door. A second later, he yawned. "I wanna sleep for about a year." He laughed. "I was *dead*, near enough. Why do I wanna sleep?"

Because they worked you harder than they'd work even a slave. I didn't say it. He was no dope; he'd see it for himself. I did say, "I'll have my lawyer call you tonight. His name is Wally Baker. He'll bust his tail for you."

"He—?" Jethroe didn't go on, or have to. He smiled when I nodded. "All right. Obliged again." He went inside and closed the door. I headed back to the trolley stop.

227

He owed me more than he could tell me, he said. Whether that ever translated into any real money for me, I'd have to see. It would depend on how hard Wally could squeeze O'Flannery and Muldoon. He'd get a fair chunk of that dough himself, of course. He wasn't in it for his health, any more than anyone else was. But if that made him work harder, so much the better.

It was dark outside when I woke up. I could hear Dora moving around in the front room. That might have been what woke me. Or it might not. I'd had strange dreams. In the way of dreams, I didn't remember as much as I thought I should. What I did remember was bits and pieces, none of them connected.

Eyes. Beards. A stern scowl that made me think of "Ozymandias." You read it in school, too. You know. This bit:

Half sunk a shattered visage lies, whose frown
And wrinkled lip, and sneer of cold command
Tell that its sculptor well those passions read …

Only "Ozymandias" talks about ancient Egypt. Shelley didn't get that right, or else I was more confused than usual.

Before I could sort things out, Dora walked into the bedroom. "I thought I heard you stirring," she said. "Did things go well while I was … absent?"

"They did, yeah. Frank Jethroe is a live person again, and he's a live person who I think'll get quite a chunk of change from the people who used him while he was a zombie."

Dora was a silhouette to me. I couldn't see her expression. But she sounded wistful, or as wistful as a vampire's ever likely to, when she answered, "This is a possibility my kind does not have. We are as we are, with no going back, not ever."

"It's … easier for your folk now that there are blood banks and things," I said.

We'd talked about that before. Even so, I should've kept my big trap shut. I didn't help; I made things worse. "Is it … easier for your folk now that there are machines to do the things they were bought

228

and sold to do?" She made a nasty mimic. I hadn't heard her really mad before, either, but I sure did then.

I worked not to get mad myself. "It is easier, yeah. Not easy, but easier. Things are better now than they were when my great-greats were slaves. Not as good as they ought to be, but better. That's all I meant."

She could have thrown me out—either told me to hit the road, Jack, or picked me up and flung me out the door. She didn't. She stood there and thought for a few seconds. Then, grudgingly, she nodded. "Yes, that is fair, I admit," she said, and things between us were all right again. I can't think of many live people who could have switched gears like that.

"Tomorrow, I need to talk to Doctor Berkowitz up at County General. I'll give blood again while I'm there. You do what you can." I didn't tell her I'd passed out after I did it the last time.

"Ah?" She sat down on the edge of the bed. "It is good that you are willing to give your blood to vampires. It is very good. But do you want to give it to any hungry vampire or to one hungry vampire in particular? I am, you know. I was going to go out tonight to tend to that. If I do not need to go out ..."

And there it was. I'd wondered if it would come, and how it would if it did. I licked my lips. "Two things before I tell you to go ahead."

"Yes? And yes?"

"You won't ... accidentally take too much?"

Dora laughed. I'd been afraid I would make her angry again, but I tickled her funnybone instead. "If I took too much, it would not be by accident. I will take what the blood bank would, no more, no less. What is your other worry?"

"You won't make me into a vampire while you're drinking from me?"

This time, she didn't laugh. She'd never sounded so serious as she did when she answered, "I would never do that, never, not unless I knew you wanted it with all your heart and all your soul and all your might. Perhaps not then, either, not with you."

Either she meant it or she was lying. If I thought she'd lie about things like those, what the hell was I doing there? "Go ahead, then," the same way I would've said *Let's go, then* when we had to take some trenches in Italy.

And she did. She nuzzled my neck. She kissed my neck. Somewhere there, she bit my neck. I don't know exactly when. You know how a mosquito can get you and you don't feel it did till the next day? I think vampires do the same thing.

She's feeding from me, I thought. *I've made what she needs, and she's taking it.* Mothers who nurse their babies must think things like that while they're doing it. It's an amazing notion, when you get down to it—more intimate ... than anything, really.

(My mother fed me from a bottle. That was modern.)

She didn't need any longer than they would have at County General. When she finished, she licked the little punctures she'd made, and they stopped bleeding. I don't think a nurse at County General would have done that, but it sure worked.

"Thank you, Jack. You make me strong, and you taste very good," she said softly.

I hadn't done anything. I hadn't even got out of bed. I'd just lain there. "Any time," I said. I didn't feel like moving or doing anything. It wasn't just like when you smoke a cigarette afterwards, but it wasn't far from that, either.

She laughed again. "I will not ask you more often than the hospital would, I promise," she said. "Now, what can I give you to show you how grateful I am for what you have given me?"

I didn't answer; answering would have been doing something. But she already knew what she'd do. She slid down the bed, away from my neck, and started doing it. I wasn't sure I had enough blood left to get the most out of it, but I did. Oh, did I ever!

Afterwards, I went into the bathroom to clean up a little. Once I'd set myself to rights, I looked in the mirror. The marks on my neck were fresh, but they didn't look any bigger or deeper than any of the nips she'd given me while we made love. I don't know how that's possible, but I'm not a vampire.

When I came out, she said, "Now you should eat something. You need to build more blood."

"Okay," I answered, and made sure I didn't laugh out loud. What I wanted to tell her was *Yes, Mother*, but I couldn't, not after what she'd just done for me. To me? Take your pick.

TWICE AS DEAD

And I did eat something: a can of Dinty Moore beef stew, fresh off the hot plate. Tasted mighty good, too. Hit the spot, they say. That one hit the spot the way a thousand-pound bomb would have. After it hit, the spot was gone.

Dora watched me eat, something she didn't usually do. When she saw me watching her, she licked her lips, once. I didn't quite choke on a chunk of stewed potato, but I came close. Damn close.

Since I wouldn't be giving blood at County General, I called Izzy Berkowitz before I went up, to make sure it was okay. "C'mon," he said. "You can bend my ear, and maybe I'll bend yours, too."

I got there right around lunchtime. "You want to go to that Mexican place? They were good," I said. As I talked, I waved my hands at the wall of his office, to give the idea some sort of listening sorcery might be there.

He understood me right away. "Sure. I haven't been to El Burro Loco for a couple of weeks myself."

I ordered tacos stuffed with tongue. I love tongue when I can get it. He chose carnitas. "Isn't that ...?" I began.

"Pork?" he finished for me. Then he nodded. "Yep. I like it anyway. I like shrimp, too, and lobster. Cheeseburgers I can take or leave alone. You know what? If I eat stuff I like, the world probably won't end."

What was I supposed to say? That he'd burn in hell forever for doing something I thought was perfectly all right? He'd laugh at me. I'd laugh at myself. I said, "Ask you something?" instead.

"You were going to, right?" he said.

"Uh, yeah. That stuff the fylfot boys cooked up, the stuff it isn't smart to name, if somebody put some of that in a flask of—I dunno, bourbon, or maybe scotch—and lets somebody else have a good snort of it, what happens to the guy who doesn't know it's there with the hooch?"

Our food came then; El Burro Loco was *quick*. Berkowitz frowned as he focused in tighter on me. "You aren't making up a hypothetical case." It wasn't a question. I took a bite from a *taco de lengua*. It was damn good. He stayed focused. "That's interesting. That's mighty interesting. As far as I know, nobody's tried to mix it

231

with alcohol. Of course, I don't know how far I know, because I don't know how much the people who work with that stuff are publishing."

"Okay." I respected his caution. "Take the hooch out of the picture, then. Suppose you slip somebody a dose in water and he doesn't know it. How does he act?"

He chewed a bite of his taco, then swallowed and said, "It's supposed to taste horrible." I just looked at him. He pushed at the air with both hands: an apology of sorts. After that, he went on, "If it's a big enough dose to be effective, what happens is this …." He stared at me. He didn't move. He didn't even blink. That gave me the creeps, the same as it had with Frank Jethroe.

"If you're drugged like that, could the fellow who did it to you take you to a zombie dealer and get you unsouled? Would you be able to do anything to stop him? Would you have enough gas in the tank to sign the papers?"

Before he answered, he finished his first taco and ate some of the rice and beans that came with the order. "You do find interesting questions," he answered. "I'd say the answer to the first and third is probably yes; to the second, probably no. You wouldn't be running on all cylinders, but on some."

"If you were running on all cylinders, you'd clobber anybody who wanted to turn you into a zombie with a crowbar," I said. Izzy Berkowitz didn't try to tell me I was wrong. I thought about the schoolboy printing on the forms Jethroe'd filled out. And I thought about the people at PERSONAL ASSISTANCE, PERSONAL ASSISTANTS. They'd known. They'd let it happen anyway. Nothing good deserved to happen to them.

"Is it anything you can talk to the police about?" the doctor asked.

"You met Sergeant Jackson," I said. He twisted up his mouth and gave back a sour nod. I went on, "But he's in trouble now, and so are some of the people who told him what to do and looked the other way when he did it. Things there may get a little better."

"Or they may not," he answered. "I saw this morning that the cop who blew the whistle on Jackson and the higher-ups is facing burglary charges himself."

"Is he? Happy day!" I wished I could've sounded surprised, but I wasn't. You try to take down Los Angeles policemen and they'll hit

TWICE AS DEAD

back with everything they've got. And they've been so crooked for so long, they've got a lot.

"I wish we had honest cops. This place would be a lot nicer to live in if we did," Dr. Berkowitz said.

Wish for the moon while you're at it, I thought. I didn't say that. Instead, I asked him, "How easy is it for people who shouldn't have that stuff to get hold of it?"

"Easier than it ought to be. The fylfot boys never should've made it to begin with—it didn't do what they wanted. I think we started fooling around with it to see if we could make it do what they wanted. Gotta keep an edge on the Reds, you know." Berkowitz sounded as disgusted as he looked.

If I ran with the *Are you now or have you ever been?* crowd, I could've landed him in trouble. But I ran from those people, not with them. Only fair to let him know it: "Of course, the Reds didn't catch any fylfot boys of their own. They aren't working on anything like that stuff themselves."

"That's pretty funny. Tell me another one, why don't you?" Berkowitz got to his feet. We were both done. He set a buck and a quarter on the table. That was plenty for both lunches and a nice tip. I tried to take the tab myself, but he got hard of listening. So I thanked him and we walked out.

"Y'know," I said as we went back toward the blood bank, "we aren't a hundred percent fubar'd, but some days I swear we're doing our best to get there."

"You and me both, man. You and me both," he said. Then he asked, "You ever find that vampire you were looking for? Sebestyen, that's what his name was."

"Still looking," I admitted.

"Ah. I just wonder—I couldn't help noticing you've been hanging around with a vampire."

Hanging around with was a polite way to say *screwing*. He was a doctor. Not only that, he was a doctor who worked with blood. Of course he'd notice the marks on my neck. Of course he'd understand what they meant. "What if I am?" I said.

He held up a hand. "No skin off my nose. I wouldn't care if one wanted to marry your sister. Or my sister."

233

I believed him. He might have a carrot top, but he didn't try to hit you over the head with how white he was. Well, he was a Jew. The white folks who did that kind of stuff probably did it to him, too. I said, "I don't have a sister. If I did, I wouldn't want her marrying Sebestyen."

"Oh, neither would I. But it's not because he's a vampire. It's because he's a schmuck."

"Can't say you're wrong. I still want to find out what happened to him, though." Schmuck was a good name for Rudolf Sebestyen, or for anybody else who might want to rob a blood bank.

When I got down to the office, the zombie janitor was policing up the alley behind the building in his usual slow motion. I wondered how he'd wound up the way he had, and how real his paper trail was. I couldn't very well ask him. And it wasn't as if I didn't have other things to think about.

After a week had gone by, I called Wally Baker. He wasn't one of those hotshot lawyers who were part of a big outfit like Dewey, Beagle & Howe. He was more like me: a guy doing a job by himself. Like me, he didn't even have a secretary, just an answering service. When he was in the office, he picked up the phone himself.

"Offices of the Baker Firm," he said, the way he always did.

"What do you know, Baker Firm? This is Jack Mitchell."

"Jack!" He sounded glad to hear from me, which was nice. He had his reasons, too. "I'll buy you dinner for telling me to call the Jethroes. Frank's gonna come into a nice little chunk o' change—you better believe he is. O'Flannery and Muldoon, they don't want that story comin' out. And a quarter of what they pay Jethroe, guess whose pocket that goes into."

"Good for you," I said, and more or less meant it. Yeah, Wally liked money. Well, who doesn't? He liked spending money, though, I mean, and didn't make any bones about it. In the old days, he would've sold his sword to whomever paid him most. He does it with his shingle now.

He did think about me, enough to ask, "You'll get your slice of the pie, too, right?"

"Fees and expenses, sure."

"Fees and expenses?" He sounded as if we weren't talking the same language. I guess we weren't, because he went on, "Never mind the chicken feed, son. You got a piece of the settlement money, too, don't you?"

"Nope. I never even worried about it."

"Oh. My. Goodness," he said, just like that, and then, "Bless your heart!" It was the nicest way I've ever been called an imbecile, no doubt about it.

"Never mind that. Once you make this deal for Jethroe, he doesn't tell his story to anybody. O'Flannery and Muldoon are out some money, but they don't get in trouble for leasing him out from the shady zombie dealers. That's how it works, huh?"

"That's how it works," Wally agreed. "They're making the deal to keep Jethroe from going to court and putting it on the record."

"So nothing really happens to them."

"Don't say nothing. Money isn't nothing to a company. They wouldn't be willing to give him a dime if they weren't scared of what'd happen if they said no."

"Nothing really happens to them," I repeated. "And nothing happens to the zombie dealer they got Jethroe from. And nothing happens to the bastards at US Rubber who took him to the dealer and got him turned into a zombie. Does any of that sound fair to you?"

Wally didn't answer right away. When he did, he said, "I don't worry much about what's fair. I worry about what's possible." For a Negro lawyer working in a white man's world, that's a sensible attitude. But he hadn't finished. He went on, "I've known you a while now, Jack. As your attorney, I strongly advise you not to do anything stupid. Anything at all. You hear me?"

"Of course I hear you."

"But are you listening to your Uncle Wally?"

"What?"

I made him laugh. Then, without heat, he said, "Damn you, it isn't funny."

"I never said it was. What happened to Jethroe's no joke, either. If I didn't get lucky, he'd still be out there building the goddamn Hollywood Freeway. He'd have no more idea who he is than my desk chair does. And his wife and kids'd maybe never know what happened to him."

235

"Every word of that's true. What can you do about it all by your lonesome?" Wally had a knack for asking questions you didn't want to answer. He wouldn't have been such a good lawyer without it.

"Who knows?" I said. I wasn't in court. I wasn't under oath. He couldn't pin me down like a butterfly on display in a collection. We both hung up. I don't know which of us was more relieved.

After that, I called Izzy Berkowitz. I told him about some of the things that had been going through my head since the last time we talked. He said, "That all fits together better than I wish it did. What do you want to do about it?"

I told him that, too. Quickly, I added, "I'm not asking you to do anything. It isn't your problem."

"Like hell it isn't. What helps the bad guys most is when the good guys sit on their hands. That's how the fylfot boys got to be what they were."

"Okay. Thanks. You're a mensch, you know?" One more word I got from Al Harris. I wonder if he says ofay these days. I went on, "Let me have your home phone number, too, mensch, so we can talk whenever we need to."

He gave it to me. That by itself would've told me he took the whole megillah seriously. Megillah? Al has a way of rubbing off.

Once we'd said our goodbyes, I made one more call. I didn't know whether Rob Grau would want to talk to me. After all, O'Flannery and Muldoon paid his salary. But he'd done solid work summoning Frank Jethroe's soul back to his body. And that was what I was interested in talking about.

"Jack! Good to hear from you! What's on your mind?" he said after I got put through to him. I wasn't The Enemy because I'd exposed something nasty his company was doing, anyhow. That seemed promising.

So I said, "When you were working there in the tent, did you notice anything peculiar about putting Frank Jethroe's pieces together again?"

"It was harder than I thought it would be," he answered at once. "Something didn't want to turn him loose, something I wasn't looking for. I've never seen anything like it mentioned in the grimoires."

"I think I know what it was."

TWICE AS DEAD

"I didn't think you were a wizard." By the way Grau said that, I was sure he'd had too many people who didn't know the first thing about sorcery tell him how to do his job. That would be part of what he got, along with the steady paycheck, for working at a place like O'Flannery and Muldoon.

"I'm not, but I think I've run into stuff like this before." I told him where and when. "If you figure I'm full of it, tell me so," I finished.

"Huh," he said thoughtfully. "That … may be possible. It matches some of what I saw, or imagined I saw, while I was working the spell. I've had some odd dreams since, too, dreams I didn't want. How about you?"

"You'd best believe it."

"Isn't that interesting?" He whistled tunelessly for a few seconds. "Okay, whatever you've got in mind, deal me in. Don't start right away, though. Give me a little time to do the kind of homework I need first. All right?"

"However you want it, you got it," I answered. I was grinning when I set the phone in the cradle. Too many things look easy beforehand but turn out not to be.

XVI

Dora and I sat in the office waiting. Old Man Mose had got used to her to the point where he didn't always dive under the sofa when she came in. Sometimes he stayed up on it and insulted her. Today, for instance, he'd greeted her with, "Think you're pretty hot stuff, don't you, when you can only come out at night?"

She'd looked through him, not at him. "Dogs say, 'People feed us and take care of us. They must be gods!' Cats say, 'People feed us and take care of us. *We* must be gods!'"

"Some people have thought so," Mose said smugly.

"Some people are fools," Dora replied. Old Man Mose licked himself in an indelicate place to show what he thought of that.

Before they could go on squabbling, somebody else knocked on the door. The cat did disappear then; strangers were liable to have cooking up a feline fricassee in mind. "It isn't locked," I said.

In came Dr. Berkowitz. He took Dora in stride. For one thing, he'd already noticed the marks on my neck. For another, he dealt with vampires at the blood bank all the time. In fact, he said, "We've met once or twice, haven't we?"

"I believe we have, Doctor, yes," she answered. I wondered how Old World her attitudes about Jews were, and never mind the ones who kept an eye on Vampire Village from sunrise to sunset.

TWICE AS DEAD

Whatever she was thinking, she didn't show it. That's all that matters, as far as I'm concerned. White people who spot what I am are welcome to hate me as much as they want. When they let me know they hate me, that's when we start having trouble.

Five minutes later, we got another knock. "C'mon in," I said, expecting Rob Grau. And come in he did. I hadn't expected him to have company, though. His companion was a short, thin, swarthy woman with gray hair. She was darker than I am, in fact, but her features would make people who cared about things like that call her white.

"This is Maryam Tuama," Rob said. "She's a curator in historical thaumaturgy at the County Museum of Natural and Unnatural History. We've known each other a long time."

I introduced myself, then Dora and the doctor. "Very pleased to meet you all," the scholar said. I was pleased to meet her, too. If she knew the kinds of things I hoped she did, she might end up saving our necks.

Izzy Berkowitz had an old Ford. "We'll all fit if we're friendly," he said.

"If crowding is a trouble, I can fly down and meet you there," Dora said.

"I brought Maryam in my Buick," Rob said. "It'll hold us fine."

He was right. It wasn't as fancy as Gallagher's Cadillac, but it was just as big. Rob and Maryam sat up front, the rest of us in back. Rob put it in gear, and away we went. We got where we were going faster than we would have on the Red Line, I will say that. And a car would be better if we needed a quick getaway.

Rob parked across the street from the US Rubber factory, in a lot that belonged to a restaurant already closed for the night. The tire factory wasn't closed. I don't think it ever closed. During the war, people had had to make do with the tires they already had. New rubber went to the Army. The plants had been working around the clock even after since peace broke out, trying to catch up.

I felt eyes on me before we got halfway across Scrying Crystal Road. I wasn't the only one, either. "Hel-lo!" Grau said. "This place is alive! It sure isn't dead, anyway."

"This building ..." Maryam Tuama shook her head. "I knew of it, of course, but I never saw it till now. I never wanted to. I never

239

dared to. It is not of our time. I wonder if the men who made it had any idea what they were doing. Did they believe they were only ornamenting it when they built it so? Or were the old gods, the old demons, whispering in their ears back then?"

Even Dora seemed sobered. "This is old and dark and bloody, more so than anything I knew on the far side of the ocean. Older, darker, bloodier than I dreamed anything in this land could be."

"This is not of California, not of America," Maryam said. "I was born in Mosul. This is from not far from there. From Nineveh or from Asshur. From Asshur, I think. It feels more ancient than Nineveh, and yes, darker."

We stepped up onto the sidewalk on the factory side of the street. "Can we do what we want to do?" I asked. "Or do we start yelling for a Special Wizardry Assault Team or for the Army?"

"How long will that take? How much money will US Rubber spend to convince important people we're talking nonsense? How many lawyers will they throw at us, either on their own or because those *things* still have hold of them?" Dr. Berkowitz said.

Those were all good questions. But so was mine. What happened if the Assyrian things got us, not the other way around? I'd asked myself questions like that as we ground our way up the Italian boot. The best answer I'd found was *Somebody else will take care of it if I can't.* It wasn't great, but it kept me going. My guess is, the fylfot boys felt the same way while we were grinding them down. They sure didn't show much quit, not till the very end.

"Let's give it a shot," Rob Grau said. Nobody told him he was nuts, so we went forward instead of turning around and driving home.

Streetlights and factory lights shone on us bright as the sun. Those winged, bearded figures on the walls would've known we were there any which way. But I didn't want us to be so obvious to anybody going in or just passing by. I longed for something like the tarncapes the Lightning Rune soldiers had used to hide themselves in plain sight.

When I said so, Rob's laugh was as harsh as a fiddle bow scraping strings instead of playing. "Jack, it won't matter much," he said. "If we can't do this fast, we can't do it at all." I remembered that from Italy, too, much too well.

TWICE AS DEAD

Maryam Tuama was already chanting in a harsh language full of odd vowels and guttural consonants. Dr. Berkowitz looked intensely interested. "I feel like somebody who speaks Spanish hearing Latin for the first time," he said. "Every now and then a word makes sense, but most of it just zips over my head."

Rob pointed at one of the things on the factory wall. "Come forth!" he cried, and made the kind of pass a bullfighter would have envied.

"Is this a good idea?" Dora Urban asked. I didn't *think* she was reading my mind, but I sure had the same thought.

Whether it was a good idea or not, our sorcerer got what he wanted and then some. All the things on the walls—not just the one he'd pointed at—stepped off them and went from low reliefs to full three-dimensional beings. Only ghost images of where they'd been were left. They all started coming towards us, too. Since they were three or four times as tall as we were, they came mighty goddamn fast.

They weren't reliefs any more, no. Me, I wasn't what you'd call relieved, either.

But the curator from the County Museum was ready for them, even if I wasn't. She and Rob must have been practicing together, because she shouted in that fierce language at the same time as he made another virtuoso pass. And then the creatures with the beards and the wings and the commanding features had more things than us to worry about.

The narrow lawn in front of the factory wasn't made for the sudden apparition of supernatural beings. Believe me, it wasn't. The creatures that had escaped from the walls or been turned loose by Rob Grau's first spell left the biggest, deepest damn footprints I'd ever seen. So did the heroes and lions Rob and Maryam summoned to oppose them.

I think the heroes were holding on to the lions when they all first appeared together. Holding them the way I'd hold Old Man Mose, I mean—they were as overgrown as their opponents. I'm not sure, though. Things were happening fast, the way they do in combat. The heroes had the same curly beards and the same strong-prowed features as the god-things, too. This wasn't a new enmity, is what I'm saying. Maryam might be able to tell you exactly how far back it went. I can't even begin to guess.

241

If the lions had gone for us, I wouldn't be here to spin out this yarn. They were the heroes' hunting hounds, though. They attacked the winged things off the wall as if there were no tomorrow. Faster than I know how to tell you, almost all the winged creatures were down, with the lions snacking on their carcasses and the heroes sticking swords into them to make sure they *were* carcasses.

One, though, one ran along Scrying Crystal Road with a hero and a couple of lions in hot pursuit. He squashed a couple of parked cars and made power lines spark when he plowed through them. I wondered what the hell the Sheriff's Department would do if he got away.

Dora touched my arm. "Look," she said, and pointed toward the factory.

I looked. The ghost images of the winged, bearded creatures had disappeared as they perished, leaving the stonework as flat and blank as if it had never been carved at all. I wondered what old photographs of the place would show, and whether brochures and magazine articles from bygone days were rewriting themselves to reflect revised reality.

Those ghost images had disappeared, yes—all save one. The one who was still on his enormous feet and trying to get away? No sooner had that thought crossed my mind than Maryam Tuama scampered across the torn-up lawn toward that image. She took from her handbag something I couldn't make out. Later, Dora told me it was an old-fashioned lady's hatpin. Whatever it was, Maryam jabbed it into the ghost image's left foot.

The creature with wings and beard that was still trying to get away let out a shriek of pain that almost deafened me, even though it had run a hell of a long way down the street. It grabbed at its left foot as if something had stabbed it. Then the hero and the lions caught it, and that was the end of that.

That was the end of that in more ways than one, in fact. The last ghost image still on the wall gave up the ghost and vanished.

A bell started clanging inside the factory building. Or maybe it had been going for a while, and I only noticed it just then because so much other stuff was happening at the same time.

Maryam bit her lip. "Now we see how many so-called modern men, modern but long steeped in Assyrian savagery and blood lust, will come forth to seek their vengeance against us."

TWICE AS DEAD

"We do what we can," Rob Grau said. "That's all we can do."

But nobody came out of the factory. Instead, over five minutes or so, half a dozen ambulances with flashing lights and screaming sirens pulled up in front of the place. People jumped out of them and rushed into the buildings. Some were carrying doctors' bags, some wizards' carpetbags, and some—the enlisted men, you might say—had stretchers.

I'd thought about tarncapes not long before. We might as well have been wearing them after all. None of the people from the ambulances seemed to notice we were there. Nobody looked at us. Nobody paid us the least attention. Even stranger, nobody seemed to see the carnage on the lawn. I'd thought that would draw a double take from a zombie, but no.

Before long, they started bringing people out. One of those people looked familiar, not least because his hair was as red as Dr. Berkowitz's. Where had I seen him before? In the diner across the street while I was trying to find out what happened to Frank Jethroe?

Then I remembered who he was. Pat Brannegan, that was his name. Babs had called him out to the reception hall for me. He'd been Frank's boss. Was he somehow involved with how the guy who'd worked on his line had wound up a mindless, soulless laborer building a freeway for O'Flannery and Muldoon? That was how it looked to me.

The doctors and sorcerers and medics made two or three trips in and out. They didn't spot us or the chaos we'd caused on any of them. Maybe that had to do with the way the factory walls didn't show the winged, bearded creatures any more. Or maybe I didn't have the slightest idea what the hell was going on.

They brought out enough people to stuff the ambulances the way you stuff sausage meat into skins: till they bulged. One of the last men they hauled out, a bald guy with a gray fringe who was wearing what to my eye looked like a Savile Row suit, kept groaning, "Vepratoga! For God's sake give me vepratoga!"

That was interesting. I wondered if it would fetch the LAPD, or if everybody monitoring that net of sorcerous snoopery was either behind bars or out on bail. With luck, we'd be gone before I could find out.

243

I asked Dora, "You all right?" Vampires and the Lord's name can mix like water and sodium.

But she gave me a nod, if a shaky one. "Yes, thank you, for the most part. It was not aimed at me."

One after another, the ambulances sped off into the night. Their sirens dopplered off into the distance. Then I realized those weren't the only sirens I was hearing. The others sounded more like fire engines. They didn't seem to be heading straight for the US Rubber factory. They weren't that far away, though. I pointed southwest. "Is something burning over there?"

"Yes." Dora sounded certain.

I believed her. She saw better at night than I did, or than any live person could. A couple of heartbeats later, something else occurred to me. "Isn't that about where …?"

"Yes," she said again.

If everything went well at the plant, we'd planned on visiting PERSONAL ASSISTANCE, PERSONAL ASSISTANTS next. Now maybe we wouldn't have to. Was that a coincidence? Was there any such thing as a coincidence? The deeper I got into this whole knotted-up business, the more I doubted it.

Since we didn't know for sure, we all piled into Rob's Buick to find out. He'd turned on to Jellison when Dora and I said the same thing at the same time: "That is the place."

Rob parked the car. We got out and walked toward the blaze as if we were a handful of ordinary rubberneckers.

"It burns very hard," Maryam Tuama said.

It did. It had the kind of red, red, *red* glare I'd seen a few times during the war and then again, not so long ago, when my apartment building went up in flames. Dora recognized it, too. As we had a minute or two before, we spoke together: "Salamander."

Izzy Berkowitz whistled softly. "Somebody doesn't *like* those people."

He wasn't wrong. All the same, I said, "Somebody doesn't give a damn about all the zombies they had in their storeroom there. And somebody is probably real happy all their files are gone for good."

Dora made a small, stricken sound. "Rudolf's records! If he was made into a zombie there, how will we ever find out what became of him?"

TWICE AS DEAD

Chances were, we wouldn't. From everything I'd heard, she was the only one in the whole wide world who cared at all about the vampire she called her half brother. From everything I'd heard, Sebestyen didn't deserve to have even one person caring about him even a little bit.

A red car with a flashing light on top shot past us, heading toward the blaze. The door had crossed torches on it, painted in gold. If the County Fire Department used the same heraldry as the Army, that was the mark of their Pyromancy Squad. They didn't think the zombie dealership was going up in smoke by accident, either.

Nothing we could do there, so we went back to the Buick. Rob drove up to Scrying Crystal Road, then turned left to take us back to our own part of the urban sprawl. When we went past the US Rubber factory, we all exclaimed. The walls had lost their reliefs, yes, but every trace of the wild rumpus that went with that had also disappeared. I wondered how long we'd be able to go on remembering it.

Almost every trace, I should say. The cars that last fleeing creature had stomped on were still squished, even though the creature itself was as one with Nineveh and Asshur. What would their owners think when they saw them? What would their auto-insurance companies think?

When Rob stopped in front of my office, I said, "I've got most of a bottle in one of my desk drawers, if anybody's interested. Matter of fact, I've got it even if nobody's interested."

Nobody said no. The office was jammed with all of us in there. I sat in my chair. Dora, Maryam, and Rob sat on the sofa. Izzy perched on my desk. "Only a little bit," he said when I passed him the bottle. "I have to make it home in one piece." And the nip he took was a small one.

"Same here," Grau said. "Doggone it." He went easy, too.

So did my undead lady friend. Bourbon wasn't her tipple of choice, as who had better reason to know than I did? That left more for Maryam and me. No matter what I drank, it didn't hit me very hard. I'd seen that after bad times in Italy, too. Fear and excitement burn away the booze before it can bite.

"We did it. We really did it," I said. Even in my own ears, I sounded as if I had trouble believing it, mostly because I did.

245

Among us, we killed the bottle. Izzy Berkowitz took off. So did Rob and the museum curator. After they left, Old Man Mose came out from under the couch. "You people are crazy. I almost got squashed under there," he said.

"We'll do better next time," I told him. He could take that any way he pleased.

When Dora and I walked back to her place, I had to pay attention to where I put my feet, so maybe the Wild Turkey got to me after all. It didn't bother her. We were almost there when she said, "I wonder what the newspapers will make of what happened at the factory."

That hadn't occurred to me. "We'll find out," I said brilliantly. The bourbon must have been helping me think, too.

I had breakfast about two that afternoon: coffee and canned corned-beef hash. The hash was quick and easy and cheap. It didn't taste too bad, even without a sunny-side-up egg on top. And it spackled over the empty I woke up with.

That done, I headed for the office. On my way, I gave a short-pants kid a dime for a *Mirror*. I sold papers when I was a kid. There weren't so many machines then. And he was browner than I am, so the odds against him were steeper. The *Mirror* cost a nickel, but I didn't wait for change.

"Thanks, Mister!" he squeaked after me. I waved and kept on.

The story I wanted didn't make the front page, so I had to wait till I was at my desk to find it. It was on page four, and I had to start reading it before I could be sure it was the right one. The headline read "Food Poisoning Sickens 13 at Tire Plant." Food poisoning? Was that what they were calling it?

That's what the story said. If you believed what you read in the newspaper, that was why those ambulances showed up there. Floor supervisor Patrick Brannegan and senior vice president Wilbert Swindell were said to be in especially serious condition. Was Swindell the fellow who'd been groaning for vepratoga? Not a word about their trying to swallow a big dose of ancient Assyrian wizardry.

The story did note, "Two cars in the area were also mysteriously vandalized. Both seem to have been crushed from above. A sher-

TWICE AS DEAD

iff's spokesperson declined to speculate on how this might have happened." No hint that that might be connected to the food poisoning that wasn't food poisoning.

For that matter, no hint that it was related to the fire at the zombie dealership. The fire got its own little story, on page seven: "Arson Suspected in Business Blaze." The squib mentioned arson, yeah, but said nary a word about a salamander. And it talked around what kind of business had burned, the way it would have with a cathouse.

If you don't look at the horrid thing, it isn't really there, right? Right.

Nobody had looked at us, which was good. I thought so, anyhow, till the phone rang a few minutes later. When I answered it, the woman on the other end of the line said, "I have Mister Victor Howe here. He wishes to speak with you, Mister Mitchell."

"Put him through," I said, even though I was a long way from sure I wanted to talk to US Rubber's boss lawyer.

"That you, Mitchell?" Howe growled after a couple of telephone clicks.

"Yes, unless your secretary dialed the wrong number," I answered.

He paused. He grunted. "That's right. You're a funny man. Heh. I don't know what you did last night, Mitchell, but it opened some eyes."

"I don't know what you're talking about. Do you mean US Rubber?"

"I'm not likely to mean anything else."

"I just saw the story in the paper a little while ago," I said, which was true. "If you think I can arrange food poisoning on cue, you're crazier than I gave you credit for." That was also true. Put 'em all together, though, and they spelled *misleading*.

Except Howe wasn't misled. The way he said "Food poisoning!" told me my friends and I weren't the only ones who remembered what the US Rubber factory used to look like. He went on, "You know damn well that isn't what was going on."

"Who told you? Was it—what did the newspaper say his name was?—Swindell? Uh, Wilbert Swindell?" I did my best to show him I was looking at the *Mirror* story. I was, too, but I remembered the name without checking.

"Funny man," Howe said again. "You aren't half so funny as you think you are, funny man. Will Swindell and I have been friends for more than twenty years."

247

You deserve each other. I thought it, but I didn't say it. *Was that before or after he started messing around with Assyrian demons?* I swallowed that, too. I was a good boy ... till all of a sudden I wasn't. I couldn't help asking, "Did he find the stuff he wanted so much?"

A short silence stretched into a long one. At last, Howe said, "I don't know what you're talking about." I know he was a lawyer, but I've sure heard lawyers who made better liars.

"Okay, fine. Ask him next time you talk, then." I know I sounded tired. Hell, I was tired. I added, "Oh, by the way, the guy I was looking for who worked for US Rubber, I found him. Somebody there drugged him and had him made into a zombie. In case you hadn't heard, I mean."

"I am aware of the allegation, yes," Howe answered. "Naturally, as the legal representative of the company and of the fine, upstanding men and women it employs, I deny that the claim has any basis in fact."

"Naturally." Oh, boy, was I tired. One of the things I was tired of was lawyers who kept on lying in spite of everything. When folks from down South talk, one of the things they do is make *lawyers* and *liars* sound the same. Damned if they don't have something there.

"Good day, Mister Mitchell." Victor Howe hung up on me. He'd done it before. If we had to talk to each other some more, I figured he'd do it again. Or I'd do it to him. We hadn't quite taken to each other. No, not quite.

I hoped Wally Baker would squeeze O'Flannery and Muldoon and US Rubber till their corporate eyeballs popped. That was mostly because Frank Jethroe deserved every dime he could get, and ten times more besides. And—I won't turn myself into a liar or lawyer here—I wouldn't have minded at all if I saw a little of the money that fell out of the sky for him.

Of course, the people who really deserved to pay Jethroe piles of loot were the sons of bitches who'd run PERSONAL ASSISTANCE, PERSONAL ASSISTANTS. Zombie dealers are bad enough any old time. When they're zombie dealers mixed up with those ancient Assyrian *things* ...

I wondered whether the dealers and wizards who'd worked at that joint were still able to look down at the grass. As opposed to looking up at it, I mean. If they just happened to be in with the zombies when the salamander did its bit, how would anybody sort out what was left of them from what was left of their clients?

Oh, I suppose a forensic necromancer might be able to use the laws of similarity and contagion to establish whether they'd been there. A good one, a really, really good one, because the dealers' presence would have been in that room whether they were there when it went up in flames or not. The other thing I wondered was whether anybody would have the will to make that kind of investigation. Dead men tell no tales, which is why some men wind up dead.

I looked at Old Man Mose. "How come Siameses and tabbies don't fight each other all the time, or Persians start a war against Russian Blues?"

His yawn showed off those needle teeth. "How come you think we're stupid like people?"

Well, he had me there. Cats are stupid all kinds of ways. A lot of those ways make us laugh, which helps keep us from going after cats with shotguns more often. But cats *aren't* stupid like people.

Saturday night. Central Avenue was cooking, let me tell you. Dora and I did our best to add to the shine, if that's how you want to put it. I still hadn't got many glad rags to replace the ones that burned in my apartment, but it didn't matter as long as she was on my arm.

She looked so good, I didn't even have to tip the maître d' at the Hotel Dunbar to get into the show. So much good music, all on that one block—the Dunbar, Club Alabam, the Last Word, other joints, too. But I wasn't going anywhere else then, not for anything. Lady Day was there. No chance I'd miss that, not if I could get in.

Yes, she'd had her troubles. Yes, she drank like a fish. Yes, she was a junkie with a monkey the size of a gorilla on her back. I knew all that. Anybody who paid the least little attention to the world couldn't help knowing it. But dear sweet Jesus God, she could sing.

When she came out, she said, "I got some old stuff for you, an' I got some new stuff, too."

If you think I didn't bang my palms together when I heard that, you better think again. Some people don't like anything but what they already know. I'm not like that. I don't understand those folks. If they only like the old stuff, how'd they ever listen to anything to begin with?

Before she sang "Strange Fruit," she waved the room to quiet. Some of us knew what that meant. The ones who didn't found out. She wanted that number *heard*. The only light in the place was a tight spot on her face. It got tighter and tighter and dimmer and dimmer, and went out when the song ended. For fifteen seconds, maybe half a minute, the place was as dark as the tomb, and as silent.

Then the lights came up. The cheers came with them, and damn near—*damn* near—tore off the roof. "Strange Fruit" hit too close to home for too many people in there.

"She knows pain," Dora said, in the tones of a connoisseur. Which she was, I suppose. But Lady Day was a Negro woman born in the United States. How could she *not* know pain? And she was a genius, which let her show other people what hurt and why.

I'll tell you something else, too, something I didn't know then. The fellow who wrote that song billed himself as Lewis Allan. For years, I thought he had to be a black man. Nope. His real name was Abel Meeropol. His folks were Jews who got out of Russia. You never can tell.

And Abel raised some Cain, yes he did. He likely had people who got hanged from trees in his family, too. The shit end of the stick is the shit end of the stick, no matter who gets hit with it. He made the world see that.

Which is its own kind of genius, I suppose.

I wondered what Lady Day could possibly go on with. She waited a minute, till things calmed down some. Then she said, "I don't reckon you'll have heard this one before. I call it 'The Vepratoga Blues.'"

Dora and I stared at each other. One of her sidemen set down the viola he'd been playing till then. He picked up an electric guitar. The jagged chords he struck from it couldn't have come from any other instrument on earth. That voice couldn't have come from any other throat.

"I've used horse, and it's a gas," Lady Day sang, "but the happy, it just leaves too fast. I've tried coke—now coke's okay—but the happy, it just goes away. I've smoked reefer and guzzled booze. Got me now them vepratoga blues."

She went on from there. If you look at it a certain way, she didn't say anything I hadn't heard from Dr. Berkowitz the first time we had lunch at that tiny Mexican place near County General. But Izzy was talking to my brain. Lady Day went after my heart and my guts and my balls. And what Lady Day went after, she got.

A gal at the table table next to the one where Dora and I were sitting turned to her boyfriend and asked, "What's that stuff she's singin' about?"

He shrugged. They were both years younger than I am, even if he'd grown himself a thin little mustache. "I dunno. Some kind o' dope," he said, which wasn't wrong but wasn't helpful, either.

The hand she got wasn't as big as the one she thought she rated. You could tell. Probably more than half the people in the room were like the couple by us: they didn't know what she was talking about. If you did, though …. If you did, oh, my.

Again, I wondered if the LAPD would come down on the Dunbar and haul away everybody who'd heard Lady Day sing the secret word. The cops stayed away. With so many of their big wheels in trouble for this, that, or the other, they were in disarray themselves.

She cut her set short. I wasn't the only one who noticed; there was grumbling when they started clearing the house. I wondered if she was miffed because the new stuff hadn't gone over the way she wanted. I'd heard she had a temper. Of course, you hear that about four musicians out of five. Maybe this time it was true.

As we spilled out onto Central, I asked Dora, "Want to see what's going on at Deacon's?" She nodded, so we went on over there and worked our way forward along the boardwalk.

Deacon Washington smiled when he took our cover charge. "You're in luck. I've got something special for folks tonight," he told me. That big, deep, rich voice sounded as if it should've been pouring out of a radio speaker, same as always.

We found places to sit and ordered drinks. Acolyte Adams glided by, so we said hello. The house combo played background music. Jonas Schmitt was back on piano. Maybe the cat with the konk drank too damn much to stick. I decided I wasn't going to let

Schmitt chase me out this time. The Deacon didn't say special unless he meant *special*.

And I didn't see Marianne Smalls there. Didn't miss her, either. I was still a long way from proud of that little bit of business, no matter how well it paid.

Some lights went up. Some went down. The gauzy curtains swung and shifted so most people got a better view of the stage. Deacon Washington seemed to materialize there. Even though he was a great big man, he had that gift for popping out of nowhere.

"Hello, friends!" he boomed. "Hello!" No mike, but he boomed anyway. "It is a privilege, a great, great privilege, for me to be able to tell you my little place here has been honored by a visit from the one, the only, the sublime—Lady Day!"

This gig had to be part of the reason she'd clipped her appearance at the Dunbar. She'd come straight over; she was still wearing the same green silk dress she'd had on there. I don't know how many times she'd played the hotel. Not a few, I'm sure. She seemed more at home here, though.

She did more new things at Deacon's. The only old ones I remember were "Strange Fruit" and "God Bless the Child." Dora listened to that without flinching much—as before, it wasn't aimed at her. This time, "The Vepratoga Blues" tore up the place. Well, it deserved to. I don't think she sang it any better than she had at the Dunbar. She just had a better crowd.

After she took her bows and went offstage, Deacon Washington brought her over and introduced Dora and me to her. I stammered like a kid; I'd never met royalty before. She had a big tumbler full of whiskey and a bit of ice, but she was royalty anyhow. And she could be gracious as a queen when it suited her—and when she wasn't loaded.

She wasn't now, or wasn't yet. "The Deacon says you know about vepratoga," she said to me.

"About it, a little. I know some people who've had trouble with it," I answered. "Never tried it myself, though."

"Oh." That made her lose interest in me in a hurry. She swung toward Dora. "How about you, sweetheart?" I wondered how she meant that. If you kept your ear to the ground, you heard things about her switch-hitting.

Evenly, Dora replied, "One of the people Jack talked about is my half brother."

"Oh," Lady Day said again. "I like the stuff myself." She went off to find someone else to talk with. And that was my brush with fame.

Dora and I looked at each other. We both said, "Should I be jealous?" at the same time. And we both laughed and laughed. If you're going to be with somebody, be with somebody you can laugh with. Believe me.

XVII

I hadn't been in my office longer than ten minutes before somebody knocked on the door. "Come in," I said, wondering if it was Dora. Twilight lingered in the sky, but the sun had set.

The door opened. It wasn't Dora. It was Clarice Jethroe. "Hello!" I said. "How are you doing? How's Frank? It's good to see you."

"Frank is doin' fine," she answered. Just like her to think about her husband, talk about him, before she worried about herself. She went on, "He got himself a new job at the Goodyear plant. He didn't want to go back to US Rubber, not after what happened, an' the new one's way closer an' pays better anyways."

"That's great!" I said. "I wouldn't go back to US Rubber on a bet, not me." While Patrick Brannegan was still in the hospital with "food poisoning," the County DA had arrested him on some kind of illegal-sorcery charge. He was out on bail at the moment, if I remembered straight.

"I told him the same thing," Clarice said. "An' I wanted you to know we're both mighty grateful for everything you did for us."

"I'm glad to hear it." And I was, even if gratitude was worth its weight in gold.

"Did that lawyer fella you found for us tell you he made a settlement with O'Flannery and Muldoon?" she asked.

TWICE AS DEAD

"No, Wally hasn't said a word about it," I answered. He might not have got around to it, or he might not have figured it was any of my business. You never can tell with Wally.

"Well, he did. He got us twenty thousand dollars for what they did to poor Frank workin' up on the freeway. Part o' the deal is, we can't ever say anything to anybody about what happened, but I reckon it's okay to talk to you on account o' you already know."

"That's a lot of money," I said.

"We don't get to keep all of it ourselves. Mister Baker, he tol' us right from the start he was gonna take his cut off the top o' whatever the builders finally coughed up." Clarice gave a wry shrug. "That still leaves us fifteen thousand. Pretty good. Enough so maybe we can buy ourselves a nicer place, move outa the old rat trap we been livin' in."

"You can sure do that," I said. The price of houses has gone through the roof here, same as it has everywhere else, but fifteen grand will still get you something pretty good.

It also occurred to me that Wally might not have told me he'd settled with O'Flannery and Muldoon because he didn't want me to know he'd made five thousand bucks from something where I did the hard, dangerous part and got paid fees and expenses. Yes, that just might have been on his mind.

Clarice hadn't finished, though. "Frank an' me, we been talkin'," she said. "We both reckon you oughta have more than what we gave you so far. So I've got this here for you." She took an envelope out of her handbag and set it on my desk.

It was a nice, fat envelope. I didn't even look to see what was inside it. "Thank you very much. You didn't have to do that," I said. I knew damn well most people would've kept every last nickel for themselves. If I'd got that kind of settlement, I probably would have myself.

"We didn't do it 'cause we had to. We did it 'cause we wanted to. *I* wanted to," Clarice said, and that told me more than I needed to know about what all she and Frank had been talking about. She went on, "I purely love that man, an' you got him back for me. This here's only money, but it's what I can do."

"Thanks," I said one more time, and looked down at the new green blotter on my desk so she wouldn't see my face till I could pull it straight. Would anybody ever say anything like that about me? The way things looked, odds were against it.

"God bless you, Mister Mitchell. I better get on home now." She didn't wait for me to answer. She just turned around and walked out. Good thing, too, because I have no idea what I would have said.

My bottom desk drawer had a new bottle of Wild Turkey in it. I took the level down some—a little, not a lot. I haven't drunk because I was embarrassed very often, but I did then.

After that, I opened the envelope. Inside were fifteen crisp, new fifties, so fresh they might've come straight from the bank. Folded around them was a sheet of paper with *Thank you!* written on it. I would have bet the whole stack it was her handwriting, not his.

I could picture them arguing after their girls had gone to bed. *We've got to give the detective somethin'. No, we don't. Yes, we do.* And she would've wanted to let me have a grand, and he would've come up maybe a hundred at a time to five hundred, and they would've stuck there for a while. And finally he would've thrown his hands in the air and gone, *Hell, let's split the difference an' forget it.* And she did love him and had to live with him, so she would've said okay.

No, I can't prove it happened that way, but it looks like that to me. *You bastard! I rescued you from being a zombie and you screwed me out of two hundred fifty bucks!* I thought. I was laughing when I did, though, honest. If you don't laugh sometimes, you've got to start screaming instead.

I was sure Wally was laughing, too, laughing all the way to the bank. Even with the money the Jethroes didn't have to give me, he was still raking in better than four times as much from their troubles as I was.

He's told me himself I don't know anything about money. He's right, too. Those new fifties there, they'd help me get as close to out of debt as I'd been since I took off Uncle Sam's uniform and started trying to make like a grownup all by myself.

Old Man Mose came in through the cat door. He knew about making like a grownup all by himself ... except for sponging off me, anyway. His pink nose twitched. Sniff! Sniff! "A real live female, not your friend from the boneyard," he said.

"Don't worry. Dora loves you, too," I said.

TWICE AS DEAD

His lip curled. I know, I know—cats don't really have lips. His curled all the same. "You gonna get in trouble for hanging around with this one?"

"No, it's business." I tapped the envelope with my finger. "Some of this will keep you in canned tuna for a while."

If I don't understand anything about money, cats *really* don't understand anything about money. "Why don't you just steal things when you need them?" Mose asked.

He would have made a good politician. Or an LAPD cop. "There are laws," I said sadly. He did that impossible lip-curling thing again. I tried my best to explain: "You know how sometimes you can't steal something you want because whoever's got it also has a big, mean dog with sharp teeth?"

His tail had been up. It went down. Old Man Mose doesn't understand laws, but he thinks dogs should be illegal.

I went on, "People use laws the same way they use dogs. If laws have sharp teeth, people have to do what they say."

"Till they do what they want while the laws aren't looking." Yes, Mose definitely should have joined the LAPD. He'd be an assistant chief by now, and too rich to hang around with the likes of me.

Or maybe he's already an assistant chief, and just hasn't shown me his badge yet. Why would he deign to shed on my worn-out sofa, then? Either because he likes slumming or because he's gathering evidence for when the department lands on me with both feet. LAPD is snafu enough, neither would surprise me one bit.

The Saturday night after that, Dora and I were coming back from Deacon's ... which means it really would have been Sunday morning. Sunday morning for sure, since the eastern sky was starting to get the color that isn't any color at all, the color that will turn to red and orange and gold and eventually to sunrise, which she would never watch again without finishing.

I wanted to stop at the office for a minute before we went on to her apartment. I needed to grab Frank Jethroe's file so I could check something in it for Wally. He'd already seen the damn thing, of course. And he'd already settled with O'Flannery and Muldoon.

But he needed it again, because he hoped he could pry more dough out of the sons of bitches who'd run PERSONAL ASSISTANCE, PERSONAL ASSISTANTS if they were still alive or out of their heirs and assigns if they weren't. Lawyers.

And me. Naturally, I'd remembered this in the middle of Slim Gaillar doing "Cement Mixer (Put-Ti, Put-Ti)." Not like remembering it in the middle of one of Lady Day's songs, but even so ... I hadn't drunk enough to forget it again, either, not at Deacon Washington's prices I hadn't.

So there I was with Dora, mad at myself for stopping but meaning to stop anyway because grabbing the file would only take a minute. We walked across where the alley behind the building opens out on to the street. Something in the alley moved.

Dora stopped in her tracks. "Who is that?" she asked sharply.

I peered down the alleyway. I couldn't see much—not as much as she could, I knew—but I recognized that slow, deliberate shuffle. "It's just the zombie the guy two doors down leases out," I said. "I don't know why it's there now. He doesn't usually turn it loose so early."

"Who *is* that?" Dora repeated, as if I hadn't opened my mouth at all. She started down the alley to find out. I followed in her wake. After a second or two, I was dogtrotting, but still not gaining any ground. She might have flown faster if she'd turned bat, but she might not have, too.

She came up beside him. He went on sweeping as if she weren't there. As far as he was concerned, she wasn't. Sure as hell, he was the same old zombie he'd always been. White guy, no particular age, expressionless face, dead eyes. Kind of a beaky nose, dark hair that looked as if it hadn't been combed for months. It probably hadn't. Worn-out coveralls. Push broom. Sweep. Pause. Step. Sweep. Pause. Step ...

"What do you care about—?" I began.

I stopped, because she still wasn't paying attention to me. She was paying me even less than she had before, in fact. That wasn't easy, because she hadn't been paying me any before, but she managed. Now all the attention she had was focused like a burning glass on the poor, sorry, shambling shape next to her.

TWICE AS DEAD

"Rudolf!" she said, and the sorrow she said it with pierced me to the root.

I was tired. I'd had a bit to drink. All the same, I knew what she was talking about. "This guy here, this guy's your, uh, half brother?"

"He is," she said, and then something in Magyar I of course couldn't understand. After a few seconds, she realized as much and came back to English: "I never thought to see him in such a sad state."

"Are you sure you're seeing him in such a sad state now?" I asked. "Because I've watched this guy pushing his broom in broad daylight."

No, she hadn't been paying attention to me. All of a sudden, she did. I watched her head swing my way. I could see it better now than I would've been able to a couple of minutes before. Whether she liked it or not, dawn was moving closer. She couldn't stick around very long, not if she wanted to do anything after that. Her eyes had the look of a trapped animal's.

"You are sure? There can be no possible mistake?" she said.

"Honey, I'm sure," I said, and she didn't even get mad at me for the first word. "I've been as close to him as we are now. I've had his broom hit my shoe. Nobody's pulled the old switcheroo on him since."

"That is not possible." Dora caught herself, because it plainly *was* possible. She tried again. "That should not be possible. How can it be possible?"

I had no idea. I just said the first thing that popped into my head: "Maybe he found the, the stuff he was looking for. Maybe that's what does it." Even tired, even tipsy, even knocked out from finding Rudolf Sebestyen'd been right under my nose all along, I didn't say vepratoga out loud.

Neither did Dora. "It could be," she replied after a few seconds' thought. "It makes better sense than anything that occurred to me. But what can we do to bring him back to himself, as you did with Frank Jethroe?"

I was starting to be able to see her in color. Yeah, sunup was coming on fast. I put my hands on her shoulders. "What you're going to do is go home and lie down. We'll talk about it when you wake up tonight, okay? Your half brother isn't going anywhere till then. It's Sunday. The guy who leases him won't be in today, and I don't know how to get hold of him at home."

259

Of course she could've shaken me off. She could've knocked me for a loop if she decided to. For a split second, I thought she would. She wanted what she wanted, and she wanted it *right now.* Then she sighed and nodded. "You are thinking more clearly than I am. Tonight."

And then she was gone, at least in human form. A bat flittered south and west, in the direction of Vampire Village. And beside me, Rudolf Sebestyen, the vampire who walked like a zombie, went on with his slow-motion sweeping. I stood there watching him and smoking an Old Gold till the sun had risen, no two ways about it.

He didn't fall to ash. He didn't catch fire and run down the alley screaming till he finished. He just swept. One of the things he swept up was my cigarette butt. I lit another smoke. He swept up my dead match, too. Shaking my head, I started for VV myself.

I didn't want to do that, you understand. I wanted to call Izzy Berkowitz or Rob Grau or both of them at once. I made myself hold back. When the phone rings before seven on Sunday morning, even if it doesn't wake you up the first thing you think is *Who died?*

By the time I got back to Dora's apartment, she'd lain down in her coffin and closed the lid. I realized how tired I was myself. I put on my one and only pair of pajamas and climbed into bed. Back before the war, I would have laughed at the idea of going to sleep while the sun was up. Slogging north toward Milan, though, I'd learned to grab shut-eye wherever and whenever I could. Knowing how to do that is useful. It's come in handy since.

I woke up once because I had to take a leak. Staying with another live person, I would've worried about waking her, too. But I knew damn well Dora wouldn't notice anything till the sun went down again. I lay back down and fell straight into slumberland. No more Assyrian-flavored dreams, either. That was nice.

Next thing I knew, it was getting close to four in the afternoon. I'd made a fair stab at sleeping the clock around. I peed again, then fixed myself some coffee and a can of beef-vegetable soup. I figured I'd get real food later. This would wake me up and keep my belly from growling too much in the meantime.

TWICE AS DEAD

I finished cleaning up and sat down with *The Naked and the Dead*. The guy who wrote it, he'd been through the mill, all right. That was what drew it to me to begin with. And that was what made me want to put it down and forget about it every time I picked it up. I hadn't yet. It was a big, fat book. I figured I'd get plenty more chances to.

Before I'd made much headway this time, the coffin lid creaked open. Not creepy—just a lot of weight on the hinges. Dora sat up and ran her hands through her hair. "How do I look?" she asked.

"Babe, you always look good to me," I answered.

How she looked right then was exasperated. Vampires can't see themselves in the mirror, either, of course. Makes it hard for a pretty woman to stay at the top of her game. Dora said, "In the old days, in the old country, I had servants to keep me looking as I should—and to keep me fed if I required it."

"Now you've got me," I said.

"Yes." By the way she said that, I wasn't an ideal replacement for the scared peasant girls she must have ordered around in the good old days. She hadn't complained when she was hungry, though. Oh, no. And neither had I, not while she was feeding or afterwards. What she did next was gesture imperiously. "Come brush out my hair, anyway."

"Okay." I did my clumsy best. While I ran the brush through that thick, honey-blond mane, I reflected that it probably wasn't an accident so many vampires had to get out of Hungary in a hurry when the old Empire fell apart after the first war and the Reds took over for a few bloody months.

"How is my makeup?" she asked.

"Your mouth's a little smeared," I said.

"Wipe off what does not belong, please," she told me, so I did, with a Kleenex. She put on fresh lipstick by feel. When she finished, she said, "How is that?"

"It's perfect." I'd watched her put on paint before. It amazed me every time. "If I tried to do that, I'd look like a circus clown. If I was lucky, I would."

"I have had rather more practice than you," she said, and she wasn't wrong. "Now we will go to your office. You have telephone calls to make."

261

We will go. Yes, she was used to being obeyed. But I also knew we needed to do it, so away we went. After sunset, Vampire Village comes to life …. Mm, no. Let me try again. It gets livelier …. Hmm. No again. A lot more goes on there when the sun isn't in the sky. That works.

I wondered whether Rudolf Sebestyen would still be sweeping the alley—sweeping it again?—when we got to the office, but he wasn't. He was probably standing in a closet, or else propped against the wall like his broom. I winced, remembering my own time in the closet across from Jonas Schmitt's place. Sebestyen wouldn't remember his.

Dr. Berkowitz was at the County General blood bank when I called. He spent a lot of time there. I wondered how his family liked that. None of my beeswax, of course. I stuck to what was: "I found that vampire I was looking for."

"Is that good news or bad news?" Izzy asked. I was sure Dora could hear what he was saying. Since her half brother'd wanted to knock over the blood bank, though, she couldn't very well get offended.

"Probably," I said, and Berkowitz chuckled. I went on, "The interesting thing is, he's not just a vampire these days. He's a zombie, too, and I've seen him working in broad daylight."

"Really?" He sounded the way a pointer looks when it sees a goose. "I wouldn't have thought that was possible."

"You aren't the only one who's had trouble believing it," I replied. On the sofa, Dora nodded. I said, "I was wondering if it could have something to do with the stuff I still don't want to name. I know for a fact he was looking for that stuff."

"Yes, you said so before." Berkowitz paused. I imagined the faint sounds on the phone line were gears spinning and meshing inside his head. "I don't know that we've made any experiments along those lines. I don't know that the fylfot boys did, either. But this is another one of those places where I don't know how much I don't know."

Dora gestured for the phone. I gave it to her. She said, "Doctor Berkowitz, this could be important to my folk. If we find a way to face the sun without finishing, it would change so much for us."

I leaned across the desk so I could hear Izzy's response: "If the stuff does to vampires what it does to live people, getting a dose of it may cause more problems than it solves."

TWICE AS DEAD

I took the phone back then. "They gave Frank Jethroe some before they took him over to the zombie dealership for unsouling, remember. It left him goofy so he couldn't do anything about that, but he's pretty much his old self now that Rob reversed the spell."

"Interesting. Interesting," Berkowitz said. "A low dosage, maybe. Or something else with it, to modify the original effect. When will you try to bring Sebestyen back to himself? I'd like to be there when you do."

"I was hoping you'd say that—it's why I called you," I answered. "I'll talk to Rob next. Then I have to deal with the guy who leases the zombie. Once everything's fixed up, I'll get back to you." We said goodbye to each other and hung up.

Before I could find Rob Grau's number, Dora said, "We will revive my half brother regardless of whether the person who leases his carcass agrees. We will, do you understand?"

That left no room for argument. "Do you want me not to talk to him, then? My thought was, he wouldn't mind if we paid him something. But if you just want to lift Sebestyen next time he's out in the alley with nobody around to spot us when we do, we can go that route, too."

"Yes. We should do that," she said. "I cannot bear the thought that this live person might tell us no. One of my kind should not be demeaned in such a way."

But it's all right for live people? I wondered. Some of my ladylove's attitudes were ... interesting. That I am what I am didn't bother her. She didn't have much of a chance to get attitudes about Negroes before she came over here. To be fair, if she had one about Jews, she didn't let Berkowitz see it.

When I called Rob at O'Flannery and Muldoon, they told me he'd gone home for the day. I waited till it got past seven thirty before I used that number, to give the poor guy a chance to eat dinner in peace.

He answered the phone himself. There were squeals and yells while he said, "Hello?"—little-kid noises. He shushed the younger shades of Grau as I was telling him who I was. Then he went on, "What's up, Jack?"

263

I told him about Rudolf Sebestyen. "So I was wondering if you wanted to help turn another one loose. It'll probably be one more middle-of-the-night job." I explained why.

He laughed. "Do you ever do anything ordinary?"

"Once in a while, I guess." For a private eye, getting nasty photos of Marianne Smalls and Jonas Schmitt was pretty ordinary. I went on, "This kind of stuff is more fun, though. Are you in?"

"Paying work?" he asked.

I looked a question to Dora, who was listening in. She nodded. "You bet," I told Rob.

"I'm in. If I call in sick the next day at my downtown job, they'll have people to cover for me." He paused. "This call'll come out of the blue, right? The phone'll ring and you'll want me there in twenty minutes."

" 'Fraid so. You and Izzy both. He knows more about the stuff than anybody else I hang around with. And he's interested in something that might let vampires stand sunlight. So is Dora."

"I can see that. We done?" When I didn't deny it, he continued, "Okay, I'm gonna go read the kids *The Churkendoose* before they tear this place down around my ears."

"The what? Do I want to know?"

"You don't have children, do you? You may find out one of these days. Talk with you later." He hung up. Before he did, I heard those shrill voices going, *Churkendoose! Churkendoose!*

"Now we have to find a night when Rudolf is in the alley. Then we will restore him to himself," Dora said.

"I guess," I said. She looked at me. If we hadn't been lovers, that look would have scared the kapok out of me. It scared me some anyhow. Even so, I went on, "Remember, he wanted the stuff. He was looking for a way to turn into something like a zombie. How happy will he be after we bring him back?"

Dora started to say something. I could tell it would be something like *Of course he will be glad we rescued him.* She stopped herself before it came out, though. "I had not thought of that," she admitted, her voice troubled. "He may not be grateful. Even for my folk, he is not one to whom gratitude comes naturally."

From everything I'd ever heard about Sebestyen, she had that right. "Still want to go on?" I asked.

"Yes," she said after no more than the barest hesitation. "If he resents me, I will bear it. And if he wants to crawl back into the kind of oblivion he found once, I am sure he can find it again."

She had that right, too. Junkies who got clean but not clean enough can always score a hypo full of horse when the craving's bigger than they are. Has to be the same way for vepratoga. It may be harder to come by than H, but anything you can find once, you can find twice.

"You're the boss," I said. I meant it, too; she knew more about being a vampire in general and about Rudolf Sebestyen in particular than I ever would or could. Only after the words were out of my mouth did I realize I'd said the same thing in the same tone of voice a couple of times to the lieutenant running my platoon as we got close to the Po. Back then, it meant *I hope like hell you know what you're doing.*

It meant the same thing here. I got lucky. Dora didn't call me on it.

We visited the alley every night after that, usually between eleven and midnight. When we hadn't had any idea Sebestyen was there, we found him. When we were looking for him? Forget about it. Night after night, nothing after nothing.

"Maybe I should talk to the guy who leases him after all," I said.

"Only if you are sure he will say yes," Dora answered. "If he says no and we take Rudolf anyhow, he will understand exactly what has happened. And we are going to take Rudolf anyhow."

I shut up. Night by night, we kept going out to the alley. Night by night, we kept finding nothing. Well, one night, a possum toddled away from us. Good Lord, but possums are ugly! Another night, we surprised a raccoon climbing out of a trash can with half a sandwich in one handlike front foot. He surprised us, too. But no Rudolf Sebestyen.

And then, just past eleven on a slow Tuesday night, there he was, dead face, tattered coveralls, push broom, and all. Dora had everything figured out. "Go call Grau and Berkowitz," she told me. "I will wait here and make sure there is no trouble before they arrive."

I had to stop myself from saluting and going *Yessir!* The Army does strange things to you. "I'll do it," I said. "Then I'll come back out and stay here with you." She nodded absently. She needed me the way a salamander needs a Zippo, and we both knew it.

Luckily, neither Izzy nor Rob had hit the sack yet. They both said they were on their way. "I didn't want to sleep tonight anyhow," Izzy said gaily. With his work habits, I was inclined to believe him.

I went outside again. Nothing had changed. Oh, Sebestyen had got to the end of the alley and was coming back the other way, but nothing that mattered. Way off in the distance, I heard a pistol shot. There are parts of town where people figure a noise like that is a firecracker. I knew better.

Rob got there first. The Buick stopped at the mouth of the alley. Then we had to figure out how to get Sebestyen into it. He was a machine with only one setting: sweep. Turning him around was easy enough. Moving toward the car was the same as moving away from it for him. Getting the broom away and bending him enough so he'd fit into the back seat .... If we hadn't had Dora's strength on our side, we never could've done it.

She and I had planned that, if we needed me to, I'd wait and guide Izzy to her apartment after she and Rob went there with her half brother. But the adventures we had making him go inside the Buick meant we were all still there when the Ford pulled up.

I hopped into the Ford's front seat as Rob drove away. "Follow that car!" I exclaimed. I always wanted to say that. It made me feel like a detective!

Berkowitz's grin said he knew he was playing a game. "You got it, Mister," he answered, and away we went.

Rob nabbed a parking space right in front of Dora's building. In Vampire Village, that's harder to do at night than it is during the daytime. Izzy and I found one down the block. We went back to help extract Sebestyen from the Buick's back seat.

That might have been even more fun than shoving him in there. As far as he was concerned, he was still sweeping the alley. We banged his head on the door frame two or three times before we finally managed to get it out instead. Not that he noticed.

Hauling him up the stairs was one more delight. His zombie shuffle was made for flat ground, and he kept trying to push the broom he wasn't holding any more. Along the hall. Into Dora's

266

apartment. Sebestyen "swept" till he fetched up against a wall. His feet kept moving then, but the rest of him didn't.

"What can you do for him?" Dora asked Rob.

He was already rummaging in his carpetbag for the asson. As he pulled out the dried calabash rattle, he glanced my way. "You'll backstop me again?"

"Sure." I nodded. "Should be more straightforward this time. No ancient Assyrian interference."

"Yeah. Or we hope not, anyway." Rob gave his attention back to Dora. "I think I can bring him back to what he was before he became a zombie. From some of the things you've told me, I'm not sure that's doing him a favor, but I will if it's what you want."

"Do it," Dora said. Rob Grau looked as if he wanted to snap to attention. She had the voice of command, you bet.

Out came the little bongos. Rob handed them to me. He started to shake the calabash at Rudolf Sebestyen. As I had in the construction-site tent, I followed along as best I could. From the corner of my eye, I saw Izzy Berkowitz watching us like a hawk. This wasn't the kind of wizardry a blood-bank doctor ran across every day.

Rob chanted in Kreyòl. At the construction site, Jerry Gallagher had called it: almost French but not quite. This was the part that worried me. Rob was summoning Sebestyen's soul back from Over There to Over Here. But did vampires *have* souls? They gave up *something* to become what they were. Don't ask me. I'm not a sorcerer or a theologian.

Grau didn't seem to have any doubts. I had to hope he knew what he was doing. Working for O'Flannery and Muldoon, he certainly had experience with zombies. I hoped it would carry over to zombies who were also vampires.

And it did, or I suppose it did. You know how, when you're fishing, sometimes you can feel a trout nibbling at your bait even before it takes the hook? This was like that—more like that than anything else I can think of, I mean. Rob had made a cast, and *something* was on the other end of the line.

"Come back! Come back!" he called, as he had before. No, I still don't know what language he used. All I know is, I understood it.

So did Sebestyen's soul, if that was what it was. It accepted the summons, though I don't think it was thrilled. Back toward the mundane, material world it came. Rob reeled it in, if you like.

Or he did at first. Then it tried its best to get away. When Rob went after Frank Jethroe's soul, something Over There wanted to keep it from coming back and rejoining his body. This was different. Rudolf Sebestyen's soul did all it could on its own to stay Over There. It didn't care what happened to the undead carcass it had left behind. It was happier far, far away from anything connected to this world.

I don't know if Rob ever went fishing off the Santa Monica pier. He was a white man; he could do that without any trouble if he wanted. He sure played Sebestyen's soul as if it were a fish on a line that might be too light. He'd let it run away a little, then reel it in more than it had fled. One step back, two steps forward.

Fish get tired after a while. So did the soul. I was only backup, but I could feel that. Pretty soon, Rob would get it into the net and the game would be over. Pretty soon, pretty soon …

Then he did it. I felt a psychic *pop!*—I don't suppose I really heard it—as the soul went back into Rudolf Sebestyen's poor zombified body and found it had no choice but to take up residence there again. The inside of Dora's apartment came into sharper focus for me as I also returned fully to the material world. I'm sure it was the same for Rob, too.

Sebestyen abruptly stopped trying to sweep up trash that wasn't there with a push broom he wasn't holding. His face didn't look dead any more. It looked … *foxy* is the first word that jumps to mind. He had the kind of expression that made me want to put my hand on my wallet so I wouldn't get my pocket picked, the kind of expression that made me wonder whether putting my hand on my wallet would do me any good.

He looked around. He recognized Dora right away, and Dr. Berkowitz a moment later. He said something in Magyar. Dora answered in the same language. Sebestyen said something else, something furious. The fylfot boys' machine guns spat bullets so fast, the individual rounds blended into a noise like ripping canvas. That was how Rudolf Sebestyen sounded just then.

Rob and Izzy and I all looked at Dora. I'd wondered whether Berkowitz knew any Hungarian, but he didn't. Dora looked ... as troubled as a vampire's ever likely to. "He ... would have preferred being left as he was," she said.

"You stinking, stupid, meddling sons of bitches," Sebestyen added. His accent was thicker than hers, but none of us had any trouble understanding what he meant.

XVIII

"Do you know you've been working under the sun, not just at night?" Izzy Berkowitz asked him. "How did you do that? Did it have something to do with the drug you took before you became a zombie?"

"The vepratoga?" Nobody'd told Sebestyen not to name it. "I don't know, and I don't care, either. It made me go away, and now you bastards have brought me back. I'll have to go and look for more of it."

"But if it can make vampires exist more safely in daylight—" Izzy persisted.

Rudolf Sebestyen fell back into Magyar. I think it was only noise to Dr. Berkowitz, but I recognized it because Dora'd aimed it my way. It was the Hungarian endearment that meant *A horse's cock up your arse.* In English, Sebestyen went on, "What difference does that make?"

"It could change the way your folk go on. Along with blood banks, it could turn you into people pretty much like everybody else," Berkowitz answered.

He was earnest. He meant well. I've heard earnest white people who mean well say pretty much the same thing about what advances in civil rights will do for Negroes. The nicest thing I can tell you

TWICE AS DEAD

about 'em is, they're optimists. Some things may get better, but ain't gonna be no pie in the sky by and by.

But what bothered me wasn't what bothered Rudolf Sebestyen. He looked at Berkowitz as if he wanted to tear his throat out. He said something else in Magyar, something that made Dora lift one eyebrow a quarter of an inch. In English, he went on, "You understand nothing. You are an idiot studying to be a moron and failing the examination. Why would I wish to make forever twice as long?"

"You're right. I don't understand." Izzy was a doctor. He'd given his life to making people last as long as they could.

That wasn't what Sebestyen meant, though. "*There is no ending*, fool. Unless I go into the sun or have a stake driven through my heart, *there is no ending*. I go on and on and on. It is too much. It is too long. Now you tell me even the sun may not finish me? I hate you for that. When I was a zombie, at least I didn't know it was going on, or care. You—every damned one of you—you stole that from me."

"We do not all feel this way," Dora said softly.

"I'm not the only one who does. Nowhere close," her half brother answered, and she didn't try to tell him he was wrong.

I looked at my watch. I was surprised to see it was getting on toward five; Rob and I'd spent longer bringing Sebestyen's soul back from Over There than I'd figured. I said, "If you can't stand staying here, the sun'll come up before too long."

The look on Dora's face .... That wasn't something you said to vampires, not if you had manners, any more than you called black people a particular name. But it didn't faze Rudolf Sebestyen, not a bit. "What do you think I'm waiting for?" he said.

"You shouldn't do that. You shouldn't do anything you can't undo." Izzy went right on talking sense to somebody who didn't want to hear it.

Quietly still, much more to herself than to anyone else, Dora said, "I fear I may have made a terrible mistake. It was my obligation, but still it was a mistake." Rob and I'd already figured that out.

"Foster sister, you don't begin to understand the mistake you made," Sebestyen snarled.

Outside, the sky began to get light. I'm sure both vampires noticed long before I could. Dora wanted to go on with her undead existence. Rudolf ... didn't. If becoming a zombie looks better to you than staying what you were, what you were has to seem the worst thing in the world for you, regardless of whether you're alive or undead.

Dora got into her coffin ten or fifteen minutes earlier than she needed to. The thump of the lid coming down had a dreadfully final sound. I think she was saying she didn't want anything to do with the world in general and her half brother in particular for a while. When she came out again after sunset, she could be pretty sure Rudolf Sebestyen wouldn't be in her apartment any more, anyhow.

In fact, he wasn't there for more than five minutes after she retreated. "Let the sun end me, then!" he shouted, and stormed toward the door. If that was what he wanted, he wouldn't have long to wait.

"You can't!" Izzy jumped in his way. Berkowitz was a doctor from the soles of his feet all the way up to his curly red hair. Saving life came first for him, nothing else even close. He didn't ask himself whether what Sebestyen had *was* life.

He didn't ask himself whether vampires were stronger than live people, either. Sebestyen gave him a forearm shiv that sent him flying into the wall—almost flying through the wall. Then Dora's half brother was out the door and running for the stairway.

He could have flown, but he didn't. I could have gone after him, but I didn't. Neither did Rob Grau. We were both more worried about Berkowitz, who was down on one knee. "You all right, man?" I asked—not one of the smartest questions I ever came out with.

Izzy gave me a shaky grin. "Did you get the license number of that truck?" he wheezed. Then he took stock of himself. "I ... think so. No knives when I breathe in or out, so he probably didn't break any ribs." He made it to his feet. "What's he doing?"

Rob went over to the window and looked down. "Standing in the middle of the street, waiting for the sunrise. Won't be long now."

You could stand in the middle of the street in front of Dora's apartment building and wait for the sun to come up without worrying about cars. Not as if a whole lot of vampires were driving off to work then. Berkowitz said, "We should still stop him."

"How, exactly? How approximately, even?" I said. He gave me a dirty look, but he didn't answer. He didn't try to go downstairs after

Rudolf Sebestyen, either, which was good, because I wouldn't've let him. Instead, he mooched over to the window to see what happened next.

I looked down at Sebestyen with horrified fascination. I'd never actually watched a vampire get struck by the sun, but I'd seen enough movies to have an idea what it's like. I'm sure you have, too. I happen to know they use magnesium strips and thermite for the trick photography. Hot, really hot, and dangerous to get close to.

As Rob had said, Sebestyen stood in the middle of the street. He faced east, and he'd thrown his arms out wide. He looked as if he were on a cross, which, considering that vampires react to crucifixes and holy names almost as well as they do to sunrise, probably wasn't what he had in mind.

He waited. We waited. For a little while, there could be room for doubt. Had the sun come up, or hadn't it? Another few minutes, though, and doubt vanished with the night. It was daytime, no ifs, ands, or buts.

And Rudolf Sebestyen stood there still. He threw his head back and let out the most bloodcurdling shriek of despair I ever heard. The sun wouldn't set him free. Whether he wanted to be or not, he was stuck in this sorry old world.

He didn't come back up to the apartment after he failed to finish himself. I don't know where he went. Right then, I didn't much care.

Rob, yawning, went home. "I'm gonna call in sick," he said, which struck me as a sensible attitude.

Izzy, yawning, went up to County General. "I pulled all-nighters plenty of times when I was an intern and a resident," he said, which struck me as insane. I couldn't talk him out of it, though.

Me? Yawning, I went to bed. The sun was up. By then, I didn't care. If I was sleepy, I slept. If I wasn't, I did things. Since I was …

I woke up just past three thirty in the afternoon. I fixed myself coffee and something out of a can. I'd tell you what, only I can't remember. I cleaned up and put on some clothes. I'd go to the office later, if I went at all. If I didn't, Old Man Mose could take care of himself for a night.

Dora's coffin opened. I heard weight shift as she sat up. "Hi, babe," I said. She'd given up telling me to stop. I held out a hand to help her stand. She needed that the way she needed an extra head, you understand, but my mother raised me to be polite no matter what.

And Dora took that hand as if it were no less than her due. She asked, "What happened after I went away?"

So I told her. I finished, "Five gets you ten we'll have more trouble from him sooner or later. He's not the kind who can do anything without making trouble, is he?"

"I fear he is not. That he went into the White Fire .... That he went into the White Fire and did not perish ...." She shook her head.

"Would you like to be able to do that?" I asked.

"Not the way he did it," she answered at once. "Some prices are too high to pay." She hesitated. "If I were aware all the time, I might also come to feel as he does. The pause when I must stop .... It is not the same as sleep, not from what I remember of sleep. But it does more or less the same thing."

"It didn't seem to for your half brother."

"Existence became too much for him. That happens with us—not always, not even often, but it does. I have been lucky enough to avoid it so far. I keep finding ways to amuse myself. They have not palled yet." When she smiled at me, her lips pulled back enough to let me see the tips of her fangs. They're not much longer than live people's eyeteeth, but they're a lot sharper.

"I'm glad to help keep you interested in things," I said.

"For a while." She looked at me as if I were a foolish child. "For a little while."

I knew all about being afraid I'd die. If a year slogging up the Italian boot taught me anything, it taught me that. But suppose Dora and I stayed together the rest of my life—call it another forty years. She'd watch me get old and shuffle off this mortal coil. How many other live lovers had she watched get old and die, or die before they could get old? How many more would come after me? After a while, how much trouble would she have, remembering just which one I was?

And how much would she change while all those years rolled by? No more than she'd changed in all the years since the vampire who made her and Rudolf Sebestyen what they were did that to them.

274

Yeah, I knew all about being afraid I'd die. But, till I heard Sebestyen shriek when the sun hit him and nothing else happened, I'd never imagined being afraid I wouldn't die, couldn't die.

"Well, however big a skunk your half brother is, he taught me something this morning," I said.

"And what is that?" she asked, though the way she asked it made me guess she was half a dozen jumps ahead of me. I explained anyway. She nodded—at least I wasn't being foolish any more—and said, "Yes, it is a problem with my folk; no denying that. As I told you before, it does not afflict all of us. I have met someone who grew up speaking Latin. He says he was in Rome when Brutus killed Caesar. I do not know he was telling the truth, but I have no reason to doubt him. As far as I know, he still exists today."

"That's amazing! Has he ever talked to live historians?" I said. Vampires mostly don't, but every once in a while somebody will. A lot of books get rewritten when that happens.

"Not so far as I know," Dora said indifferently. She didn't care about history. Why should she? She *was* history. I started to say something else, but she held up a slim, elegant hand—she hadn't finished. "I have met someone who grew up speaking a tongue so old, living men have no name for it. She believes she is older than the Pyramids. I have no reason to doubt her, either. I think she still exists, too."

"The things she must have done!" I said.

"She existed. When the hunger got to be too much, she fed. She mostly stayed away from live people otherwise. Live people are dangerous—they move about while we must lie quiet. The sun never struck her." Dora paused. "It seems only yesterday that any live people thought my kind should be allowed to go on existing like other folk."

There are still black people alive who were born slaves. There were more of them when I was a kid. I met one or two—and paid no attention to them, because they were old and wrinkled and gray, and I *was* a kid. The vampire Dora was talking about wouldn't have changed, not to look at, in those thousands of years.

Somewhere, there might be a vampire who remembered the Neanderthals. There might be a vampire who *was* a Neanderthal.

"It is good that here in America we do not always have to feel hunted. In America, and in a few other places," Dora said. "But who can guess how long that will last? It may be one more passing thing."

When I was a kid, white men would march in KKK robes. They still thought we should be slaves. They mostly don't do that any more, except in the South. Could they start again? You never can tell.

Dora went on, "The years pile up. Some of us have ways to deal with that. For others, like my half brother, they grow too heavy to stand. It might happen twice as fast if we could bear up under the fire from heaven. It might not happen at all if we could fully join the daylight world. Or it might vary from one of us to another."

"Would you want to find out yourself if you could use the drug without turning into something like a zombie? You would, wouldn't you?"

"Yes. I said as much to the *zsidó* doctor when we talked on the telephone," she answered. "It is exciting. But it is frightening at the same time. Any change that cannot be changed back is frightening when you risk regretting it forever."

When she said forever, she meant *forever*. If she found out she regretted going out by day and night, she'd still be regretting it when the wizards figured out how to put a man on the Moon. Or on Mars. Or on some planet going around Arcturus. Three score and ten meant nothing to her. Not a thing.

I did go to the office for a little while, to make sure Old Man Mose didn't starve to death and to remind him which side his canned mackerel was buttered on. As he dug into the glop, I said, "Beats the hell out of lizards and grasshoppers, doesn't it?"

He looked up at me as if he thought humans were stupid. Well, of course he thought humans were stupid—he was a cat. After he cleaned off his pink nose with his tongue, he said, "The stuff you give me tastes fine, sure. But it just sits there in the bowl. I don't get to chase it down and kill it. Takes half the fun out of eating."

"If you say so," I answered.

"I *do* say so." Mose sounded at least as regal as Dora did. Cats and vampires both have very high opinions of themselves. Cats and vampires are both convinced they're entitled to have those opinions. Since they compare themselves to live people, who's to say they're wrong?

TWICE AS DEAD

Mose leaned down and started feeding his fuzzy face again. He drank some water from the other bowl. He used the catbox. He did cover up what he'd done there. He was good about that, as good as the average human is about flushing the people box. Not all cats are, God knows. Of course, not all humans are average or higher, either.

Then he hopped up onto the sofa. I scratched the sides of his jaw and under his chin. He liked that; he rolled over onto his back so I could rub his tummy. I did, cautiously. He enjoys it, then all of a sudden he doesn't and decides he has to murder my hand. I jerked it away before he could grab it with his front feet and use his back legs to rip its guts out.

The exercise brought him back on to his stomach. He curled up and got ready to go to sleep. I went back to my desk. There's always paperwork, and I'm always behind because I hate it even more than I hate canned spinach. Eating spinach is good for you—hey, ask Popeye. So is doing paperwork. I've heard that, anyway. I don't really believe it.

Only Old Man Mose didn't go to sleep. He stuck up his head and stared at a stretch of wall near the door. His ears pointed that way, too. I didn't see anything or hear anything. He might have spotted a little moth or a gnat. Or he might have been looking at nothing, or nothing a mere human could observe or comprehend.

I didn't see anything or hear anything ... till I noticed some of the flowers on the wallpaper seemed not to be quite lined up with the rest, as if a patch of air between me and the wall had curdled. As Mose and I watched, the curdled patch moved.

It was about as tall as a man. About as wide as a man, too. If a ghost wanted to visit, I couldn't do much about it. Who was I gonna call? A priest? A rabbi, if it was what was left of somebody Jewish? Sure, it could read my files without opening drawers, but I didn't have anything all that explosive in there.

Besides, the more I looked, the more familiar the outline of that curdled patch seemed. I might have been imagining things (you do, with ghosts, a lot of the time), but I didn't think so.

"That you, Eb?" I asked.

I imagined that the ghost turned its head toward me. Unless I didn't. I might have imagined the long-dead Pinkerton man's New

277

England accent as he answered, "Ayuh. Ain't nobody else." How did he have a New England accent when he couldn't really make a sound? I don't know. I'm just a live guy. But he did.

"What can I do for you?" I said. Ebenezer'd always been square with me. He was with Missing Individuals, though, and Missing Individuals was part of LAPD. So I had my reasons to be leery of trusting him too far.

"I hear you found someone who's been missing a while," he said.

"I do that for a living. Not a great living, but I do. Are you talking about Frank Jethroe or Rudolf Sebestyen?"

"Jethroe won't cause any more trouble. They threw enough money at him to keep him quiet. You had something to do with the big thing down at the tire factory, didn't you?"

"Who, me? I have no idea what you're talking about," I said. Yeah, Eb'd been square with me, but I wasn't going to admit anything I didn't have to. I did answer in a particular tone of voice, though. If he wanted to testify to that, I could always say he'd misunderstood me.

I heard, mm, the ghost of a chuckle. I don't know what else to call it. "Go ahead, play 'em close to your chest," Eb said. "I would, in your shoes. But I came to call on account of Sebestyen. How'd you scrape him off the ash heap?"

I told him the story. The worst I'd done was aid and abet absconding with a leased zombie, and I didn't think that was enough to get the powers that be upset at me. Besides, Sebestyen wasn't an ordinary zombie. Now he wasn't an ordinary vampire, either.

Eb understood that. "The way I hear it, he's been runnin' around in broad daylight today."

I nodded. "He sure has."

"That's disgusting!" Old Man Mose exclaimed. "Vampires are bad enough at night. If I have to watch out for them all the time ...." He shuddered. He didn't need to worry, or I didn't think he did. I remembered what Dora'd said about how cat blood tasted.

"How come he don't go up like fiyawuhks?" Eb managed to say the last word as if it had no R's at all instead of two.

"I don't know, but I think it's because he had some of the drug that helped turn him into a zombie. You know—the drug I don't want to name." I wasn't about to say *vepratoga* in my office. I didn't want another visit from Elmer V. Jackson, or from whoever was minding the store for him while he stood trial. Oh, yeah, the LAPD—more fun than you can shake a stick at.

"Huh! Ain't that somethin'?" Ebenezer thought for a little while. "Reckon that stuff'd do the same thing for any old vampiyuh?" He might talk funny, but he could see what counted.

"I wouldn't be surprised, but I can't say for sure because I don't know of any other vampires who've taken it," I answered.

"Huh," Eb said again. "Talk about big things, though, that could be one all by its lonesome."

"I expect it could, yeah." I didn't want to talk about what Dora'd had to say there.

" 'Course, it *would* be a son of a whore like Sebestyen who got it. If he's out day and night, he'll make twice as big a stink as he could have before," Eb said. I would've said *son of a bitch* instead of *son of a whore*. Aside from that, I agreed with the ghost straight down the line.

"Well, now you know," I told him.

"Now I know," he agreed. "Reckon I can disappear." When a ghost says something like that, he means it, same as a vampire does. All the air in the office uncurdled. It was just me and Old Man Mose.

"You know the strangest assortment of people," the cat said.

"I know you, for instance," I said helpfully.

"I'm not a people!" To show how offended he was, and to prove his point, Mose stuck one hind leg in the air and started licking his rear end.

When I got back to Dora's apartment, she wasn't there. She didn't leave a note to let me know where she was or anything; to her way of thinking, it was none of my business. Maybe she'd change her mind after she kept me around for a few years, or maybe she wouldn't.

Nothing I could do about it now. I sat down with a *Saturday Evening Post*. Somebody had a story in there about going to the Moon with rockets, not sorcery. I think it was pretty good—almost made you believe we could do that one of these years. But I had trouble paying attention to it. I was worrying about Dora. Her half brother was out there somewhere, and he wasn't happy with her or with anything else in the world that wouldn't let him finish.

She came in a little past midnight. She didn't bother opening the door—it was her place, and she could come and go as she pleased. "Hello, Jack. Did you tend to your conceited fluffball?" she said.

"Yeah." I nodded. "I'm glad you're back. Rudolf's prowling around. Who knows what he's liable to do?"

"I can watch out for myself, believe me." She sounded like a mother humoring a little kid.

"How about when the White Fire's shining?" I said. That sobered her. She wasn't used to a vampire who could move around and do things during the day. Neither was anybody else. Eb had it right— Sebestyen could make twice as much trouble now as he ever had before. I went on, "I'll take care of you the best I can, hon."

Dora drew herself up, the picture of affronted dignity. The idea that she'd need a live person, a mere miserable mortal, to defend her! But after a moment she got down off her high horse. "Thank you," she said. "That is generous." She was trying to tell me she was grateful, I think, but gratitude doesn't come naturally to vampires.

"It's nothing," I said. And then my mouth, living its own life, wild and free, tacked on, "I love you, you know."

Even if I hadn't expected to come out with it, I meant it. Well, the way she flinched, I might've slapped her in the face. "We have talked of this before. You cannot! You must not!" she exclaimed.

"How come? Not like we haven't done the kinds of things people do when they're falling in love." I touched two particular scars on my neck. I had a bunch of little ones by then, but I knew which two those were. "Not like we haven't done some things most people never think of, either."

If she weren't a vampire, I swear she would have blushed. "You are not thinking of that," she said. "You are thinking of what came afterwards."

What came afterwards was me, spectacularly. I shook my head anyhow. "No. The other was pretty special, too. Part of me is part of you now."

"You are quite mad," she said. And maybe she'd remember me after all, even when I lay five hundred years in the grave. *Jack Mitchell, yes. The one who was so crazy, he imagined he loved me.*

280

TWICE AS DEAD

The grin I gave back probably looked a lot like the one I wore when one of the fylfot boys' fancy machine guns started spitting death at my buddies and me. "Did you need so long to figure that out?" I asked.

"Love is not something vampires are capable of," she said, now as if to an idiot. "Pleasure, yes, but not love. I remember the difference .... I think I remember the difference."

"You may surprise yourself. Or you may do something so horrible, I won't want to love you any more."

"You know as well as I do, the second is much more likely than the first."

"I'll take my chances. And I'll take care of your half brother if he decides to try something while the sun's up." *You bet I'll charge that pillbox, Sarge!* During the war, guys really did charge those pillboxes. A lot of them bought a plot doing it, too. But, one by one, the pillboxes fell.

She eyed me the way you'd look at a Chihuahua puppy that barked at a bullmastiff. But if all you had was a Chihuahua puppy, wouldn't you do your best to get the most out of it? "You are foolish, but you are brave," she said.

"Must be love. You see? I told you."

You don't find an exasperated vampire every day, but I did then. And Dora came up with a way to change the subject. It wasn't a way that made me love her less, but it did make me shut up for a while. That seemed to suit her well enough.

I wondered if she'd tell me again how pretty soon I'd meet a live woman I loved, and how then I'd want to pretend our fling never happened. She didn't say a word. Then I realized she didn't need to. She'd got to the point where I could hear her voice in my head whether she said anything out loud or not. Or I'd got myself there.

But, even if I heard her voice in my head, I didn't have to listen to it. And I damn well didn't.

The trials of all those corrupt cops filled the papers for weeks. The ones who hadn't been taking dough from madams and prostitutes had been taking dough from gamblers. Sex and money—what else sold copies? All the juicy testimony got printed so all the righteous citizens could reach the proper stage of moral indignation. If even a quarter of it was true, those guys had earned long stretches in Folsom or San Quentin. And I had no doubt way more than a quarter of it was true. You don't indict cops unless you've got the goods on them.

That's what I thought. God help me, I'd lived in Los Angeles all those years, and that's still what I thought. My mama told me she didn't raise dummies. If you felt a little earthquake when the verdicts started coming in, that was her, turning over in the grave at how stupid her only child turned out to be.

Not guilty. Every damn one of them, not guilty. Not guilty, from Sergeant Elmer V. Jackson all the way up to the assistant chief of police. One by one, they walked out of courtrooms with big, fat smiles pasted on their big, fat faces.

And, just to put a cherry on top, the honest cop who landed them in trouble when he talked to a grand jury without getting permission from the people it was looking at, you know what happened to him? He managed to beat the phony burglary rap, but he got charged with conduct unbecoming an officer and thrown off the LAPD anyway, that's what.

When I heard that, I swear I tried to drown myself in Wild Turkey. Before I got to the point where I couldn't talk, I remember saying to Dora, "Well, they were right, the rotten, stinking sons of bitches."

"What do you mean?" she asked. She didn't get upset about the whole scandal the way I did. The difference was, I went into it with hope. Fool that I was, I thought things might get better. She didn't. She always figured the powerful people would take care of their own.

On the evidence, she was right, too.

But, before I hit the bourbon blackout, I had one spark of wit left. "What do I mean?" I said. "I'll tell you what I mean. In the LAPD, telling the truth *is* conduct unbecoming an officer."

She nodded. I remember that. And she kissed my forehead with her cool lips. I remember that, too, and how she answered me: "Someone wise, I do not know who, once said, 'No good deed goes unpunished.' Here we see this truth once more."

TWICE AS DEAD

No good deed goes unpunished. That was the thought I took down to eighty-six-proof oblivion with me. That was the thought I woke up with, too, a long time later. And the way I felt when I did wake up let me see that truth once more, too.

I had aspirins. I took … I don't know how many I took. A lot. I poured cold water on my head. I made coffee, and drank too much. All that helped a little. None of it helped much. Nothing helps much with a hangover like the one I had.

I was on my own, too. Dora'd long since gone into her coffin. The sun was bright, bright enough to hurt me almost as if I were a vampire myself. It shone impartially on the crooked cops who'd walked and on the honest cop who'd got canned. Stupid goddamn sun.

Eventually, I took my courage in both hands and walked up to the little Mexican place near my old apartment building. I got a bowl of *menudo*. It soothed my sour stomach. Nothing did much for my head. The waitress watched the way I spooned it up. "You hurt yourself last night, *Señor?*" she asked sympathetically.

"'Fraid so," I said. "'Fraid so."

Dora didn't laugh at me when she came to herself after sunset. She just asked, "How do you feel?"

"I may live," I said. I almost added, *I may even want to*, but I didn't. I'd found out live people weren't the only ones who wrestled with *To be or not to be, that is the question*. Instead, I found my own question: "You put me into bed, didn't you?" I sure didn't remember doing it myself, and we'd been talking in the front room. I thought so, anyhow.

She nodded. "I thought you would be more comfortable there than on the floor." That answered that.

"Nice to know you care," I said. She made a face at me. If she did care, she wasn't about to admit it to a live person.

Aspirins or coffee or *menudo* won't cure a hangover, only blunt it a bit. Time eventually does. After a day or two, I resumed the uneven baritone of my ways. I found a reason to go downtown to check on something in the long, narrow strip of land between Vermont and Figueroa that connects the rest of LA to San Pedro and gives our unfair city a major port. I didn't find what I needed to know, which was par for the course. I didn't even get all that upset.

As long as I was there, I stopped in at Al Harris's dirty-book den. Al hears things. By now, he knows that if he tells me some of what he hears, it won't get traced back to him. He needs to be sure of that. He's too fat to run fast.

Nobody prints dirty books or dirty magazines. Nobody poses for dirty pictures. Nobody takes them, either. And nobody ever buys any of that stuff. Nobody ever goes into the stores that sell it. Somehow, Al keeps eating. Eating pretty well, in fact.

I went in. I ignored the other guys and looked at this and that. After a while, I was the only one in there besides Al. His chins bounced when he nodded to me as I went up to the counter. "Saw a friend o' yours yesterday," he rasped. Those damn cigars of his have smoked his voice for real.

"Who?" I asked. Nobody goes into those stores, so anybody might.

He made a disgusted face. "Everybody's hero, Sergeant Elmer V."

That disgusted me, too. "What did *he* want?"

"The usual Vice Squad rake-off, natch. Nobody came to collect it for a while, 'cause all o' their guys was in hot water. But I paid him no sweat, on account of I set it aside, like. I figured somebody'd show up sooner or later. Those scumbags, they're like cockroaches. They always come back."

"Business as usual in the big city," I said.

"Business as usual, yeah. That's just what he told me." Al made as if to spit. "At least he was only after the regular dough. He didn't ask me nothin' about the stuff." Dirty-book dealer or not, no flies on Al. He wasn't going to come out with *vepratoga*, either.

"You paid him, but you still *fargin* him the money, huh?" I trotted out the word I'd picked up from Doc Berkowitz.

Al kinda looked at me. "Another wise guy. This stinkin' town's full o' wise guys."

"Yeah." I couldn't very well tell him he was wrong.

www.ingramcontent.com/pod-product-compliance
Lightning Source LLC
Jackson TN
JSHW020215130125
76927JS00002B/2/J